Basket Weavers

Aaron Lebold

Copyright © 2025 by Aaron Lebold

13 Days Publishing

All rights reserved.

No part of this book may be reproduced in any form or by any electronic or mechanical means, including information storage and retrieval systems, without written permission from the author, except for the use of brief quotations in a book review.

Chapter One

Laying flat on my back with my eyes closed, I could feel the world around me transforming. It was a familiar feeling. A journey I had been on countless times before. A smile crept across my face as I gave in to the sensation of the waves. I opened my eyes and fixed my gaze on the ceiling. Wherever I was, it had elements of magic. Potentially dark magic.

The bits of plaster shifted around and melted into each other. A wall of kaleidoscope colors hiding behind the off-white. Begging to come forward and bring some much-needed life to the otherwise stale room. Deeper meaning and stronger connection always came with the colors. They remind me that beauty always exists, even if only in fragments.

I looked down at me feet. My toes were bright pink. They contrasted significantly against the stark white pants I was wearing. My shirt was white too, buttoned up all the way to my neck. Suddenly I couldn't breathe. I clenched the collar and undid the button, and a wave of oxygen filled my lungs.

I sat up, possibly too quickly. I felt a headrush and for a moment my vision blurred. I closed my eyes tightly and held them like that for close to a minute. Maybe I was hoping that when I opened them, I would be somewhere else. As it turned out, I wasn't.

The room was small and mostly empty. The walls pulsated slightly, in rhythm with my heartbeat. The door was ajar, and a small stream of artificial light crept across the floor. The more I watched it, the more it began to dance. To call out to me. I sat up and put my feet on the floor, entranced by the sign that presented itself.

I stood from the bed and took a few steps towards the door. Once I reached the light I crouched down and placed my hand in it. It changed colors as it hit my skin and I could feel its warmth. The longer I kept my hand there, the more heat the light seemed to generate. It was like a magnifying glass focusing energy into a single location. I soon feared that it may start a fire.

I pulled my hand away and stood back up. I decided to investigate my surroundings a little further, and if that light ended up causing a structure fire I wanted to be as far away from it as I could when it did. I opened the door slowly and peered outside. There was a long hallway with numerous doors. It was painted a taupe color, and the floors were cladded in a plain white vinyl.

Each step I took I could feel my feet sinking ever so slightly. The walls were dripping very subtly. Like beads of sweat that lingered and nearly evaporated before they had the chance to fall. I kept a steady pace and did my best to keep silent. I wasn't sure what I was up against, and I tended to err or the side of caution.

I had made my way down most of the hall when I heard one of the doors behind me creek open. I turned my head to

Basket Weavers

see what was going on. My feet were still sinking slightly into the floor, and I

didn't want to risk getting stuck trying to change direction. A man wearing a white outfit quite like my own emerged with a sense of urgency.

"Hedburg! Hedburg!" His eyes looked crazed; they were the brightest green I had ever seen. He had a bald head and exaggerated chestnut eyes. "Hedburg!"

He reached down and pulled his shirt open, revealing some sort of tattoo or marking. It was hard to make out exactly what it was as the walls began to melt at a faster pace. I assumed it had something to do with the man's energy. He began to move towards me, and I froze. I could tell that he was the type of adversary who couldn't see me if I didn't move.

"Heburg, care bear! Care bear Hedburg!"

My plan worked and he ran right past me. I could see the floor splashing with each impact of his feet. He didn't seem to notice and skidded into a turn at the end of the hallway. His rambling continued for a moment and then stopped as quickly as it had begun.

For a moment I debated retreating back to the safety of the small room, but I needed to gather information. I went back to putting one foot in front of the other and doing everything I could to keep my steps light. The idea of being stuck in the floor motivated me to keep a swift pace and a long stride.

The end of the hallway grew steadily near, and the walls seemed to return to their previous state of melting. It was back to a slight blistering and felt much more serene. I pressed on and soon enough I came to the end. There was a sharp corner where the strange man had disappeared, which became my next obstacle.

I peered around slowly. It opened into a large room. The screaming man was standing near a desk that was encased in glass. A dark-skinned woman in a white shirt was on the other side. I could tell she was important. She was some sort of display piece protected by an invincible barrier. Protected from the chaos that was surely lurking all around me.

I pulled my head back and placed it against the wall of the hallway. I felt certain that I hadn't been spotted and I needed to decide if it was safe to make my presence known. I took a deep breath and held it in. I could feel bacteria in my lungs. My insides began to tingle, and I exhaled. You never knew what kind of particles were floating around in the air.

I decided to venture into the unknown. My curiosity was swelling greater than my need for safety. I kept to the plan of moving slowly so that the man from the hallway wouldn't see me. I kept my eyes fixed on him as I approached the protected desk. He was opening his mouth and lifting his tongue as he stared ahead at the woman in front of him. A subtle cloud drifted from his mouth. Some kind of phantom spirit.

He turned and once again we were facing each other. I froze in place, but it was too late, he had seen me. His shirt was still unbuttoned, and he opened it again with excitement. Being much closer I could see that the marking on his chest was a heart. It looked more like paint than

permanent ink. I knew right away that it was probably some sort of metaphor for the soul he had eaten. War paint. Blood souvenirs.

"Hedberg care bear!"

He ran past me and once again vanished into the corridor. A moment later I heard a door slam shut. I could only assume that he had some sort of nest in the corner of his room. Likely to hide the body that once owned the soul and wore the heart that he now adorned. He was evil. I could tell.

The woman behind the desk spoke with a raised voice. "Mrs. Timmerman, clean up required!" She must have noticed me startle. Her tone calmed noticeably. "Is that you, Mister Ferguson?"

I snapped my head back in the direction of the desk. The woman was talking to me. She could see me even when I was motionless. The protective barrier was likely equipped with some sort of heat sensors. I walked slowly towards her. "Yeah?"

She had a smile on her face, and she had nice hair. Something about it seemed too fake for me. It was a facade of normalcy. It was like she had put on the uniform that created the illusion of a functioning member of society with no hidden secrets or demons. She looked at me through the glass. "Good timing, Mr. Ferguson. You've come for your appointment with Doctor Ranck?"

I could feel the sweat starting to form on my brow. I knew I had to keep my heartrate down or I was at risk if it turning acidic and melting my face. I took another deep breath. "I'm not sure."

I stood closer to the glass so I could see what her bunker looked like. There was a slot and some holes at the front. Beside her was a cabinet with a lock and a cooler filled with water. It was the type of water that gets stolen from the mountains and tainted with the essence of human consumerism. The worst kind of poison.

She smiled again. "Remember you are scheduled to meet him at three thirty." "What does he want?"

"He just wants to talk. He wants to get to know you.

You seem a little different than you were this morning. Is everything alright?"

I wasn't sure how to answer. If she knew of my elevated perceptions and abilities, I would lose my advantage. I tried to act like them. I tried to put on a phony persona and a fake smile. "Yes. Everything is going well. What was up with that guy?"

She got a confused look on her face. "I'm sorry, which guy?"

She knew who I meant. I could sense it. "The guy that was screaming and running around with his shirt open."

"Hedberg? He's a funny guy, I just gave him his medication. Why do you ask?"

I had to keep up the charade. I couldn't tell her that I watched a soul escape from his lips. I couldn't let on that I knew he had a body in his room, entangled in a nest to be consumed later. "Is he safe to be around?"

"Tom, you were playing cards with him only a few hours ago. Don't you remember? Are you alright?"

I felt a powerful wave flow over my entire body. I couldn't remember anything from the morning. I had to keep that to myself. I knew that if I admitted it, it would be used against me. They always seek out your weakness. Prey on it and exploit it. Twist it around and smash you in the face with it. "Of course. I thought that was him."

"There aren't many people like Hedberg, Mister Ferguson. Are you sure you're alright?" "Yeah."

"Alright, well why don't you go back to your room for a few minutes and lay down? I'll come get you when Doctor Ranck is ready for you. I'll be sure to tell Mark you were out here on time."

I nodded and started back down the hallway. Why did she want me to go back there? Who the hell was Mark?

Basket Weavers

What was in that room? The floor was getting softer, and my feet sank further with each step. I slowed my pace and focused on my breathing. If my breaths were shallow, I always became lighter.

I got about five feet from the door. I knew it was the same one I had come from because I had left it open. I looked down and I was ankle deep in the vinyl. I knew I didn't have much time before it swallowed me, I had to make a decision. I looked at the distance to the door and back at my feet. I took one giant step and dove towards the opening.

My right arm and shoulder landed on the threshold, but I could feel the lower half of my body sinking fast. I threw my other arm into the room and began to pull as hard as I could, trying to free myself from what felt like a tar pit. It took all the energy I had, but soon I felt myself come loose. I rolled onto my back and scurried in reverse until I felt resistance from the bed.

I looked down at my legs. The white material of my pants concealed any of the remaining liquid vinyl flooring. I could see a few drips, but nothing seemed to be accumulating on the floor. I focused on my breathing and tried to collect myself. I stared at the walls and hidden symbols and messages began to appear. It was enough that I knew they were there, but not enough that I could clearly identify them.

Then there was a knock at the door. "Mister Ferguson, the doctor is ready to see you now." "I'm not going back out there."

Chapter Two

Did I ever tell you about the first time I dropped acid? It was back in the nineties. I was a teenager trying to make my way through adolescence. I was jaded for sure, but I also struggled with depression. I would never admit that to myself, or anyone else at that time. I had two close friends, Corey, and Dylan.

Dylan got into drugs first. He always had connections and seemed to have the means to use every day. Due to my circumstances, I had a house basically to myself with no rules or accountability. Corey was a typical teenager and looked up to me at that time, doing whatever I thought was a good idea.

The three of us had developed a consistent routine. We would hang out at my house after school and smoke whatever Dylan brought over. It wasn't long before he started experimenting with new, stronger drugs. He would never push it on me, but it wasn't a secret that he was selling LSD. He would buy a sheet at a time and sell the hits off to people he trusted.

He started doing it often, usually by himself or with the

other group of people he hung out with in my town. I quickly developed an interest in trying it myself. I had already found comfort in drugs, and I had no fear at the thought of stepping it up a notch. Corey on the other hand, was reluctant.

When I would talk to him about the idea of trying it, he would always agree, but whenever I tried to actually get him to do it he didn't seem to want to. Sometimes I would forget that not everyone thought the same way as I did. I had an underlying death wish and tended to live a bit less cautiously than most. Eventually, Corey gave in. I think he may have just been worried that I would lose respect for him if he didn't do it.

I was more excited than I had been for a long time when I thought about the new experience, even though I really had no idea what I was committing to once that paper was on my tongue. Acid was cheap, it was five dollars for one hit. Our first time we both opted to take just one and waited for the weekend to put our plan into action. Corey's parents were typically away every weekend at their cottage, which gave us access to another unsupervised house.

We took it at my place. I remember the metallic taste in my mouth and the anticipation that was building inside of me. I had been looking forward to it for so long and I knew it was about to actually happen. We soon ventured down the street to Corey's place. We waited for about an hour before feeling any effects, constantly checking in with each other to see if the other had noticed anything.

Once it took hold, there was no denying that the world was changing. The first thing I noticed was a change in my perception. Everything seemed sharper. It was all the same, but somehow different. I imagine that it was like the way a very young child would see the world. Becoming suddenly aware of yourself and the things around you. Seeing things that you've seen a million times, but in a new light.

We sat around for a while and compared our experiences. We were both in a good state of mind and couldn't stop smiling. After a couple hours, we decided to go down to the basement and take a picture of ourselves with Corey's parents' Polaroid camera. Back then you had to get pictures developed, but the Polaroid was basically instant.

We did this mostly to mark the milestone in our lives. We were doing something new for the first time and loving it. It was a sort of souvenir of our first trip together. We went into his parents' office and snapped a few pictures. I still have them somewhere. We looked like spaced out kids, trying to be bad ass but at the time we thought they were great.

Not long after, we went back upstairs to his kitchen, and something miraculous started happening. I started seeing three dimensional squares floating around the room. I was reluctant to mention it to Corey at first, but once I did, he was relieved. He had been seeing them too.

It was so real, and so fascinating. Cubes of light showing up out of nowhere and drifting around weightlessly. We started trying to catch them with our hands and following them around the room. Even when one would seem to touch my fingers, I couldn't feel it. We must have chased them around for at least a half-hour. The fact that we could both see them and experience the surrealism of it all made us feel even more like we were on the same journey.

In my later years I realized what was likely going on. When you take acid, it forces your pupils to grow as big as they can, and they will not dilate at all. Your eyes are naturally designed to adapt to the light in your environment, your pupils will get smaller in bright lights, and bigger when it is dark. This prevents damage to your vision. With our pupils forced to capacity, my guess is that they couldn't adjust to the sudden burst of light from the camera flash. The flash bulb was a square, which was most likely why we were both seeing them at the same time.

Anyway, our night went on once the squares disappeared, and we decided to play ping pong. It stared out pretty normal but with all the extra energy we had and our lack of coordination, we abandoned the traditional rules and created only one. If the ball stops moving on your side of the room, you lose.

Corey and I found ourselves diving all over his cement basement to try and keep the ball in circulation. Even if it seemed like it was moving a tiny bit, it would get smashed towards the other side of the room. Soon enough it really wasn't ping-pong at all, but it was a lot of fun.

The night went on with music and more conversations about the amazing world we had discovered with LSD. We both agreed that it had been the greatest night we ever had. For Corey, it was a good time, but for me, the world of acid became my new obsession. I couldn't quite

place it, but I knew I was onto something relevant. I knew there had to be more to this new revelation than just fun.

Corey confided in me the next day that he had planned on throwing the drugs away and faking his whole trip. He said he was glad he didn't. That statement should have made me feel like a bad person, like I had pressured him into doing it, but it didn't. After experiencing it, I thought everyone should try it. If anyone were to bring it up in conversation, I had no problems telling them that LSD was the best drug on earth.

As it started to be a prominent element of my life, I got a

lot more used to it. I knew what to expect when it was first coming on, and how long it would normally take. One of the first signs that I would see was the floor moving a little when I would take a piss. Something about that old linoleum would always tell me that it was good, and I was about to trip out.

My friends and I would usually plan an entire night around it. I remember once I got a call from a woman I did some landscaping for to mow her lawn. I had already made plans that night to drop acid with my friends, so I tried to get out of it. I was told that it was my responsibility and I needed to do it, so I raced through it just to get it done. Needless to say, I didn't do a great job and I had to re-do the whole thing the next day. I just couldn't wait to get the drugs into me, so I was okay with starting over.

That night I was hanging out with my friend Steve. Typically, when we got high we would stay inside, but as time went on he started wanting to go out more. We ended up going out for a walk. Something about being out in public really put me inside of myself. I would get paranoid of people, like they were somehow the enemy.

That night we ended up running into one of Steve's friends, who was with his girlfriend. We paired up with them and walked around town. I was already feeling nervous from the drugs and being around people who were sober made me question everything. How would I normally act? What would I normally say? They already knew that Steve and I were high, and they thought it was cool, but it didn't change the way I felt.

We ended up walking past an abandoned building that had a lot of the windows already broken. I took notice and pointed it out. Steve's friend apparently saw it as an opportunity to show his rebellious side and threw a rock of his own. It smashed through one of the windows. Again, I started over-thinking. How loud was that? Is anyone near by?

We left the area quickly and ended up in some sort of parking lot for transport trucks. They must have had some sort of refrigeration units in them or something because it sounded like they were all running. I had no idea where we were, or why we were suddenly surrounded by what seemed like fifty running transport trucks. My first reaction was to feel like we had just walked in on some crazy truck cult or something. My friends had to reassure me that there were no people in them.

As we continued our way, Steve's friend picked up another rock and threw it as a car went by. My paranoia was still at the forefront, and I thought he was throwing it at the car. I told him that,

trying to gain some reassurance that he wouldn't do that, but instead he picked up another rock. "Like this?" He threw it at the road, leaving no doubt that it had hit the passing car.

I felt panic all over, but the car didn't stop. My relief was evidently his disappointment because he then picked up an entire handful of rocks. He tossed them all at the next car that went by. Most of them clearly hit, and no driver could have mistaken that for anything but what it was. Intentional.

I couldn't tell you if the car stopped or not. We were all on the same page and the four of us started running. I didn't look back. I had never run on acid before, but apparently, I was moving pretty quickly. It was a strange feeling. I didn't get tired or worry about what was ahead of me in the darkness. I just ran. It felt like the whole world of energy that came with the trip was all concentrated into that single action.

At some point we all stopped. I had no idea where we were, or where we were going. I didn't live in that town and wasn't familiar at all. We were on a backroad; it didn't have much traffic, but it had streetlights. The girl that was with us started to try and mess with me. As we passed under the lights, she would tell me when my shadow was going to get bigger, and then it would. Smaller. It did.

With my head full of acid, I couldn't comprehend how she was doing it. I think the idea of simplicity was completely gone for me. Everything had to be more sophisticated and more meaningful than it was in real life. Basic concepts didn't make a lot of sense. When we arrived at Steve's house, I was a bit surprised since I didn't know how we got there.

The girl looked at the clock once we got inside and pretended that she was surprised at the time. Apparently, her father was supposed to be picking her up somewhere and there was no way to get there in time on foot. Steve had a car that his parents had bought for him, and she was trying to convince him to drive her.

I reminded everyone that Steve was also on acid, and probably shouldn't be getting behind the wheel of a car. Even though I could be impulsive and reckless sometimes, I always had pretty good core values. Steve seemed strangely drawn to the idea and agreed to drive anyway.

I decided I would stay back. I tried to convince myself that Steve's friend was just showing off, but part of me really felt like he had ruined my whole trip. Acid was sacred to me, and I wanted to make every experience as positive as it could be. My thoughts continued to darken after they all left. I was alone in a house that wasn't very familiar and wondering if Steve would even make it back.

I found a pen and some paper and started writing and drawing. All the darkness that was in my head transferred to the paper in a way that I couldn't explain. I didn't feel the need to explain. I knew I was bound to have a bad trip at some point, but the creativity that I felt resulted from it made me want even more. It was a channel of expression that I had never been able to tap into before.

When I heard Steve open the door, I tossed the papers under the bed like I had been caught doing something wrong. I'm not sure why I felt that way but the whole experience led me more towards creation, and less towards the company of others.

Chapter Three

I pressed my back up against the edge of the bed and dug my heels into the floor. It was the lady from the forcefield desk. How did she get out? How did she manage to make it all the way down the hall without sinking into the floor?

"Mister Ferguson, I told you I was coming. It's time for you to see Doctor Ranck. Let's go, now."

I locked eyes with her. I couldn't see anything evil at first glance. I knew I had to be a chameleon. I had to blend in with my surroundings if I had any chance of figuring out what was going on. I felt like I was in the middle of a bad dream. I decided I would play ball. "Alright." I stood up and followed her out the door.

As we walked the vinyl flooring seemed to stay in place. I kept a small distance behind her and watched her feet. She wasn't sinking at all, and I wondered if she had some kind of control over the density of objects. She turned around a couple of times, seemingly to make sure I was still there. Possibly to make sure that the floor hadn't consumed me. It was hard to say.

We passed by the desk, and I tried to examine it. I still couldn't tell how she could have escaped it. I poked the glass, and it had no flexibility.

"Tom? This way, please."

I looked back to see that she had gotten pretty far ahead of me. I took one last look at the glass and then caught up to her. We walked down a hallway with only a few doors, one stood open.

She knocked on it as she spoke to the man inside. "Doctor Ranck, Mister Ferguson is here for his appointment."

"Send him in, Gladys."

She turned to me as she extended her hand towards the open door. "Right this way, Mister Ferguson.

I was apprehensive, but I knew I had to play along. I needed to find out where I was and how I got there. I couldn't remember anything. I walked past her and gave her a nod. I turned to face the room and saw a man sitting at a desk. He had dark hair, and he was wearing a grey suit. His tie had bright colors that I could already see were moving.

He gestured towards a chair that was across from him at the desk. "Come on in, Mister Ferguson, have a seat. I'm Doctor Ranck. Mark has told me all about you."

That name again. Who the hell was Mark? I walked slowly into the room and looked around. There were framed paintings on the walls. Some were art, and some were people. I recognized

Sigmund Freud. My first thought was that the guy was going to ask me if I had sexual dreams about my mother. I already didn't like him. I sat in the chair across from him and moved it backwards with my feet.

He shuffled through some papers on his desk. "So, you just joined us today?"

I nodded. I had no idea.

"Right, so this is basically just an introductory meeting. I'm not going to put much on your plate yet. We like you to settle in for a bit. I understand you have had an eventful weekend. How has today been?"

Again, I had no idea. "Fine."

"That's good to hear." He smiled the fakest grin I had ever seen. "We will meet once a day to set a plan and discuss your progress. We will review your medications and review all your behavior reports. Simple enough?"

This guy had no idea what I was capable of. I could read between the lines. I could take someone's words and dissect them in an instant. He wanted to control me. I needed to keep it together until I could remember more. "Sounds fair."

He nodded. He took his tie between two of his fingers and looked at it. The colors were starting to swirl onto his hand. "Do I have something on my tie?"

I shook my head. "I don't think so." The blues and greens started dripping down onto his desk, but he didn't seem to notice.

He let it go and pursed his lips a bit. "Okay, well I won't keep you too long. Just wanted to get acquainted. We'll meet again tomorrow. Have you had a chance to meet some of the other guys?"

"Hedburg."

"Hedburg? Oh, Annunziato. He's a delightful fellow."

I hated the gap I was having with my memory. What the hell was a-nun.. whatever? I just smiled and pretended like I knew exactly what was going on. "It was nice to meet you." I stood up from my chair, assuming that we were finished.

"Make sure you see Gladys before bed for your medication. Have a good day Mister Ferguson."

I headed towards the door and didn't look back. I went back the way I had came until I was back at the desk. Gladys was back behind it. She didn't seem to notice me, so I started to wave. I wondered if she was really there, or if she was just some kind of a hologram.

"Hello, Mister Ferguson. That was fast." She kept her eyes on whatever she was doing.

I pushed my finger against the glass again.

"Why don't you join the others in the common room for a while? May do you some good to socialize a bit."

I tilted my head in confusion. The whole place was a mystery to me. She pointed behind me. "Down there, to the left. Remember?"

I smiled and gave her a slight wave before turning around to try and find the place. It turned out to be only a short distance from her desk and around the corner. At first sight it was overwhelming. There was at least eight people in the room. Some were watching a television set that was projecting plastic people uttering nonsense to each other.

Before I had time to process, I was accosted by a strange little man with a lot of hair. "Hey Tommy, where ya been?"

I stared at the man. His teeth were rotten, and his eyebrows were bushy. He looked like he hadn't shaved or had a haircut for quite some time. The smell was overwhelming. Body odor and hot garbage. He had the same outfit on as I did but it was covered in blood.

He placed his hand on my shoulder, and I felt my flesh burning. "'Tommy? You alright? It's me, Benny. Remember? From before? You disappeared."

I projected a look that said I was having a revelation, but

Basket Weavers

I had no idea who the guy was. "Yeah, Hey Benny." I stepped back a bit to get his hand off me.

"Want to come paint with me now?" He pointed to a table that had some paper and pulsating colors. There was a large pool of blood on the surface. Black and white drips were crawling on the floor near an empty seat.

He started walking over to the table and I followed him. There were three chairs and he sat in one. I sat down close to him and looked at what he was working on. It was all done in blood. A smiling man and child with a red sky. The apocalypse foretold. The blood of the innocent reshaping into the souls of the wicked.

"Like my painting? Red's my favorite color. That's me and my dad."

"It's nice." I figured that the gross guy was an ally, so I took a chance. 'Hey, Benny, how do we get out of here?"

Benny used his fingers to add more blood to his painting. "Get out of here? I don't know. I don't think we can."

I watched him shaping a sphere above the wretched. A black hole that sucked in all life in its purest form and regurgitated it back as a toxin. "Does anyone here get special treatment? Stuff you don't get?"

He kept his finger on the painting. "Like my sun? Special treatment? We all get treated real nice."

"Nothing stands out at all? I need to know."

"No. Well, the only thing I can think of is maybe the basket weavers. But they need it."

"Basket weavers?"

"Yeah, they've been here a long time. There's a few of them. They like to make baskets all day, but they have their own room."

I nodded. I needed to process. Whoever the basket

weavers were, they were my ticket to freedom. I took a paper from the table. "Can I paint one?"

He looked up with a huge smile, possibly happy that I was changing the subject. "Sure, you can. But you have to use your fingers, or a sponge."

I placed the paper down in front of me and thought about what I would paint. Benny moved the jar of blood closer to me, as well as a jar filled with blue. I dipped my fingers into the blue and began drawing. I wasn't entirely sure what it was, but I was hoping it would jog my memory.

I began with a huge circle. From the top left of the circle, I started a line down, and then a bit before the bottom I went to the right, all the way to the inner edge. I dipped my finger back in the paint and started again from the top right and went straight down until it met up with the other line. Lastly, I put two partial horizontal lines in the space between.

"What is it?" Benny was looking at my painting.

"I'm not sure." I took some of the blood and began drawing random points and swirls on the outside of the circle. It was all starting to boil and melt. I couldn't tell what I had drawn but I knew it meant something.

I broke my gaze from my artwork and looked back to Benny. I was about to ask him more about the basket weavers, but we were interrupted by Hedberg pulling out the third chair and sitting down with us.

Benny looked up and smiled. "Hey, Nunz. Get all that paint off?"

The man smiled a large grin and then reached over and grabbed the blue paint. He stuck his entire hand in the bottle and started smearing it all over his face and bald head. I noticed another phantom demon escape from his nostrils as he titled his head back to rub the paint in.

Basket Weavers

He jumped up from the chair and started yelling. "Heburg, smurf! Smurf Hedburg!"

A woman came to our table who was wearing a navy outfit. Her hair was blonde, and she had the aura of an innocent. She looked flustered. "Annunziato we just got you cleaned up, what have you done?"

"Hedburg smurf!"

The woman placed a hand on her hip and looked over at us. "Benjamin, please don't let Annunziato get into the paint. I've asked you several times today."

Benny looked down at the table like a scolded puppy. "I'm sorry Mrs. Timmerman. He just started doing it again."

The woman placed her hand on Hedburg to get him to stand. He jumped from his chair and ran out of the room. She followed him and left me alone with Benny again. "Why do you have to watch him?"

He shrugged. "Mrs. Timmerman and I have an understanding. I'm her helper."

I could feel my eyes starting to squint. The guard was using the captives to do her bidding. She likely had access to some sort of mind control. Maybe she even had some sort of cloaking device to make herself appear as an innocent. Hide from me in plain sight.

I stood from the table and looked around the room. Everyone seemed so docile. Possibly trained or under duress. I had to figure out where I was and how I got there. I had to find out how to get out. I knew it all started with the task of seeking out the basket weavers. They were the key.

I started to walk away and took one last look at my painting. In the middle of the circle there were three letters. It had to mean something. How did I know to draw it? It wasn't conventional lettering, but it clearly read, LSD.

Chapter Four

When I was fifteen years old, my girlfriend was pregnant. I had been happy with her for a few months, but she slowly became more and more controlling. One night she was over and planned on going home by around ten. She told me I wasn't allowed to do drugs anymore, since we were going to be parents.

I had spoken to Dylan earlier in the night and we had made plans for him to come over around nine with some of his other friends. We were all going to take acid together and hang out. They all came by, and I dropped a few hits, figuring that my girlfriend would be gone by the time they started to kick in.

Once she realized that I was having people over, she didn't want to leave. She didn't like the idea of me socializing with anyone but her. She called her mother and asked if she could get picked up by a friend instead and spend the night at their place.

I went into a bit of a panic. I knew her mother was intelligent, and I didn't think she would believe such an obvious lie. Unfortunately, she did and gave permission for my girlfriend to return home in the morning. With my friends already there and the chemicals taking hold of my system, I wasn't sure what to do.

The result was her getting what she wanted. The two of us stayed in another room, while Dylan and his friends all hung out and had fun. I did my best to act normal so she wouldn't know I had taken drugs and she never mentioned anything. This turned out to be the first night I would have sex under the influence of LSD.

It was a pretty intense experience, but it wasn't something that really stood out. I remember walking to the bathroom after we were done and having to pass by all my guests that I had been ignoring all night. I was embarrassed that I couldn't stand up to my girlfriend. When I made it to the bathroom the moving linoleum showed me that the drugs were in full effect. I ended up spending the night having conversations that I didn't understand and pretending to sleep.

Around the same time, I had a friend named Brett. We had met the year before and gotten along well. One night we stayed up outside by the fire and talked about real things. Feelings, traumas, that sort of thing. I looked up to him after that for a long time.

The thing with Brett was that he was a womanizer. He always had different girlfriends at the same time, and I would watch as he lied to them and focused only on getting laid. The way he would make connections with women was the same way he connected with me. He would confide in them and make them feel important in their conversations.

It wasn't long before my daughter's mother and I broke up. Soon after I started seeing Mary. She was a bit younger than me, but I thought I saw someone who I could really connect with. I used Brett's technique, thinking that it was the best way to build a real bond like I had with him. The first time I hung out with Mary our conversation went in the direction of trauma and understanding.

She told me that she had been molested at a young age by a man who reeked of whiskey. She would never want to disclose who it was, or many details and I respected that. It started off our relationship on a level that made me feel was deep. With that as the basis, we moved forward as a couple and soon enough we were taking acid together.

One night we went over to hang out with one of Mary's friends. There was often a party going on at the house with some regular guests. I learned that night that Mary had apparently been with the boyfriend of one of my friends. I learned this when we ran into them while on acid. The vibe was hard to explain, amplified by chemicals it was even more of a challenge.

It was like a huge negative energy washed over me and I had to pick a side in that moment. My friend or my girlfriend. We found ourselves crossing paths with them and stopped mid-stride and turned around, walking away. That action made it clear who I was choosing, and it really got the night off to a bad start. I wanted to reach out to my friend after that night and talk, but I never did, and we never really spoke much again after.

Later in the same night we ended up in Mary's friends' room, just talking and hanging out. Suddenly her friend's dad came in with intensity. He pointed at me, and Mary. "You two, get out. Now." I still have no idea to this day what prompted this, we assumed it was because he found out that we had taken acid.

I asked for the phone and called my mother. I remember my leg was shaking uncontrollably, and I imagine I looked really sketchy. My mom told me that she couldn't come and get us, so our next option was to call Mary's mom. We both preferred to have my mom drive us, as we figured she wouldn't notice or care that we were high.

While Mary called her mom, I could feel a lingering tension in the room. It felt like her friend's family were just sitting there watching us as we tried to find a way home. And wanting nothing more than to get us out of their house. I felt like a spectacle and an outcast. Waiting for Mary's mom felt like a long time, and we were both doing our best to act normal.

When she got there and picked us up, we were both somber. Still filled with chemicals and unsure of what we did to provoke such a reaction. Mary's mom put on a country music station and turned the volume up loud. Being on acid, neither of us could figure out if that was normal, and we weren't sure how to react.

It got even stranger when we got back to Mary's place and her mother had some fun by driving across the front lawn with the car. Again, we had no idea what was happening, and found ourselves both asking, "Is this normal?"

When we got out of the car, we both talked about the evening, and tried to figure out if everything we had experienced was even real. It seemed like strange things would always

happen when we took acid, or maybe the acid just made them seem strange. I feel I will never really know.

I would question my own thoughts a lot on this drug and challenge my own perceptions fairly often. How would I normally react to this? Is it weird that I didn't mention that? Did they do that because they know I am high? All questions that always seemed very relevant at the time.

These nights almost added to the allure of LSD, it gave

me a story to tell and made me feel like my life was interesting. The more I did the more my mind would venture into new territory. When I was under the influence, I felt liberated, and I felt that I was opening my brain up to brand new concepts.

Often when I would come off the drugs, the things I remembered as being mind altering and life changing were nothing more than regular thought process and common knowledge. Despite this, I was not anywhere near ready to even consider giving it up.

A while after that night, and countless trips later, Mary and I were invited to go to Niagara Falls with my sister. When we got there, we found that the only room available for Mary and I was the Honeymoon suite, which had a giant heart shaped Jacuzzi.

The whole thing just reeked of tourism, and I felt like the whole city was just a giant cash grab. We did our best to have a good time, and for the first day it worked out well. The second night we were there my sister went out to see the lights, and Mary and I opted to stay in the hotel and take acid.

Once the drugs began to take hold, the world started looking like it was some sort of scene right out of a bad movie. The fake atmosphere of the hotel room was enhanced ten-fold by the heart shaped Jacuzzi tub. My thoughts began to race in different directions, and I felt like I was having an intense revelation.

Since I had first taken LSD, I had been doing it as often as I could. It was starting to feel like one trip was a continuation from the last. It wasn't even fun anymore, it felt closer to the lines of a spiritual journey. I felt that some of the answers I was looking for were coming soon, and I continued to venture further down the rabbit hole.

I started rambling intently about the world, and how there was a realm of people that were trying to pull us in to a world that we didn't want to enter. I concocted a giant conspiracy about a subtle battle between good and evil. I was getting to the point where LSD had altered my way of thinking to a pretty serious extreme, but I was embracing it as fact. I felt like I could see things that the rest of the world could not.

I kept looking to Mary for reassurance, assuming she saw all the same things that I did. That was the night that she broke down. She told me that a lot of the things she had shared with me about her past in our first conversation were fabricated. She had never been assaulted and had no real trauma in her past at all.

I'm not sure why it was so important to me. In an instant I felt alone. I had no idea how to process the information when I was already out of my mind and drawing intense conclusions about the world we lived in. I froze up a bit and suddenly began keeping all my intense thoughts to myself, allowing them to resonate in my brain. My paranoia kicked in and I had no idea what to think.

The rest of the night was a bit of a blur. What stands out to me more was when we woke up the next day. My paranoid thoughts continued to haunt me more than ever. Typically, when you take acid, you can still feel some underlying effects the day after. You're not really high but you still feel like your reality is skewed.

We wandered around the city, which was full of tourist attractions and fun houses. I remember one specific conversation with Mary. It felt like the idea of an evil group of people trying to lure me into their reality was the definite conclusion I had come to, but now I was unsure as to which side she was on.

Basket Weavers

We were staring at a haunted house, and I remember saying that it must have been a crappy attraction, because nobody was going in. It was like under the guise of a regular observation I was actually talking about the sinister world that I had discovered. She responded by saying that it may have been so good, that nobody was leaving once they had gone in.

I felt like she was admitting that she was part of the dark forces and was trying to convince me to enter the world that I perceived as being evil. I was holding my ground and saying that I would never go in. Though we both used the fun house as a reference, this conversation may have been completely fabricated in my head. To this day I have no idea.

At the time it felt very real, and I began to question my entire world. Every time I have been to Niagara Falls since then, that night has crossed my mind and made me feel a bit crazy.

Chapter Five

I looked around the room for anyone I thought I may be able to trust. There were two couches, one had three people and on the second sat only one. I could tell that he was glancing back and forth between me and the television. I walked over and stood next to him. "Mind if I sit?"

"Shh.."

I nodded and took a seat beside him. I could feel myself sinking into the furniture and hoped that when the time came, I would be able to get back up. I looked up at the screen and right away the control machine was clear. People pretending to be someone else, engaging in a fictional conversation. Listening to the words, reading between the lines, it was all about keeping the people placid.

I looked over at the man, he seemed nervous. "You know, they put this shit on there to keep your eyes off the real problems. Our own free will is nothing more than a clever illusion, projected by our own eyes. Our senses have been poisoned and our brains have been conditioned to absorb this kind of bullshit to generate someone else's idea of what life should look like."

He looked over at me as though something I said made sense to him. His eyes were a chestnut brown, and his hair was disheveled and a bit long. He just stared for a minute before he opened his mouth, revealing his crooked teeth. "Smash the control images, smash the control machine."

He leapt up from the couch and started to jump up and slap the screen of the television. The men on the other couch all began grumbling and telling him to sit down. He continued to do everything he could to break the glass, but it was protected with some kind of forcefield. I imagined it was similar to the one that encased Gladys's desk.

"That's enough now, Matthew."

I looked to see the blonde in the blue outfit walking over. She was trying to control Benny, and now she was trying to control my new friend, Matthew. I wanted to intervene, but I was afraid of showing my cards. I couldn't let anyone really know the things I knew. I watched as Matthew abandoned his campaign and stared at the blonde.

She looked at me with annoyance. "I'm pretty sure Mark asked you not to engage with him." She looked back to my friend. "Come with me, Matthew."

Matthew followed the blonde out to the hallway. He looked defeated. I've seen the look of defeat before and it always pulls at your heartstrings. The men on the other couch started clapping. They were clearly oppressors who supported the control mechanisms. It was really starting to bother me who this Mark character was. He was clearly in a power role but it sounded like I

already knew him. I couldn't risk admitting that I had no idea who he was. I thought I may be able to ask Benny.

I lied back on the couch. I could feel my head sinking

into the fabric. I looked around the room and noticed what looked to be surveillance cameras in several locations. We were being monitored. I tried not to stare at them, I didn't want to alert our captor that I realized they were there. I tried to watch the television, but I couldn't stand it.

I tried to get up, but the couch had swallowed me. I was in partial paralysis, and I took it as a sign that I needed to do some reflection. The walls in the room were the same taupe as the hallways. The flooring was the same white vinyl that I already knew could develop quicksand properties when it was instructed to. I felt trapped.

My heart started racing and my energy started going bad. I was about to scream for help when I felt a wave slip under me and free me from my prison.

"Tommy, what was that all about?"

Benny had sat down beside me. I had never been so happy to smell something so awful. I leaned over to him and kept my voice quiet. "Matthew knows about the control machine. He tried to make a stand and they kidnapped him."

"Kidnapped him? I saw him leave with Mrs. Timmerman."

"Where is she taking him?"

"He'll get a time out in his room; he'll be back soon. What did you say to him?"

I could tell that Benny had been brainwashed. His thoughts were always so simple. He did seem like a good source of information, so I decided to try to dig a bit further regarding the basket weavers. "Hey, Benny, can you introduce me to the basket weavers?"

He got a look on his face as though he had just been scolded. "They don't really talk much, and we're not really supposed to go in there while they have the room."

I was intrigued. "Authorized personnel only? Do they have powers?"

"Well, they sure do make nice baskets. I think because they have sharp things. They've been here for a really long time but nobody else can have the stuff that they have."

No, I was certain that they were my way out. If they weren't directly in charge, they would surely know who was. Whose eyes were watching the feeds from the camera's. Who was holding me captive. Before I could finish my conversation, a loud burst of noise filled the air. I sprang from the couch and dropped to the floor, covering my head. It was an air-raid siren. I held tight to myself and braced for an explosion, but it didn't come, and silence was restored.

I lifted my head just enough to see Benny crouched up beside me. He looked like he was crying. "Are we okay?"

"I don't know. That sound."

"The dinner bell?"

"What?"

"That's the sound that the walls make when it's time for us to go get dinner."

I looked up and saw that the room was nearly empty. We were being conditioned like Pavlov's dogs. Wherever I was, it was more sinister and sophisticated than I had given it credit for. I stood slowly and Benny followed suit.

He was reluctant to walk past me, but I motioned for him to continue. "Lead the way."

He nodded and I followed him out into the corridor. The rest of the group were a little way ahead of us. He gave me a nudge and looked to his left. There was a door with a small window. "That's where they work." He looked down at the floor and tried to act like he didn't say anything.

I knew I needed to cease the opportunity, so I slowed my pace. Benny kept walking and when he got far enough ahead, I turned around to go check out the door. It looked like an average door, but the window was made of ice. A large crack ran through the middle of it. I placed my hand on it, and it was cold to the touch.

I peered inside and saw the blonde Timmerman lady placing tools into a safe of some sort. There were partially finished baskets lying all over the floor and three chairs where the weavers were likely working. She picked up the baskets and placed them on a shelf that hung from the wall.

I was fascinated by what I was seeing. I got lost in the moment and soon enough she noticed me. She locked the safe with a key from her keyring and approached the door. I tried to step away, but I knew it was too late.

"Mister Ferguson, what are you doing? It's dinner time. The lunch hall is that way." She pointed to the left.

I nodded, pretending that I didn't see anything. I started walking and before I knew it, she was right beside me.

"What did you say to Matthew to get him so worked up?"

She was on to me. She probably already had Matthew on her radar since he seemed to be the most aware of what was actually going on. "I just told him that I don't like TV."

"Okay, well just don't get him worked up like that, alright? He almost had to miss dinner."

They starve the educated. They deprive the free-thinkers of their basic needs in order to lower their inhibitions. I needed to be careful. "I'm sorry."

We arrived at the lunchroom. Everyone was already seated. It looked like a soup kitchen with all the scruffy men sitting around. I scanned around and saw Matthew sitting by himself. Mrs. Timmerman noticed that I was looking at him. "Let Matthew sit by himself, please. He needs some more time to calm down."

It was starting to make sense why Matthew could see the big picture. He was clearly the victim of control and manipulation. I decided to avoid any conflict and went and sat near Benny.

"Hey Tommy, were you getting in trouble?"

"Trouble? No. I'm just being oppressed. Being told where to go, where to sit, what to say. That sort of thing."

He got a look of confusion on his face and didn't seem to know how to respond. "Oh, okay."

The sound of indistinct chatter filling the room sounded like static in my head. White noise. The tables were all metal, and I noticed they were bolted to the floor. Utensils sat at each place, but they were made of plastic. It was clear that many measures were in place to keep us from defending ourselves in the event of an attack.

The room fell silent as a woman in a white uniform wheeled out a plastic cart with plates of food on it. Two others helped her place individual portions in front of each of us. When a ration was placed in front of me, I struggled to understand how people were remaining so calm.

There were two long meat logs, and they both had tiny eyes that were blinking every few seconds. Next to them was a pile of orange worms that were still squirming around all over the plate. A pile of curdled milk finished it off, with a small mouth that kept opening as if it were about to speak but couldn't. As I stared at the monstrosity before me, the woman came around again and filled my plastic cup to the brim with some sort of piss.

I picked up my plastic utensil and jabbed at one of the meat logs. Its eyes went wide as I penetrated its flesh. Oily blood spilled out and landed beside the worms, who devoured it with no hesitation. I looked over at Benny, who had worms dangling from his lips. He was chewing happily and didn't seem to realize what he was doing.

Glancing around the room, it was the same story. They were all eating the fleshy milk and gnawing on the tiny meat creatures. At that point I realized how serious my situation really was. What kind of a place could convince rational people to consume such a brutal feast?

Benny noticed my apprehension. "You not eating Tommy?"

I stared at my plate. I really wanted to act as though I belonged, but I had limits. There was no way I could bring myself to put any of that in my mouth. I looked back to him. "I'm not really hungry."

He leaned in and whispered. "Can I have your sausage?"

I assumed he meant the strange winking meat tubes. I knew what sausage looked like, and that wasn't it. "Yeah man, sure. I owe you one."

In a quick motion he jabbed his plastic spork on my plate, spearing one of the creatures. Again, the oily blood jumped from the wound, and I watched him jam the whole thing in his mouth. As he chewed the juices trickled down into his beard. He was eating as though he had been starved. Thinking back to Matthew, and what the blonde had said, maybe he really had been starved.

He swallowed hard and smiled. His face dripping with greasy residue from the fresh kill. "We aren't allowed to share food."

I nodded. The pieces were coming together. They brought each man his own personal meal and he was the only one who was allowed to consume it. They likely loaded it with toxins that would target specific neurological attributes. If they found out what I was thinking, they would surely give me something to chemically lobotomize me.

Aaron Lebold

I looked over to Benny. "Do we have to stay here?"

He had another worm hanging out from between his teeth. "Don't you want desert?"

I shuttered to think what desert may be. I looked up to see a second cart being wheeled out. I stood from my chair and walked in that direction. The cart was filled with bowls filled with brown sludge. Possibly some sort of tar mixture, or maybe even feces. Whatever it was, I wasn't interested. I had to keep myself from throwing up as I headed towards the exit.

Chapter Six

I started my first real job after high school in 1999. I was nineteen years old, and I had moved in with my sister temporarily. At that point I had been taking LSD as often as I could for about four years. It had become my second world. It was a place where I could escape to and feel like I meant something.

Leading up to the new millennium, there was a lot of talk about what would happen when the clock hit midnight. There were all kinds of talk about computers only being set to handle two digits for the year, and when they flipped, they would go from 99 to oo with devastating effects. People were convinced the world was going to end, and some even stocked up on canned goods and made shelters to prepare for the apocalypse.

I never believed in any of that type of thing, but in the back of my mind part of me was hoping to watch the city spontaneously burst into flames when the clock hit midnight. I figured I should go a bit more extreme on New Years than I normally did to mark the occasion.

Mary and I made plans to hang out with a couple that

Brett and I had met at a bar. Naturally we decided that we would all take acid. I had found a new connection in the city, and the blotter I got was stronger than anything I had ever tried. I dropped nine hits for New Years that year. Everyone else took two or three.

The night began well, just hanging out and having fun. It wasn't long before I felt like they were dropping subtle hints about doing something sexual. I felt like I was being paranoid, but at the same time I felt like there was a lot of pressure being put on me. I wasn't sure if it was the drugs, or if I was going crazy, but it felt like the same thing that had recently happened with Brett.

All sorts of memories started flooding back to me. A continuation from my other trips. I thought back to Niagara Falls and the way I saw Mary. I would look to her to help me make sense of what I was feeling but she seemed to be putting pressure on me as well. The whole thing felt huge in my head. I thought back to the funhouse. Maybe it was just a metaphor, but once you go in, you don't come back out.

The night went on like that for a while, and I got to the point where I was ready to give in because I felt so much pressure, but I had no idea what to do, and thankfully did nothing. I still felt a sense of shame for the idea that I was almost willing to put myself in a position that I really didn't want to be in, for the sake of what I felt others wanted. I felt like I was being manipulated by the forces that I couldn't see, but I knew were out there. Not the people per say, but something bigger trying to draw me in and change me.

I remember going to the bathroom and looking in the mirror. Staring at my reflection through acid-soaked eyes made me appear to myself as though I wasn't even human. It was very surreal, and my paranoia started to intensity. I was getting to the point where it was hard for me to distinguish which thoughts I should trust.

When I was sober, I felt depressed and alone, and completely lacking in self-confidence. I think that's why I tended to believe that the world I saw through the eyes of LSD was the one I wanted to put my faith in.

The apartment building we were in was high up, likely more than twenty floors off the ground. I went out to the balcony right before it hit midnight and waited with anticipation. While I stood there, I imagined the city burning, building exploding, people screaming. I tried my hardest to will the apocalypse upon us. It seemed like an easy way out. If all of humanity died in the Y2K thing that had become so popular, I would never have to figure out what was real.

Mary and I walked back to my apartment that night, it was late, and we didn't really talk. The whole thing left me feeling awkward and ashamed, even though I didn't actually do anything. It was a long night without a lot of sleep. It still didn't convince me to put the brakes on my acid use. I still didn't know which reality I could trust.

Despite the fact that my mind was starting to go in a lot of different directions, I still felt that Brett was the one person I could always trust and rely on. He invited me over to his girlfriend's place one night. When I got there, I saw that the couple from New Year's was also there. Using the same logic as I typically did, I made the decision to take acid again that night, and again my mind picked up where it had left of on my previous trip.

As soon as I walked in, I had a strange feeling. Shortly after getting there, Brett just got straight to the point and asked me to sleep with him and his girlfriend. He did this thing where he touched the tip of my nose with his finger, like people often do when they are trying to be cute with their girlfriends. To this day that gesture still makes me cringe when someone does it to me. "Boop."

To me the whole thing was a lot bigger than just sex. All the acid-soaked thoughts and ideas created a much bigger picture that I felt more than thought. I had made it as clear as I could that I wasn't interested, yet Brett kept pushing. All the thoughts that filled my head in Niagara Falls about an evil force trying to lure me in pushed their way back to the forefront of my mind.

I left the house and walked back to my sister's apartment. When I got there, I called Mary right away and tried to explain my situation as best as I could. While I was on the phone, Brett continued to call. I answered a couple times and told him I would talk to him later, but he kept calling over and over. I hung up with Mary and hit *67 to disable call waiting.

I called her back. I knew that if Brett kept trying to call, he would get a busy signal. Surely that would get my point across. I thought he had received my message clearly, but it turned out I was wrong. About thirty minutes after I disabled call waiting there was a knock at my door. My sister knew I was freaking out and told me she would take care of it. When she opened the door, it was Brett, his girlfriend, and the couple from New Years all standing outside.

My sister started to tell them that I didn't want to see them, and to talk to me later. Brett kept insisting, and they all made me feel like I was overreacting. I ended up getting a bit frustrated

and told them all to leave. I will never forget the response I got from Brett. He looked at me with a look I had never really seen before and said, "I will call you tomorrow."

The way that it came across was like he knew that he could get me back on the line. He knew that he would be able to manipulate me to forgive and forget, like I had always done in the past. It sent a chill down my spine, and I suddenly had a revelation.

I thought back to different moments in time where I had raised a bit of a flag in my mind, and connected all the dots. I realized how much Brett had lied to me about everything, and I saw the need he had for complete control. I realized that the feelings I had towards him were implanted on purpose, and I was nothing more to him but practice.

I thought back to all the things that stood out in my mind over the years. Him telling me he was a serious alcoholic as a teenager, his girlfriend being a recovering cocaine addict. He told me he could buy guns and once he was supposed to be getting acid for a bunch of people and he said he got robbed at gunpoint. I had always believed him when nobody else did, and suddenly I felt like a complete idiot.

I called Mary back to fill her in on what had happened, and I started going off on a paranoid tangent. I was still out of my mind on acid, but I felt like I had a massive awakening. I remember telling her my conclusion. Brett was just like Charles Manson; he would recruit people into his control and get them to bend to his will. The people in his circle would do anything for him, and that had always included me.

I had almost killed a complete stranger for no reason a few years before, just because Brett had suggested it. I had placed all my faith in him and regarded him as a deity for years. In that moment it became clear that he cared nothing about me, and just tried to push the limits as to how far he could persuade me in his desired direction.

I spent that night with minimal sleep, and overwhelming thoughts. It basically changed my entire life.

After that, I wish I could say that I was able to move on as though nothing happened, but that was not the case. The paranoid thoughts continued to manifest, and I felt afraid for my life. I didn't want to break communication with Brett right away because I was afraid of how he would respond.

I was convinced that he was a type of cult leader, and that he had manipulated me and taken advantage of me since we had met. His girlfriend had called me not long after and tried to see my side of things. It was hard to explain to someone the magnitude of what I was thinking without sounding like a crazy person. To her, they were just a couple trying to branch out sexually. The more I tried to explain, the more confused I became about reality.

I started seeing traits of my perceived evil world in other people, everywhere in my life. I got to the point of isolating myself from just about everyone, and only left the house when I needed to. I suddenly found myself second guessing the large majority of what I believed in, and feeling like my entire world was a lie.

I equated these feelings to the idea of one day seeing a small defect on the side of your house, and after some investigating finding out that the foundation itself was actually made of Styrofoam, instead of cement. I was asking myself how the whole thing hadn't crumbled sooner, and how I could have possibly not noticed it for so long.

I could tell that one of two things were happening; I was either starting to see things that others couldn't, or I was getting close to becoming an acid casualty. I still had about 35 hits left from the most recent sheet I had purchased, and I had to figure out if I was going to go deeper down the rabbit hole, or retreat from the drug altogether.

Over the years LSD had become a best friend to me. A portal to a world where I was special. I could feel things and see things that most people couldn't comprehend. Since I had alienated all my other friends, it was difficult to consider parting ways with the one that had always been there for me. At the risk of losing my mind, I made a decision.

Chapter Seven

I started heading back in the direction of the locked door. I needed more information if I had any chance of reaching the weavers. As I moved the walls started distorting from the energy of my speed. I hardly even noticed the man in front of me and when we collided it nearly sent me on my ass.

"Whoa there." He had a green uniform and dark hair. "Oh. Hey, Tom. How are you settling in?"

I took a step back and examined him. I had no idea who the man was. He had a large growth on his chin, it was brown and pulsating. He reached out to touch my shoulder and I couldn't help but flinch.

"Are you alright? It's me, Mark. We spent the whole morning together, remember? Like, twelve hours ago?"

Mark. I had to remind myself that everyone told me I knew the man. At least I now knew what he looked like. It also occurred to me that he likely had information about the room and the weavers. He seemed like he wanted to engage so I decided to take him up on the offer. "Right, of course.

I'm not going to forget you, Mark. You just startled me. How are you?"

"I'm fine, I was just going to grab some dinner. Where are you headed in such a hurry? Come join me and we can talk about your first day."

I nodded. I was reluctant to return to that lunchroom but decided it was worth it if I could get some answers. I walked with him and sat at an empty table while he went and grabbed a plate of nightmares. He returned and sat across from me, immediately picking up some of the curdled milk with his fork. "Are you not eating?"

"I'm not really hungry. I had slugs for lunch."

He laughed as though I was joking, but I wasn't sure if I was or not. Some of the strange substance fell to his chin when he opened his mouth and the growth on his face opened its tiny mouth and consumed it. I tried to keep it together.

"So, have you had a chance to meet everyone?"

"I met Benny and Hedburg. Also, a guy named Matthew."

"Right. You were playing cards with Benny and Annunziato this morning. I told you about Matthew too. You didn't say anything to set him off, did you?"

I had to think fast. "Accidentally. We were talking about TV."

"Right, well just keep your distance from him while he settles in." I nodded.

"How did your meeting go with Doctor Ranck?"

I wasn't interested in small talk, so I figured I would just get to the point. "It was fine. Hey, what do you know about the basket weavers?"

"Basket weavers? Oh, you mean the Johnson brothers? I

told you everything already. Are you sure you're feeling alright? You seem off."

"Yeah, I just want to get to know those guys a bit."

"Well I told you, they've had a rough go, and they don't talk."

I was intrigued. The weavers were mute. That alone told me that they operated on a different level. Only someone who saw the truth about the world could have the willpower to shut down communication and keep their secrets. "Can I meet them?"

Mark shrugged as he bit the head off of one of the meat creatures. "Well sure, but they don't socialize much. They craft for two hours twice a day, and when they aren't doing that they usually just sit in their room. Why the interest in the Johnson's?"

I kept my eyes on the table, avoiding having to look at his plate. "I was hoping I could maybe weave some baskets one day. I like crafts."

"Well, for now, you just focus on getting settled in. You only have a couple of weeks with us, and you need to get yourself back on track."

I glanced up at his face. He looked like he had secrets. I wondered what would happen to me after two weeks. I assumed that they would see how much I knew, and if it was too much, they would make me disappear. The fact that he was trying to get my focus off the weavers also spoke volumes. He knew I was onto something. I tried to smile. "I'm going to go lie down for a bit."

"Alright, as long as you're going to your room. The common room is closed until six for cleaning."

I stood from the table, acting as natural as I could. I headed back down the hallway and stopped in front of the locked room. I peered inside and saw that it was empty.

Only chairs, half-made baskets and the safe could be seen. I tried the door, but it was locked. I knew my time was limited by myself, so I went back to the common room. It seemed suspicious that they would have to lock it to clean it.

I peered inside the window and saw the Timmerman lady searching through the couch. All the cushions were piled on the floor. She was checking to see if anyone had left anything

incriminating. Any information about things they had learned or occurrences they witnessed. The whole place was designed for secrecy and malevolence.

She looked up and we locked eyes. All my nervous energy congregated in my stomach and I could feel myself starting to sweat. She started walking in my direction and my fight or flight response came to the forefront. I was done with flight. I prepared myself for battle as she cracked the door open.

"Hey Tom, I'm just cleaning up in here, you'll have to come back at six. Did you get some dinner?"

I couldn't figure out why everyone kept asking me the same thing. They had an agenda that included me eating that plate of organisms. I decided to lie and see how she would respond. "Oh yes, it was very good. Did you get some?"

"I usually bring my own food from home. I have to get back to work now, come back at six."

She closed the door in my face. I kept watching for a minute. I was sure she knew I was there, but she pretended not to. She went back to searching the couches. In that moment I hoped that I hadn't left anything incriminating. I couldn't remember anything from the first half of the day, it was hard to say what I had or hadn't done.

I headed back towards Gladys's station, hoping she

Basket Weavers

would be there to talk. My impression was that she may be the type of person who had more information than they realized. She may not have been in a position of authority, but she saw the daily goings-on of the base.

I saw her behind her glass barrier, she was preparing pills of some sort. She noticed me coming and gave me a wave. I took it as an invitation to go talk to her. "Hey, Gladys. How are you?"

"Hey Tom, just prepping the evening meds. Did you find the lunchroom?"

Her too. I needed to keep up the facade. "Oh yes, the worms were very tasty. Did you get some?"

A strange thing happened to her face. Her typically smooth ebony complexion collapsed slightly in on itself for a brief moment. "Worms? I thought they were serving carrots and sausage with mashed potato?"

I had to give her points for creativity. "Oh yeah, well whatever it was, I ate lots. Feeling super complacent."

"Okay.."

"Say, Gladys, who watches those cameras in the common room?"

She smiled. It was an uncomfortable grin, as though she was concerned with my inquiries. "Well, I have a monitor right here." She turned a screen towards me, and I could see Timmerman

vacuuming the floor. I could tell it had some sort of filter in it so they could gather small fibers and skin samples for later analysis. She turned it back before I could see much else. "We just use them to make sure everything is going alright in there, and that everyone is getting along."

I nodded. I had more questions, but we were interrupted by the sound of footsteps coming down the hall. It was a symphony of tap shoes and obstructed conversations.

I turned to see nearly everyone exiting the lunchroom at the same time. Benny and Hedburg both approached me.

"Hedburg pills!"

I felt a wave of confusion and looked over at Benny.

"Tommy, get out of the way so Nunz can get his evening meds."

I realized I was still standing in front of Gladys's bunker. I stepped aside and watched as Hedburg stepped up to the window. Gladys handed him a small paper cup and a plastic glass filled with what I assumed was water. "Here you are, Mister Hedburg."

"Hedburg pills!"

He emptied the contents into his mouth, followed by the liquid. I could only speculate on what I was witnessing. Perhaps they were brain-melting pills and a shot of liquid nitrogen. It certainly would explain the man's behavior. I watched in awe as he opened his mouth wide and lifted his tongue in front of Gladys. "All gone!"

As fast as he had arrived, Hedburg was gone. Benny stepped up to the window and Gladys handed him the same type of small paper cup. I knew I needed to get out of there before they tried to give me anything. I took a few steps in the opposite direction, nearly bumping into someone.

I looked up to see a large man, his eyes spread very wide apart. They were almost touching his ears. His face was scruffy, and he looked at the floor. He was with two other men who had a similar appearance. Something about them looked familiar like I had seen them before.

"Excuse me."

The man didn't answer. He kept his gaze on his feet and continued down the hallway. It hit me; I remembered where I had seen those men. They were the basket weavers.

Basket Weavers

I didn't recognize them out of their element. It was my chance to try and get in with them. I followed them.

As soon as I felt my feet sinking, I knew exactly where I was. The vinyl tar pit was still trying to suck me in. The three men moved at a slow pace, so I had to figure out how to stay with them and not fall victim to the floor. I walked beside one and tried to start a conversation. "Hey, I'm Tom."

When he didn't respond I felt a little deflated, but Mark had mentioned that they don't really talk much. I decided to go for it. "Look, I get it. I wouldn't have anything to say to me either. The thing is, I know who you are. I see you. I see you when others don't, and I think we can really put our heads together to understand the confinement that we have found ourselves in."

The man paused for a moment and stared at me. He remained silent but the look in his eyes told me that he was interested in what I had to say. They all filed into a single room, and the last man left the door open. I knew it was an invitation for me to follow them.

I was glad to be back on solid ground once I crossed the threshold. The room looked similar to mine, except it had three beds. The three men all sat down and crossed their hands across their laps. The first two stared at the floor while the third looked at me, clearly waiting for more information.

I wasn't sure how much time I had, so I needed to get straight to the point and choose my words carefully. "Alright, I know how important you guys are. You are the key to getting free from this place. If we work together, we can remove the shackles that have been placed on our minds and finally see the ultimate truth."

The other two turned their heads to face me, but still, no words were spoken. With their attention on me, I continued. "The first step is agreeing to work together. Next time you guys are in that room, watch the window. If you see me looking in, open the door. I'll take it from there."

They all continued to stare at me but didn't give me a response. I could tell that I had got through to them and just hoped that they would follow through with their end of the plan. I could see it in them, they were sick of being slaves. They were just as fed up with the system as I was. It was time to take a stand, which we could only do as a united unit.

"Alright, I'm going to go so they don't see us talking. Remember, watch for me and open the door. Together we will combine our efforts and liberate ourselves from the prison that is being forced upon our minds, and our spirits." I stepped back and closed the door. My feet started sinking as soon as I was back in that damn hallway.

Chapter Eight

For a few months, I stuck with two hits a week. It was enough to keep one foot in both worlds without cutting out either one completely. I felt like I needed retribution. Once the fear wore off, it was replaced by anger. I felt completely manipulated, and like people saw me for a fool. I needed a plan to get back at Brett, and whatever sinister part of the universe that was pulling his strings.

I contemplated several ideas as the months went on. Often times I would drop acid and have what I thought was a perfect plan, but when I sobered up, I noticed flaws that I had previously overlooked. The issue was that my ability to restrain continued to diminish. Once the sheet I had was gone, I went and bought another.

First it went up to two hits three times a week, and before I knew it, it was every other day. Despite not having formulated an exact plan, I had a pretty good idea of my direction. Something explosive, with a wick. One night I was sitting in my apartment and noticed the incense I had burning. It would make a perfect time delay.

Aaron Lebold

I had already concluded that putting aluminum foil on a battery could cause a fire or explosion, and that aerosol cans would also combust. I decided to make a prototype. I placed a stick of incense in a circle of batteries that were taped together. I attached a piece of foil close to the bottom of the stick, so when the ember went through it it would free the foil to fall on the batteries and make them explode.

I was able to get it to work, but I stopped it before any explosions happened. I was confident that it would work, and that I could put one on Brett's porch. The idea brought a smile to my face. It made me think of the bigger picture. The poison that circulated through the atmosphere. The hand that urged good people to the dark side. I needed to do something bigger than just killing Brett. I needed to send a bigger message.

The more acid that I did, the more the picture became clear. There was a cul-de-sac a few blocks from my apartment. The houses were massive, and the occupants clearly had money. It only made sense that they were an elite group. For people of such financial prosperity to all be gathered in a small section of an otherwise middle-class city, there was an obvious connection. A connection I hadn't seen before.

Whatever the forces were that drove people to the point of narcissism and self-service were clearly at work there, just as they were in Brett. They were his people. It was his side of the battlefield. I headed out one night to count the houses and scope out the security measures. There were nine houses, and nothing stood out as being an issue. A few cameras, but I could tell where they were pointing.

With my new intel, I needed to figure out what materials I would need. I figured at least four batteries per house.

Basket Weavers

Including Brett's, that was forty batteries. I figured if I added at least three

aerosol cans to each package it would increase the force and cause more damage. Thirty cans. Tape, and incense. I was peaking and decided that the easiest way to obtain these materials was to just take them.

I waited until the weekend. On Friday night I dropped around seven. By ten thirty I was confident. I went to the corporate everything store and picked up a basket. I loaded it with everything I needed, acting as normal as I could. Seeing the other customers made me feel like I was in a play, or a movie. They were all exceptional in some way. Some dressed to impress, but most looked like they could have been planted there by someone who knew nothing of normal human behavior.

I casually made my way towards the front door and waited for my moment. When nobody seemed to be looking, I darted into the parking lot with the basket. I didn't look back, I just ran. It reminded me of the night that I ran after Steve's friend had thrown the rocks at the car. Nothing existed except flight. I ran all the way back to my apartment and locked the door behind me.

I paced around for a few minutes, checking out the window for any red and blue lights. Eventually I felt confident enough to get to work. I spent the better part of the night preparing the ten bombs. Taping the batteries together, a stick of incense placed in the middle. Three spray cans of oven cleaner taped around the whole thing. The stage was set.

A thought occurred to me before I set out on my task. My daughter was almost four years old at that time. I decided that I needed to write her a letter, for her to open when she got older. Just in case. The thing was that I still didn't completely understand the forces that I was rising up against. I could feel them, clear as day. I knew they existed, but they were hard to label. With this in mind, I figured that they would be working against me that night and may even find a way to kill me.

I grabbed a lined sheet of paper and a pen and sat down at my kitchen table. I tried to think about what I wanted to say but decided to go with spontaneous prose. I liked the idea that words were like rivers. Once the water passed a certain place, that was it. It would never be back there again. Once a statement is made, it's made.

Chloe:

If you're reading this, it means I am not around. I am about to embark on a mission that I can only tell you is for the greater good. Through my life experiences I have realized that a great evil exists in this world. Promise me that as you grow, you will not succumb to it's siren call. There will be temptation, and people who tell you that they can be trusted. Trust no one and keep your guard up. Pay attention to the little things and always follow your instincts.

Love, Dad.

I folded the letter and placed in in an envelope. I sealed it and wrote her name on it. I slid it into the top drawer of my desk and took a deep breath. It was time. I loaded all the bombs into a backpack and made my way towards the front door. The LSD amplified all my senses and I

could feel my heartbeat in all of my extremities. A thought crossed my mind, I was worried enough to write my daughter a letter, I should also plan for my own fate.

I went to my stash spot, I had around a half of a sheet of blotter left. I picked it up with the tweezers and cut it in half. I put the twenty-five hits in a small zip-seal dime bag and made sure it was closed all the way. I swallowed it.

Basket Weavers

Whatever happened, at least I would have one more good trip in me to help me figure out my next play.

I left the apartment, and my focus became razor sharp. The stairs leading down to the parking lot didn't seem to want to stay still and on a few occasions I nearly tripped. I kept it together and decided to hit the cul-de-sac first. I wanted to savor Brett's death. I wanted him to come out and confront me just as the bomb went off. I wanted to scrape chunks of him off my sweater.

The thoughts made me smile as I walked along the street, but my focus changed after I saw the world. Few cars drove by, but when they did their headlights left tracers in their wake and the streetlights poured out a fog of neon light. I watched my shadow grow and shrink, just as I had seen before. The world was an ugly place, and it had so many components that the majority of civilization either couldn't see or chose to ignore.

I was about to make a statement that could not be ignored. It would generate conversation and open people's eyes to the real reality. It may not have been the head of the snake, but the butterfly effect would certainly shake things up in the offices of the manipulators. The liars would be exposed, and their masks would fall to the pavement, splashing worms and centipedes for miles.

When I reached the target location, I was relived to see only two porch lights on. I decided if I moved fast enough in the darkness, I could avoid tripping any motion censors or being caught on camera. I went house to house placing bombs on the porches. I lit the incense about halfway to allow for a shorter wick. With the exception of a couple barking dogs, I felt certain that I had floated through the cul-de-sac like an illusion, leaving no trace.

As I walked away from there, I felt indestructible. My

eyes were squinted slightly, and everything contorted to my will. It was time to go after the man who tried to recruit me into eternal corruption. The man who had given me my first flicker of light, only to try and use it to feed his own flame. I saw him as a deity, and he saw me as a mark. He was about to learn that not all birds are meant to be caged.

I arrived at his girlfriend's house and went to work. I placed the bomb on the porch and lit the stick of incense. I stretched out my arms and began spinning on the front lawn. "No rest for the wicked." I repeated it loud and clear until I saw a light turn on. I stopped spinning at looked up, expecting contact. "Only the truth will set you free, Brett. You can return to your God and explain your failures."

Silence filled the air.

"You were sent to break me. You were tasked with driving me mad. Madness is nothing more than the beginning of wisdom!"

Still, nobody emerged from the house. The next thing I knew I was surrounded by flashing lights. The red and blue that filled the sky blinded me to much else. I felt someone tackle me and my face collided with the lawn. Instead of allowing myself to feel the cold steel on my wrists, or the knee pressing into my back, I decided instead to focus on the grass tickling my face.

There was purity in the world. Nature. Even nature had a breaking point. People mess with nature for too long, eventually they get a tornado or a cyclone. Floods and fires to purify and reclaim what had been taken. There were so many loud voices and sirens that I went into a strange state of awareness. My defense mechanisms keeping the ugly truth at bay.

After that, things were a bit surreal. Being thrown in the back of a cruiser, officers trying to ask me questions. They were so ignorant, like newborn babies who knew nothing about the world that they lived in. When we got to the station I could hear things, but I was dissociated. They put ink made from raven's blood on the tips of my fingers and pressed them down hard.

They put their hands all over me.

"I've got his wallet. Thomas Ferguson. Obviously intoxicated on something, what do you want to do?"

"Make sure he's clean and toss him in a holding cell. Shot callers can make the decision in the morning when he sobers up and makes sense. Hopefully."

The man again placed his hands all over me before escorting me down a hallway. It was dark with a few lights flickering along the way. I was pretty sure it was purgatory of some sort. I was tossed in a small room and a steel door closed behind me. I was trapped. I sat on the floor and curled myself into a ball, my thoughts sounded like a room filled with desperate poets.

The night was long.

Chapter Nine

I walked as quickly as I could through the vinyl swamp. I was focused on my feet and wasn't paying attention. I collided with something solid and fell to the floor. When I looked up, I saw Hedburg. He was just standing there, staring at me. I reached out, expecting him to grab my hand and help me up, but he didn't.

He opened his mouth wide and at least three spirits drifted out like a heavy cloud of cigar smoke. His eyes looked possessed. I could feel myself melting into the floor and I was getting desperate. I feared that I may have my soul extracted from my body by the clearly deranged man that stood before me. He was one of them.

I rolled to the left with all my force. I kept rolling until I crossed the threshold of another room. I was on solid ground again, but I feared for my life. I waited for a minute against the wall, out of sight from the hallway. I wanted so badly to look and see if he was still there, but I was afraid of what I may provoke. Finally, I got the courage to crawl over and check the hallway. It looked empty, but was it?

"What are you doing?"

I nearly jumped out of my skin. He found me. I turned around and saw Matthew sitting on the bed. His knees were tucked up to his chin ad he was hugging his legs. "Oh shit, Matthew. Am I ever glad to see you."

"This is my room. Are you going to hurt me?"

"No, no of course not. I had to get away from Hedburg. Did you see that?"

"No."

I wasn't sure how much I could trust Matthew, or how much of the truth he could take. I stood from the ground and closed the door. He started shaking, and then screaming. "Open!"

His sudden change in demeaner caused my energy to buck. I quickly opened the door. "Sorry man, you don't like it closed?"

"Need to stay safe."

I knew right then and there that he saw the same dangers as I did. Keeping the door open was his way of monitoring the halls and making sure that his soul remained intact. I took a couple steps towards him. "Hey, Matthew, have you ever seen Hedburg act, strange at all?"

He looked nervous as he nodded.

I wanted to keep some subtlety, but at the same time I needed him to know that we shared the same wisdom. "Matthew, I can tell that you're a smart man. Smarter than most."

He seemed to relax a little.

"Remember what we talked about before? The control machine?" His eyes glazed over a bit; I had clearly hit the nail on the head.

"Well, we both know how far that machine can reach into our world and twist the fabric. It's a concept that most people aren't able to see. It takes a kind of trans-dimensional insight for anyone born of flesh to be able to comprehend it on even the most basic level. I see you, and I know you know what I'm talking about."

He nodded. It was a subtle nod, but in that one simple gesture I saw hope. I knew where he had come from. A world that had no desire to really open its eyes to see the division that it created. I had come from the same world.

"I've been devising a plan. You in?"

Before he could answer, Timmerman appeared at the door. "Only one person in a room at a time guys."

The control machine at work. We both knew it. I turned to face her. "Sorry, just stopped in to say hello."

"The rules were all explained to you this morning, Tom. Why don't you head back to the common room before bedtime?" She gestured for me to follow her.

I glanced back at Matthew. I saw a slight nod and I knew he was in. As I left the room, I felt my feet sink in the floor again. I walked at a good pace but by the time we reached the end I was sinking deep. I fell flat on my face a few feet away from Glady's fortress. Timmerman stood a few feet in front of me and I saw her shaking her head. She looked to Gladys. "I thought this one was supposed to be easy."

I pretended not to hear, but I knew what that meant. I was in a brainwashing facility. They wanted to convince me that the truth was actually manufactured in my own mind. They wanted me to feel confused and question my own belief system. Whoever made her think I was going to be "easy" would soon discover the true abilities that were granted to me by the forces of good.

"You alright, Tom?"

She was patronizing me. I stood back to my feet. "Yes, thank you."

She shook her head again. Condescending narcissist. "Alright, well you have about an hour before it's time to take your meds and head off to bed, alright? There are a few guys still in there you can hang out with."

"Meds?"

She rolled her eyes. "Tom, Mark explained all of this to you this morning. We've prescribed you medication to help you sleep."

I found it insulting that they thought they could actually get me to take pills. Did they think I was an amateur? "Uhm, no thank you."

"Is this going to be a problem Tom?"

"Not if you don't try to force me to take pills." "Okay."

I felt as though I had made my point. I walked past her and headed towards the common room. I could hear Timmerman say something to Gladys, but I couldn't make out what it was. I knew it didn't make much difference; my mind had been made up.

I went into the common room and saw Benny sitting by himself with a deck of cards. He lit up when he saw me come in and started waving. I headed towards him and sat down beside him at the table.

"I thought you went to bed."

"Nah. Hey, Benny, do they make you take pills?"

"They give me pills to help me. You saw me get them after dinner, remember? Annunziato and me both did."

"Oh, right. Do they help you sleep?"

"You ask a lot of questions. Do you want to see a card trick?"

I could tell as soon as I met Benny that he was a good person. He wasn't being controlled or placed on a mission to manipulate and exploit. He had a good heart. I figured I probably had been asking too many questions. "Sure, I like card tricks."

He fanned the deck out in his hand, face down. "Pick a card."

I pulled out a card and looked at it. It was the four of spades.

"Okay, now put it back in the deck." He turned his head and closed his eyes.

I slid the card back. "Alright, it's back in."

He placed the deck on the table and rested his hand on top. He got a very concentrated look on his face. He cut the deck and flipped over the first card. It was the seven of hearts. "That's your card. Pretty neat, eh?"

It took me a minute to process what I had just seen. It was clearly not my card, but he was convinced that it was. I didn't like to lie, but at the same time I couldn't bring myself to crush his spirits. Energy was such a major element in my mood and thought process and something about the look of pride on his face made me feel so much lighter. I felt that I owed it to him to pretend. "Wow, that is my card. How did you do that?"

He smiled slyly. "Want to know the truth?" "It's actually the only thing I really want."

"It's magic. That's the truth. I only learned that I could do it since I've been here. Almost every person that I show it to, I get it right. I think I have powers."

In that moment everything changed. He did get it, even if he didn't realize it. His power was shifting my energy and helping me see the light that I wanted so badly to protect. I had been so focused on fighting the negative forces that I had become engulfed in them. If I let myself fester in the battle for too long, I would become nothing but a bloodthirsty soldier. I would become the very thing that I wanted to eliminate.

For the first time that I could remember, I smiled. I looked at Benny's face and I smiled even more. "You truly are a magician my friend. You have helped me more than you could know. Thank you."

He blushed. "It's just a card trick, Tommy. But you're welcome."

I felt a tap on my shoulder. Benny's demeanor changed in an instant. I turned to see Mark standing behind me. He made a motion with his finger, wanting me to follow him.

He stopped just outside of the common room with his arms crossed. "Why am I being called in from home for something we already discussed, and agreed upon?"

I was still feeling light and free. "What do you mean?"

"Seriously, Tom? You're going to make a big stink over taking medication? This was clearly discussed this morning. Now I have staff calling me to come in and deal with this. They said you looked possessed. They said you were in Matthew's room and then you tripped over nothing in the hallway. Do I need to be concerned?"

"No. I'm actually feeling a lot better. Has Benny ever showed you his card trick?"

"Are you going to take your meds, or not?" "Do I have to?" "Yes."

"How do I know what I'm taking?"

"Because we went over it in detail this morning. It's a sedative to help you sleep and calm your nerves." He had a look of frustration on his face. "You know, Tom, given your circumstances I would think that you would be showing a bit more effort here. Are you really going to risk everything over a couple of sleeping pills?"

Basket Weavers

My energy started to shift again. Why did I have so much on the line? I knew I wanted to play ball but having me take some random pills was a pretty big ask. I looked in in the eyes, I gazed so deep that I connected with his soul. It was a lie detector test that nobody could beat. "Can I trust you?"

"Of course, you can trust me."

It felt sincere. 'Alright, I'll take them."

"Good choice. We're going to go together, right now so you don't change your mind."

I followed him over to Gladys's safe haven. Timmerman stood against the glass and they both had a look on their face that made me feel as though they were the enemy. I approached the window with Mark right behind me. Gladys didn't speak, she just put a little paper cup down with a glass of water.

I paused for a moment. The energy was bad. I could feel it radiating all around me. I was the enemy. Maybe they knew my true intentions. Maybe they knew that I was searching for a weak link in the corruption chain. I couldn't take the vibes any longer and picked up the little cup. I tossed the pills in my mouth and used the water to swallow them down.

Timmerman was wearing a set of gloves. "Open up."

For a moment I wanted to lash out, but I was outnumbered. The heavy piercing energy of three pairs of eyes burning a hole right threw me made it impossible to resist giving in to direction. I opened my mouth, and she stuck a gloved finger inside to sweep my gums and under my tongue. It was violating and the taste of the glove reminded me of the dentist.

I turned to face Mark and he nodded. "'Thank you,

Tom." He pointed to the hallway. "You may as well get to bed; you have an early day tomorrow."

I gave a half-hearted nod of my own and headed towards my room without looking at either of the women. My mind felt like a mess. Was it the control machine that sent me on that

rollercoaster, or was Benny there to help me stay grounded? I needed some time to reflect. I stepped into the hallway and felt my foot start to sink. I hated that hallway.

Chapter Ten

I can't say if I got any sleep or not, but I know my eyes were closed for a while. Acid has a strange way of keeping your conscious alive while your body feels like it's shut down. When I started hearing people in the building, I assumed that it was morning. I can't say for sure how long I waited, but it was probably at least an hour or two.

I heard the door to my cell open. "Come on, Ferguson. Some people want to talk to you."

I got up and followed the officer. He escorted me to a small room with a table and a few chairs. A camera was perched on the wall. It was an interrogation room. He motioned for me to sit, and I did so without words. He didn't tell me who I was waiting for, or how long I would have to wait before he left the room and closed the door behind him.

I planted my forehead on the table and tried to gather my thoughts. I was back in the real world, at least for the most part. I knew I was likely facing some pretty serious charges. The night before was a bit of a blur. I remembered planting all the bombs, but I couldn't remember them exploding. I knew it wouldn't be long until I was given an official body count.

I tried to tap into the leftover chemical energy, but I couldn't immerse myself. When I was floating on LSD, I always felt a lot more confident, and sitting there waiting to find out my fate was a lot more difficult with lingering doubts. Had I made a mistake? Was I losing my mind? Those were questions I never asked myself when my pupils were the size of dinner plates.

I lifted my head when I heard the door open. One uniformed police officer and two men in suits walked in and sat down in the three chairs that had been placed across from me.

The cop spoke first. "I am Officer Caudle, how are you feeling today?" "I feel alright, I guess."

"You've put us in a predicament here, Mister Ferguson. You scared the hell out of a lot of people last night."

I dropped my eyes to the table and said nothing.

"I'm going to tell you what you're being charged with, and these gentlemen are going to fill you in on our plan. Sound fair?"

I nodded.

"Alright. You are being charged with theft from a retail store, prowl at night, criminal trespassing, and public intoxication." He proceeded to read me my rights. He then pointed at one

of the men beside him. "This is Mister Jack. He is your appointed lawyer, and he has already advised us that you do not wish to give a statement at this time."

I looked over at the lawyer. He was well dressed but didn't look like he had slept well for at least a week. I was confused. "I didn't even ask for a lawyer yet."

Basket Weavers

"I retained him for you." The other man in the suit looked much more put together. He had a growth on his chin that I tried not to stare at. He continued. "My name is Marcus Wolf; I am a social worker from Hillside Manner. It's a rehabilitation center of sorts."

"I don't understand."

The officer and the social worker both seemed to be looking at the lawyer. He must have felt it too. "Let me be straight with you, Mister Ferguson. The charges that are being placed against you are a gift. You could be facing a lot more."

I was starting to feel a bit skeptical. Wondering if I was being played, or if they were going to ask me to do something in return. "So, what? You guys just all really like me?"

"No. The truth is that the devices you placed at ten homes last night posed absolutely no danger. It looked like you had attempted to make explosive devices, but there was really no chance of a few batteries blowing up, even if the foil landed on them and managed not to get blown away. The cans of oven cleaner would need a significant source of heat to explode, so even if by some miracle the batteries started a fire, it wouldn't have been enough."

I felt like he was mocking me. I looked over at the other two and they looked pretty serious. I looked back to the lawyer. "If that's true, how could I be charged with anything else?"

"You scared a lot of people. The bomb squad had to come out and check each device. With the number of houses you targeted, you could be looking at terroristic activity. Even though the skill wasn't there, the intent was. All the court needs to prove is that in your mind, those bombs were going to detonate."

The man with the growth on his chin cut in. "Mister

Ferguson, we got a call from the station this morning requesting to give you an evaluation. We need to know what you were thinking last night, and from there they will decide how to handle your case. Just because you have minimal charges right now, doesn't mean that more can't be added."

"Evaluation? What kind of evaluation?"

The lawyer went on. "Hillside Manor is a minimum-security psychiatric facility. As your lawyer I have arranged for Mister Wolf to take you there this morning. Essentially you will be leaving here on bail for the charges against you. You will stay there for at least two weeks and using the reports we receive about your progress; a decision will be made about to proceed with your case."

"Psychiatric unit? Like a nuthouse?"

Marcus sighed. "We don't use terms like that. It's minimum security, which means you have freedom to move around and a private bedroom. I will be your acting social worker while you're there and you will meet with our Psychologist Dr. Ranck on a regular basis to discuss last night."

"What if I say no?"

The officer smiled. "Then we move forward with all the charges. Terroristic threats, ten counts. Conspiracy to commit murder, ten counts. Starting to get the picture? You'll wait in jail until the trial."

I looked over at the lawyer and he slid a piece of paper across the table. It was a contract to a voluntarily psychiatric assessment at Hillside Manor for a minimum of two weeks. He handed me a pen, which I accepted and used to sign the paper. I handed it back and all three men started getting up.

Marcus motioned for me. "Good choice. Let's go get your property and get moving." "Now?"

Basket Weavers

The officer looked at me with a scowl. "Right now."

I stood up and followed the men out of the room. We went towards the front and my property was handed to Marcus in a brown paper bag. He thanked the officer and together we walked out to the parking lot.

He looked over at me as we walked. "How are you feeling?" "I'm not sure. Is this normal?"

"Studies have shown that locking people up isn't the best method of rehabilitation. They are always trying other ways if they can. Apparently, you were pretty far-gone last night. Do you remember much?"

We stopped at a blue van, and he opened it with a key fob. We both got in and he started the engine. I tried to think back to the night before. "I remember some things, but once the cops showed up it was a bit of a blur."

"You're lucky they didn't kill you. What the hell were you on?"

We drove through the city, and I started watching out the window. I had permanent tracers. The residual acid was wearing off as time went on, but some things never went away. I didn't trust people. I didn't trust society or authority of any kind. "What did they tell you?"

"You were uncooperative. We're going to have to get a urine sample from you when we get there, so I'll find out anyway."

"What if I refuse to give you one?"

"Did you even read that contract you signed? Any questions like that all have the same answer, and you know what that is. Look, Tom, I'm trying to help you. If I was out to get you, we wouldn't be here right now."

I felt defeated. "I could still be a dick if I wanted to. You won't find anything in my piss."

"I find that hard to believe."

"You'll believe it when you see it."

He shook his head. I found it hard to look at him and not stare at his chin. "Alright, so you were completely sober last night?"

"I didn't say that."

"I'm not interested in playing games with you. If you don't want to talk, don't talk. Just know that I write up the majority of the reports that will be sent back to the police."

"I was on acid."

He nodded his head in understanding. LSD is consumed in such small quantities that it doesn't show up on urine tests. Even blood tests can't confirm that it's been used. "How long have you been using?"

"Six or seven years, I guess."

"You know that stuff can cause some serious permanent damage, right? Some people take so much that they never come back from it."

I rolled my eyes. "Marcus, have you ever done drugs?"
"No. And you can call me Mark."

"Okay, Mark. There are a lot of scare tactics out there. You ever hear the one about the guy who had a pet python that used to sleep in bed with him?"

He looked at me out of the corner of his eye. "Something like that happened in my hometown, but probably not the same. What's the rest of the story?"

"So, the guy wakes up to see the snake stretched out beside him. He thought it was just sleeping but as it turned out, it was sizing him up to see if it could eat him."

"Yeah, that's the same story I've heard."

"Everyone's heard it. It's not true. You ever actually confirm that it happened in your hometown?"

"I guess not."

"Right. So, back in high school there was a similar story

about a guy who did too much acid. They said he woke up in the hospital and started ripping his clothes off and yelling that he was an orange and begging people not to peel him. Ever heard that?"

"Not exactly."

"But some variation perhaps? People make shit up. Acid has helped me gain perspective. It's helped me see things that most people can't. It makes me wise beyond my years."

He chuckled. "Sorry. I know what you mean, but it obviously didn't help you understand anything about building explosives."

I wanted to be mad, but he brought a valid point. "All I'm saying is that I'm really not too worried about long term effects."

"Well, that I can tell you is not a scare tactic. I've seen it myself. It doesn't really matter anyway, because you won't be doing any drugs while you're in Hillside, right?"

I nodded. "Right."

We drove in silence for a little while. As I looked out the window and saw all the light trails and subtle irregularities I started to wonder if I had done too much. I had never really considered it before. If I learned anything from the drug, it was that things made sense when they were supposed to make sense. With that in mind I decided I would at least try to be open.

After driving for about forty minutes, we pulled into a parking lot. It didn't look much like a nuthouse. Not what I pictured one to look like at any rate. It was very discreet. I guess I was picturing a huge mansion with a spooky aura surrounding it. The name Hillside Manor on a large bronze banner bolted to the twelve-foot fence. It didn't look like that at all.

He parked the van. "Well, you ready?"

Chapter Eleven

It was dark in my room. I knew I was supposed to be sleeping but it didn't really feel like a viable option. I tried to close my eyes, but the light was still on in the hallway and there was an ominous shadow creeping across my floor. I watched it for a while, and it started taking a new shape.

It looked like an ice pick, or a screwdriver or something. I wasn't sure what it was trying to tell me. The longer I watched it, the more it seemed to transform. A small face appeared in one of the corners. It was just about too small to see but the detail was intensifying. It was ink shadow black, but it had an eye and a pointed chin. It looked a bit like some kind of demon crocodile.

The more I watched it, the more I saw its jaws begin to move. I focused all of my energy into it, and I could hear a muffled voice. "Don't.. believe..."

I was a bit astounded. I knew that a sign was coming. I felt completely unafraid. I spoke in a whisper. "Don't believe what?"

"Don't believe that things can get better."

"I don't understand, isn't that the whole point?"

"They will never get better. Stick with Matthew. Keep to the plan." "I don't really have a plan; I'm still working on it."

The shadow started shifting again. It went back to the screwdriver, and then into a demon. It was a demon I recognized; I had seen it slip out from between Hedburg's lips. It was starting to make sense. "Okay, but what do you mean it will never get better?"

I got no response. It shifted into a few more shapes before returning to its original form. I slipped out of bed and placed my hand on it. It felt like the floor. I followed it to the door; it looked like it was being cast by a small sensor box. I imagined it was an alarm that would sound if I tried to leave the room. I waved my hand in front of it a few times but heard no sound.

I went back to the bed and laid down. For the first time in a long time, I was confused again. I tried to analyze what had happened with Benny. How something so insignificant could seem so relevant. That was always the nature of things. People tended to overlook blatant signs that were right in front of them. That had to mean it was significant.

I heard a loud creaking noise and looked over to see my door opening. A woman I didn't recognize was shining a light into my room. "Bed checks. Did you get up?"

"Am I being monitored?"

"We have sensors on the doors that tell us when people leave their rooms. It's just a precaution. Have a good night." The beam of her flashlight disappeared.

I started to feel strange. Like an energy force was trying to counteract my own. I looked over at the door and focused on the sensor. They were watching me. They knew when I got out of bed. If I had to take a piss, they would come and make sure I hadn't fallen in or crafted a lethal weapon from the toilet seat.

My eyes felt like they were getting heavy, but my brain was still on overdrive. I sat up and took a deep breath. I stared back down at the shadow, but it wasn't moving. My thoughts were a strange mixture of cloudy and aggressive. It took me a minute to remember the pills I had taken. They were going to kill me if I fell asleep, I had to resist it.

I stood up and went back to the door, placing my foot across the threshold. My toes started to sink in the vinyl, and I pulled them back in with haste. I stood there for a minute to see if the woman would come back. It wasn't long before she did. She got startled when she got to the door and saw me standing there.

"Is everything alright?"

"How do you do it?"

"I'm sorry, do what?"

"How do you walk down that hallway and not get sucked into the floor? Every time I step on it, I start to sink."

She looked a bit confused, and maybe a little nervous. "I just work the night shift. It's my job to make sure everyone is safe."

"Well, I have to pee. If I step out of this room, I become unsafe, because that floor will drag me down until I drown in liquid vinyl."

She got a confused look on her face and stomped her foot lightly. "It's solid, see? I'll walk with you to the bathroom if you want."

"I'll try to hold it. Listen, I'm having a hard time sleeping. Can I have some paper and a pencil?" "I can give you a crayon, but we don't allow pencils. Will that work?"

A crayon? Seriously? "Uhm, sure, I guess so."

She vanished for a minute and returned with a journal

and a black crayon. I felt like I was being treated like a child, If I had a pencil, I would have jammed it into her throat. "Thank you."

I laid down on the floor to use the light from the hallway. The first thing I wanted to do was write. I figured that I wouldn't be able to once the tip had worm down. I was never a big fan of poetry, but at the same time I didn't mind writing it. I know that sounds a bit contradictory, but a lot of poets are drama queens. They look for depth when they don't have eyes for it. It's annoying.

I liked my poems to rhyme. Most of my experience had been in writing lyrics, so I was used to the flow. I felt like I had a lot to say and sometimes the free flow of a song would help me organize the chaos that could bounce around in my head. I put my crayon against the paper.

The world we perceive is a misconception
Trees and flowers and beauty connection
The darkness hides in the souls of the masses
Spreading like plague with each day that passes
I see their deception, I see their disease
Corruption and greed and the selling of sleaze
They have beaten me down to the point of exhaustion
But they are sloppy sometimes and forget their precaution They've shown me their weakness, their Achilles heel
I'm not dead yet and soon my wrath they will feel

I rolled over onto my back and thought about what I had just written. My own words guiding back to the path I knew I had to follow. Something had to be done about the way that human beings treat other human beings. I stared at the ceiling for a few minutes. I was starting to have trouble with my thoughts.

I figured that part of the problem was that my bladder was beyond capacity. I decided I would brave the hallway and I stood up beside the door. I stepped out and my foot sank faster than usual. I pulled it back in and shook it off before trying again. It sank even faster. I knew there was no way I could make it all the way to the bathroom.

The night woman appeared again, now looking annoyed. "Just walk over to the bathroom, you won't sink in the floor."

I was starting to feel a little delirious. I was afraid and confused. "Can you get a wheelie chair and take me there, please?"

"Are you serious right now?"

"Please, night lady? I have to pee and I can't go on that floor."

She sighed and crossed her arms. "My name is Delores, by the way. If I do this, will you finally go to sleep?"

"I promise I'll try."

She sighed loudly and disappeared down the hallway. She returned a minute later pushing a rolling chair. "I can't believe I'm doing this." She pushed it to the edge of the door, and I sat down, lifting my feet. She rolled me down the hall to the bathroom. "Alright, ride's over."

I hopped off the chair and into the bathroom. The florescent lights gave the room an eerie vibe and it smelled like bleach. There were a few showers and in one of them I could see bits of blue in the corners. Hedburg. The demons. He likely swallowed the souls of the pure and processed them in his intestines. Regurgitating them back in the atmosphere as the corrupt. They would fly around and take on a new host, poisoning it with the essence of humankind.

I started to relieve myself and it was amazing. I must have stood there for five minutes. I washed my hands and went back to the door. Delores was gone but the chair was still there. A new dilemma that I would have to sort out. I stepped on the floor again, but it was still sucking me in. I needed a paddle of some sort to row the chair back to my room.

I searched the bathroom and found the toilet plunger. It was perfect. I went back and hopped on the chair, sticking my legs up away from the floor. I started using the plunger to propel me forward, and it was working. It wasn't the fastest, or most efficient way of transportation but it was better than the alternative.

I made it about six feet when I felt myself being pushed. "Are you serious right now? Give me that plunger."

I looked over to see that Delores had returned. I handed her the plunger. "I thought you left." She pushed me back to my own room and I dismounted safely. "Thank you, Delores."

"Yeah, yeah. No more getting up. You promised you were going to sleep. How are you even awake with all those meds in your system?"

"I don't know."

"Yeah well, I'll have to talk to Marcus about that. Now get into bed."

I walked over and sat on the bed. She continued to stand there so I laid down. She watched me for a minute, but once she was gone, I got back up and resumed my position in front of the door. I picked up the crayon and flipped the page on the journal.

I started drawing. The visions in my head were that of the shadow. It's words to me. Things are never going to get better. I scribbled the best likeness to the crocodile shadow creature as I could, and then flipped the page. I proceeded to draw the screwdriver thing that it had shown me. I had to peel the paper off the crayon.

I kept scribbling. It made sense that my only color was

black. It was a good representation of how I was feeling, and how I knew the true characteristics of the average human being looked. I drew, I flipped the page, I drew some more. I couldn't tell you exactly how long I did this for, but I couldn't stop.

I kept flipping pages until there were none left. The crayon was worn down to a nub and I could tell I was developing a blister on my finger. I felt so much. I started to cry as I thought about everything. The world was supposed to be a beautiful place. People were a virus, and the more they spread the more the natural elegance of peace and tranquility are blanketed by their feces. I felt the rage building up inside of me again. It was the same feeling I had on the night I was going to blow everybody up. The world needed some bloodletting.

I started to hear voices coming from down the hall. It quickly dawned on me that it was morning. I hadn't slept at all.

Chapter Twelve

Mark got out of the driver's seat, and I followed him. I was nervous. I had never seen the inside of a funny farm before and I wasn't sure what to expect. The exterior looked nice. It had flower beds and actually seemed pretty welcoming. When we got to the door Mark had to use a card to get it open.

"Minimum security?"

He looked back at me as he swung open the heavy door. "Yeah, not zero security. You can't be surprised that there are precautions."

I nodded. He had a point. I followed him inside. The place had a sterile feel to it, but it didn't really feel like a hospital. On the right was a woman behind a desk, it was surrounded by Plexi- glass and had a small opening for communication and exchanges. Mark started walking in that direction.

"This is Gladys. She works three to four days a week."

I raised my hand in a waving gesture. She was a middle-aged woman with ebony skin. She had an aura of kindness about her.

"Hello, you must be Thomas. I have some clothes for you." She handed a paper bag through the slot, which I accepted.

Mark pointed to the hallway to the right of Gladys. "Your room is down here. I'll show you where it is so you can get changed. Everyone at Hillside has to wear the uniform, so don't even bother asking."

I looked down at my clothes, they were filthy. "No complaints."

"Good." He started down the hall, and I followed him. The walls were a typical taupe. Seemed to be the popular choice for institutions. The floors were a white vinyl. A series of doors were scattered along the way, and we stopped at one. He motioned with his hand. "This is you. Go ahead and get changed, bring me back the clothes you have on, and we'll have them washed."

I went into the room and looked around. It was pretty bare. It had a bed and not much else. I took off my dirty clothes and slipped on the white uniform, it actually fit pretty well and wasn't too uncomfortable. I took a minute to try and gather my thoughts, I was feeling much more sober as the day progressed. I slid my old clothes in the bag and took it back out to Mark.

As we rejoined in the hallway, I saw a blonde orderly walking by, she stopped at another door and knocked a few times. Mark looked over at her. "That is Mrs. Timmerman. She works long days as well; you'll probably see a lot of her."

I watched as the woman opened the door and three men emerged. They all looked similar. Their eyes were spread apart, and they all looked very focused. I looked over to Mark. "All three of those guys have to share a room?"

He waited until they walked past us before he responded. 'Those are the Johnson brothers. They've had a

Basket Weavers

hard go. They were born with Fetal Alcohol Syndrome and were soon diagnosed with non-verbal autism. They have basically spent their entire lives in one institution or another and they can't be separated."

"Where are they going?"

Mark sighed. "At a previous placement they were forced to make baskets for twelve hours a day. We've tried to break them of the habit but it's a compulsion. We've got it down to two two-hour sessions a day where they are given the tools and allowed to do it. It seems to keep them happy."

I thought about the life the men must have had, and it made me feel embarrassed about the problems I struggled with. I nodded to Mark, and we headed back down the hallway. He handed my old clothes to Gladys on the way by and we proceeded to go past her desk. He pointed to a room. "That's my office, we'll go in there in a second."

We went down to the next door. "This is Doctor Ranck's office. I have scheduled you to meet with him at three o'clock today. Gladys is aware but I'm hoping she won't have to come and get you."

"Meeting about what?"

"You just landed, so he's going to keep it light. Just an introduction and a check-in."

He turned and headed into his own office. I followed. He sat down at his desk, and I sat across from him. The office was adorned with the usual things. Pictures of his kids and a few trinkets on his desk. He looked over at me. "So, we'll keep this short. I'll introduce you around, but I have some appointments this afternoon, so you'll be on your own."

I nodded. "How many people are here?"

"Right now, we have twelve, including you. For the most part they are all friendly. We have one client right now that is on a trial basis, like yourself. He is a paranoid schizophrenic, but as long as he doesn't get worked up, he seems to be fine. His name is Matthew, please let him have his space."

"Alright. Anything else?"

"Lunch is at twelve, supper is at six. You'll hear the bell go off when it's time to eat and you are expected to be in the lunchroom." He paused for a moment. "I've also decided to place you on some sleeping medications for your first week. They are pretty strong, but I worry that all the drugs you did may keep you awake."

I felt my stomach turn a bit. "I'm not a fan of meds, but I'll do it."

"Perfect. Unless you have any other questions, I'll take you to the common room and introduce you around."

"I'm good."

He stood up and I followed suit. We went into the hall and passed by Gladys again, this time turning the other way. I started to feel a bit nervous about meeting my peers, it sounded like they could be an interesting bunch. When we got to the common room it looked pretty comfortable. There were a couple of couches and a television mounted on the wall.

There as a guy sitting alone on one of the couches, he looked like he was lost in his thoughts. Mark gestured towards him. "That's Matthew." He pointed to a table with two men sitting at it. "I'll introduce you to these guys, they are always happy to meet new people."

I followed him over and observed two men playing cards. They both had big beards and looked a bit homeless. One of them extended his hand to me." Hi, I'm Benny."

I accepted it. "Hey Benny, I'm Tom."

"Tommy, eh? Cool beans." He nodded his head towards

the other man at the table. "That's my friend. His name is Annunziato but nobody can ever say it right, so they call him Hedburg."

The second man at the table looked up from his cards. "Hedburg eights!" I nodded. "Nice to meet you both."

Mark put his hand on my shoulder. "So, this room closes during supper for cleaning. We always have to make sure it's safe so they do a quick check for anything that may have gotten in here. You are free to travel between here and your bedroom. You are not to go into anyone else's room. Got it?"

"Got it."

"Alright. I have an appointment to get to, why don't you play some cards with these guys and get acquainted."

"Thank for everything, Mark."

"Thank me by following the rules. I'll check in with you later." He headed back towards the hallway.

Benny motioned to an empty chair at the table. "Have a seat, want me to deal you in?" I sat down, still feeling a little uncomfortable. "What are you playing?"

"Hedburg, eights!"

Benny nodded. "Yep. Crazy eights. You in?"

"Sure."

Benny dropped his cards on the table. "Give 'em back Nunz, we're starting over."

Hedburg dropped his cards on the table and Benny looked over at them. "Hey, you said you didn't have any sixes!"

"Hedburg eights!"

Part of me really wanted to ask what the deal was with Hedburg, but then I remembered that I was in a nuthouse. Benny dealt the cards, and we played a few rounds. I didn't have a lot to say but Benny seemed pretty interested in getting to know me. "So, where ya from?"

"A few towns over. How about you?"

"Here, mostly." He laughed. "Sunnybrook before that." We tried to play a few rounds, but Hedburg couldn't seem to grasp the concept. Eventually Benny tried to change things up. "Hey, we have some paint here. Do you like to paint?"

"Sure."

He smiled and jumped form his seat. He went over to a cabinet and put the cards inside, trading them for some basic paint colors and a few sheets of paper. He came back and set them down. Hedburg immediately stuck one hand in the black and one in the white. He started smearing them on his face. 'Hedburg penguin!"

It didn't take long for Mrs. Timmerman to take notice and she came over to the table. "Benny, you know how Annunziato gets when the paint is out." She put her hand on Hedburg's back. "Come on now, let's get you cleaned up."

'Hedburg penguin!"

As I watched Hedburg being escorted out of the common room, I started to feel my insides twisting. I tried to remember the last time I had used the bathroom. I was having a lot of issues with my memory, but I figured I still had the remains of my trip still swimming around in my system.

'Hey Benny, where's the bathroom?"

"'There's one down the hall near the bedrooms, and another just outside of here. Hedburg usually gets washed up in the bedroom one."

"Thanks Benny." I stood from my chair and walked out into the hall. The bathroom was pretty easy to find. By the time I got inside I could barely contain myself. I ran to the first stall and dropped my pants before the door was even closed behind me.

Basket Weavers

I felt a great sense of relief, but also a strange pain. It felt like something was cutting me as it was evacuating. When I was done, I stood up and looked in the bowl before I flushed it. There was something plastic mixed in with my excrement. I knew it was gross, but curiosity got the better of me. I tried to remember what I may have eaten that was plastic.

I pinched it with my fingers and pulled it out. My eyes went wide when I realized what it was. It was a dime bag of acid. Looked to be about twenty-five hits. I contemplated for a minute. An opportunity was in front of me that I wasn't sure I should take. On the other hand, I may never get the chance again. I still felt like I had some unanswered questions in my LSDimension.

I flushed the toilet and went to the sink. I washed my hands and then looked at the bag again. I took a deep breath and before I knew it, I was opening the seal. The entire thing was in one piece, and I didn't have any scissors. I had never taken that much acid at once before, but if it was to be my last trip, may as well go big.

I put the whole piece of blotter in my mouth. The chemical taste was so familiar, and it made my heart race. I smiled before going back into the stall and flushing the empty bag. I took a long look in the mirror and promised myself that it would be my last time.

I knew I had about an hour before it started to kick in, and I was exhausted from lack of sleep the night before. I headed down the hallway, waving to Gladys as I passed. I went into my room and laid down on the bed. I was asleep in minutes.

Chapter Thirteen

I peered out of my room. It was hard to tell what time it was because the light was all florescent. I looked down at the vinyl floor. My nemesis. I stepped on it lightly and it seemed a bit less squishy. I decided to go for it. I ran as fast as I could towards the main foyer. It was a tough run, but I made it.

When I got there, Gladys was there with Delores. She looked me up and down. "Hey there, Tom. I hear you had an eventful night last night."

Before I could answer Delores looked at me with a scowl. 'How did you make it here with a chair?"

I looked down at my feet. I wasn't sure why she was mocking me, but it made me want to lash out. "I had to run, actually."

She shook her head and looked over at Gladys. "All night."

Gladys looked at me with what looked to be pity. "All night? Tom, did you sleep at all?"

I could tell by her tone that she would scold me if I hadn't. I had to keep it together. "Of course."

Gladys shook her head. "Tom, if you didn't you need to be honest. Those meds you took were pretty strong. If you didn't sleep, it could result in a psychosis."

I tried to focus on her face. Her eyes kept sinking down towards her nose and then crawling back up to their original location. "Slept like a baby after I went pee."

She looked skeptical. "Alright, well it's too early for you to get up yet. Go on back to your room and we'll talk to Mark about it later when he comes in."

I sighed. "Alright." I turned around and looked down at the floor again. I braced myself in a runner's stance and took off to try and keep from sinking. I ran down the hall but instead of going into my room, I took a detour. It may have been the only opportunity I got to fill Matthew in on the things I learned throughout the night.

I dipped into his room, and I saw him awake with a start. He had a violent expression on his face, but it seemed to recede when he noticed it was me. "You awake?"

He sat up in his bed and I went and sat down beside him.

"Okay, things are clear. I saw it last night in the shadows. Premonitions of the future and a way to take a major stab at the control machine."

"Smash the control images."

"Right. So, there I was in bed, right? And this shadow crept across my floor. It was a prophecy. It shaped and contorted itself into the answers that we've been seeking. It showed me things, not all of which I have figured out."

I could tell I had his attention.

"You know Hedburg?"

He looked over in the general direction of Hedburg's room and nodded.

"So, he is actually a biological soul converter. I've seen it myself. He absorbs the spirits of the one's who crave a pure world. Somewhere in his guts he twists them and spins them like a washing machine. Once they have been polluted, he releases them from his mouth so they can seek out new bodies to inhabit and corrupt. I've seen it myself."

He had a look on his face that I couldn't quite figure out. "Smash the control machine."

I nodded. "C'mon, I'll show you." I stood from his bed, and he followed me. I stopped at the door and looked back at him. "Be careful, the floor might try and swallow you." I stepped with huge strides, and he followed me, looking at his feet. We ended up in front of Hedburg's room and together we peered inside. He was still sleeping.

I watched as one of his loud exhales was accompanied by a corrupted soul. It vanished before I could see where it went.

"Hey! What are you two doing?"

I turned to see Gladys. She did not look happy.

"Tom, I told you to go to your room, not wake up anyone else. Matthew, what are you doing up?"

Matthew got a look of rage on his face. He spoke loudly. "Smash the control images, smash the control machine!" He ran back towards his bedroom.

I tried to head back to mine but I started to sink. It got so bad that I fell over and one of my shoulders started to go down. I started flailing to try to get loose and Gladys just stood there and watched.

"Tom, get up."

As I struggled to release myself from my vinyl prison, I watched the soul that had emerged from Hedburg slip into Glady's ear. I went into panic mode. "They got you! They corrupted you!" I

rolled around and with the extra adrenaline I was able

to free myself from the quicksand floor. I dove into my room and pulled the covers off my bed to make a cocoon.

I could hear a presence in the room. I knew it was Gladys, but I was afraid to look at her. "What are you doing, Tom? I swear you must not have slept at all."

I peered out and saw her picking up my journal. Her eyes went wide as she flipped through the pages. I could tell she was different. Her eyes slowly darkened until they were jet black. "What is all of this? I'm going to call Mark to come in early and talk to you."

With that, she left. I huddled deep into the bedsheet. My heart was pounding a mile a minute. Gladys was such a nice person and now she had become a victim to the dark side. I knew it wouldn't be long until she saw the plans I had sketched the night before and came to the only conclusion that she could. I knew.

I'm not sure how long I stayed there for. I got lost. Swirls of color consumed my vision and thoughts of a demonic takeover left me no peace. I was startled when I felt a tap on my shoulder. I knew it was the end. Death itself had stepped into our world to stop me from fighting back against the massive machine that was set on destroying all that was beautiful. I accepted my fate and moved the sheet.

"What the hell is going on with you? You haven't slept?" It was Mark. "I had to come in last night for you, and now again today. Get up and meet me in my office."

I hesitated for a minute. I didn't think Mark had been corrupted but there was really no way to be sure. I took a deep breath and stood up. I almost fainted but I caught myself. I headed to the door and stepped out. I had forgotten to prepare myself and my left leg sank considerably into the vinyl. I needed to get it together.

I pulled it out and ran down the hall. I could feel the

backsplash hitting me in the neck. When I got to Gladys's desk I put my eyes on the floor, I couldn't care to look at her. I walked past and headed down the hall to the offices. I couldn't remember where I was going, and I passed by.

"Hey, in here."

I followed the sound of his voice and went into the room. He had my blueprints on his desk. I stumbled as I tried to sit.

"You want to tell me what's going on?"

The thing on his chin was pulsating. His eyes had dark bags under them, and he looked like an interrogating fleet officer. I knew I had to smooth things over, I had a plan, and I would stop at nothing to implement it. "I had a hard time sleeping, but I did."

"Are you sure? The night report says you were acting strange. Do you think the floor is some sort of quicksand or something?"

He knew full well that it was. This was his organization; he probably knew everything. I was just about to lose my cool when there was a quick knock on the door. Timmerman came in looking timid. "Just me, sorry, need to grab the Johnson keys."

The weavers. The time was approaching. I calmed myself down and tried to come up with something. "I think I was having a bad dream. Must have kind of slipped into reality or something. I'm sorry you had to come in early, I'm fine, really."

He looked like he wanted to believe me. He pointed to the journal on his desk. "What about this?"

"Just trying to tire myself out. Nothing important in there." I knew that even if he could see all the obvious clues and information, he would have a hard time calling me on it without blowing his cover.

He looked like he wanted to believe me. "Alright, Tom. Here's the plan. I'm going to bring you back in here in two hours. If you're still acting strange, I'm going to have to sedate you. I'm worried that lack of sleep is affecting you. I'm sure you didn't sleep well in the holding cells so if you didn't sleep here either that's pretty concerning."

I nodded. "That's fair. I just need a bit of time to wake up is all." "I hope so."

I got up and headed back into the hallway. I passed by Timmerman, who was taking the keys back to Mark's office. I knew it was my chance. I walked quickly, but calmly towards the weaver's room. I peered inside and saw them all working on baskets. I smacked my hand against the glass.

The one I had spoken to the day before looked up and saw me. I waved and tapped the glass again. I knew he was on the side of virtue. I could feel it radiating off of him when we had spoke the night before. I was right. He got up and opened the door. I slipped inside.

"Alright guys, it all come down to this. I need your permission. I know you are the key. I have a plan to knock out a relevant cog from the wheel. It will reduce the power of the enemy exponentially. I am missing one piece, and the forces have informed me that you are in possession of it."

They looked at each other, likely communicating telepathically. The man from the night before handed me the tool he was using. My eyes widened. It was as the prophecy foretold. It looked like a screwdriver, but it wasn't. I accepted it. "Thank you, great weaver. Time is of the essence; you will be rewarded greatly for your sacrifice."

I spun around and opened the door. I headed towards the common room and saw Matthew. I motioned to him. "I have the final element, and the weavers consent."

"'Tom"

Basket Weavers

I looked over to see Timmerman walking towards us. I slipped the tool to Matthew and stepped away from him, towards her. "Yes, Mrs. Timmerman?"

"You didn't go in that room, did you? I thought I heard the door close." "What room?"

"The Johnson's room."

"No Ma'am."

She came over and patted me down. It was like everything was happening as it was supposed to. If I hadn't handed the tool to Matthew, it would have been confiscated. Funny how the world works sometimes. Once she was satisfied that I didn't have anything on me she shook her head. "Alright, you can go."

I went into the common area and saw that Benny was by himself at the table. Matthew was on his regular couch, and Hedburg wasn't there yet. I walked past Matthew and gave him a subtle nod before making my way to join Benny.

"Morning Tom, sleep alright?"

"That seems to be the question of the day. How are you today?" He smiled. "Want to see a trick?"

"Sure."

He placed his right hand in front of him, thumb bent. He took his other hand and placed it overtop to hide where his second thumb lined up with the first. He moved his left hand, and it looked like he was pulling his thumb apart. "Look at that, pretty cool, eh?"

For some reason I found myself smitten by his innocence again. He separated his hands and lifted his right thumb, showing that it had put itself back together. It seemed like no matter how fucked up the world was, or how dire his situation, Benny was always able to find a way to be happy. I admired that about him. "That is amazing, Benny. How did you do that?"

He leaned in close to me. "Remember I told you, I'm magic."

I developed a strange feeling of contentment. Something about him really was magic. It was hard to pinpoint, but also hard to ignore. In that moment I started to question my own plan. Something about the power of a pure soul really shined a light on everything I was fighting for.

I looked up to see Hedburg coming into the room. I started to get up to tell Matthew to hold off, but it was too late. Matthew jumped from the couch with the basket weaving tool in his hand and started jamming it repeatedly into Hedburg's neck. Blood spattered everywhere, I got it all over my white suit and felt the warmth on my face.

Everyone else in the room started screaming. Timmerman, Gladys, and Mark were all there within a minute, but Matthew wouldn't stop. Once Hedburg was on the ground he started stabbing him all over his chest and face. It was surreal. Mark was able to get Matthew restrained and Gladys ran to get some needles.

Timmerman pointed at me. "Get him too!"

As soon as the plunger was pressed, Matthew was out cold, or dead, I wasn't sure. Before I knew it Mark was on top of me, and I saw the blackened eyes of Gladys looking at a syringe. I felt something jab into me and then everything went dark.

Chapter Fourteen

I woke in a room that I didn't recognize. I was restrained to the bed. I looked down and saw a catheter protruding from my white uniform. I looked to the left and saw that I had an IV in my arm. There was a camera on the wall.

I tried to clear the fog from my thoughts, but I was confused. I felt like I had been sleeping for a long time. I laid my head back down and heard the door open.

"You're finally awake. I'll get Mark." I looked to see Gladys vanishing from the door.

I sighed heavily. I felt awful and my memory was a bit of a blank. It didn't take long for Mark to get there. He stood at the end of the bed. "How are you feeling?"

"I'm not sure. What happened?"

"Well, that's what we're trying to figure out. You've been asleep for three days. You were sedated, but that would have worm off after a couple of hours."

"I was sedated?"

"You don't remember much, do you? Here's the thing, Tom. We are pretty sure you are responsible for what happened here, but we are also fairly certain that you were in some sort of psychosis. You are very close to losing your deal and going back to jail, but I'm not ready to give up on you just yet."

I tried to remember, and it was coming back to me.

"The key here, is honesty. We can't help you if we don't know what's going on. I'm giving you one week to prove that you're buying into this. Anymore of this and you're out of here. Understood?"

"I think so."

Alright. I'm going to give you some time to think and wake up and then we'll go from there. I'm leaving you restrained until I feel comfortable."

He left the room, leaving me alone. My thoughts started coming back. The key is honesty. Was that really true? I was starting to question my own beliefs. Maybe my way of thinking was causing me to be the darkness I hated. I felt so confused. The one thing I knew for sure was that people were cruel. The world was cruel, and I was sick of being hurt by anyone that I was stupid enough to trust.

Now I was being asked to trust Mark. Would I even be able to do that? I hated the fact that there was so much I didn't understand. I needed an explanation as to why people treated each other the way they did. I sighed again and all I could think about was trying to get my hands on some LSD.

About the Author

Aaron Lebold is an author of psychological horror, sometimes dabbling in extreme elements. His love of the genre began at an early age with all the best slasher films. After falling in love with expression and lyrics, and a failed attempt at doing music, he got off drugs and went to school to be an addictions counselor. This has been a fifteen year career with a brief hiatus in 2017.

Writing had always been something of interest but it was after making the decision to leave an 8 year position at a youth facility that he needed something else to evoke passion. Writing came naturally. Since that time he has completed several novels and novellas. His work can be found with 13 Days Publishing, Uncomfortably Dark Publishing, D&T Publishing, Shadow House Press, and

Broken Brain Books. His short stories can be found in various anthologies by various publishers. Some of his short stories have been narrated for the Cryo-Pod Podcast. His novel "Born Sick" took second place at the Godless 666 awards for best novel of 2022.

Also by Aaron Lebold

Balm of Gilead

Black House

Born Sick

Genocide

Pennyroyal Tea

Popular

Quarantine

Rorschach

The Sheriff of Salem

Made in the USA
Middletown, DE
19 January 2026

26794012R00071

Made in United States
Orlando, FL
23 January 2022

Support Us

We hope you enjoyed reading *Cossmass Infinities*. Please consider supporting us:

Subscribe

https://www.cossmass.com/subscribe/

Preorder the next issue

https://www.cossmass.com/preorder/

Become a Patron

https://www.patreon.com/cossmass

Newsletter

https://www.cossmass.com/newsletter/

Donors

A huge thanks to all our supporters on Patreon. Join them:
https://www.patreon.com/cossmass

Destroyers of Infinities

Anonymous

Aaron Sisto

Orla Hayes

Jessica Hyslop

Scourges of the Realities

Myra Campbell

Elizabeth Campbell

Deanne Fountaine

Jeffery Reynolds

Patrick Sullivan

Maybe today will be the day she sees green shoots sprouting through the mud, at last, or hears birds singing, or sees a squirrel scamper up a tree. The signs of something healing.

When they come, perhaps the seeds she planted over Haf will sprout, too.

She's waiting, she realises, for the first good day.

She will not know it when it comes.

© 2022 JL George

Science Fiction - 4896 words

About the Author

JL George lives in Cardiff and writes weird and speculative fiction. Her work has appeared in *Fireside*, *Curiosities*, *New Welsh Reader*, and various other magazines and anthologies. Her first novel *The Word* won the New Welsh Writing Awards and is published by New Welsh Rarebyte.

kettle on. For an old lady, Mrs Roberts has hearing like a bat, and a single creak is enough to wake her.

It'll be light soon. Almost March. It's been a year since the dust came. Elin will be up soon, and her husband Gav, and the three of them will head out to help with the rebuilding effort. Dani's been helping plan community gardens. There's a quiet satisfaction in seeing them take shape, in digging her hands into the waiting earth and planting seeds. When she's working, Dani's present in a way she can't remember feeling since she was a kid. Solid, wanting for nothing.

One of the other volunteers, Shaz, is a scientist. It's her job to help them find sites, testing the soil to be sure the toxin from the dust is gone. She catches Dani's eye and grins, sometimes, her hand lingering on Dani's shoulder a moment longer than necessary.

Dani doesn't know if she's ready to do anything about it. She thinks about Haf a lot. The memories still come in flashes of dark and light, sometimes, but more often they're a marbled whole, the good and the bad, the soft words and the barbs, the sparkling excitement and the suffocation, all swirled together until there's no unpicking one from the other.

She isn't sure how you mourn a love like that, except quietly, piecemeal, without explaining. She has time to figure it out, she guesses.

Elin is quiet a moment, eyes thoughtful. She sighs, a rasping noise through the respirator, fogging up the plastic in front of her eyes. "You can come with, if you want. We've got space."

"Really?"

"Sure." Elin jerks her chin up. "Got to stick together, haven't we?"

Without another word, she turns for the 4x4.

A moment later, Dani follows.

"D'you ever wish you'd known?" she asks Elin, as they wind through the lanes, away from the Roberts's place.

Elin frowns at her. "So we could've stopped it, you mean?"

"Not really. More like—somewhere back there was the last good day you were ever gonna have, and you didn't know it when it went. Don't you wish you had?"

Elin shrugs. "I try not to think about it." And then, an afterthought: "Anyway, who says it was the last?"

Dani snorts and says nothing more.

———

She wakes early. It's still dark, but she opens the curtains anyway, peering out at the mud where the front lawn used to be. She creeps downstairs in her socks to put the

Pulse throbbing in her throat, she creeps toward the house. The front door's still locked, so she tries around back. "Hello?" she calls, barely more than a whisper. Her voice feels rusty. She hasn't spoken in days. "Mr Roberts? Mrs Roberts?"

There's a clatter inside. Coming from the kitchen by the sound of it. On instinct, she hefts the rock.

The back door opens. There's a woman standing there, most of her face obscured by a respirator, pale blue eyes looking Dani over and narrowing in recognition. "You're one of the neighbours, aren't you?"

Dani nods, the rock tumbling from her grip. "Elin," she realises. The Roberts's eldest. She used to come down and help them out regularly until she had the baby last year. Dani remembers her as a soft, comfy sort of person, agreeing with everyone, always making cups of tea. The human equivalent of a marshmallow.

Now, she looks Dani up and down with assessing eyes. "Just you, is it?"

Dani looks away. "Yeah."

"Mam and Dad said you'd been round to help them when this all started. I'm guessing it was you who left the food?"

She nods, can hardly bear to ask: "Are they—"

"Dad's gone. Mam's up at our place. Asked me to come down and get some of her things, now that it's stopped."

She buries Haf after three days. Somehow, she doesn't think anyone will be coming around to collect the dead anytime soon.

The radio broadcasts have started up again, and they're saying something about the toxin in the dust losing its potency over time. A few more weeks and it'll be safe to go outside without a suit again.

She lays the shards of the shattered mug in the grave, along with Haf's copy of *Wuthering Heights* and the sundress she wore on their first anniversary. There are no flowers, so instead Dani plants seeds, leftovers she had no room for in the conservatory.

Maybe the dust will kill them before they sprout. Or maybe in a few months when the dark part of the winter is past and the poison gone from the earth, they'll come to life, put out tendrils.

When she's done, she locks up the house and drives over to the Roberts's place.

There's a 4x4 in the yard, startling red against the dusty landscape. It's been so long since Dani saw another person that her heart rockets into her throat, and she wishes she'd thought to bring a length of wood, the poker from the old fireplace, anything for a makeshift weapon. She glances around for inspiration and ends up grabbing a stone that's fallen out of the wall, wondering if she has the strength or the stomach to bash someone's brains out with it.

at last, with nobody to send you to detention or just disapprove at you until you did what they wanted.

Her last class of the day was English Lit. She turned up a few minutes late, hazy from the two pints she'd drunk at lunchtime, and stopped and stared in the door of the classroom. The woman standing in front of the whiteboard couldn't have been more than a few years older than the students. And she was stunning, all of her: the wide soft bow of her mouth, the waves of her strawberry-blonde hair, the freckled curve of her neck.

She pivoted to face Dani, one eyebrow cocked. "Joining us?"

Dani gulped. "Um, yeah." She shoved herself into the nearest empty chair, the strap of her messenger bag tangling around her ankles.

"And you must be Danielle?" the woman asked, glancing down at the list on her desk. She'd written her name on the whiteboard. Ms Williams.

"Yeah," Dani said. "But, um, everyone calls me Dani."

Ms Williams nodded. "Dani," she repeated, with a small curve of her lips, and warmth kindled in Dani's belly.

That was definitely a good day.

———

She realises she's run the scourer over the same spot a dozen times.

She gazes down at the mug in her hand, the neat blue pattern of waves rendered into geometric absurdity.

Then she flings it hard at the wall. The shards scatter like snow, like dust.

Outside, the dust stops falling.

————

Dani's first day of college. Kerry whined endlessly that it wasn't fair she still had to wear a school uniform while Dani could go in jeans and trainers. She met her friends Matt and Anwen at the bus stop, and the three of them chattered with excitement as the bus bumped toward campus. Dani let her eyes roam over the girls who got on the bus, not quite ready to name the possibility that flickered inside her.

Everything was new. The smell of weed wafting from the knot of students smoking in the car park; the lecturers who talked to you like you were an adult, no scolding about homework or tucking your shirt in. At lunchtime, Matt grinned and said, "Let's go to the pub!", and they did, and nobody kicked them out or even spared them a second glance.

This was what it felt like to be grown up, Dani decided. Possibility everywhere. In control of your own decisions listening to the world around her, opening doors without thinking. The same inattentiveness Haf used to snap at her for in college.

She remembers the argument they had after she got back from Kerry's, and after Haf finally got tired of giving her the silent treatment. "It always feels like you're looking over my shoulder," Haf complained. "Looking for the next thing, and when you find it you'll ditch me." And she sighed. "It's my fault really. I know I'm too old for you."

Stumblingly, Dani tried to explain she'd never meant to make Haf feel that way. She'd only wanted a few days with her sister, a small corner of her life to be just her own, because Haf's presence at the centre of it suffused everything and sometimes she felt like she was choking on it.

It didn't work, of course. It never worked. Dani never could seem to explain herself in a way that didn't get tangled up, that didn't come out sounding childish and selfish and thoughtless.

Now she never will.

Dani stares for what feels like hours at the coffee soaking into the carpet, every contour of the stain, every speck of lint. After a while, she closes Haf's eyes and picks the mug up from the floor. She collects the water glass, too, takes them downstairs and washes them in cold water at the sink. Her hands are stiff and aching, like an old woman's.

Haf dies on a Wednesday.

It's her least favourite day of the week. Even back at college, she used to bitch about it and give everyone an extra five minutes' break because she needed that extra coffee to get her over the hump. Dani's downstairs waiting for the kettle to boil when it happens. She doesn't hear anything, sense anything. There's no deepening of the quiet, no whisper of loss.

Oblivious, she climbs the stairs, Haf's favourite mug with the wave patterns on it held carefully in both hands. Haf is gazing sightlessly at the ceiling, one hand hanging off the side of the bed, water glass on its side on the floor.

Dani drops the coffee, too, and the stain seeps deep into the carpet. She presses her fingers to Haf's throat, her wrist, and leans in close to her chest, listening for breaths that don't come.

Yesterday, she decides, was the last good day, even measured out in coughing fits and cups of tea, painkillers and recriminations. The last day Haf was here.

Or it was the day before that stupid argument in the porch, though it had been identical to almost every other since the dust came, so nondescript it might never have happened at all.

If she'd only known, Dani would have taken the time to savour even the petty little annoyances and the tension in the air. To pay attention, commit it all to memory. But that's always been the problem with her, hasn't it? Not relaxed into the evening, the fizz of nerves in her belly giving way to a loose, easy drunkenness.

Walking back to Haf's place, later: "You haven't told anyone you're seeing me yet, have you?"

Dani's shoulders stiffened at the question. "Not, like, officially. I mean, not yet." She risked a glance sideways. "Is that a problem?"

She half-expected it would be. She already knew Haf didn't suffer fools, and it probably wouldn't be any different for cowards.

But instead, Haf stroked the back of her hand. "Don't worry. I know not everyone's family's supportive. But they'll come round, if they love you. They'll see that I do, too."

The suddenness of it shocked a laugh out of Dani, and she stifled it straight away. "Sorry. I wasn't expecting—you really mean that?"

Haf nodded, and the nerves were back, a little dip of the stomach like when you're about to hit the drop on a rollercoaster. "Me too," Dani breathed.

It was early days yet. That's what her mam would've said. Don't get carried away. But she was already surfing the wave, and it lifted her up, up, until the air shone all around her.

———

dance floor, and it would be easy. She rarely called them after.

That had all changed the night she saw Haf. Haloed in neon-pink light, strawberry-blonde hair tumbling over her shoulders and a bead of sweat shining in the hollow of her throat. An electric cherry goddess. Dani hadn't recognised her at first. Then she had, and she'd been reduced to a teenager again. Fumbled over her words, coordination deserting her so she'd spilt cider and black down the leg of her jeans.

Miraculously, it hadn't stopped Haf from spending the whole night talking to her, drinking until they were both swaying on their feet, or from offering her a lift home the next day.

And now Dani was heading out to meet her, the boring local pub turned golden by the promise of her presence. She still couldn't quite believe her luck, heartbeat thrumming in her throat with a pleasant kind of nervousness.

They giggled as they put songs on the jukebox. The cheesiest, most obnoxious pop they could find, just to piss off the regulars. They talked about books, music, who else at the college had come out of the closet. Dougie Price was no surprise to anybody; Mrs Evans History had been divorced in the Eighties and lived with the same woman ever since. Dani hadn't expected that one. Haf smirked at her surprise and said, "Hey, not all lesbians are as hot as you, you know. Wouldn't be fair on the blokes." Dani

"I can do it," Haf huffs. Dani strips off the suit and follows her back in anyway, as though filling the bath and running the sponge over Haf's shoulders as she soaks will wipe away the sick feeling that creeps up inside her whenever she thinks about the dust in the porch.

She'll go and check on Mr and Mrs Roberts tomorrow, she tells herself.

But in the morning, Haf begins to cough.

———

The first time Haf told Dani she loved her. That was a good day, she's sure of it.

They'd only been seeing each other a few weeks. They both still lived in Bangor at the time, Haf teaching at the sixth form college. Dani hadn't quite made the transition in her head, and sometimes she still defaulted to thinking of Haf as Ms Williams.

She hadn't told Kerry yet, or her parents, knowing that having to explain would spoil the thrill of it. Her one-time teenage crush turned into an adult relationship. Like something out of a soap opera.

Dani posed before the mirror as she got ready, jeans slung slow on her hips, short hair artfully messed, a bit of a pout to her lips. The look served her well on the occasions she managed to catch the train to Liverpool or Manchester for a night out. She could catch a girl's eye across a crowded bar, raise her glass like a question, slink up to her on the

That would be Dani's cue to backtrack, normally, to apologise and soothe with compliments. Today, she snaps. "Are you pretending you care what I think?" And she storms to the door, slamming it behind her as she lets herself into the porch.

She fumbles on the makeshift suit and the hated respirator, swearing under her breath. Right now, she doesn't care much whether Haf hears, though later, when the anger and nausea have boiled away, she will. Still borne along on the wave of emotion, she opens the front door.

A hand grabs her sleeve and yanks her back.

Dani stumbles, stares. The door thumps shut again. It's breezy outside, and dust already swirls around her binbag-swaddled ankles and Haf's bare feet.

"What are you *doing* out here?" she says, to cover the terror spreading out from her core. "I didn't see you, you should have *knocked*." She trails weakly off, her anger fading to guilt. Perhaps Haf did knock, or say something, and she didn't hear? She should've been more alert, less wrapped up in her own stupid feelings.

Haf folds her arms. "I had to come after you. You weren't listening."

"I did listen, I just..." Dani trails off, protests withering and falling away like deadheaded flowers. "Let's get you in the bathroom. Need to make sure there's no dust sticking to you."

reflection of the ghostly sun? Are they still alive in there, desperately hoping for a video or a voice over the airwaves? The radio stopped broadcasting a few days after her excursion, and now there's no way to tell what's happening across the rest of the country.

"Look," says Haf, "I know you want to help them. It's great, it really is. 'S why I love you."

Those words used to make Dani feel full up with sunshine, fizzing inside like a firework, but lately, they mostly get trotted out when Haf wants to persuade her of something.

"But things are different now. It's an emergency. Got to look out for number one." Haf puts her hand on Dani's arm. "And two, of course."

Unbidden, the idea floats into Dani's head and settles there like dust. A world with just the two of them in it. Sometime after it's stopped—because it has to stop eventually, right?—traipsing from house to house and finding nothing but dust-coated bodies, the only two beings left under the dead sky.

The thought of all that emptiness chokes her.

She shakes off Haf's hand. "You can't stop caring about people because things are hard."

Haf's expression curdles into a scowl. "Are you calling me selfish?"

It never seemed to help. She always talked herself into knots. Started out complaining, and ended up defending Haf and wondering how she'd turned her into a monster in the telling.

"Well," Kerry said, "if you change your mind…"

"Yeah."

"C'mon, I've had enough paintings. Let's get a coffee before you've got to catch the train, yeah?"

Grateful for the change of subject, Dani gave a weak smile and followed her out.

The last time she heard from Kerry was a week after the dust came. Dani had been conserving her phone battery because the power was out, and they didn't exactly have a ton of fuel for the old backup generator. A couple of minutes a day, long enough to check for news updates and messages. The latest one from Kerry read *We're managing, don't worry. :)* That was it.

Dani sent back a smiley face of her own and switched her phone off. The next time she turned it on, the signal, always spotty, was completely gone.

———

The Roberts's never did email or text messages, even before the network went down. Dani can't stop thinking of the light she saw in their window when she dropped off the food, a few weeks ago now. Was it really a light, or the

Dani had danced with a blonde girl a year or two younger than her, undercut and arm muscles and a lip ring that winked in the light when she smirked—and extricated herself with an apology and an explanation that she was with someone. The morning after, she and Kerry nursed hangovers in some Northern Quarter hipster café and mooched around the art gallery.

Haf hadn't answered her texts all weekend, and by Sunday afternoon Dani had been checking her messages reflexively, hand twitching toward her pocket even as she gazed up at Hylas and his pale-titted nymphs.

Kerry caught her eye. "Everything okay at home?"

"What do you mean?"

"You know." Kerry fiddled with her bracelet. "I know people didn't exactly approve at first, what with her being your teacher at college and all. Christ, *I* didn't. Might make it hard to admit if there's a problem."

And she gave Dani the shrewd, sidelong look that meant she knew she was right. Sometimes Dani forgot Kerry wasn't her naïve kid sister anymore.

She thought about shrugging it off, but the effort felt too much, suddenly, and instead, she sighed. "Fuck knows with her these days."

"Wanna talk about it?"

"Not really."

she says. "We could heat this up with some of the tinned tomatoes. Did you get pasta?"

Dani nods. "They didn't have the wholewheat stuff, sorry." As if it was a normal shopping trip. Ridiculous.

"Not to worry," Haf says. Then: "You were out a long time today."

Dani's shoulders stiffen, old accusations ringing in her ears. "Took some stuff to the Roberts' place. They didn't answer, though."

She tries not to watch Haf's face too closely, not to analyse every microexpression, but still feels the sudden lightness when Haf's lips don't turn down, when she nods and says, "Hope they're okay."

"Yeah," Dani says, "me too," and she opens the sweetcorn.

———

Maybe it was the last day she did something for fun. When was that?

About a month before the dust started. She'd trained it up to Manchester to visit Kerry, made a weekend of it. Took the bus out to the Trafford Centre, which Dani had never really been into—those big, shiny monuments to capitalism all blurred into one endless maze, eventually—but Kerry was always after an excuse to shop, and Dani didn't mind indulging her. They'd gone out drinking that night, Fab Café followed by a stagger down Canal Street.

Dolgellau and wedges herself through a broken window, heart racing as she pats the arms and legs of her makeshift suit to make sure it hasn't ripped open. She loads herself down with tinned and dried goods, scrubs them in the porch before she carries them inside.

She leaves a small cache outside the Roberts's back door. There's no answer to her knock, but she thinks she sees a light on in an upstairs window.

The dust is still falling.

The day before the first dust warning—was that the last good one? Dani can hardly remember it. She shopped, she thinks, and started a new batch of soap, the downstairs windows propped wide to let out the lye fumes. She glanced at the news once or twice, anxiety biting when the presenter talked about stay-at-home orders in London, respirator shortages up north, and changed the channel. A quick phone call to her sister, Kerry, while she cooked, protected by the noise of the extractor fan. Haf always got shirty if she spent too long on the phone.

She doesn't remember what they talked about, or what she made for dinner. Did she read a book, watch a movie, step outside to breathe in lungfuls of clean air and let her eyes roam over the mountains?

She doesn't think so. A nothing kind of a day. She wouldn't have called it a good one at the time.

At home, she fills the cupboards while Haf peers at labels, trying to put together a half-civilised meal. "Sweetcorn," doesn't rain. What would happen if it did? She pictures treacly sludge dripping from the sky, gumming up the footpaths. Dust and mud, a world of greys.

But as she tramps home, the sky blooms colours. A dust sunset in hothouse reds and pinks, indigo shot through with orange flame. She can't help but stop and stare and think that even the apocalypse gives out consolation prizes. A bouquet handed to the ageing diva, humanity, as it dodders offstage, voice and memory shot.

This isn't the end of the world, Dani reminds herself. The stern voice in her head is Haf's. It just feels like it, enough so that a good day is a rare, startling thing.

Is this a good day? She isn't sure she knows what one looks like anymore, or when was the last.

By the time she reaches home, the sunset colours have faded and the press of the respirator across her forehead is giving her a headache. At the unlit upstairs window, she sees Haf's outline, and then the curtains twitching closed, tight as disapproving lips. Dani sighs, fortifies herself for the coming row and enters.

———

The last good day. It becomes a sort of puzzle. Something Dani worries at while she works, busying herself with the vegetables and the cooking, keeping up with the news on TV and, when they stop broadcasting, fiddling with the radio to search for updates. When it becomes evident the shops won't be reopening anytime soon, she drives into

That's what she keeps telling herself, anyway. Easier than thinking about the work, the weight, of changing things.

Here, with only one foot to put in front of the other until she reaches the Roberts's, there is a freeing blank. Dani walks hard, thoughts circling like tame birds, a good ache in her limbs.

She finds Mr and Mrs Roberts huddled around the electric heater in their front room, its two bars giving out a thin halo of heat. Paltry compared to the open fire, but they can't use that. She helps them tape bin bags over the fireplace to seal up the chimney, and then the front door.

Before she leaves, Mrs Roberts tries to press a packet of biscuits on her. Bourbon Creams from the stash in the kitchen cupboard, the Best Before date only a couple of weeks past. Dani shakes her head and clasps her hands around Mrs Roberts', the skin paper-dry, the knuckles swollen.

"We're alright," Dani promises. "You might need them. Don't know when the shops'll be back open, do we?"

Mrs Roberts huffs. "Well. You'll come and see us properly when all this blows over."

Outside, the dust is still falling. "Yeah," Dani says. "When it's all over."

She finds a broom so Mr Roberts can poke the tape back down over the bottom of the door when she leaves, slaps some more on from the outside to be sure and hopes it

But worry nudges her toward the door, and the edge of the sky is pearly-pale with a false dawn above the slate-grey of the dust. Dani imagines the crisp bite of the morning and aches to be out in it.

Haf throws up her hands. "There's no talking to you sometimes."

For all of five seconds, Dani considers a retort. Then she lets it slide and reaches for the bin bags, the government-issue mask. Time enough for that later.

Even with the respirator strapped tight over her face, leaving a sweaty indent across her forehead, Dani's breathing comes easier once she's out of sight of the house. Not a car or another person to be seen, only the cold, the crunch of her footsteps, the distant ridge of the mountain like the back of a great beast. Something scaled and primordial, opening a curious eye to check whether the human nuisance is finally gone.

The thought surprises her. It's been a while since her mind wandered this far, or this fancifully. Always taken up with minutiae, practicalities: the part-time marketing job she does remotely, swearing when the internet goes down; the handmade soaps she sells online; Haf and the endless work of managing her moods, the vigilance they require. The way these things expand when they're your whole world. Dani snorts at herself, half-amused. Lesbian fuckboi to desperate housewife: not a transformation she ever planned on, but it is what it is.

On TV, they're broadcasting instructions on how to seal up doors with gaffer tape and bin bags, but Mrs Roberts can barely hold a pair of scissors with her arthritis, and Mr Roberts' back certainly won't allow bending down to tape along the bottom. Dani pictures them immobile and dust-coated in their front room. Poisoned in their armchairs, cardigan sleeves rimed like winter gutters.

Haf's eyes narrow to half-moons. "After I've spent all that time taping up the doors?"

The cross pucker of her mouth makes a knot form in Dani's stomach. She knows what that look means. If she pushes, the argument will be exhausting and the night sleepless, Haf shifting and huffing beside her and resolutely facing the wall. Sometime tomorrow, she'll be unable to bear the tension-thick silence any longer and dredge up an apology, and she'll feel like the concession has carved out a small portion of her innards, even as Haf rewards her with small-talk over dinner.

She doesn't know what they'll eat. They finished the fresh groceries last night, and the supermarkets stopped deliveries sometime last week. The cabbage and celeriac starting in the conservatory are nowhere near ready, the tomato seeds not yet planted. She isn't even sure they'll grow, with the dust blotting out so much of the light.

Maybe Haf's right. She ought to worry about putting together their next meal, assembling something palatable out of the pantry cans, and not go trekking over to the Roberts's.

The Last Good Day

JL George

Even here in the lee of Cadair Idris, the dust has found them.

It falls over everything, soft and grey and killing, muffling sounds and the shapes of dead livestock—a pillow pressed over the face of the world. Dani stands at the window, watching it like a first flurry of snow, until Haf takes her by the elbow and draws her away.

"Don't," Haf says. "You'll drive yourself nuts. Nothing we can do."

Dani shakes her head. "I should go over the Roberts's place. See if they're alright."

The Blackbirds in My Sister's Chest

© 2022 Katherine Westermann

Fantasy - 6059 words

About the Author

Katherine Westermann is a nonbinary witch living in Portland Oregon with their wife and a coterie of artistic roommates. When they are not writing, they spend their time coaxing their urban garden to grow vegetables and managing the squabbles of four fussy backyard hens. Their short fiction has appeared in Chrome Baby, and Kaleidoscope Literary Magazine.

lays its ears back if I get too close. It is only Feliz who still regards me with soft looks.

"We can only see and touch one blackbird, but I feel the others out there, soaring," said Feliz, after a week with only one heart. Then she took my hand, for the first time since that night, and twined her fingers through mine. I knew then, she'd forgiven me, and some of the fear went out of me.

I have not lost my sister's affection. Though she *is* smaller. Her frail shoulders are hunched, and her eyes watch the ground. She smiles less and cries less too. She loves us less than she did before, I can feel it in her embrace. And her dark eyes almost never light up with glee.

But the advantage to a cold-blooded heart like mine is pragmatism—being able to take the good with the bad. Her hair has returned, thick and glossy, her blackbird sings in the dawn each morning, and lately she's been well enough to attend school. Does it matter if she doesn't dance or sing anymore? Mother and the rest of the family are bitter at what we have lost, but a heart like mine can appreciate that even a fractured Feliz is infinitely better than no Feliz at all.

last one spread its wings, ready to fly, but Feliz caught the blackbird between her two hands and pressed it back inside. She closed her chest with a soft click, leaving her last bird safely tucked away. And together, we watched the freed birds disappear into the wide azure sky.

"How do you feel?" I asked.

"Smaller," she replied. And I understood her meaning as only a sister can. She was saved. But forever diminished.

"I'm sorry," I said, unable to think of anything better to say.

Feliz took my hand and squeezed. I knew I should feel worse, guiltier, but Feliz would live and that was all I could care about.

"I'm happy." I blurted it out, not thinking, and instantly realized how insensitive it sounded.

But Feliz smiled and said, "I'm happy too." She shook her head, disbelieving. "But Mother will never forgive you."

————

She was right, Mother has not yet forgiven me, nine months hence. I catch her sometimes looking at me with horrified revulsion. Like I'm an insect in her food. She believes I am cold, unfeeling. It is the fish in my nature she suspects. Connie and Father are different with me too—Father avoids me and Connie's cat-heart hisses and

I touched her shoulder and she shrugged my hand away. "Feliz, please." The fish inside me yearned for her.

"I can't kill anymore. I understand what the doctor said but I won't do it." She dropped her hands from her face and gave me a defiant look.

"Would you let them free?" I asked. "Keep one close, and let the others…" I made a vague flying gesture.

She looked me in the eyes, her lashes full of tears. "I dream of them flying free," she said, almost too quiet to hear.

"Feliz?" I asked.

"Okay," she said, "At dawn. They can't see well in the dark."

We sat together on the moist ground, hand in hand, watching the world light up. The dead birds stiffened. I would have covered them, but we had nothing suitable. Feliz trembled with cold, and I wrapped an arm around her skinny shoulders. As the sky turned blue, Feliz got gingerly to her feet. With deft fingers, she unbuttoned the front of her pajamas and smoothly opened her chest. I peered into the dark cavern at her center and saw four pairs of wary eyes gleaming out at me.

"Which one are you keeping?"

"They'll choose," she said and arched her back. Three blackbirds erupted from her chest—one, two, three. The hammered in my hand and I saw the frantic pulse in its naked neck. I positioned the scissors over its spinal cord and snicked through tendon, skin, and bone. Its body tightened, spasmed, and went limp. A fat drop of blood slid down my knuckles.

I lay the bloodied bird next to its dead sibling and, without looking at her, extended my hand to Feliz for the other sick bird-heart. There was a long terrible moment, and I looked up at her.

Feliz had stopped crying—she just looked at me with horror. The whites of her eyes shone with the light from a waning moon, and I felt her pain. She pressed the last sick bird into my blood-streaked hand. Smelling death, it struggled against me, weak and frantic. I looked away from my sister, forcing myself to feel nothing and think only *mercy killing*. I pinched the bird's face between my thumb and forefingers. It squawked, terrified, and fought me when I pulled its neck out. I severed its spine with one quick motion of the scissors. The birds inside Feliz screamed in protest, and she crumpled to the ground. I thought she'd fainted, but then she began to cry audibly.

"Alma," she moaned.

Still holding the dead bird in my hand, I went down on my knees before her. Cold dew soaked through my pajamas. I laid the dead bird aside.

"Alma," she repeated. "The pain is gone. I feel so guilty, but I can breathe again."

"I know," she sobbed. "I don't want to die too. It hurts." She put a hand to her chest. The four healthy birds twittered and squawked inside her.

I lifted the two birds whose skinny bodies still wriggled with life and told Feliz to bring the dead bird with us. She followed me down the rickety stairs, crying softly when I collected shears from the kitchen and walked outside. Feliz followed holding a hand to her chest.

The night was cold and full of stars. Our breath, human and bird alike, rose in white puffs. Feliz lay her dead heart on the dewy ground amid sprouting grass and the closed pale crocuses.

I told her what I was about to do, and she nodded, understanding.

"I'm sorry," I said and handed her one of the sick birds. She cradled it in her hands and kissed the top of its patchy head.

The tear tracks on her face shone like snail trails and I thought of us playing together as children in the garden. The fish inside my chest darted in terror, and I felt the water rushing through its gills. She kissed the bird again. I looked away, understanding that watching her face would hurt too much.

I put a finger under the bird's chin and, trusting me, it let me stretch out its neck. My hand holding the shears shook. *To save Feliz*, I thought hard. The scissors opened with the sharp sound of metal on metal. The bird's heart

At night, Feliz cried, and I lay awake listening, my fish heart throbbing with pain. I was frozen with worry and unsure what she wanted. *Go to her*, I often told myself, remembering when we were young. When I would crawl into bed with her and sing her to sleep whenever she cried. She had always felt so much.

Mother began taking long morning walks, and Connie took to writing in a journal that she and her cat guarded always. Father receded further into the background. All I can remember of him from that time is a stooped figure trudging to and from work, more of a specter than a father. Feliz has since told me that I was the only one who stayed with her. The rest of the family disappeared inside themselves.

That must have been why she came to me that night, cradling three sick blackbirds in her arms, and sobbing. "Help me, Alma." She laid the three sick birds on the bed beside me.

I rubbed the sleep from my eyes and inspected them. In the moonlight, shining through our attic window, her bird-hearts looked almost translucent. They were nothing but bones and skin with a few spiky, black feathers. One bird was unmoving. I picked it up and it was cool to the touch.

"It's dead," I whispered.

"I may not have my heart on display all the time, but I'm healthy. I'm fine."

"Sick hearts need to be treated at a hospital," said Ms. Crawford, talking fast. "I'm happy to talk philosophy all day, but if there is something going on with your heart, or…or someone else's heart, that's serious."

I shook my head and muttered, "I was just trying to talk, you know." With a forced, high-pitched laugh, I dashed from her classroom, and Ms. Crawford watched me leave, a stunned and worried look on her face.

I couldn't go against my sister's wishes and tell anyone because I believed her when she told the doctor she would rather die. Ms. Crawford would force Feliz into the hospital, and once the doctors got control, she might never see her birds again. According to my medical books, wasting hearts are often separated from their hosts and kept in 'care facilities'. Pictures on the school computers showed animals in incubators, with wires coming out of their chests and feeding tubes down their throats. I saw an eagle hooked up to an iron lung with his talons crumpled and twisted, like arthritic hands. I saw a glassy-eyed goat, with his hair shaved, his horns cut off, and on life support with the heading, 'Hearts on life support (pictured above) can live for years while alternative wasting treatments are researched.'

After that, I stopped using the school computers.

———

like her heart's. She fixed me with her keen blue eyes and waited. Her interest in me always took me off guard. I blurted out the question eating at my mind.

"Why do hearts get sick?"

"For the same reasons that our bodies get sick."

"No, I mean the wasting illness. Our bodies don't just waste away for no reason."

Ms. Crawford sat down at one of the student desks and gestured for me to do the same. I sank into the hard chair, half afraid that I was in trouble.

"Wasting is complicated," said Ms. Crawford. She spoke slowly, weighing her words with care. "There is the bio-psycho-social model of heart disease that says its biological, psychological and social." Seeing the look of dismay on my face, she gave a quick shake of her head and changed tactics. "Why do you think wasting happens?"

"I don't know," I said, standing up. "I'm already late for math. I'm sorry."

"Wait," said Ms. Crawford, standing too. "Is your heart alright?"

She held out her hand to me and I took a step back. Of course, she thought I was just concerned for myself. My face flooded with heat and frustrated tears stung my eyes, but I blinked them back.

aqua-hearts. She spoke wistfully of island nations, long ago colonized, enslaved, and destroyed, where most people had aqua-hearts and mothers gave birth in tubs of freshwater, with oceanwater standing by, just in case their baby's heart needed seawater to breathe. Ms. Crawford ranted in class against what she called 'anti-aqua-heart bias' and smiled at me knowingly. She seemed to think we were in some nebulous struggle together.

At home, when I thought of Ms. Crawford, I wanted to align with her and accept the premise that her catfish and my minnow made us the same—heart-mates even—but in her classroom, she was just another white woman who didn't understand me or my family. I couldn't bring myself to trust or confide in her, but I did linger in her classroom after the bell. I slid my books into my backpack one by one and made a show of eying the blackboard after class. Eventually, my passive tactics worked, and Ms. Crawford asked me how I was doing lately.

"Your sister is missing a lot of school lately," she remarked and waited for me to fill her in, but I just shrugged, staring past her at the catfish tank. Her heart had long whiskers and a downturned mouth.

"Is it weird not being able to fit your heart in your chest?" I blurted out the question then immediately felt embarrassed, like I'd crossed a line.

"Not for me," she said. "I don't even remember what it was like to have a heart in my chest." Her face was pale and lined, and her mouth naturally slopped downward, physical. She felt her heart dying with every breath. In class, I would watch her shake with repressed pain and emotion. She never let us see her sick heart and mostly kept all the blackbirds crowded inside her. She lost weight, and her once lustrous black hair thinned. I heard the birds rasping and squawking, as if in protest at being locked away, and I suspected that the illness was spreading.

I lived for those rare moments when laughter and birdsong rang through the house. Moments of distraction or industry, when we'd cook thick winter stews and Feliz would grin at me through her pain and fear. I tried to be cheerful for Feliz and my family, but the doctor's grim assertion that my sister's hearts would die one by one and take her with them weighed on me. I thought of calling the hospital, begging the stag-hearted doctor to make a house call. Maybe try talking to Feliz again, or Mother—the hospital must have translators. But I was too afraid to even look up the number on the school computers, let alone make the call.

Ms. Crawford, my humanities instructor, was the only other aqua-heart I knew and the only outsider who tried to intervene. She had long white hair that she always wore swept back in a bun, and her catfish heart lived in a tank behind her desk. She wanted to mentor me, or so she claimed. It was hard for me to believe I was anything special. She enjoyed my writing and left encouraging comments, but I suspected she liked me mostly for my aqua-heart. Ms. Crawford was a strong proponent of

All sorts of people knocked on our front door and Mother served them tea and told the story of Feliz's youth: birds nesting in the rafters, singing all hours of the day and night. Then the inevitable turn in the story. Her daughter's illness. The doctor's ruthless examination and misdiagnosis. Her complaints changed, but her certainty that the doctors were wrong never wavered. At first, the visitors were real doctors, with black medical bags and grave expressions, but they all gave the same gruesome news that Mother didn't want to hear, and she kicked them out. Doctors stopped coming, replaced by healers in long flowing robes or wizened old women who burned incense, held Mother's hand, and took cash. Then they would give their complex advice—green tea at 2 am, raw eggs cracked over her head, and a diet of liver. However absurd or banal the advice, mother would meticulously carry it out, bursting with hope that this advice would surely work. Nothing helped. Feliz kept the sick heart mostly hidden away in her chest, but the drawn expression on her face betrayed the pain she felt.

I borrowed medical books from the library. They were heavy dry texts, full of grey diagrams and Latin phrases. I read them in snatches and bursts when Mother and Feliz were not around. Mother was disgusted with traditional medicine. To her, my books were further evidence of my frigid nature.

The frosted earth shattered into bloom while Feliz wilted before our eyes. She suffered. The wasting of her heart, she told me once, felt like loneliness and loss turned

"¡Ella tiene un destino demasiado grande para solamente un corazón!" Mother yelled over the cacophony of lamenting birds as if I hadn't heard this speech my entire life.

"Mama, stop!" I said cutting her off. "Is a myth really worth Feliz's life?" I asked, repeating the doctor's cruel logic, hoping to get through to her. But she just stared at me like something caught in a drain and, for the first time in my fourteen years, I felt like I disgusted her.

"Deshonras a nuestra familia," she said, her normally inscrutable face blotchy-red with rage.

"Mama," I begged, "Please, we have to do what the doctors say is best."

"¿Como puedes decir eso?"

"I'm scared." I held out a trembling hand to show her. "Aren't you scared?"

"I don' know you." Mother pronounced the English words with contempt and led Feliz, still weeping, downstairs, away from me.

After my birthday, the house, the schoolyard, and even the privacy of our attic room changed. The world tinged grey. Mother sat by the heavy black phone waiting for friends to call back with news of miracle doctors, obscure healers, and recommendations from great-grandmothers.

"Think!" I cried, blocking the door open with my body. "Were you listening to him?"

Face flushing with emotion, Feliz said, "You don't understand. I—I—" Tears spilled down her face, and she began to shiver, like someone in the grips of a deadly fever.

"¿Que hacen ahí arriba?" called Mother.

"¡Nada Mama!" yelled Feliz, but pain edged her words and Mother came running. In the hospital waiting room, I'd let Feliz obfuscate the truth of her situation and reassure the family that she would be okay. But at the sight of our Mother's wide oblivious eyes, I told her in a rush of English and Spanish.

As I spoke, Mother's face settled into a frown, and she shook her head no. Like she didn't believe me. Then her gaze turned to Feliz's tear-streaked face, and her disbelief hardened into anger.

"No," she said when I was done explaining. "No vamos a matar una parte de Feliz."

"But Mama," I said, unable to keep the quaver from my voice. "She could die. All of her could die!"

Feliz covered her face with her hands, and the birds inside her chest began to squawk, a discordant rasping sound I'd never heard the blackbirds make before. Mother stepped between us in a protective posture, like my mere proximity was a threat.

hearts. The sickness spreads through the cluster and, if action isn't taken, the host will die with them."

"You keep your heart near you," I said, eyeing his stag with its antlers full of blackbirds.

"Why leave my safety to nature? A stag in the forest can easily be a dead stag."

"You don't love your heart?" asked Feliz, her voice hoarse and low.

The Doctor's shoulders dropped, and his body relaxed visibly. He looked tired.

"Feliz," he said, his voice soft and coaxing. "The sick bird at the very least should be euthanized." He spoke to her back, as Feliz refused to turn. "To be safe, you should pick one and eliminate the others. I know it's painful. But multiples are susceptible to the wasting sickness. Is a myth worth your life?"

"I'd rather die," she whispered.

When we got home, Feliz, claiming a headache, tried to retreat to the attic, but I followed her.

"We need to tell them," I said in a hissing whisper. "We have an appointment tomorrow to…" I trailed off, too anxious to utter the word *euthanize* out loud.

"Give me a minute," said Feliz, trying to close our bedroom door in my face. "I need to think."

ragged, molting feathers. He inspected its curled black claws and shined a light into each of its glassy eyes.

"It's wasting," he said, handing the bird carefully back to Feliz.

"What's the cure?" I asked.

"Kill it," said the doctor. "Before the disease spreads."

Feliz gasped and turned away from the doctor, shielding the bird with her body.

"Common medical practice with multiples is to kill all the hearts but one, when the child is an infant. That way they don't remember the pain, it's far less traumatic."

"But doctor," I said, my voice steady despite the cold ache of the fish behind my ribs. "Multiples are blessed with a destiny too big for one heart." Mother's and Grandmother's words sprang readily to my mouth and the doctor smirked at me. His blue eyes locked with mine, and I held his gaze, telling myself I was not afraid.

"Yes, there are a lot of myths surrounding different kinds of hearts. Multiples have grand destinies, predator hearts are easily corrupted, rodent hearts are timid. Some cultures think hearts should run free, far from their hosts, some believe they should be kept close.

"But none of that is science. Multiple hearts are eleven and a half times as likely to grow sick and die as regular across the long, tiled floor and up elevators. Until we ended up in a wing of the hospital called Heart Care.

I was afraid of the doctor—a tall angular white man with a stag for a heart. The stag's sharp horns and spindly legs cast shadows across the floor.

"Feliz Ruiz," said the doctor. The stag watched us like a woodland sentinel. We all stood. The man smiled at our frightened faces. "Just the patient please."

"I need my sister," said Feliz, gripping my arm.

The stag bowed his horned head in consent, and we followed them across the marble floor, down a long, carpeted corridor, into a white stainless-steel exam room.

The doctor nodded at Feliz to show him the problem. With quick nimble fingers, she unbuttoned her shirt and opened her chest. Six healthy birds erupted from her in a flurry of feathers and song. They circled the room, settling on the stag's horns. The hart rolled his eyes up to look at them and sighed, nostrils flaring.

"A multiple," the doctor said, opening a manila file and thumbing through it. "Seven," he said, with a quick shake of his head, as if seven was somehow excessive. "Show me the sick one."

Feliz held out the twisted little bird, and the doctor snapped on gloves before holding it in his big square hands. He pulled out each wing and made note of the

She stood and went to the corner. Mother followed. "Un momento, Mama," said Feliz, gesturing for space. Mother stood close behind her, waiting. Connie crept closer. My heart thrummed with cold watery breath.

Feliz turned, holding out a heap of trembling feathers and sharp pink joints. The bird's dark beak was open, panting and struggling to breathe. My eyes fastened on the bare patches of skin, covered in pockmarks where feathers should have been. I'd never seen any part of Feliz so pink and raw. Mother burst into tears.

We drove to the doctor's office in silence. Father tapped the steering wheel and mother watched us in the rearview mirror. Our car drifted over the icy road like a sleigh, and I told myself a story about drifting back in time, to the early days of man, when we were animals, the same as our hearts. I may not have survived in such a time.

In stiff, halting English, Mother told the nurse that we didn't have an appointment but one of her daughter's hearts was sick. The blonde nurse cocked her head, pen hovering over the clipboard.

I interrupted. "We have an emergency!"

Her brow furrowed with concern, clearly understanding me better than Mother.

The hospital was a labyrinth of glass and stone, perched atop a hill, overlooking the city. We followed the nurse

The Blackbirds in My Sister's Chest

Feliz nodded, and as if by design—perhaps her heart was unwilling to lie—birdsong started in her chest. A long low whistle, barely audible over Sinatra's velvety croon. She crossed her arms, trying to muffle it, but we'd all heard.

Mother's mockingbird fluttered down from the rafters to perch on the table, and Father lifted the needle off the record. Connie stared at Feliz, mouth full of muffin.

"Liz," she blurted, crumbs falling from her lips.

Mother's expression darkened. She'd never heard that shortening of Feliz's name before. The harsh Anglo sounds of our nicknames—Liz, Ally, Connie—were meant to stay trapped in the concrete walls of the schoolyard. We already stood out with our brown skin, dark eyes, and the occasional lapses into Spanish. We gave ourselves nicknames teachers could pronounce and remember— names that could be called on the playground without someone snickering. We used them out of necessity, except Connie, who I suspected preferred her nickname.

Mother shook her head to rattle the nickname out. "¿Por qué estás mintiendo?" she asked.

I reached for Feliz's hand under the table, and we twined our fingers together.

"I'm sorry," she whispered to me. "I didn't want to say anything on your birthday…" Feliz trailed off, her eyes shining with tears. I squeezed her hand, trying to communicate that she needn't feel guilty. Feliz had never asked to be the center of our family, she just was.

My ceremony was silent, our breaths rising in white clouds. Cold hands held cold glass. I watched the shifting discomfort on their faces as they were each reminded of my fragility. The heart no one can touch. Father passed the basin to Mother. I ached with emptiness.

―――

With my heart and all the accompanying apparatus tucked safely back inside me, the party could start. Mother put Frank Sinatra on the record player and closed her eyes, letting the music wash over her.

Volare. She swayed with his voice. He was her favorite artist. *Cantare.* Not mine.

Connie's cat prowled the table, tail flashing, eyes gleaming, with unknown intent, while Connie danced around the table, stuffing muffins in her mouth leaving a trail of moist crumbs. Father's heart, a skinny grey squirrel, perched on his shoulder and watched the big tabby, twitching and chattering with anxiety if the cat came too close. And Mother's mockingbird, perched above us all, feathers puffed up against the cold.

"¿Feliz," asked Mother, "por qué escondes tus pájaros?"

"I'm not hiding them." Feliz took a bite of muffin. "I left them upstairs to stretch their wings."

"¿Todos?" asked Mother.

The doctor had equipped me with my first baby-sized fish tank and lectured mother about the dangers of giving birth at home.

"Señora Ruiz, this is just one of the many things that can go wrong with a home birth. Here at the hospital, we are equipped to handle complications. We check for things like aquatic hearts, injured hearts, multiples. There is no reason to labor at home."

"But my mother, and her mother before her—"

"All lost children," said the doctor, cutting her off. Mother wanted to argue, but he was not wrong.

I set the cylindrical tank on the table with a click.

"Que linda," whispered my sister admiring the flash of my scales.

With trembling hands, I unscrewed the lid of the cylinder and poured my heart out into the blue basin.

The ceremony was simple. The basin was passed from person to person and they each said a silent prayer over the fish. Feliz's seven hearts made her ceremony long and reminded us how complex she was. Connie's restive cat heart made her ceremony different each year— sometimes scratching, sometimes purring, but always the cat reminded us that Connie was fickle and wilder than she seemed.

into me, staring at the glass cylinder suspended behind my ribs and the black cords of the oxygenating unit. When I was little, I used to inspect my open chest in the bathroom mirror. My heart, a small silver fish, was only visible to me as a flash of scales in the shadows.

I untwined the wires that held the cylinder in place and slipped it out from behind my ribs. Inside, the fish glinted.

Mother had given birth to me at home, after twelve hours of labor. "Ernesto," she had said, extending her trembling hands, certain I was the boy who stalked her dreams.

Father had opened my chest, like any other newborn, and water splashed out of me. Aquatic hearts, the doctors explained later, are not safe to open until the child is fitted with a tank. My tiny heart had flopped on the wood, its soft body making a thwapping sound as the last of the moisture disappeared into the wood. The fish thrashed in desperate, wide-eyed silence. The girl child had gone silent too. Like my heart, I couldn't breathe. The heart must live for the host to live, and they had not anticipated an aqua-hearted child.

Father went to his knees and cupped his hands and scooped my heart of the drying floorboards gingerly. Mother, still bleeding, limped to the rusted sedan. While Feliz, mature even at four, carried me, purple-faced and limp, and father carried my heart, dazed and barely swimming, in a jar of cold tap water.

Father was a big man with broad sloping shoulders and a round protruding gut. His body ached from years of hard labor, and he moved cautiously, like an older man, but his face was boyish with nervous close-set eyes and dimpled cheeks when he smiled. But Father rarely smiled anymore. Now, he came up behind my chair and kissed me on the top of my head.

"¿Lista?" he asked, and I nodded, though I didn't feel ready.

Anxiety pulsed out from the center of me like cold water sliding through my veins, and the air felt raw in my throat. Feliz squeezed my cold fingers and I gripped back.

They say multiples feel more than regular people—people like me, who only have a single heart. And that may be true for every emotion except fear. Of my sisters, I am the one who knows the dizzying heights of fear. Some nights I lie awake, staring at the ceiling, unable to blink, unable able to move, I lie there, drowning in a fear as vast and deep as the ocean.

Father put the basin in front of me and took a seat. I took a deep, steadying breath and pulled my hand free to unbutton my shirt for the ceremony. I ran a finger along my ribs waiting for my body to unclench and let my chest open. Mother spoke softly, reciting the story of my birth.

"Alma nació en la tarde. Fue un nacimiento muy difícil."

I closed my eyes, focusing on the soft swishing of my heart. My chest unfolded like origami. My family peered second child and she had hoped I would be a boy—Ernesto Hector Ruiz. Mother painted an image of the young man I was supposed to grow into—broad and cherry cheeked with a lion at his side, presumably his heart. She had made boy clothes, tiny overalls, and denim hats. She had even painted the crib robin-egg blue. But lionhearted Ernesto Hector Ruiz had never arrived.

The family didn't know what to call me. For months, I was 'la bebe', until Grandmother started calling me Alma, literally Soul in Spanish, to make up for the cold disappointment of my heart.

"Siéntate," said Mother, pulling out the heavy carved chair at the head of the table.

With a muttered "Gracias," I sat, watching the flickering candle flame. Thin lines of blue smoke mingled with the steam from the muffins, blurring Constancia's and Mother's smiles.

Feliz sat next to me and took my hand beneath the table.

"¿Dónde está tu padre?" Mother asked, exasperated. "¡Hector!"

She half rose from her seat, lips thin with frustration. Wood creaked in the ceiling and we heard his hurried footsteps.

"Aquí estoy, Amor," huffed Father appearing at the foot of the stairs, carrying the blue basin we used for my birthday ceremony.

more genuine with her. I am Mother's least favorite daughter.

Feliz—named for the great joy she brought our family—was born at dawn to the ecstatic singing of birds. Mother's heart, Feliz's seven hearts, and robins in the fields. She was delivered outside on a stained quilt—the same as Mother and her mother before her. And when they opened her chest and seven baby birds squawked inside her, Mother wept, Mother prayed, she loved our father again, and Feliz's birth ushered in three years of perfect joy. Multiples are rare and, according to Father Mark, they are blessed. Seven hearts. No one had seen such a thing in this desolate, uninspired part of the country.

Constancia was born breach. According to Father, her feet appeared at the stroke of midnight, as if on purpose. And the moment her chest appeared, before she'd taken her first breath, the kitten inside her broke loose. It leaped onto a tray of birthing tools and sent them clattering to the floor. The nurse jumped and yelled for someone to bring clean tools, but before they could arrive, Connie emerged screaming and red-faced, covered in blood and amniotic fluid. The nurse laughed and told my mother she'd never seen a breach come so easy. As it turned out, there was no need to break tradition and deliver Connie on the sterile hospital cot.

The story of my birth—dutifully told each year on my birthday—did not make Mother smile in her private way or cause the sparrow inside her to whistle gayly. I was her was also a bird, needed big windows and natural light. She refused to mount curtains, and the naked windows revealed the vast January desolation—bare trees, brown garden remains, and an icy lane that snaked off into the flat, gray distance. I inhaled the smell of fresh bread, wishing I could skip the ceremony and just enjoy breakfast.

The floors were bare, scarred wood, and the furniture was heavy, durable oak, handmade by Mother's great-grandfather. The only soft place to sit was a yellow, sagging couch where Father usually slept. In recognition of my fourteenth year, Father had folded his quilt and hidden his pillow in Mother's room, and Mother had draped the hulking dining room table with thick ivory lace. Tapers burned in the tarnished candelabra. Mother, carrying a steaming tray of muffins, rushed into the dining room with our little sister, Constancia, on her heels.

"Alma!" cried Mother, pecking my cheek. "Catorce años! Eres creciendo a ser una mujer. ¿Qué hare cuando te vayas?"

"No te preocupes Mama, siempre seré tu hija."

Mother grinned at my expected response. Ever since my tenth year, mother has told me I am growing into a woman, and I have told her that I will always be her daughter. It is a ritual that felt more genuine with Feliz, and last year when Constancia turned ten, it also felt by both our beds, our breath rose in white clouds and our noses were numb and runny.

My birthday is often the coldest day of the year.

"Wake up darlings," said Feliz, and two shiny heads emerged, nervous and twittering. The birds ruffled their feathers against the cold. "Come on," said Feliz, petting them on their dark heads, "never too cold to fly." And she arched her back to roust them. A flurry of black iridescent birds erupted from her chest. School papers flew off our desks, pencils clattered to the floor, and I closed my eyes against the frantic beating of wings. The birds twittered in the rafters, flitting from beam to beam. Feliz noticed me watching her and closed her chest—a fast, anxious motion. I looked at her, startled. She usually left herself open, not shy or embarrassed by the dark cavern in her center. She was not frightened of breaking open, coming apart, unlike me, who only opened my chest on my birthday—the one day of the year it was expected of me.

"What's wrong?" I asked.

She pulled the sheet over her face so only her tussled hair was visible. "Nothing," she said. "The cold was getting inside me."

And I believed her. She had never lied to me before.

———

Downstairs, the woodstove glowed red, and the kitchen was steamy from Mother's baking. Mother, whose heart

The Blackbirds in My Sister's Chest

Katherine Westermann

Every morning, my sister opened her chest and let the blackbirds fly out into the daylight. We shared a rickety attic, with a high beamed ceiling and east-facing windows. Feliz—whose heart had fourteen wings—wanted to be close to the sky, and I wanted to be close to her.

The day it began, I woke up to the soft, fleshy click of her torso unlatching and I rolled over to watch her chest swing open like a cabinet. The morning was cold and grey, and even though Mother had placed space heaters

Sombra

© 2022 Julio Angel Ortiz

Science Fiction - 9443 words

About the Author

Julio Angel Ortiz has written short stories published in several collections by Obverse Books as well as an audio drama for the original science fiction series The Dome. When not banging his head against his laptop in order to string words together, Julio works in Information Technology.

Aurelio screamed, rushing forward to his dad, but there was blood everywhere. He looked around frantically, seeing the woman on the riverbank, quivering as she lay facing away. Aurelio looked back at his father, whose eyes rolled into the back of his head.

"Help! Help me!" Aurelio screamed. He continued to scream until his voice was hoarse and so raw that he could taste blood.

He heard something in the distance and sat silent. A humming sound that soon signaled the approach of a vehicle.

Aurelio heard a click behind him, where the woman lay, and looked back. He saw a light envelop the now-still woman, and she vanished.

Aurelio sat, mouth agape. *What madness have we found?*

Soon, the vehicle arrived, and border patrol agents approached Aurelio, guns drawn. He tearfully raised his hands, forced to allow his father's lifeless body to slump into the water. They were screaming, but their words meant nothing to Aurelio. He simply looked down, watching his father's blood dilute into the river water, innocence washed away in a canticle of tears and horror.

immediately regretted it as he looked over at his father, fearing a scowl or a smack. Instead, he saw his father appear perplexed and looked in the direction of the flash.

He did not expect to see a woman standing there, much less one that was bleeding.

"Where the hell am I?" the woman screamed. Aurelio was confused. He knew a little bit of English, from what they had taught in school, but this woman was frantic and speaking quickly. He was having difficulty understanding her. She was clutching her chest, and then Aurelio noticed her gun.

Aurelio's father must have noticed it at the same time, because he immediately placed himself between the woman and Aurelio.

"No te entiendo!" his father said, panic creeping into his voice.

The woman was yelling at them, and Aurelio could only discern something about helping her. However, she was pointing the gun at them, moving her aim between father and son, and Aurelio was terrified.

His father acted, rushing towards the injured woman to grab her gun. He was too slow.

A shot rang out and Aurelio saw his father stiffen, before twisting the woman's arm. Another gunshot rang out, and both of them collapsed.

He searched his memory. He remembered seeing himself get shot, and barely recalled some pain when it happened to him originally, but the scar...it was new.

Or was it?

— 2017, Chrono-past. —

Aurelio held onto his father's hand, as he struggled to keep up with him through the water.

"Papa!" he said.

"Shhh." His father motioned for him to be quiet. There was no anger in his eyes, but Aurelio saw something else. Something new.

Fear.

Aurelio nodded and resumed following his father in silence. He knew they were taking a risk—his father had told them as much—but Aurelio was tired of walking, his feet aching and wet. They continued to lay low and move ahead.

They came to a bend in the river and moved along the banks, finding some comfort in the tall grass that was becoming more commonplace. Aurelio wanted to ask if it was much further now but thought better of it.

A flash of green light surprised them, appearing without preamble. Aurelio yelped in surprise, and then apartment. Aurelio replayed the conversation during the debriefing over and over in his mind. He could hear the disappointment in Overwatch's voice that the Precept's Unknown would remain as such, despite his admonition that it had been proven that you cannot change history.

Though Aurelio's own memories of those events were hazy, he had offered a possible reason: it was very rare for Agents to be dispatched to interact with their own pasts. There could be some as-yet unknown physiological phenomena that results from someone having two different pairs of memories of the same time period. That answer appeared to appease the Research division, and they made their copious amounts of notes as they were wont to do.

But it didn't matter. Byron was still dead. He had failed in his true mission.

He sighed deeply, one that took root in his soul and threatened to physically break him. He washed his face then looked in the mirror.

Something caught his attention.

He noticed the scar on his arm, a horizontal graze that left a distinct if thin line across his bicep.

Aurelio struggled to remember.

That was never there before.

— 2034, Chrono-past. —

Aurelio turned around to face the stranger speaking to him.

"What do you mean about Byron?" he asked.

But no one was there.

"What the hell?" he said, to no one in particular.

— 2060, Chrono-present, —

Aurelio stepped into his apartment and, as was often the case, it was dark. It was just past 2am. He threw his laptop bag onto the couch and walked to the bedroom.

His body ached, and he felt as though he hadn't slept in days.

Or years.

He stripping down to his boxers and stepped into the bathroom, flicking on the light.

Aurelio looked at himself in the mirror and felt like he was staring at a stranger.

The debriefing had been longer than usual, and though they offered for him to spend the night in one of the Agency's spare rooms, he opted to drive out to his

Zannah looked to the source of the orders and saw law officers rush towards her. She moved to tap something on her shoulder—*her extraction device*, Aurelio reasoned—but as she did more shots rang out.

Aurelio saw Zannah struck, her face twisting in pain as she was enveloped in light and vanished.

"Where did she go?" came a confused cry from an officer.

Aurelio ignored it for now. He looked at his past-self, who was grabbing his shoulder but waving away onlookers. He heard his own protestations, that he was only grazed and was fine.

He looked back at the wounded Asanka, as people already swarmed around him. Asanka's injuries were more serious, but to Aurelio's consternation, law enforcement were already tending to him.

I can't reach him now.

Aurelio moved swiftly and approached his past-self, taking care to not draw attention. He came up and placed a hand on his uninjured shoulder, but kept himself from being seen by himself.

"I'm fine, I'm fine," he heard himself say.

"Listen," Aurelio said, "don't let Byron go to Sri Lanka. Don't let him cover the uprising."

Aurelio heard the click of his extraction device activating, and tried to say something else, but then he was gone.

Which lead right to Asanka.

Ten seconds.

Aurelio ran in a perpendicular angle away from Zannah, and one that kept him out of his own past-self's line of sight.

Five seconds.

Aurelio slid on the ground. *I need to talk to the Tech division about lengthening that timer.*

Time snapped back to a normal pace.

Aurelio was disoriented briefly as the gunshot appeared to come from two distinct directions. He looked at Zannah, the shock on her face, then at Asanka. Who had been hit in the back.

His past-self flinched and fell.

Shit!

Aurelio rushed towards where his past-self lay, his head a dizzying swarm of fear and ideas. He hazarded a glance at Zannah, who locked eyes with him, and her shock turned to anger. She raised her gun again, but cries cut into the panicked voices around them.

"Terrorist!"

"Drop you weapon!"

"Basically, what if I could kill Hitler?"

"Indeed."

I don't give a damn about Tophet, Aurelio thought. *It may be my only chance to save Byron.*

— 2034, Chrono-present. —

Thirty seconds.

Aurelio never considered himself much of a tech guy. He loved using the gadgets provided to him, but he never claimed to have any great insight into how the devices worked. He would occasionally help with the design or provide calculations. At his core, he was still something of a scientist—and assisting the Agency with those tools satisfied that part of him.

He carried Zannah—whose frame and size did nothing to hint at the muscle mass she must contain as Aurelio struggled—as quickly as he could, careful to not knock anyone over. It was proving to be a challenge.

Twenty seconds.

Aurelio was approaching the spot. He placed Zannah down, more haphazardly than he cared to as she almost toppled over. He grabbed and righted her quickly. He turned her, doll-like, to aim down the hall, in an unimpeded line of sight.

"Fragmented? Confabulatory?"

"No matter," Aurelio said. "The point is, while I remember those events, I don't remember them as well as I should."

"And that affords us an opportunity to test one of Precept's Unknowns."

"But actually, *changing* history?"

"Aren't you curious?"

Aurelio paused. "I'm more concerned with the potential reality-shattering fallout."

"The current theory says that we will not 'blink out of existence'. Misremembered information is common throughout history. Events are remembered differently by people. I believe this phenomenon was referred to as the 'Mandela Effect' in the early 2000's."

"I'm very familiar with it."

"You should be. It was your research into this concept that gave rise to the possibility of this Precept being proven."

"Or *disproven*."

"You are uniquely qualified for this test case. You and Asanka have history together. Casual Event 1 was a steppingstone. Imagine if you could stop Asanka before his Tophet Movement wrecks their havoc across the globe."

Aurelio noticed the bullet from Zannah's gun had just poked out from the barrel, but most of it was contained therein.

I don't have much time.

He reached forward, grabbed Zannah by the waist and ran.

— 2060, Chrono-past. —

"It'll never work," Aurelio said, but he knew it was a lie. He had *hoped* it would work. Or at the very least, provide an opportunity.

He basked in the chrono-fluid of the tank that contained him, naked save for the helmet that he wore allowing him to communicate with Overwatch. The helmet was tinted, but Aurelio could still make out the gorgeous teal of the fluid that he currently bathed in.

"But you agree, correct?" Overwatch asked. "The talk in 2034...that is most likely a Causal Event?"

"Based on my faulty memories of the event, yes."

Aurelio thought he heard an actual *humph* escape Overwatch.

"You are not a machine. Your memory is not 'faulty'."

"Then what would you consider it?"

lives. We believe that it is the *only* moment where you can possibly change history. I aim to find out."

"We investigated the same possibility, but it was a dead end."

"Bullshit. Your presence here says otherwise."

"You got me."

In a breath, Aurelio twisted, bringing his arm down and into Zannah's gun hand while spinning his body away. He struck her arm with such force that it swung out in an arc but she maintained her grip on it. As he spun, he reached into his own jacket and removed his own gun. As Zannah whirled back to face him, Aurelio saw she was bringing her gun towards him, finger beginning to press the trigger.

He already had his gun out and fired.

Time, quite literally, slowed down to a crawl all around him.

Aurelio looked at the verdant sphere of energy that had been fired from his gun as it floated in the air between Zannah and him. Its surface roiled like a miniature sun, with tendrils of energy spiking out all around it. It emitted a pulse in the air, the movement of particles just barely perceptible to him, and Aurelio began running a countdown in his mind.

"Figured you were lying about not interfering," Aurelio said, glancing at her. "Do you work for Tophet?"

She gave a non-committal shrug.

"I already told you that you can't change history."

Zannah shook her head. "Your Precept Project is not the only one who has been conducting their own investigations across history."

"I wonder how your group procured temporal technology. It's not exactly licensed and on the market."

"Espionage comes in many forms, Sombra. Regardless, Asanka—not this one, of course—made the same discovery you did."

"Which was?"

"How his sister died. You were there, Sombra, right?"

Aurelio gritted his teeth. "What are you getting at?"

"Imagine if I could kill you—your past-self—here and now. That would prevent you from initiating the circumstances that lead to his sister's death."

"You're wasting your time."

She tutted at him. "I don't think so. You see, we have a theory, and I am almost certain that you and your lot have the same one. This right here is what you call a 'Causal Event', that key moment that impacts multiple people's

Aurelio's smile vanished. "I'm sorry, you are mistaken." He turned to leave. "Now if you'll—"

Asanka reached out, gripping Aurelio's arm, his smile never wavering. "I understand the motivation to use time travel to investigate the past, and to uncover the truths behind previously unsolved mysteries. But why not push further?"

"Further?" Aurelio looked at Asanka in concern. "What do you mean?"

"Why not use it to change the past, to right wrongs? History doesn't have to be immutable."

Aurelio shook his head, shaking himself free of Asanka's grip. "That's where you're wrong. Every test we've been able to perform on Novikov's Self-Consistency Principle has proven it to be correct. The past cannot be changed."

"Humanity once thought a weapon as powerful as the atom bomb was impossible, or landing on the moon. This new frontier is just another one waiting to be conquered."

— 2034, Chrono-present. —

A realization struck Aurelio, and he began to move, but Zannah was there next to him, holding onto his arm while clandestinely jutting something against his ribs.

"Easy now," she said with a smile.

He stepped down off the podium, shook hands with some of the attendees as he passed, and nodded to others who gave approving comments and smiles. He reflexively reached into his pocket to pull out his smartphone to see if Byron had texted him during the presentation.

"Excuse me, Mr. Sombra?" came a stranger's voice.

Aurelio turned and found a sharply dressed man emerging from some of the attendees, a toothy grin as he reached forward and offered his hand. Aurelio responded in kind and shook the stranger's hand.

"Hello?" Aurelio offered with an uncertain smile.

The man nodded. "Asanka. A pleasure to meet you."

"Same. Please, call me Aurelio."

Asanka nodded. "Thank you. I must say, you gave an impressive presentation."

"I appreciate that."

"I'm something of a businessman. I find a lot of potential value in your work."

Aurelio raised a hand, smiling. "Oh, it's all just theory right now."

Asanka laughed. "You're being too modest, Aurelio," he said. "After all, I'm aware of your work on Precept."

but maintaining a line of site with my past-self and our other guest." He allowed her to absorb his words. "You're waiting for a specific moment."

Zannah smiled, and he found no insincerity in it. "Fair enough, Sombra." She reached over and picked up one of the refreshments and drank. "Do you ever wonder what this means?"

"Define 'this'."

"Us being here and how it relates to Fate."

Aurelio scrunched his eyes in surprise. "Really?"

She extended the arm with her drink, motioning to the room. "You are here, in your own past. We, as a species, can traverse time now. In a universe in which we can witness and possibly alter our own future, is there room for a deity? Or did such an entity merely establish the clockwork of the universe, and here we are, roaming about the cogs and wheels."

"There's a fallacy in your logic. This is my *past*. What's happened here has already happened."

Zannah flashed him a look of innocence. "Of course."

— 2034, Chrono-past. —

Aurelio was relieved that his talk was over.

"Ah," he said smoothly, "you haven't aged a day since 2001."

She made a show of examining his head and face. "I wish I could say the same for you. Trying a new haircut? Can't say the glasses suit you."

Aurelio shrugged. "I'm trying new things. It's the Thirties, after all."

"Uh-huh," she said playfully.

Aurelio extended a hand. "I'm sorry, I don't think we ever got a chance to formally meet."

She took his hand with a firm grip. "Zannah," she said. "And I know who you are, Agent Sombra."

Aurelio did not let his surprise show. "This is going to end with us fighting again, isn't it?"

Zannah smiled. "No, no. I'm simply here to observe."

"I doubt that very much."

"*And* to make sure things proceed as expected." Zannah gave him a knowing smile.

"I find that doubtful," Aurelio said.

Zannah feigned hurt. "Why do you say that?"

Aurelio gave her a stern look. "You're keeping your hands at your side, which tells me you're armed and ready to use the weapon in an instant. You're keeping close to me

His younger self was speaking with several people at the convention, and Aurelio found it curious that he had had very little memory of doing so. He remembered arriving at the hotel the night before, and preparing the notes for his talk until late, but aside from waking up and preparing for his talk, he was unable to recall many details.

"I'm in place," Aurelio said, whispering into his comms device.

"Understood," came the ever-present voice of Overwatch.

Aurelio causally walked up to a table that contained several pamphlets and pens. Beside it was a placard that contained his name and the subject of his talk, *Theories on Temporal Forensics*. He sighed, remembering how much happier his younger self was during this time.

"Things were simpler," he found himself whispering.

"Can you repeat that?" came Overwatch's voice.

Aurelio rolled his eyes. "Disregard."

"Remember, Agent Sombra: you are to observe and, if possible, engage in Causal Event 2."

Aurelio looked back. "I shouldn't be here."

"Wrong. You are the best person to test this Unknown."

"I'm not—" he said before recognizing the woman next to him.

Aurelio felt his body go numb, and suddenly the memory of that morning's dream was gone.

He sat before the closed casket, staring at the picture of Byron that was propped up on top. He felt empty, weightless, and could barely discern what people said as they passed by and paid their respects. Aurelio found himself rooted to the chair and did not move until long after everyone else left and night fell.

Aurelio moved like a ghost to his car, driving home and barely remembering the experience. He entered their—*his*—home, and sat on the sofa, alone in the dark. After a few moments, he turned on the television and instantly regretted it.

"The Tophet Movement is claiming responsibility for the murder of Byron Thorne," the reporter droned, *"as a show of defiance in the face of recent sanctions. We are hearing reports that the leader of the movement, Asanka, personally handled the execution—"*

Aurelio turned off the television and sat in a darkness that offered no solace.

— 2034, Chrono-Present. —

Aurelio watched himself with unease from across the room, obscuring himself with glasses and a shaved head.

Byron chuckled, and then kissed Aurelio's ear. "Yeah but I know about the project. Isn't that already breaking secrets?"

Aurelio shook his head. "No. It's already a matter of public record."

"The *name* is a matter of public record," Byron said. "But not the contents. Not what it's about."

Aurelio smiled. "If you were working on something that could fundamentally change our understanding of existence...would you give that information away so freely?"

"Auri, it's *literally* my job to ask those questions."

"I know, love." Aurelio squeezed Byron's hands. "I know."

"I have to go," Byron said.

Panic set in. Aurelio tried to grip Byron's hands tighter, by they slipped away. He turned and saw Byron's back, his husband already dressed and ready for an assignment. He did not turn around; he had his laptop and camera bags in hand as he approached the door.

"I'll call you when I land, okay?" Byron said.

Aurelio felt the energy drain from his body. "No, you won't," he whispered.

"I'll see you soon. Love you!" Byron said as he slipped through the door.

Aurelio exploded, the calm demeanor collapsing in an instant. "Did you know? Did you know that was going to happen? Was Eromi always supposed to die with me there?"

A pause.

"Causal Event 1 has been determined. Return, Agent Sombra."

Aurelio heard the *click* of Overwatch closing the channel and pulled the vehicle over. He began venting his frustrations at the wheel, punching it repeatedly until his knuckles bled and part of the wheel snapped off.

It did not make Aurelio feel better, but it would help when he saw Overwatch next.

— ????, Chrono-past. —

"Why are you so secretive about Precept?" Bryon's voice lilted through the air to Aurelio's ears and was soon followed by Byron's arms wrapping around him from behind into a warm hug.

Aurelio was staring out the window and closed his eyes as he sank into Byron's presence. He raised his hands and placed them on Bryon's, which were interlocked around his waist.

"You know I can't talk about the Project," Aurelio said.

One of the men reached over, grabbed Eromi's hair and yanked her to her feet, hard. Still fighting, arms flailing, she smacked uselessly at his arms.

And then her hands found purchase on his firearm.

Eromi pulled the gun out and aimed it towards the guard.

"Eromi, no!" Aurelio cried. A gunshot rang out.

Eromi slumped to the ground, like a doll. Aurelio looked down at her, at the smoke from the fresh bullet hole in her head. Eromi's eyes stared at nothing. They said everything about the despair of her final moments.

One of the guards was speaking into a walkie-talkie, and the other grabbed Aurelio by the arm.

"Mr. Sombra, it's best if you were leaving now," he said.

Aurelio nodded, silently allowing himself to be led out of the room, down the hallway and away from the nightmare he had found himself in.

"I will be heading back," Aurelio said, calm but stern.

The guard said nothing, but escorted Aurelio outside to the valet, who promptly retrieved Aurelio's rental car. Aurelio drove off and waited a good two minutes before tapping his hidden comms device.

"Overwatch," Aurelio said.

There was a buzzing sound. "Overwatch here. Report."

Aurelio's heart froze, and he gently but firmly removed Eromi's hand. "Look, I'm sorry. I thought maybe I could buy you some solace, some peace for a moment. But—"

There was a heavy knock at the door, followed by the beep of the keycard and the door opening. The same guards from earlier entered the room.

"Session time is up, Mr. Sombra," one of them said.

"But it's early," Aurelio protested.

The man shook their head. "Time's up," he said, in a tone that left no doubt as to his intentions.

Aurelio nodded and stood, buttoning his suit. "Understood." He turned to Eromi. "Thank you for the evening." He turned to leave.

"No!" Eromi cried.

Aurelio barely had time to react when Eromi rushed into him, knocking him off balance. Both of them nearly fell to the floor.

"Eromi, no!" he said, but his voice was drowned out by her screams.

"I won't do it! I won't live this way anymore!" She was frantic, eyes mad with despair and the glint of hope that Aurelio had mistakenly offered.

She's broken, Aurelio reflected bitterly. *And I can't help her.*

"Not alone," Eromi said, a hint of a smile finally appearing. "I had my brother, Asanka."

Aurelio kept his tone even. "Asanka?"

"Yes. My little brother."

"Do you know what became of him?"

Eromi shook her head. "They kidnapped me when I barely just became a teenager. He was younger…old enough to remember me, I'm sure, but what could he do? We were trying to survive without a home, without a family. I don't know what became of him." She paused. "I hope he made it out."

Aurelio nodded. "I'm very sorry."

Eromi looked at him, and Aurelio saw it in her eyes: *desperation*. His heart sank before she even uttered a word.

"You could take me away from here!" she said. "Please!"

Aurelio was shaking his head. "Listen, Eromi. I can't. They wouldn't let you leave with me."

"Yes, they could! You're rich. You have to be if they allowed you to come to the island! You could just…just buy me! Please, I'll do whatever you want. Just take me away from here." Eromi began to grip Aurelio's arm and jacket.

"I'm not going to hurt you," he said.

Eromi wiped away tears. "You're not the first to tell me that."

"But I'm the first to mean it."

Eromi looked at him, her eyes betraying a curiosity.

Progress, Aurelio thought.

"So, what are you doing here?" she asked.

"I want to talk to you."

"'Talk'? That's it?"

Aurelio smiled and nodded.

"About what?"

Aurelio shrugged. "I don't know. How about...where did you grow up?"

Eromi scoffed, a cynical laugh that Aurelio felt had the weight of years and regret behind it. "I was born in Sri Lanka. Lived there for years before...before all of the shit."

"How about your parents?" he asked gently.

"Both died when I was younger. Dad first, then mom during all the fighting and cleansings."

"Must have been tough all alone."

of the men used a keycard to open it and nodded to the woman. Quietly, she entered, and Aurelio followed suit. He looked back at their detail and nodded at the men before shutting the door.

Aurelio turned back to the woman who was already sitting on the edge of the bed. He slowly walked over to her, and she still would not look at him. As he approached, she reached for the straps of her dress and begin to pull them down.

Aurelio quickly put his hand on her shoulder. "No," he said gently.

This caught her off-guard. She finally looked up at him.

"It's okay," Aurelio said, favoring her with what he hoped was a warm smile. "What's your name?"

She stared back, her eyes wavering between relief and distrust. It was a long while before she answered.

"Eromi," she said.

"Nice to meet you, Eromi." Aurelio sat beside her on the bed.

She nodded dumbly but said nothing.

Aurelio made a show of looking at the bruise on her face. "They treat you pretty shitty here, huh?"

Eromi said nothing, but he saw tears welling up.

Aurelio gave the man an annoyed look. *Finally, I don't have to act.* "Are you rushing me?"

The maître d' raised his hands, stammering as he spoke. "No, no, of course not, sir! I just imagine you would be eager to join the rest and enjoy your evening."

Aurelio looked back across the room. "What if I wanted private accommodations?"

"That can be arranged. The price, however—"

"Is not a problem," Aurelio said, putting an edge in his voice.

"Of course."

Aurelio looked at the women again, and his gaze settled on one, of Asian descent. "She'll do," he said.

The maître d' nodded to the burly men who stood nearby, extending a hand to his side. "A fine choice, sir. Come this way."

Aurelio looked at the woman, and he could see that she was making no pretense of enjoying herself. Through the makeup and styled hair, he could see the ghost of a woman hiding in a shell. He noticed the makeup covering up a barely noticeable bruised cheek, and Aurelio clenched his fist momentarily, before quickly reigning his anger in.

The men lead them down a short flight of stairs and a nondescript white hallway, before stopping at a door. One

Aurelio nodded, but found himself unable to take his eyes off the television and the violence unfolding on the screen, even as Byron held his hand and lead away to the bedroom.

— 2006, Chrono-present. —

"Please, Mr. Sombra, take your time," came the gaudy voice of the maître d'. Aurelio had to, once again, refrain from punching the smug rotund man in the mouth.

Aurelio fidgeted with the cufflinks, his immaculate suit feeling oddly confining despite the custom fit. He remained silent, only nodding to the maître d' with an almost-disinterested expression. It was not a terrible stretch to feign his lack of interest in being here. Aurelio felt exhausted.

He had barely had enough time, from surviving his ordeal in 2010, to get his bearings back home before being debriefed, outfitted and sent to this year. Aurelio wondered when the last time he slept was and found himself unable to remember.

He casually glanced around the wide room, ornately decorated, the subdued light offering the lie of privacy. Around the room were similarly dressed men—and one woman—of all ages and nationalities, and the women they had chosen.

"Everyone is enjoying themselves, sir," said the maître d'.

on Precept, and my job at the Press keeps me flying everywhere. When are we going to find time to raise a family?"

"We'll make time, I promise."

Byron shook his head. "They're sending me to Sri Lanka."

That brought Aurelio up short. "What?"

"I just got an email confirmation. They're sending me to cover the Tophet Uprisings."

"You can't go."

Byron's face twisted with anger. "No, we're not doing that. You *also* knew I was a journalist when we got married and that my ass could wind up going anywhere at any time."

"But it's dangerous right now in Sri Lanka."

Byron shrugged his shoulders. "It wouldn't be my first time in a warzone."

Aurelio was at a loss for words. "It's just…I don't know." He looked back at the television. "This feels different."

A look of sympathy crawled across Byron's face as he slipped his arms around Aurelio. "That's very sweet of you to worry. But it's not my first time, okay? I'll be fine." He kissed Aurelio on the lips. "Okay?"

Aurelio looked at Byron blankly. "I...Uhm..."

"Exactly," Byron said, rolling his eyes and pulling away from Aurelio.

Aurelio winced. "No, look...I just meant that I thought you were warming up to the idea."

"That's not how you asked it."

"I'm sorry, okay? That's how I meant it."

Byron sighed. "We're just not there yet. *I'm* not there yet."

"We've been married for six years now! When will you get there?"

Byron whirled on Aurelio. "I'm sorry, I didn't realize there was a time limit on deciding whether to have kids or not."

Aurelio grunted in frustration. "That was unfair of me. I shouldn't have said that."

"When we got together, we both weren't sure if we wanted to have kids. And when we got married, I was very clear that I wasn't sure I wanted to. *And you were okay with that!* I never guaranteed children, okay?"

"Just...what is the hang-up? Do you just not like children? That's okay, I just want to know."

Byron shook his head. "No, that's not it. You know it's not. Look at my sister's kids. They're great and I love being their uncle. But let's be honest, Aurelio. You're working

That stopped Byron, who turned to Aurelio and favored him with a tense smile.

Uh-oh, Aurelio thought to himself. "What?" he said at length.

Byron put away the bread. "I thought we were going to hold off on talking about that?"

Aurelio raised his hands defensively. "I was just looking up a few more things. I'm not trying to imply we're going to start jumping in next week."

Byron nodded. "Okay."

"Unless you wanted to start soon?"

The smile vanished from Byron's face.

"Soon-ish?" Aurelio appended.

Byron sighed and scratched his temple. "Aurelio, we need to talk about this."

"What?" Aurelio said, struggling to keep his tone even. "Don't you want to have kids?"

"You know that's a loaded question," Byron said. "And honestly, not a fair one."

Aurelio stood and moved around the counter, placing his arms around Byron. "I'm sorry. That didn't come out the way I meant."

"So how did you mean it?" Byron asked.

"How do you do that?" Aurelio asked.

"You mean have you haven't figured it after all of these years?"

Aurelio scoffed, but his tone betrayed light-heartedness. "I guess not."

"You'll learn, babe."

Aurelio smiled and looked back at the television, which flashed images of soldiers and social unrest.

"Another day of unrest in Sri Lanka as the Tophet Movement coup attempt enters its sixth day."

Aurelio took another sip of coffee and noticed Byron had stopped at the refrigerator, is only briefly, before resuming opening It and putting away the eggs. Aurelio put down the coffee.

"Hey, you okay?"

Byron flashed him a weak smile. "Yeah."

Aurelio considered pressing it, but he knew better. He opted to move in a different direction.

"So, I was doing some more research last night."

"Oh yeah?" Byron said. "On what?"

"Adoption."

Aurelio closed his eyes from the explosion, but heard the no-less thunderous clamor, followed by the tumult of the elevator racing unimpeded down the shaft. He considered keeping his eyes closed, but opted to open them, seeing the endpoint of the shaft racing away at high speed.

If I'm going to die, I'll stare it in the face.

One thought kept going through Aurelio's mind.

Byron.

And then there was a flash and a cacophony of metal crashing.

— 2039. Chrono-past. —

Aurelio wanted to turn off the television, but every time he reached for the controller, Byron kept moving it.

He was seated on a stool at a kitchen counter, occasionally glancing at the television while finishing up his eggs and toast. Byron was putting away some dishes, and Aurelio kept wondering how Byron knew he was going for the remote.

Randomly, Aurelio reached out for the remote, but only got as far as brushing against the corner when Byron, while reaching for a cabinet, would arc his free hand down and shift the controller several inches, before returning to putting away dishes.

the field's effect. He would be stuck in a miniscule moment of time forever.

Unless…

The field extended almost to the roof of the hotel. He understood these fields were spherical. They were over half-way up the building so the bottom would be around the second floor.

That would do.

Aurelio dropped back down into the elevator and lay down on the floor, so his torso was positioned directly beneath the hatch. He set the temporal extraction to activate with a countdown timer feeling his fingers beginning to succumb to the slowness surrounding him.

He removed the miniature explosive device from his bag, it was relatively newer tech for the Agency, essentially a programmable bomb. Aurelio punched in the yield and added an EMP burst so that the emergency locks for the elevator would fail.

Am I committing a high-tech suicide? Aurelio wondered, not for the first time.

He performed two actions in quick succession.

Aurelio threw the explosive through the hatch, watching it sail through the air, and followed this by activating the countdown timer for temporal extraction.

in places, like motes of kaleidoscopic light floating throughout the hallway.

"Agent," came Overwatch's voice, "immediate extraction is advised. The anomaly is approaching the Xeno Threshold. We won't be able to retrieve you if you are caught in it.

A living, infinite Hell, Aurelio thought to himself. Or so the theory went.

Aurelio pulled out his device to initiate a temporal extraction but immediately saw the issue. It was reporting a failure to establish a link to the Chronostream. Aurelio cursed in frustration.

Overwatch's voice was filling with static. "Agent Sombra, you will need to find a way to distance yourself from the spatial field."

Aurelio considered his options and had an idea.

He stepped back to the elevator and pressed the button again. The door opened, and upon entering, he began to feel around the ceiling and pressing on it until he was able to find the emergency hatch. He pushed up on it, moving the panel and unlatching it. Aurelio climbed up onto the roof of the elevator and looked up in dismay.

Far above him in the shaft, Aurelio could make out a shimmering in the air, and realized it was the limit of the distortion field. Even without determining the height, he knew it would be impossible to climb it in time to escape

Right back out in front of his hotel room.

"Shit."

Aurelio turned right to the other exit, feeling the same drag on his body but continuing to fight. When he stepped through the door, he was surprised that he had not exited his hotel room again, but through the *other* stairwell door, back into the hallway.

"Overwatch," Aurelio said into his comms device, maintaining a level voice.

"Overwatch here. We are detecting increasing-"

"Whoever they are, they have me trapped in a spatial loop."

"Understood. Please stand by."

Aurelio grunted in frustration and moved back down the hallway. He stopped by the elevator, and after considering it for a moment, he pressed the button to summon it. After twenty seconds, the door opened. Aurelio entered, pressed the button for the lobby, and waited.

The elevator door refused to close. Aurelio pressed the button several times, but it did not react.

Aurelio exited the elevator and noted with irritation that the elevator door closed. He looked around the hallway and felt the heaviness getting worse and wondered if his eyes were deceiving him when the air began to shimmer

There was a long pause. Aurelio began to wonder if the connection had dropped or if his contact was spooked. After a long while, there was a response.

It's a reminder of my past. A reminder to me of what I've lost.

"Overwatch here," came a voice over Aurelio's communicator.

"Sombra here."

"We are detecting third-party chrono-interference building in your location. You are advised to immediately head to extraction."

"Acknowledged," Sombra said briskly.

He turned his attention back to the chat session. *I'm sorry, I can't help you. Too much risk.*

After hitting SEND, Aurelio closed his laptop, unplugged the Ethernet cord and shoved it into his satchel. He exited the hotel room, turned left and began to head down the hallway.

That's when he realized something was terribly wrong.

The air felt heavy, a pressure that rooted itself to his chest and did not let go. His steps were labored but far from impossible, as though someone had dialed up the gravity. He gritted his teeth and made his way to the stairs and opened the door, stepping through.

Understood. But what guarantees do I have? It was Aurelio's turn to pause. *After all, $100K is not a small amount.*

Aurelio looked at UnderW0rld's avatar. He noted that it had changed from the generic outline of a person. It was now a drawing of a bear, frowning, with one of its ears missing. Aurelio made a note of this.

A speech bubble appeared, and judging by how many times it appeared, disappeared and then re-appeared, Aurelio expected a rather long reply.

Don't you want to expose them?

Aurelio was amused by the curt response. He began to type but received another message.

You can see, can't you? The world is sliding towards fascism. Towards ultra-nationalism, towards the slow decay of the rights of the people. The ultra-rich will consume the other classes, leaving only a broken poverty class and despair, while they continue their trafficking and debasement. The world doesn't want to see it, but I do. I know what they do. Who they sacrifice.

"Yep, that was what I was expecting," Aurelio said in a whisper.

Aurelio typed back. *Why is your avatar of a bear with one ear?*

While the hotel did have wireless, it was still slower than connecting via hardwire, and Aurelio didn't want to deal with troubleshooting old WiFi issues.

Once connected, Aurelio fired up the virtual app layer of the chat program he was to use. Once booted, Aurelio logged in with his credentials—*how quaint*—and watched his friends list populate. His contact still was not online, he waited.

It did not take long for Aurelio to hear the tell-tale ding of the message notification.

Aurelio opened the chat window and found a message from 'UnderW0rld'. *Did you read over the agreement?*

Aurelio respected the lack of pleasantries. He responded in kind. *I did.*

And? Though text could not always convey emotion, Aurelio imagined impatience in his contact's tone.

You're asking for quite a bit of capital with little guaranteed return on my investment, Aurelio messaged.

I understand your hesitation, but I promise you, the results will be worth it.

Aurelio frowned at this but messaged back, *I imagine you tell everyone this. ;-)*

There was a pause. *You are not the only investor I am communicating with.*

Aurelio found himself nodding, then raised a hand as though waving hello. "My name is Aurelio."

The man nodded, placing a hand on his chest. "Byron. Maybe I'll catch you around."

Aurelio nodded and watched Byron walk away down the path towards the Walker building. He noted with amusement Byron's casual attempts to look back at him without being noticed.

For a moment, Aurelio forgot what he had been thinking about and found himself feeling grateful.

— 2010, Chrono-present. —

Aurelio felt like a caveman plugging in the hotel Ethernet cable into his laptop.

The Agency-provided laptop was state of the art, even if the shell was made to look plain and antiquated, maintaining legacy networking ports and protocols for obvious reasons. The latest developments in the operating system used by the Agency allowed a dynamic artificial intelligence to analyze and adapt itself to the current time period the technology was being used in, all the while maintaining a suite of encryption and security tools for the jobs at hand.

He looked up and locked eyes with the young man standing before him. The great mop of hair, his dark green eyes, the backpack and a notepad in his hand.

"Can I help you?" Aurelio said, his voice even.

The man shrugged nonchalantly. "Just transferred here and I don't know where the Walker building is. Was wondering if you knew?"

"What makes you think I would know?" Aurelio immediately cringed inside. His voice came off sharper than he wanted.

The man shrugged, his face betraying a slightly taken aback look. "Hey, sorry to bother you."

The man turned, but Aurelio raised a hand and spoke quickly. "No, I'm sorry. I didn't mean to be rude."

The man looked back at him with a quizzical look.

Aurelio chuckled self-consciously. "Uh...would you believe me if I told you I've had a rough day so far?"

"It's cool, I get it."

Aurelio pointed down the path to the building on the far end of campus. "It's over there. That's...what, for English majors?"

"Journalism," the man said, smiling sheepishly. "We'll see but that's my goal.

though calling to him. *I should really just get back to studying.*

He considered where to start. Aurelio perused a mental list of upcoming tests and papers that were due, and the most pressing—Physics, of course—was not one he felt mentally invested in perusing now.

He looked back up at the sky, letting the warmth dance across his face and taking in the cerulean beauty. Inevitably, the image took him back to that day by the river all those years ago.

Dad.

The river.

Sister?

As ever, the fog refused to lift on the events of that day. Like claps of thunder, the images crashed into his mind. His father, and then splashing, and his sister laying nearby, her face away from him. *Why? Why can't I remember her?*

Reflexively he reached for his temple, and gently rubbed, suddenly self-conscious as though the world were razor-focused on him now. But as always, Aurelio looked around and found no one noticing him.

Except for the guy in front of him.

Aurelio sighed. He felt that he could resume his mission without issue but understood the protocols and the need for strict adherence. Still, he wondered about the woman, and why she had engaged him. Her technology and combat skills were indicative of some rival power and was not something he had previously come across.

Who else would be sending people into the past? Then a troublesome thought crept into his mind. *And do they know about the Project?*

Aurelio shook his head. He wouldn't find the answers here or now. He would have to wait.

He pressed a button and merged back into the timestream.

— 2029, Chrono-past. —

Aurelio sat by a tree on the university campus. As he observed his fellow students walking, joking and communing on the gorgeous spring day, he couldn't help but feel lingering anger.

They are so carefree, he thought.

Sitting on the grass, he knees hunched up and his arms lazily slung around them, he caught himself scowling at some of the people, then looked down before anyone could see him. Aurelio looked aside at his bag, seeing his Physics and Mathematics books poking out the top, as avoiding additional punches and kicks. As he rolled into a standing position, he saw the woman standing a safe distance away, punching and kicking into the air as parts of her vanished in the process.

Spatial portals. Damn, I hate those.

Aurelio reached into his jacket pocket, grabbing a slim disc with a button in the center that he clicked. He tossed it just short of the woman, who looked at it with a weary gaze just as energy exploded from the disc. She was surrounded by tendrils of energy from a dozen spatial pockets around her, and she flipped backwards to avoid them. Taking advantage of her distraction, Aurelio hurriedly pulled out a transponder from his pocket, clicked it and threw it at her. The transponder swiftly arced through the air, avoiding the strings of energy lashing about, and landed on her shoulder. There was just enough time for her to look down at it before a flash of energy overcame her and she vanished.

Aurelio sighed and looked around to make sure no one had witnessed their spectacle. He then reached for his comms device.

"Overwatch," he said, "I was engaged by my stalker. I'm fairly certain she was also non-Chrono native."

"Understood." There was a distinct pause. "The window for non-temporal contamination has passed. Disengage and await further instructions."

Aurelio tried to mentally trace the accent. *Middle Eastern?* "I figured I'd at least try to get to know who's trying to kill me."

"Who said I was trying to kill you?"

Aurelio dangled a finger on the left side of his head. "Gunshot? That was you, I'm assuming?"

"If I were trying to kill you, I wouldn't have missed."

"There are much easier ways to getting a hold of someone. Call, maybe an SMS?"

"I forgot my smartphone at home."

'Smartphone'. This is interesting.

Aurelio kept his cool. "What do you want with me?"

"Why are you trailing her?"

Aurelio shrugged. "Don't know who you're talking about. I was just out for a stroll on a beautiful London evening."

The woman shook her head. "I see you're choosing the hard way."

He heard a device click in her hand and she punched behind her. He felt the punch in the *back* of his head.

Aurelio allowed his momentum to carry him forward, turning back to see a fist, hovering in the air, vanish. His confusion intensified when he received a kick to the side of leg, causing it to buckle. Aurelio rolled onto the ground, the shadows here and could hear the rapid footfalls of his pursuer. He crouched and waited.

The figure came into sight, running past without seeing him. Aurelio took the opportunity to reach down into his boot and removed the slim throwing knife he kept concealed, and threw it at their back.

Aurelio wasn't expecting for them to twist in mid-run, grab the knife out of the air and throw it back with uncanny precision.

He barely leaped out of the way in time, the blade clattering against the stone wall. He was barely in his new position when the pursuer, who he could now identity as a woman, jumped towards him, her right leg thrusting out and connecting with his ribs.

Aurelio grunted in pain as he reeled back but maintained his composure. He moved forward, leaning into his attacker's momentum and ramming his shoulder into her stomach and tackling her to the ground. Once on the ground, he lifted his arm and punched down hard—into the macadam. She had narrowly slid out of his grasp to the side and scurried away several feet before standing up and facing him. He bit down the pain in his fist and stood, squaring himself as he faced her.

"Impressive," he said at length.

"Trying flattery now?" she said.

Night always accentuated this feeling, and Aurelio allowed himself to revel in it. The life he lived allowed him rare gifts and benefits that few others enjoyed, and Aurelio richly embraced them.

He also suspected that some of the thrill this time came from the fact that he was being followed.

That's...a pretty new feeling.

"Overwatch," Aurelio said, speaking into his hidden comms device, "I have a tail."

Another pause. "We are not aware of any other chrono-incursions into your current time frame."

"I know, but I figured I'd give you a head's up."

"Proceed with following the mark at a distance, until circumstances change."

The gunshot that rang out and the bullet narrowly missing his left ear, was reason enough to satisfy 'circumstances changing' for Aurelio.

Aurelio ducked into an alleyway, racing through the shadows until he reached the end, then hazarded a glance back to see a figure in pursuit. He picked up the pace, weaving through cars and streets but the figure remained persistent. Aurelio turned down a street where the buildings morphed into a rougher part of the neighborhood, before heading into a lot with half-standing walls of indeterminant age. Aurelio receded into

Aurelio involuntarily shuddered at the sound and shrunk back in his cell.

The soldier held his gaze for a moment longer before proceeding. Aurelio felt the abyssal tug of despair as he remembered that he was utterly alone. He tried to remember what happened to his dad, and the pain returned.

Water. Dad was trying to carry me…We were trying to get somewhere, and then water and pain and my dad lying dead…and my…sister? Where is my sister?

Aurelio slumped to the cold, unforgiving ground, and welcomed the sleep that encroached upon him.

In this cold, alien place, Aurelio wondered—not for the first time—what would become of him.

— 2001, Chrono-present. —

No matter the time period, London was always magnificent.

There was something in the air and in the streets, an energy that permeated the stone structures that never failed to invigorate Aurelio.

I wonder if it's the history. Could history be tangible in a way we feel, or perceive? Does it bleed off the streets and buildings like an invisible stream we are always wading through?

guns that looked larger than any Aurelio had seen before. He remembered seeing something like them back home in Mexico, on TV or sometimes in the streets around government buildings. But up close, they terrified Aurelio, and as he looked around at the other children and sickly people, he wondered why the Americans would need such powerful weapons to guard them.

And why are we even here?

A headache took root, and Aurelio rubbed his temples in a vain attempt to sate the pain. It was not the first time since arriving, but they were not getting any better.

Aurelio saw a guard walking nearby and decided to try again.

"Hola?" he offered. "Uh...excuse...eh, help me," he began, his voice thick with accent and confusion. He did not know English beyond a few phrases on TV and the limited exposure at school. They hadn't allowed him access to any kind of translator, and his inability to communicate frustrated him.

The guard looked down at Aurelio, and his heart froze with the look of indifference.

"Shut up, wetback," the soldier said and, as though to highlight his intent, bumped the stock of his gun against the bars, resulting in a *clang* that reverberated throughout the facility.

The length of time it took Overwatch to respond surprised Aurelio. Even if it was a beat of several seconds in length, it was uncommon for Overwatch.

"That's disappointing. Temporal abatement about to cease. You'll have ten real-time seconds once abatement ends to extract."

Aurelio nodded. "Understood."

Already he could begin to see the process of the temporal slowdown coming to an end. A faint shimmer of light in the air; the fire outside beginning to flutter strangely, like a leaf in a hurricane. Aurelio removed a small device from his pocket and pressed a button. In a breath, Aurelio merged into the timestream.

— 2017, Chrono-past. —

Aurelio found the cold marble floor the most welcoming thing about this place.

He began to lose count of the days and could no longer remember how long it had been since had been brought to this building, the prison that had been home for what now seemed like an eternity.

Aurelio looked through the bars that formed his cage and saw other people, mostly children like himself, each cooped up in a small cage of their own. Between the blocks of confinement, soldiers patrolled armed with

Aurelio looked through the shelves in the upstairs room, gently pushing aside the children's books and crayons. He looked back at the unkempt bed and cracking pale walls. He noticed a poster slack on the floor, folded over to conceal its contents. Aurelio considered moving forward and turning it over but thought better of it. Time was limited, and the information would most likely be of little value.

He pressed a button on the comms device on his chest. "Overwatch, this is Agent Sombra."

There was a pause, and then a distinct heavy voice responded. "Overwatch here. Report."

"Three events to note. First, the mother was shot in the leg and chest."

"This is consistent with the limited records we were able to uncover."

Aurelio withheld a sigh. "She was alive for approximately two hours before expiring. There's reason to believe she spent that time speaking with the subject."

"That…is new," Overwatch said.

"Second is a toy bear was discovered, with one ear."

"Noted."

"And the sister is nowhere to be found."

Sombra

Julio Angel Ortiz

— 1991, Chrono-present. —

Aurelio moved like a ghost through someone else's life.

Through one of the windows, he could see the damage and chaos, muted into a tableau of horror. Some Tamil soldiers breaking into a nearby building, while others were dragging women and children through the street. A fire's rage was captured as a still frame, consuming some unfortunate house. Aurelio wondered, not for the first time, if Chavakachcheri had ever been beautiful.

"Temporal abatement will cease in one minute," came a voice from the device on his chest.

The creature next to me takes my hand and we all leave, a river flowing through the door. The porch outside has been covered with a thick blanket of flowers. The salt is hidden or cleared away. There is nothing to stop me leaving this house now.

I step out onto the cool grass and run to meet my mother, the Queen of the Forest Folk, who has come to rescue me at last.

© 2022 Jessica Lévai

Fantasy - 5244 words

About the Author

Jessica Lévai has loved stories and storytellers her whole life. After a double major in history and mathematics, a PhD in Egyptology, and eight years of the adjunct shuffle, she devoted herself to writing full-time. You can find her work on *The Overcast*, *Strange Horizons*, and *Tor.com*. Her first novella, *The Night Library of Sternendach*, is a vampire romance in Pushkin sonnets. She has begun work on her second long-form piece and dreams of one day collaborating on a graphic novel, and meeting Stephen Colbert. Check out her website, https://JessicaLevai.com/, for links and more.

Nanny, they give her poker less and less room. They purr like cats.

They crossed salt and iron to come for me. They will kill Nanny now for revenge. I know this deep inside, just as I start to remember who I am. But with this understanding comes the knowledge that once I am whole, once the salt is gone from my body and the iron is no longer there to weaken me, I will not remember other things. The little kindnesses Nanny did show me. The pain and loss that drove her to make her horrible mistake.

"You cut off my wings," I say, stepping closer. "And poisoned my food. Trapped me in iron. You tortured a child and thought that would get you back your own."

Finally I come to stand in front of the woman. She sinks to her knees so her face is just at my height. The rumbling behind me gets louder. Out of the corner of my eye I see them stretch their claws, test the keenness of their teeth with their tongues. Not much longer now.

Nanny—Nell—is shaking. "I'm sorry," she says so quiet I can't hear it. I just see the words. I know she means it. I know it shouldn't matter. I lean forward and give the woman a kiss on her sweating forehead. "Good-bye, Nanny," I say as I step back. One of the creatures hisses and I lift up my hand. They all stop, silent, and look at me. I shake my head. I look at Gerry's body on the couch. The vacant child's room upstairs. "It's enough," I say. "I would like to see my mother now."

touching my back with his finger. He makes a chittering noise and others come to stand where he is.

Some of the monsters start to snuffle loudly. Others have tears in their eyes. They show me spots on their arms where the scales have been burnt away, where their wings have been singed. Nanny is still swinging the poker, and the monsters won't even get close to it because when they do, they stumble and fall down.

I think about the salt in my porridge and the metal that my bed and braces are made of. The creatures' claws are tracing the lines on my back. The scars.

I was scared and I was sad but now I'm angry. I'm furious. The monsters aren't trying to hurt Nanny, because I told them to stop, but they're not crying anymore. Nanny looks at me and I show her my teeth.

"Child, please, you have to understand. We only wanted our little girl back."

As I walk closer to her, the monsters—my mother's servants—part around me like water.

"We thought…we thought that if we caught one of you, you would trade her back to us. We didn't mean any harm to you."

The servants are moving closer to Nanny. There are more of them. They come in through the front door, climbing over the bodies of the ones who fell, crushing them into the last of the flowers, and as the mass presses closer to monsters will eat her. I don't know what to do so I just scream "Stop!" as loudly as I can.

And the monsters stop.

Their little heads turn and look at me all at once, all their yellow eyes blinking at me. I should be scared of them, and my legs should shake. But I'm not scared of them. I take two steps down the stairs and my legs are good. I feel so strong.

The monsters are still looking at me, and then one of them sort of falls on his face. The one next to him falls, and the next, and soon they all have their faces on the floor. I hear a little thump behind me. It's the one from my room, who came in the window. He opened the door and now he has his face on the floor, too.

I breathe in all the good smells of the flowers as I get to the bottom of the stairs. The monsters are little. Not even as big as me. And now that I see them up close, they're not scary. They're funny. They're familiar.

One by one they pick themselves up off the floor and come to stand around me in a circle. One of them touches the skin on my arm and shrinks back. Then another touches my hand. These are the best, softest touches I've had in a long time so I let them. They sniff at me and wrinkle their faces. They trace the red lines the braces left on my legs and look at me like they're sad. Something stings on my back and turn around to see the monster from my room, standing on a stair above me. He was

The bird thumps against the window again. It does it again and the glass cracks. It thumps one more time and the bird crashes through. I cover my eyes because there is glass everywhere, but when I look again it's not a bird. It has feathers and a beak and claws but it is not a bird. I turn to run away from the room and the monster and I hear a huge crashing noise from downstairs and Nanny screams. The monsters found us. They're coming into the house.

The monster in my room is little but it's coming for me. I grab my brace that I can reach and swing it at the monster. Then I fall backwards out of the room and close the door before it can get me. I'm safe. But what about Nanny?

From upstairs I can see that the front door is open. That was the crash, I think. The door is hanging against the wall and from up here I can see that there are flowers and flowers and flowers and they smell so good. But there are also little shadows, and as I get closer I see that they're monsters like the one in my room. Some of them are lying in piles and not moving, and the others climb over them. There are some with scales and claws and some with feathers and wings and long tails.

Nanny is stuck in the corner, swinging at them with the poker and trying to keep them away from her. She's crying and they're making this rumbling noise. They show her their sharp beaks and all the teeth in their wide mouths. I know she's going to get tired and then the

"Are the monsters coming?" I ask her, my mouth all full of mushy bread.

"I don't know." Nanny doesn't look so lost any more. She picks up the broom but puts it back and grabs the poker from the fireplace instead. "I think you should go to your room, child. Get ready for bed."

"But I'm not sleepy," I say, and I'm not. "I don't want to be upstairs by myself."

"I'll tuck you in soon. Just go get into bed. You'll be safe there."

"But..."

"Please," says Nanny. She's never said please to me before. I decide to be helpful and go to my room. At least my flowers are there. When I see them and smell them I feel better. I don't want to go to bed. The bed is uncomfortable and I hate it. But if I'm supposed to be getting ready anyway...

I have never taken my braces off so fast. The first one falls on the floor with a bang and I worry that Nanny is going to come up and yell at me. But she doesn't. So I take the second one and throw it against the wall, where it makes a really loud crash which I like. I breathe deep down to my toes. Suddenly I'm not scared anymore. I hear a thumping at my window and I know it's the bird again. I run over to the window. It's so dark outside I can only see the bird's shadow, but it came back, and now I can show Nanny.

Nanny put a tablecloth over Gerry and left him on the couch. I don't like looking at him. We didn't eat lunch but I'm not hungry, which is good because I'd have to eat in the same room as Gerry.

Nanny took the box of salt and tried to put some of it in front of the door, but she dropped it. It spilled all over the place but she didn't clean it up. Now she's just sitting on the floor and crying. I want to ask her about my mother but she doesn't answer when I call her so I think maybe she's so sad she can't hear me. She sits and sits and it starts to get dark out and now I am hungry. Finally I tell her. "I'm hungry," I say.

Nanny looks up at me with her red eyes and nods. But she doesn't move. I go to the kitchen myself and find the bread in the cabinet. Usually Nanny makes me peanut butter sandwiches but I don't like peanut butter. It's yucky like the porridge, so I just take a piece of bread and eat it. I'm making crumbs on the floor but Nanny doesn't say anything. I wonder if she's hungry. Maybe I should give her a piece of bread. But then that would mean that I'm taking care of Nanny and I don't know how to do that.

There's a sound outside the window. It's like scratching on the frame. I wonder what made that sound, but then I remember the blood coming out of Gerry's stomach and I think I know. I'm afraid Nanny didn't hear the noise, but when I look at her she's not on the floor anymore, but looking through the windows. She kicks the spilled salt in front of the door into a line.

"You think flowers are the worst they can do? Marianne is probably dead by now. We don't have a choice. We have to."

"No!" says Nanny, grabbing me by the shoulders.

It hurts. Everything hurts and I'm scared of Gerry and I'm scared of monsters. "I want to go home!" I say and start crying. "I want my mother!" I wish I could run away and out of this house but now I know there are monsters.

"Hush, child," says Nanny, and then she surprises me by wrapping her arms around me and hugging me. I yelp a little when she touches my back because it hurts but I don't want her to stop. If my mother can't be here, maybe Nanny will love me enough to keep the monsters from getting me. Nanny squeezes me and says, "I won't let them have you. I won't. I promise."

We are both crying and I wait for Gerry to say something but he doesn't. Nanny lets go of me, because I think she noticed that Gerry didn't say anything for a while. She goes over to him on the couch. He dropped his towel, and I can see the big cut on his stomach. It's very red, but it isn't bleeding so much now. Nanny is calling his name and grabbing his wrist but he still doesn't say anything and doesn't move. Nanny looks at me and then back at him and starts making this kind of moaning sound, over and over again.

Gerry coughs and says, "Jesus, she really don't remember anything we tell her. She was taken by the things that live in the woods. By those…monsters."

I think that monsters is the scariest word of ever.

"Call them the Folk," says Nanny. "Please, Gerry, you know better."

"Monsters aren't real," I say, but he just laughs at me.

"I did this to myself?" he says, pointing at his stomach, but then he lays back on the couch. Nanny gives him the new towel. This one is yellow. The first one is almost black and it drips red on the floor when she takes it away.

"Why did the monsters take your little girl?" I ask. "Was she bad?"

"She was an angel," says Nanny.

"But if she was good and I'm good then are the monsters going to take me?" I get all cold and shaky. My braces are pinching and I hate them because I can't run away if the monsters come to get me.

Gerry kind of groans but Nanny surprises me because she kneels next to me and holds my hands. "I'm not going to let the monsters take you. Not ever."

"Nell," says Gerry, and his voice is soft. "We have to give her to them. There's no other way this is going to end."

"I'm not giving up."

parley, they're not..." He stops talking and the bottle slips out of his fingers. Nanny catches it before it spills. The towel is very red now.

"What's going on?" I ask, and wish that my mother was here.

"Go to your room," says Nanny.

"No," says Gerry, and he tries to sit up a little more. "She should know what did this. I have no idea why you're trying to protect her."

"Gerry, sit down and don't talk."

"Tell her about them! Tell her..." His face scrunches up like mine does when my back hurts. He's breathing really hard and I can see all of his teeth.

I remember that they said a name. "Who's Marianne?" I ask. Nanny puts her hand to her mouth and goes to the kitchen to get another towel.

"Marianne was our daughter," says Gerry.

"She *is* our daughter," Nanny says from the kitchen. "Our little girl."

I want to know why Marianne and I can't just go back to our own mothers right now. "What happened to Marianne?"

she drops the broom and unlocks the door. When it opens, Gerry falls onto the floor in front of her.

———

Gerry isn't moving, and there is so much blood everywhere. His shirt is dark and shiny and wet and it smells. Nanny pushes past me into the kitchen to get towels. She presses a white one with blue stripes against his shirt and very slowly he gets up. She almost has to carry him to the couch and he just lies there, breathing heavy and holding the towel, which gets red spots on it. I think he lost his necklace because I don't see it. He grunts at Nanny and she brings him a bottle from the kitchen. He puts his mouth right on it and drinks.

I don't want to stay here and look at him, but it's like my braces are all locked up and I can't move at all, I can just stare. I don't think I ever saw so much blood in my life and I don't want to ever again.

"What happened?" Nanny says, her voice very small. She's kneeling next to him on the couch and her face is so pale she matches him. They look like paper.

"The flowers were a warning," says Gerry, after he swallows a huge mouthful from the bottle. "Not a truce."

"Did you see Marianne? Do they still have her? Will they give her back?"

Gerry shakes his head. "I didn't see her. It doesn't matter. This was insane, Nell. They're angry. They're not going to

Nanny wipes her nose on her sleeve again. She comes closer but I don't want her to so I just wave my hands at her until she goes away. She doesn't lock the door and I can hear her crying as she goes down the stairs. Even though she is mean to me I feel really bad about biting her. I know that I should say I'm sorry so I get up carefully and go down the stairs. The braces' straps pinch my skin.

Nanny's in the kitchen with the box in her hand getting ready to put salt into some boiling water. I stand at the table and say "Nanny?" in a small voice. Nanny turns around and I think she's going to throw the salt box at me, but she doesn't. She puts it on the counter. Her eyes are all wet and that makes me want to cry again but I say instead, "Nanny, I'm sorry I bit you."

She makes this sort of gulp noise and sniffs. She shakes her head though I didn't say anything and shakes it and shakes it until I think her head may fall off but then she says, "It's not your fault, little one. None of this is your fault."

"I don't want to be sick," I say.

Nanny makes the gulp noise again and gets down on her knees. "Little one, all of this, all of this is…"

There's a knock at the door. Nanny stands up really quickly and smoothes out her dress. "Stay right here, all right?" she says to me as she goes to the door. She grabs the broom and looks out through the little windows. Then

"Where did he go?"

"That's none of your business."

Nothing's my business ever. "Can we go outside?"

"You know you're not allowed to go outside, child."

"But I really want to. Just for a little bit, and you can come with me so I don't get sick."

"That's not possible."

"Please! I'm so bored!"

"NO!" Nanny shouts.

I am so angry I scream as loud as I can. Nanny grabs me and puts her hand over my mouth, so I bite her fingers. She screams and lets me go. I see that her skin is bleeding and I'm glad. She's awful and she deserves it.

"We should never have brought you into this house," she says, sucking at the blood on her finger. "You horrible thing!"

All of my tummy gets cold and my legs are shaky. I sit down on my bed and I think I'm going to fall over. Everything hurts like Nanny slapped me even though she didn't. My nose feels pinchy and my lips get tight and I say very softly, "I am not a horrible thing." I want to say more but then I start to cry.

I turn around so fast that my legs shake and fall and I fall with a hard bounce on my bottom. Nanny is standing in my doorway and her face is the angriest I ever saw. I want to tell her about how I was walking but now I fell down and she probably won't believe me.

She picks up the braces and stomps over to me. "Put these back on this instant!" she says. I don't move because I'm still surprised, so she grabs my foot and pulls me closer. She puts my leg in the brace and puts the straps on. She always makes them too tight and they hurt. She tightens the brace on my other leg and now I don't know if I could get up at all. I look at the flowers on my dresser. They aren't helping.

"You are never to be out of bed without your braces, do you understand me?" Nanny shouts into my face and I nod at her. I thought she would be happy that I was better but I don't know. Now that she's so close I see that she's crying. She wipes her nose on her sleeve and stands up. "I'm going to prepare some lunch," she says, "If you're hungry, you can come downstairs." I don't say anything. I just look at her as hard as I can.

She looks at me for a bit and then her face kind of melts and she shakes her head. She gives me her hand and pulls me up. I'm shaky so I lean on the bed. "Come down if you're hungry," she says.

She's going to leave when I ask her, "Is Gerry back yet?"

She sniffs and wipes her nose again. "Not yet."

and then sitting down again. Up and down, up and down, and after I do this about a million times I start to laugh because my legs don't hurt. Usually getting up and getting down is so hard I don't do it. I'm hungry because I didn't eat all my porridge but my tummy doesn't feel barfy and that's good too, so I laugh more. My mother will be happy to hear that I'm getting better. If I'm not sick, then she can take me with her to fight dragons.

But what if I'm not better? I should test it. I clonk over to the door and put my ear against it. I don't hear Nanny doing anything. Maybe she's taking a nap, or she's reading, or something else. I will be very quiet anyway. Quiet as a mouse.

My braces squeak a little as I take off the leather straps one by one. They leave red dust on my skin and I blow on the dust because if I rub it in it makes my skin itchy and that's worse than the stupid heavy braces. Once I get them off I stand up and bounce on my toes. I'm wobbly and I fall down against my bed, but then I stand up again and don't bounce. Now I'm not so wobbly.

I keep my hand on my bed as I walk around it. I decide to race myself to the window. I don't go very fast but it doesn't matter because any way I win. When I get there, I lean against the window and I'm breathing big heavy breaths but I'm here and I didn't fall down. The next time the bird comes to wake me up I am going to run over and say "BOO!" at it.

"What the hell are you doing?"

broom from the corner and sweeps the rest of the flowers off the porch. I don't know why she doesn't like them, but she's muttering the whole time.

She's so busy, and the sweeping is so noisy, she doesn't even see me when I take my bowl to the sink and push half the porridge down the drain with my spoon. I wash my bowl very carefully, hardly making any splashes. Nanny comes back into the kitchen and grabs the box of salt from the counter next to the porridge box and sprinkles salt all over the porch.

"Nanny?" I say, holding the jar with the flowers, once she comes back to the kitchen. "Is my mother coming to get me soon?"

"Your mother has something to do first before she can get you," says Nanny, who is fidgeting and looking out the window. Maybe she can still see Gerry, but if he's in the woods she can't. "Maybe soon. I don't know."

"I hope soon," I say, but Nanny doesn't answer. "Can I take my flowers up to my room?" Nanny sort of waves at me and I think that means yes, so I hold the jar very carefully in my hand and take it upstairs slowly, not worrying about the clonking noises this time.

————

After Nanny locks my door behind me, I put the flowers in their jar on my dresser. For a long time I just sit on my bed and look at them. They are the first thing I've had in there that is beautiful, and I keep getting up to smell them

"Please, Gerry. If there's a chance." Nanny looks like she's going to cry.

Gerry lets go of my arm and makes a sort of growly noise. "All right," he says. "I'll go. But I don't like leaving you alone with her if…"

"We'll be fine," says Nanny. "Please, go."

He stomps over to the corner to get his boots. Nanny gives him his jacket and a black carpenter's nail hanging from a leather cord. He puts the cord around his neck and looks once more at me before he leaves. I think he hates me. I hate him, too, and I stick my tongue out at him once he turns.

Nanny watches him go. I stand next to her to try to see the flowers some more. Then I have an idea. "Nanny?" I ask.

Nanny looks at me all sharp, before she says, "What is it, child?"

"Can I have some of the flowers?" I ask her in my sweetest voice. "I just want a couple of them to look at. They're so pretty."

Nanny doesn't say anything for a while. I make my eyes all big to see if that helps. Finally she says, "I suppose you may. I'll gather them. You go finish your porridge."

I choke down three bites of the porridge as Nanny puts a couple of the flowers in a glass full of water and puts them on the table in front of me. Then she takes the shout, but I can still hear their whispering. They catch me looking at them and go to their room, and now I can't hear anything at all.

I slide very carefully off my chair and stand up. I slink as quietly as I can. My braces creak a little so I stop, and then I start again. If I am very quiet, I can get to the door and see what made Nanny scream. I wonder if it's horrible, but what could be more horrible than this place?

I make it to the door and put my head around it. I know I'm not supposed to go outside, Nanny told me, because I'm sick and the outside air will be bad for me. But it's got to be all right if I just look, right?

I'm so surprised I almost scream myself. The porch outside is covered with flowers! Not roses like in the book Nanny reads me, but wildflowers. There are red and blue and yellow and purple ones, and they're in a big messy pile in front of the door. I don't think I've ever seen anything so beautiful in my whole life. I don't know who put them there but I don't care because they smell so good. I reach my arm out through the door, but then Gerry grabs my arm and pulls me back. He slams the door so loud it rattles the walls.

"You know you can't go outside," says Nanny. "I don't want to catch you trying again, little lady, is that clear?"

Gerry turns to Nanny and says, "We can't keep this up, Nell." His hand is hurting me.

Gerry comes running out from their room. He usually goes out in the morning to go to work or something so I don't spend a lot of time with him, which is good. Nanny is always angry, but at least sometimes she reads to me and helps me with my braces. I don't think Gerry likes me at all. I'm glad he doesn't have to take care of me, but I really wish that my mother would come and get me. I'm pretty sure she's having an adventure slaying dragons right now. But she'll be done soon, and then I can go home.

Now Gerry is standing next to Nanny and looking out. They are both quiet, but then they step back in the house and he closes the door. They're not looking at me. It's so exciting I forget to be happy I'm not eating my porridge.

"What do you think it means?" Nanny asks Gerry.

"I don't know," he says, and he sounds angry that he doesn't know.

"It's a good sign, right?" Nanny smiles, a sort of scared smile.

"They know where we are."

"They always knew where we are. They can't get in. The wards keep us safe. Maybe it's a truce. Or a…or a parley."

Then they see that I'm looking at them and get very quiet. I stuff a spoonful of porridge into my mouth and try not to gag on it. Nanny and Gerry go to a corner of the room and turn away from me, talking quieter. They're trying not to forever. (He says it's only been three weeks and I should stop complaining.) My mother left me here for them to look after while she's away. They live in this creaky old house with its dirty windows and dark rooms and I don't like it at all. But I'm not allowed to go outside because I'm sick, so I'm stuck here until my mother comes to get me. If I were that bird, I could just fly away. It must be fun to have wings.

It takes a long time to get down the stairs with my braces on, and it's very loud. Nanny stands at the bottom, watching me clonk, clonk, clonk, down each stair. She has short brown hair and her eyebrows are always frowning. She talks like she's always a little bit angry with me, even though I don't do anything wrong. Unless she's angry because I'm sick and she has to cook special for me.

"Eat your porridge, child," says Nanny as she puts the bowl on the table in front of me. The porridge is terrible. I told Nanny once that when I eat it my tummy hurts and I want to barf. She locked me in my room with no food for the rest of the day, so now I eat the porridge, but only in tiny bites. It takes forever, and she sits and watches me almost the whole time. I stare at her while I'm eating my tiny bites and eventually she stands up and goes away.

Usually she goes to the door and looks outside at the forest, which I can see through the windows. Then she goes all quiet and nervous. I like that because it means she isn't watching and I don't have to eat my porridge. But this morning she opens the door and screams.

Salt and Flowers

Jessica Lévai

I wake up in the morning and wonder if today is finally going to be the day that my mother comes to get me. There's a sound at my window like something scratching at the glass. I think it's a bird. I roll myself to the edge of my bed. That makes my back hurt so I have to stop for a moment, and that's not good, because the bed is big and metal and smells funny when you put your nose too close to the frame. But I need to grab my braces from the floor. I strap them on as fast as I can and swing my legs onto the floor. But by the time I get to the window, the bird is gone.

Nanny must have heard my feet on the floor because I hear her call up that I have to come down to breakfast. I have been living here with Nanny and her husband, Gerry,

© 2022 Juliet Kemp

Science Fiction - 3508 words

About the Author

Juliet Kemp (they/them) is a queer, non-binary, writer who lives in London. Their 'Marek' fantasy series is available from Elsewhen Press, their short fiction has appeared in venues including *Analog* and *Cast of Wonders*, and they were shortlisted for the WSFA Small Press Award 2020. They like knitting, fountain pens, and bouldering. They can be found at http://julietkemp.com, or on Twitter as **@julietk**.

"Right."

Cleo sat down on the stool. "I'll be coming out, for a while. Til she's better. If you want. You don't have to let me in."

"I always let Erin in."

"Yes, well. She's a better person than me."

There was a silence.

"Why are you here?" he asked, finally. His hands rested on the table in front of him, fingers interlaced, thumb rubbing restlessly against his knuckle. He didn't look at her.

"Because Erin's a better person than me. I don't always agree with her. But she never, ever, gives up, and sometimes she needs saving from herself." She hesitated. "And because…she keeps me honest."

"Yeah," Parrick said softly.

"So," Cleo said, eventually. "Wanna know what the kids have taken up now they're bored of graffiti?"

"Yeah." Parrick met her eyes. "All right."

really fancy getting a bit high." It was doctor-recommended, even. Maybe it would help her appetite.

Cleo visibly let the argument go, her shoulders falling. "We have. And if we hadn't, I'd go get you some. C'mon. Let's sit down. I'll finish mine on the couch, and put yours aside, and maybe you'll want it later. Or I'll cook some more."

"Thank you," Erin said.

Cleo smiled crookedly over at her. "Well. Need you around, don't I? Keeping me honest." She put an arm around Erin, and Erin let herself relax into her familiar embrace.

––––

It was fourth-sol again. Cleo went to the south-west exit, and the rover carried her and the safety-bot six kilometres to Parrick's bubble. The plants in the greenhouse above-ground, when she reached it, looked like they were thriving. Erin would know what they were. Cleo just noticed that the rover's left tread needed tuning.

Downstairs, Parrick was in the living-area, sitting on one side of a table, an empty stool on the other side.

"Is she…" He stopped. She couldn't read his expression.

"She's alive," Cleo said. "Just bloody ill. And bloody stubborn, and someone had to come out here if I wanted her not to. She needs to rest."

smash." Cleo snapped up a piece of carrot and chewed furiously on it.

"This is part of that, though," Erin argued. "It has to be. Just because it's difficult... You can't just stop when it's hard. Tibo spent five years on that damn bubble membrane."

"And *he* put a hole in it in seconds." Cleo's chin went up. "Look, on Earth he'd be dead. We just exiled him. Fuck's sake, he still has storehouse privileges."

"I know. I take deliveries to him."

"He won't *change*. He won't be sodding *redeemed*. He won't even say why he did it."

"I don't care. That's not the point. The point is not to look away. The point is to keep the door open."

"And if this is it? If he lives and dies out there. Never comes back, is never safe to come back? What's the point?"

Erin put her bowl down, and spread her hands wearily. "The point is to keep the door open."

Cleo rubbed the heel of her hand against her forehead. "You really think it's worth it?"

"Wouldn't do it otherwise. Sure as hell wouldn't right now." She shut her eyes, suddenly unable to face even just plain noodles with ginger. "Look. Can we just leave the social ethics for now? Have we still got edibles left? I

Parrick looked at her narrowly, opened his mouth, shut it again, then stood up and walked out of the room. Erin sat for a while. He didn't come back.

―――

When Erin got home, Cleo was cooking, banging pots around. Chemo had done something peculiar to Erin's tastebuds, and she couldn't cope with the communal kitchen, which was frustrating for someone who'd always been proud of not being picky. Cleo had volunteered to cook; she enjoyed it, said it was good to have an excuse to use the extra resources. Erin didn't think the pot-banging betrayed irritability with cooking.

Erin was having plain noodles, with a little ginger to settle her stomach. Ginger had coped with Mars much more readily than she'd expected. She sighed, just a tiny sigh, as she sat, and that was what set Cleo off.

"Erin. You're tired, *obviously*, because you're having *chemo*. And your hair's falling out." That was a low blow. "Why the hell're you still spending energy on that man?"

Erin was indeed tired. Tired, and fed up. She put down her chopsticks. "Because if I don't, who else is going to? Everyone says—everyone said, we don't want to be like Earth. We'll make something different. But you don't walk the walk, do you?"

"You're talking like it's just, I dunno, wilful laziness. I'm busy. We're all busy! Trying to build what he tried to

"Not sure that's much better." His shoulders were hunched.

Erin's sorrow had washed away again, leaving behind it only the loss that never quite went away. Tibo had designed the bubble plastic. She thought of them every time she stood in the gardens and looked up at the sky. David had run the creche. He lived on, she supposed, in the not-teenagers and the littler kids coming up behind them.

"I do enjoy our conversations. Just sometimes I...remember, and then I feel other things too." She gestured with her mug. "Humans are complex creatures. We feel many things at once. I can like you, and enjoy your company, and still hate you, sometimes."

Neither of them spoke for a while. Erin drank her tea, and thought about living on in the lemon trees, and the perennial kale, and, in a very practical sort of way, in the compost that fed them.

"That's the most honest you've ever been with me," Parrick said eventually. "Maybe dying suits you."

"Maybe it does." Erin traced the handle of her tea mug with a finger. "Kieran says I'm probably not dying. Except, of course, we're all dying, aren't we? The one cold truth of life. Me, you, everyone else."

"Sure. But I'm honest already. I don't need the help."

Erin squinted at him. "Are you? Always?"

surprisingly okay, for now, but...however much Kieran said optimistic things about probabilities, should she be thinking more carefully about what she did with each fraction of her remaining time?

But then, time always was limited.

Parrick commented on it, over peppermint tea. (Peppermint did just fine in Martian greenhouses. Peppermint did just fine everywhere.) "Why're you wasting your time out here with me? You've got fucking cancer."

Erin shrugged. "Nothing's changed, really. You never know when you'll go, do you?"

David and Tibo hadn't. A great sorrow washed up inside her, surprising her with her intensity. Once she'd battled it down again she said, conversationally. "Sometimes it's hard not to hate you, you know."

Parrick didn't look surprised. "Don't bother trying, then. Get on and hate me, I should."

"I suppose I've chosen not to."

His mouth twisted. "I'm not that keen to feel like a charitable project, you know."

"I wouldn't say charitable. A reflection of my ethical beliefs, perhaps. No. Not a reflection. An action. Ethics in action."

teenagers she passed, decorating another blank wall with half-empty paint buckets scrounged from other projects. She'd never see that, cancer or no cancer. The thought was oddly soothing. Mars would go on, with or without her.

The rover swung past the storehouse. She ought to stop and requisition some of the things Kieran had recommended to help her through chemo, but she couldn't face it. It pulled up outside her house and she made herself get out, swipe herself through the arch, go down the ramp, smile at Cleo.

It would all be fine.

———

Before coming to Mars, Erin had thought a lot about whether this was the right thing to do with her life. About the risk of being here, and the loss of everything and everyone she knew on Earth, everything she might have done on Earth, against what it would mean to be part of what they might build out here. Since they landed, she'd been busy: in the gardens, mediating, spending time with Cleo and her friends and the community, all two-hundred-and-change of them, including the kids. Her life was full, and it didn't seem necessary to stop and assess it.

Trundling towards Parrick's bubble after her second bout of chemo, she wondered, for the first time since Earth, about time and cost and loss and worth. She felt thought Erin wasn't looking. Parrick sat and waited, staring at his hands, and when she was done he fetched her tissues and made her another cup of rosemary tea, all without saying a word.

"I'm sorry," he said finally, as she left.

———

Leaving, she rested her head against the hard window of the rover and shut her eyes. She was bone-deep exhausted and she hadn't even started bloody chemo yet. When the rover got back to its dock, she let the safety-bot out then tapped in a new destination. She'd take it all the way back home, for once, rather than walk.

The rover pulled out and tucked itself neatly onto the vehicle path through the above-ground part of the complex, settling to the permitted speed. To one side were arches leading down to offices and workshops and living-rooms. To the other, plants. This was the annuals, here, not Erin's perennials. There was only one other vehicle out that Erin could see, a rover piled with big boxes of something; the complex was still small enough that most people walked, especially in Martian gravity. Erin envisaged the future they planned: a hugely expanded bubble complex, as resources increased. A second complex out by the mountains. Maybe another shuttle or two from Earth, even, depending on what happened down there. And eventually, maybe, the possibility of walking outside the complex without a helmet, for the great-great-grandchildren of the not-

He didn't look impressed. But then, he was hard to read.

"You've never asked before," she said.

He shifted in his seat, arms still folded. "Didn't seem important."

"Well. I might not be able to come so often in the next few months."

Parrick grabbed both half-full tea mugs, got up abruptly, and turned to the sink. "Fed up, are you?"

"I've got cancer." To her horrified surprise, her vision blurred, and she felt water in the corners of her eyes. She hadn't cried at all, all week, through all Kieran's explanations and Cleo holding her hand and trying to smile at her.

Through the blur, she saw Parrick freeze, briefly, before he put the mugs down in the sink and turned around. "Cancer."

"It's the healthy Martian atmosphere," she said, wiping irritably at her face. Next to no atmosphere, in fact, which was why they all burrowed underground, except apparently that wasn't enough. "Or maybe it's not. Plenty of people on Earth get cancer, don't they? Maybe it's just me."

Parrick sat down opposite her, and Erin put her head down on the table and cried, the way she hadn't in front of Cleo, because of Cleo's worried face every time she lemon. Coaxing the citrus into fruiting was her most cherished achievement. *So far*, she made herself add. Plenty more to come, weren't there?

"They asked, at the trial."

"Not technically a trial." A mediation. Like any other mediation she'd done, except not. Parrick on one side, refusing to talk; everyone else on the other, raging and sorrowful and furious; and her trying to hold it all, because that was the job. Her chest ached in memory; or maybe that was the chemo line settling in.

Parrick made an impatient gesture. "Whatever you care to call it. They asked."

"And you didn't answer. I remember it well."

"Is that why you come out here? Waiting for me to change my mind and tell you?"

"No. I don't expect you ever will." Did she even want to know? She tried not to. *Expectations* rarely helped anyone.

He'd never asked before. He'd sat and spoken to her, at least a little, every week, and he'd never asked why she was there. Why now?

But since he was asking... "I come out here because you're human, and you're still part of our community, whether out here or in there, and it's not right for someone to be wholly alone."

"I see a bit," Erin said. "Doesn't seem worth much time. I won't be going back. Plenty right here to keep me busy." Especially now.

"Yes well. Not like I've much else to do. Anyway. I meant the executions."

Terrorists. Erin had seen that and felt sick about the whole business, all the way through, and hadn't read past the headlines. "I saw it had happened. No more than that."

Parrick was staring off at the wall to one side, failing even more obviously than usual to meet her eyes. "You could have executed me."

On Earth, he'd have been counted a terrorist. A hole blown in the bubble. David and Tibo dead before the emergency crew got there.

"No death penalty in the accords," Erin said.

"They could have been changed."

A couple of people had argued for that, but they hadn't gone as far as proposing it. If she hadn't been mediating, she'd have been arguing against. "That's not how we do things, on Mars. Whatever Earth does. We agreed, when we came out here. You too," she added.

Parrick finally looked back at her, his chin up, arms folded. "You've never asked me why I did it."

"No," Erin agreed. "I assume if you wanted me to know, you'd tell me." She sipped at her tea. Rosemary and

Everyone. Problems and all.

Cleo sighed and put her head back against the couch, then sat up again and drained her mug. "Anyway. Top up? How's your apprentice getting on?"

"Made me a beaded bracelet," Erin said, eyes comically wide, and was rewarded by Cleo's laughter.

―――

The next week didn't go quite as Erin had planned. One routine doctor's visit turned into three, in rapid succession, and a whole host of discussions with Kieran about treatment and prognosis and next steps.

Cleo argued with her when she asked Kieran to schedule the line insertion so she would be on time to visit Parrick afterwards. Surely she needn't, in the *circumstances*, Cleo said.

Erin hadn't even started chemo yet, for fuck's sake. She wasn't going to abandon everything just because some stupid cells were trying to take over her body.

Parrick seemed awkward, that sol, drumming his fingers on the table. "Have you seen the news from Earth?" he asked, in the middle of a story she was telling him about the graffiti some of the not-teenagers had put up on the wall of the garden. (They'd gone off beading.) Most of it had stayed; some of it Erin had negotiated with them to scrub off. She wasn't prudish, but there were limits.

kids don't like that idiom any more than they like 'teenagers'. Put my social credit where my mouth is."

Cleo ignored the distraction. "Have you forgiven him?"

"That's not the point."

"David died, Erin. Tibo died. Isn't *that* the point?"

And nothing was going to bring them back. "Yes," Erin agreed, feeling the familiar tug of loss. David and Tibo had both been on the first shuttle out, with her and Cleo. Only a hundred of them. They'd all been so close. Parrick had been on that shuttle, too.

"People change their minds. I don't…" Erin paused. "I suppose, I believe that we are a community, and we need to keep on giving people that chance."

Cleo's fingers were tight on her mug. "Drain on resources. Should have sent him back to Earth."

"What, and export our problems? That doesn't work." Erin gestured, palm up. "But if you want it, propose it."

"Too expensive," Cleo said. "Drain on resources either way."

In theory it was possible to go back. They had two shuttles, one from each of the trips out from Earth, and they could manufacture fuel, if anyone proposed it, which no one had. They were out here for good, all of them; that was the point.

That evening, she and Cleo sat on the sofa in their rooms, legs entangled, with a glass of Martian hooch apiece. It wasn't exactly beer—hops, like camellia, were one of the plants that Erin and her team hadn't been able to get to thrive here—more like lightly-fermented fruit juice, whatever they'd had extra of that season. It was a spare-time project of Kieran, one of the doctors, the resource use enthusiastically authorised by the rest of the community. This batch was mostly apple, and it was pretty good.

"I don't understand why you keep going out there," Cleo said. Her short dark hair stood up around her face. Cleo still wore helmets a lot, out checking on the atmos-formers and the machinery that sustained the complex. She looked tired, today.

"Because being cut off from everyone else isn't the way to redeem people." They'd had this discussion often enough before; but Cleo always was the sort to prod at a scab, especially when she was tired and grouchy. It had been a few months since the last round, so this was about on schedule by Erin's reckoning.

Cleo snorted. "Like that's ever gonna happen."

"Well, maybe not. But..." Erin hesitated, thinking over her words. "I suppose, on principle, I don't believe anyone can't or won't change, wholly and definitely. If they're still connected. If they still have a way back. And if I believe that, I also believe I should put my money where my mouth is." She laughed and took a slug of hooch. "I bet the

"Oh, I meant to tell you," she remembered. "The Latest Trend! It's beading, this time. Total run on the craft supplies." Trends came and went more fiercely on Mars than Erin ever remembered them doing on Earth.

"Beading." Parrick sounded disbelieving.

"Yep. And the warehouse only had a tiny amount, for people who like working with their hands, you know? All went in a day. The teenagers are trading beads around like they're some kind of illegal substance. Uh, though they say they're not teenagers. They're eight and nine and ten." She still didn't know her own age in Martian without thinking about it, but these kids were growing up here. "One of the teachers tried ten-agers but they didn't like that either. Anyway. The printers are booked to make more towards the end of next week but obviously that's not fast enough." She rolled her eyes.

Parrick snorted. "The things I miss out on, huh?"

He didn't have to. Probably. If he wanted, she could mediate, again, between him and the community. Despite everything. Two deaths to his name, and maybe it wasn't deliberate murder, but he'd known exactly what he was about.

She'd still be willing to mediate. That was what she did. But he knew that already. She wasn't about to bring it up.

―――――

Abruptly, Parrick appeared at the bottom of the ramp that led up to the greenhouse. "You need a haircut."

"Hello to you too. I'm growing it out."

"Isn't that inconvenient, under a helmet?"

Erin shrugged. "I don't go outside the complex so much these days. We're all specialising more now." At the start, everyone had done some of everything, especially when they were first getting the bubble up, but things had changed since Parrick was exiled. She tried to keep him updated. To keep the door open.

He sat on his own stool, across the table from her. "Spending all of your time in the gardens, then?" They often talked about plants. Parrick had to grow almost all his own food, and Erin was responsible for the perennial crops in the community's gardens back in the complex. (Gardens aboveground, housing below, and all of it under the bubble, which was just as well since gardening in a helmet would be no fun.) It was a useful topic: safe, interesting to both of them.

"The raspberries are doing well," Erin said. "And the kitchen are drying the leaves for tea. The camellias still don't like it here."

"Yeah, well, who can blame them?"

"I like it here," Erin said, placidly. The fact that none of the herbal teas were *tea* was hardly enough to make her miss Earth.

Opening Doors

Juliet Kemp

Parrick wasn't waiting for her. He never was. Erin assumed it was deliberate, but like so many other things, she didn't ask. As the rover clicked into the airlock she could see his back, through the plastic of the small greenhouse bubble, as he bent over his plants. He must have heard the rover, but he didn't turn around.

She went down the ramp into the underground living-rooms, safety-bot at her heels, sat on a stool, and waited. Just like every other fourth-sol since the bubble had been built and Parrick confined to it. Getting on for two and a half Martian years, now.

me to have had any real relationship to Violaine. And as far as I am concerned, neither did you."

© 2022 Xauri'EL Zwaan

Science Fiction - 4947 words

About the Author

Xauri'EL Zwaan is a mendicant artist in search of meaning, fame and fortune, or pie (where available); a Genderqueer Bisexual, a Socialist Solarpunk, and a Satanist Goth. Zie lives and writes in a little hobbit hole in Saskatoon, Canada on Treaty 6 territory with zir life partner and a multitude of cats.

After considerable deliberation, the judge chose to acquit me of the charges facing me by reason of temporary insanity, provided I agreed to leave the planet immediately and trouble Violane's family no further.

During the time of my incarceration, Violaine had died. The trauma had been too much for her. I was not permitted to attend the funeral.

I saw Violaine's mother and father one last time, just as I was about to board a shuttle to take me back into orbit. It had finally dawned on them, now that they no longer had to protect their darling daughter from me, that I had gained a vast fortune from the accident that had claimed our lives, and ultimately her life. Her mother demanded that I hand over Violaine's share of that fortune to her family.

For a moment, for two, I considered it. Were they not human, like me? Had I not ill-treated them? Were they not also bereaved? Had they not done merely what they thought was right?

Then, like a specter, the image rose before me of Violaine, of what they had made of her, of the expression on her still-perfect face when I had seen her for the last time, of her dying alone, without even the comfort of the neurolink to soothe her.

I laughed in their faces.

"You have made it abundantly clear," I told them as I was being wheeled on to the ship, "that you do not consider actions and demeanour leading up to the fateful meeting, of psychiatric 'experts' discussing what a neurochemical stabilizer might or might not do to a person's state of mind. Finally, I was wheeled up to the witness stand and swore on some ritualistic relic to tell the truth, the whole truth, and nothing but the truth. Sanford Hall ran through my perspective on the events which had occurred, and then asked me the one question on which the tide of the trial would turn: "What did you feel when you saw your lover lying there, in the state in which you found her; all of her augmentations removed, barely able to recognize her, pleading with you for help?"

I had rehearsed my simple answer many times, yet I still had trouble giving voice to it.

"Imagine," my words crackled forth from my voice synthesizer. "Imagine someone you love dearly has been in a terrible accident. Imagine that it happened on one of the colonies, out in space, among my kind. Imagine that you had gone through hell and high water to try and see them. And imagine, when you did, that all kinds of cybernetic implants had been grafted into their body without their authorization or consent. Imagine that they no longer looked remotely like the person you had come to know and love. Imagine what you would do to the person who did that to them, if you could. Imagine this and you may begin to understand what I felt in that moment."

————

better, higher than they. I had treated them like yapping dogs, like flies to be brushed away, so focused on my objective that I had barely even seen them; and given the opportunity, I had lowered myself below the level even of the most disagreeable of them. Yet Sanford Hall, who had been no more than a tradesman in my employ, had thought nothing of coming to my aid. *Simple human decency*. Below all of it, and above and around and interpenetrated through, was the sight of my Self, my Violaine, on that bed, barely anything remaining of her; and the black rage I felt at the thought of it, the unthinkable violence I now knew I could unleash on those responsible, was hard to bear.

I was unused to such a catastrophic weight of introspection, and pathetically relieved when Master Hall informed me that he had secured me access to the walled garden of the prison's social network and library stack. But even once I regained my ability to connect with the world outside my skull, even though the tedious and laborious construction of letter-by-letter messages and search queries occupied every ounce of my mental focus, the guilt and the anger and the nagging questions remained.

―――

At last the day came when I was allowed before a magistrate to plead my case. I lay immobile on an upright slab, displayed publicly like a cut of meat, through the interminable legal technicalities, the testimony of doctors as to the injury I had caused, of Violaine's family about my imagine what seeing her in such a condition must have been for you, who trod the stars and planets with her hand in hand. Your reaction that day was entirely understandable, and I could not have lived with myself had I abandoned you; it is no more or less than simple human decency."

I spent many hours turning these words over in my mind as I lay, crippled and disconnected, in a cell that was but an afterthought in my confinement. I grew famished for company, and fawned desperately on the guards and medical technicians who maintained the equipment that kept me fed and breathing, who renewed the drug and nutrient packs and removed the voided waste, basking in their plain fear and contempt, grateful for once that these primals rarely used robots to accomplish such simple tasks. I would have done anything to escape the emptiness inside, the echoing cavern of my own mind and the things it reflected back at me.

Could not have lived with myself. I had done the unforgivable. I had struck other people in anger, people over whom I enjoyed a vast gap in physical prowess; possibly maimed them for life. For all their flaws, their shortcomings, their disabilities and deliberate backwardness, they were just as human as I. Dr. Xian had even showed me a degree of sympathy and kindness, complicit as he was in what had been done to Violaine. *Your reaction was entirely understandable.* My reaction had not been that of a civilized man; it had been that of a beast. I called these people 'primal', as if I was more, chatter, and my attempts grew fewer and farther between as I came to understand just how thoroughly they had isolated me. My confinement was to be solitary indeed. Throughout my life—even in the womb—I had been separated from solitude by the constant soothing whispers of the network; doubly so when I had joined the borganization and been relieved even of the burden of individuality. For the first time, I was alone—truly, completely alone.

I was visited occasionally by Sanford Hall, who had shifted effortlessly from pursuing my suit against the hospital to defending me on charges of assault causing bodily harm. He informed me in cold clinical detail of the injuries I had dealt to Dr. Xian, who had suffered several broken bones, and to Esmer Frall, the hospital administrator, who was being treated for whiplash and brain damage. He then laid out the legal options available to us. There was of course no question of my being allowed to interact with the general prison population or given back the power of the prosthetics, but I could perhaps be allowed a very restricted and highly supervised degree of network access. It was, he claimed, actually a point in our favour that I was so heavily augmented. The case could be made that I had suffered a kind of temporary insanity, exacerbated by the drugs my neurochemical stabilizer had been feeding me. I acquiesced to this avenue of attack, then thanked Master Hall profusely for standing by me. At this, he gave me a curious look. "Master Archwell," he replied, "you have been hard done by, you and your lover both. I can hardly finish a second word; I spun around, swatting him like an insect, the prosthetics lending my arm strength enough to throw him several meters down the hall. My neurochemical stabilizer's imbalance alarms were shrieking in my head as my adrenaline and acetylcholine levels spiked far beyond the redline. The hospital administrator rushed forward babbling something, and I picked him up and shook him so hard his neck nearly snapped, screaming out some half-wordless cry of indignation and rage. They had ripped everything that did not fit their pathetically narrow definition of 'Normal Human' out of the woman who had become my Self. They had violated her—violated *me*, just as surely as if it was my own flesh gone under the knife. In that moment, I could have killed them all.

Luckily for them, and doubtless for me as well, my desperately overcompensating neurochemical stabilizer hit me with a massive dose of sedatives. I folded gently to the floor; the last thing I remember before blacking out was uniformed officers of law enforcement arriving and dumping thousands of volts of electricity through my body.

I woke in solitary confinement.

My muscular prosthesis had been removed; I lay in a hospital bed, barely able to lift my arms or raise my head. I was in a wireless coldspot; none of my connection protocols could detect so much as a whisper of network living flesh; her body was plastered in thick slabs of synthskin to protect the raw muscle tissue beneath. Shockingly large holes had been drilled in her skull and scooped out of her chest; thick cables snaked from them, connected, no doubt, to crude machines that mimicked the functions of a primal human heart, lungs, spleen, gut, liver, and endocrine glands. And that was hardly the worst of it; that was only the damage I could see. In a terrible instant I understood what the doctor had meant. *Normalization.* Every cybernetic implant she had ever chosen to have grafted into her body had been surgically removed—every servomotor and processor and wire. She was being turned back into a Primal again.

I walked to her bedside and raised a trembling hand to her cheek; she had always kept her original face, beneath a bubble-shell lifemask, and so her face, at least, remained intact—the only part of her these animals felt was worth keeping. "Violaine," I whispered to her, "my Self. What have they done to you? Oh, what have they done?"

Her eyelids fluttered. They slid open, and her pupils slowly focused on me. "Richter?" she whispered hoarsely. "I had a dream…felt them all screaming…I can't feel my legs…my arms…I can't feel my selves…or you…" Her eyes widened, and a look of subtle horror stole over her face; tears leaked from the corners of her eyes. "Help me, Richter…Please…Something is wrong with me…I can't feel my *mind*…"

Dr. Xian walked up behind me and touched my shoulder. "That's enough," he started to say. I didn't even let him comfortable, that she is not in any pain, and that the transition goes as smoothly as possible." He looked away from me then, his posture indicating no little amount of shame. "It's better for her this way. You are being permitted one visit, to say goodbye to her. Then you should go back to your space stations and get on with your life. If the healing process is to continue effectively, she has to be protected from disruptive stimuli. You cannot be allowed to visit her again after this. It would be far too traumatic."

Of course I should have paid more attention to what he was saying, but I was so close; to delay even a moment longer was intolerable. I pushed roughly past him and through the doors, into a small room with a deep bed set against one wall. I looked around; for a moment, I did not quite comprehend what I was seeing, and asked them, "Where is she? Where is Violaine?". There was, of course, only one person in the room; the one lying in the bed, surrounded by bulky medical devices obsolete by generations.

She had no arms or legs. The prosthetics she had once had them replaced with, the sleek and beautiful biomechanics with 360-degree joint rotation, prehensile feet, integrated rockets and weapons and tools, were all gone; her shoulders and hips were flanked with tanks of bionutrient gel in which tiny organic limbs twitched and quivered. The airtight carapace which had once protected her body from vacuum and radiation had been ripped off, every one of the billions of nanohooks torn from her absent. As they escorted me through the building's maze-like dumb corridors, the doctor did his level best to impress on me the severity of Violaine's delicate condition, the poor odds that she would regain consciousness, and the urgent necessity of trying to avoid exposing her to anything confusing or upsetting. I barely paid attention; my heart soared as it slowly sunk in that at last, at long last I was going to *see* my co-self. To actually set eyes on her. To stand in her presence; to breathe the same air she was breathing. I experienced an unexpected and unfamiliar sensation: my lungs, beneath the patina of steroids and through the cold stimulation of the mechanical respirator, were struggling to breathe of their own accord. Slightly alarmed, I accessed information about the phenomenon through the dilapidated local search architecture, and found that it was a common reaction in natural breathers to extreme emotion, a normal accompaniment to the pounding of my still-human heart.

We reached yet another set of doors, and Dr. Xian stopped, turned, and took my hand. I was quite startled; it was the first time one of the Primals had voluntarily touched me in all of the months I had been here. He looked directly into my eyes and spoke with what my subtextual heuristics assured me was genuine compassion. "I need you to understand," he said, "that your...friend...is not as she was when last you saw her. The family has insisted on total normalization. The sight may be shocking to you. Please be assured that we are doing everything in our power to ensure that she is

Luckily, once the rest of the family had fallen into line, her objections lost considerable force, even as they grew ever more forceful and abusive. Master Hall and I went before a magistrate to plead my petition; he refused it, of course, and looked on me with distaste, but seemed taken aback by the efforts Nikoli made to quiet his mate as she poured slanders and insults against me and my kind out before the court. I barged into a family meeting with the hospital administrator to demand my rights, and was immensely gratified to hear Demeter, Violaine's youngest sister, actually take my side. I went to local press outlets, which had become interested in the scandal and drama surrounding my quest, in an attempt to publicly shame and embarrass anyone involved into complicity. The stories released were, as I expected, quite tawdry and salacious - "Comatose Spacer Trollop Caught in Sex Scandal with Cyborg Lover" was among the least disgusting titles; but they included quotes and interviews with several of Violaine's siblings, most of whom spoke of me with a degree of sympathy and several of whom hinted that they would not object to allowing me to see their sister, if for no other reason than to have the sordid business over with.

It took weeks. It took a small fortune. It took a hundred nightmares and a thousand guilt-soaked hours of emotional agony. But in the end, I succeeded; I won. I strode into the hospital braced for yet another futile shouting match, and was instead met by Nikoli, the hospital administrator, and a psychiatrist who introduced himself as Dr. Xian. Violaine's mother was conspicuously waxed eloquent to them about my deep and abiding love for their sister; I heavily implied that we had been sexually intimate, declining to reveal the irrelevant fact that we had never physically coupled our specific bodies, and only rarely physically occupied the same room since I was formally inducted into the Archwell Borganization. They could have no conception of the extent of the intimacies that I had shared with Violaine. I knew her family as if they were my own, though I saw them through the eyes of a stranger and not those of the woman who loved and cared for them; and I used this knowledge as a tool to coldly manipulate them, turn them to my side, make them feel as if maybe I wasn't all that bad...for a *cyborg*. Nikoli, her father, was not particularly difficult to handle; he was, after all, little more than an alpha male ape. I simply dominated him, physically and intellectually and in the arts of subtle social manipulation, until he gave way and acknowledged me his superior. In fact, once the moment had passed when he couldn't possibly imagine himself to be anything but my inferior, he became something almost like an ally—defending and apologizing for me as I stormed about the offices of the various apparatchiks and nomenklatura, smoothing ruffled feathers, unconsciously playing good cop to my bad. Her mother, Atasha, remained the lone holdout, and no matter how I barked and wheedled and roared, I couldn't turn her; she finally had her baby back from the clutches of the *things* that humans had become when they left the Earth behind, and there was no way under all the heavens she was letting us come in and steal her away again. Never once did she show me anything but loathing.

of the destruction of Eternity Station, and willing to assist me; and assist me he did, more ably than any daemon I could have accessed for the price. I felt frequent guilt at employing another intelligent being to do drudge research that even a simple expert system could handle; of course, I intimated nothing of this sentiment to him, as I was certain the man wouldn't appreciate hearing a profession he had spent his life learning referred to as machine work. He quickly dug up all the relevant documentation and set to work planning out several lines of attack.

I am not proud to say that I used every advantage I had, including their fear of me. I demanded meeting after meeting; imposed endlessly on the time of the family, the doctors, the hospital administrators, and the various bureaucrats involved. I brought up mountains of facts and documents, which I could access to my consciousness at will while they had to physically read and comprehend each piece like an already overstuffed restaurant patron choking down plate after plate of food. I *loomed*; carelessly lifted heavy objects; hissed and roared and made thinly veiled threats. I became their worst nightmare, to the extent that my conscience would allow me: I was there, I was heavily augmented, and they had best get used to me.

I wore them down bit by bit. First I forced the doctors to grudgingly admit that there was no physical reason why I should not be allowed to visit. Then, I began plying her brothers and sisters with drugs and expensive food. I plain as perihelion in their body stance and eye movements, though many of them at least made an effort to hide it: the fear, the disgust, the anger. They hated me, almost to a one; hated the very fact of my existence. I was an alien intrusion into their carefully preserved world of ancient primal-human dominance. I was most emphatically not welcome on Earth.

My next challenge, after clearing customs, was to gain access to the hospital where Violaine was being treated. Their society, permitting no possibility of borganization, contains no recognition of it whatsoever in their legal structure. Their courts recognize neither the Law of Space, nor the network of standardized private contractual arrangements that has grown up around it; for the execution of estates and consent in absentia, they rely primarily on genetic relationships and a kind of crude half sexual liason, half business co-op they call a 'marriage'. To them, to their society, there is simply no legally recognized relationship between Violaine and myself; and nobody but family was permitted to visit the hospital bed. I was only her co-self, only closer to her than any mother or father or sister or brother or sexual partner or child could ever be. I was not her *kin*. And the family had made it abundantly clear that I was not to be treated as such.

I engaged a lawyer—not a daemon, but a slightly senescent Primal gentleman named Sanford Hall with a thoroughly memorized and well-experienced knowledge regarding his specialty. He was sympathetic, having read and primitive, like some historical costume drama virtuality come to life; dumb, dingy, crumbling old turn-of-the-millennium buildings and half-smart pavements plied by chemical fuel-burning motorized transports that barrelled along guided by merely human brains and hands. The network coverage was spotty at best, plagued by bottlenecks and incompatible protocols and firewalled patches blacked out by government fiat—and it was costing me hundreds of credits an hour just to maintain a barely adequate degree of access and neurosensory integration; the daemons, deep databanks and contextual overlays commonly available out in the colonies were beyond even my significant inheritance, services reserved by the local monopoly markets for the richest of the rich. Without the comforting hum of information I was accustomed to feeling sleet through my mind, any desired fact available to be picked up and examined on a whim, I was ever disoriented and mentally fatigued by the mere act of trying to find the knowledge I wanted on their network's clunky search engines. The air and the water and even the *food* were interlaced with toxins, forcing my environmental samplers and blood scrubbers to work overtime; radiation from unsecured power transmission lines (*wires*, by all that is beautiful) tickled constantly at my electromagnetic sensors, and half-heard broadcast radionic transmissions leaked into my head until I was almost willing to kill for a little peace and quiet. But more than any of the myriad physical discomforts and mental annoyances, it was the *people* who continually brought back to me just how far from my home a mere trip from orbit to surface had brought me. Their emotions were technology before I would be allowed even to enter their territory—everything from my blood-borne repair nanomeds to my formal logic co-processor to my integral weaponry. I spent days fighting and begging to obtain an exemption for my neurochemical stabilizer, on the basis that I would go insane if it stopped functioning for any significant length of time. The borganizing neurolink was left untouched.

A lifetime in zero gravity, my blood oxygenated directly by nanofeed rather than inelegant and dangerous physical respiration, has left me ill-adapted to travel the planet surface. I need to wear an exoskeletal muscular prosthesis in order to stand, walk, and move my arms; a valve and ventilator pumps the soupy terrestrial air into my atrophied lungs (and thank the heavens I never bothered to have the things removed) while a cocktail of drug drips stimulates them to draw oxygen from it into my bloodstream. Though the rig, on top of my basic servomuscular augments, made me stronger than any of the unreconstructed primals I was surrounded by, I was left feeling constantly weak and short of breath, always gagging on the tubes stuck through my nose and down my throat. Strapping the things on every morning is a harassment; it is as if the planet itself rejects my presence.

After a humiliating 7-hour physical examination to ensure that I was free of 'unauthorized unnecessary prosthetic devices', I was finally allowed through customs and into the city of Violaine's birth. The surroundings were squalid body whipshuttle, and I set off immediately for Earth, the cradle of humanity. I had never been there, and neither had I harbored any intention of going; but Violaine had constantly pushed us to visit in person, though we could see perfectly well all of its wonders through our—through *her* memories and eyes.

In the final hours of my journey, Violaine's presence in my mind was torn roughly away, and I felt again, for the first time in nearly half a gigasecond, what it was to be alone.

———

On reaching Earth orbit I found out again that I would not be allowed immediately to attend to Violaine. I had known it, of course, because she had known it as she knew intimately all of the customs and mores of the place where she had been born and raised; being told again was like hearing something learned long ago and half-forgotten, an inconvenient fact one wished heartily to pretend one had not known. The Earth is still divided into a patchwork of terror-age nation-states, and each of them jealously guards their borders and the right to determine who can cross them; the culture of the region is zealously genetic-fundamentalist, and the government of Violaine's place of origin practices particularly extreme bio-conservative policies. I landed instead in a neighbouring polity, one with more relaxed ingress controls, and stayed there while each and every one of my numerous genetic and cybernetic modifications were endlessly examined and debated by a horde of petty bureaucrats. They forced me to shut down a wide swath of my integrated so intoxicating was our transcendent communion with the whole. We each spent our days bathed constantly in a warm sea of *us*, sharing the most casual thoughts and intimate details, the slightest sensations and most life-altering epiphanies.

Eternity station was our home, where the majority of us spent the bulk of our time, yet we were tied together by instantaneous quantum-ansible neurolinks. They connected us no matter where we went, how fast or how far. I was out near the rings of Saturn negotiating the purchase of water ices; Violaine was on Earth, visiting family to wrap up certain legalities. And so, in that single eternal moment of death and destruction, we were reduced to two; a symphony cut down to a duet singing across the solar system. And one of us was discordant, disharmonious, mad; confused and terrified and in terrible pain, uncomprehending and incomprehensible. At first, I found it difficult to understand that it wasn't me.

The utter and total intimacy of the link was suddenly no longer enough. I needed urgently to *see* my co-self, to care for her and hold her in my arms. I needed to find out what had gone wrong with her recovery and set it right; and I could hardly do that from across the solar system, no matter how closely connected were our minds. The surgeons protested and warned; but after all, our bodies belong to us and none other. So I drew deeply on our collective capital account, flush with insurance payments extracted by our legal software from the maker of the deadly microwave transmitter. I purchased a light one-

Normalization

Percival and Halden and Ryx, and so many others; all gone within barely a centasecond, screaming and praying and begging us not to let ourselves die. We felt every second of it; every thought, every emotion, every last particle of agony, and felt our minds and consciousnesses degrade and slip away into oblivion. Though we did not die, we died; again and again and again we died, and felt ourselves die. It was too much to bear; in the end we retreated into the cold comfort of catatonia, unable to continue to face the pain of ourselves ripped away and burned to ashes.

―――

When one is One, one can barely imagine going back to singularity again. The very forms of address, the pronouns and cases, grow stale from lack of use. It is difficult, even now, to think in terms of oneself, alone; but it's something that we—that *I* had best get used to. *I* woke, in the fullness of time, in a psychosurgical hospital on Hyperion Station, that having been the closest hab with the necessary facilities. I woke, expecting as always to feel the comforting murmur of my co-selves' thoughts in my head. And yet such a description is like sacrilege, in the way it renders the magnificence of the experience down to banality, to mere mechanical telepathy. We had been many, and yet One. Our selves, our minds, our feelings, our every sensation were intertwined to the point of near indistinguishability; and yet still we each retained our own unique perspective—though it was a thing that most of us rarely ever regarded or attended to,

Normalization

Xauri'EL Zwaan

There was no warning, no comprehension, no fear or even surprise; only the blinding pain of a body incinerated from the inside out, echoing between us all as Anando died and fell silent. Caught up in the trauma, in the shock and the confusion, we could not react. We could not make the split-second decisions that were needed, that our bond had always made so much easier but now rendered impossible. Again and again the burning agony tore into us and we felt ourselves feel it, and the terror and the mad grief echoed and built like a wave threatening to drown us in each other's pain. We died one by one, as the beam of a stray microwave power transmitter sliced down the shaft of Eternity Station, reducing body after body to ash and steam and molten silicon. Like hammer-blows our deaths came one after another, Carena and Tandi and Mora and Falion and

© 2022 Izzy Wasserstein

Fantasy - 9495 words

About the Author

Izzy Wasserstein is a queer, trans woman. She teaches writing and literature, writes poetry and fiction, and shares a home with a variety of animal companions and the writer Nora E. Derrington. Her fiction has appeared in *Beneath Ceaseless Skies*, *Clarkesworld*, *Fantasy*, and elsewhere. Her most recent poetry collection is When Creation Falls (Meadowlark Books, 2018).

A collective gasp goes up the marchers, a sudden movement in the crowd. Justine tenses, expecting the furious report of musket fire. And then she sees them, joining as a group: shadows. Dozens of them, maybe hundreds, slip into the crowd, take up positions among the other marchers. Ripples of nervous energy shiver through the protestors, through Justine. Her own shadow is there, not beside her, but not far away, either, one among many. She nods to it, and it inclines its head, then nods in return. There are so many shadows, each one the result of a pain so great it ruptured someone's life. Yet here they are.

Amidst the throng, it's hard to tell the severed shadows from those still attached. Under the yellow tribute banner Justine wove, the protesters advance. Shoulder to shoulder, they march into their uncertain future.

———

The protestors choose Royal Way, one of the widest streets in the city, for the march, and Raye has made it clear to Justine that she should keep an eye on side roads. Sooner or later, the Watch will move to close them off, and then it will be time to get clear as quickly as possible. Justine is terrified, and Mina has repeatedly assured her she doesn't have to participate. But Justine has spent weeks in the craft space, finishing her project, helping others with theirs, sharing meals and stories, wine and regrets.

Marching with the protesters won't put back together what was severed, will never mend the hole in her life where Zara had been. It is no cure. But it is a small thing she can do to help. Like her heartweave, now draped from a long pole, carried aloft by Mina, by Justine, by friends and strangers.

She is terrified, even as the crowd fills in, even as their combined presence ensures that whatever fate awaits them, they won't face it alone. There is no certainty, no easy answers. Nothing left but to put one foot in front of the other.

The Watch are still assembling themselves as the protesters begin their procession, more joining their number all the time. Up the Royal Way they march, shouting slogans demanding food, justice for the fallen, an end to the Watch's violence. Justine's voice is fragile as cracked glass, but it rises with the others.

taking in other projects, speaking to their crafters, to Raye, or to Mina, when she is present.

When the thread does emerge, she works ceaselessly, afraid of the next dry spell. Some nights she sleeps on the floor of the shared workspace, others she returns to her apartment, knowing she can no longer afford it, but not yet prepared to leave behind its absences. Her shadow joins her in neither location, though she watches for it. It has gone as inexplicably as it had returned.

The weave is nearing completion when Raye stops by to admire it. Her smile is still kind, but there is something else in her face, something determined.

"What do you plan for this when it is finished?" she asks.

Justine tells her what she hoped, and why she hesitated. It is not her place, not her right.

"Don't you have as much a right as any of us to mourn the dead?" Raye says.

"But I wasn't involved. I didn't join when I should have. I was lost in my own dreams, and then my grief." Justine turns away, fighting back sobs.

"You're here now," Raye's voice is gentle. "Are you ready to do the work?"

Justine is.

"Good," Raye says. "Then I know a way you can help."

seems to have been assembled out of scavenged pieces of broken looms, supplemented with parts reclaimed from other projects. Where the looms she has seen before were clearly purpose-built, this one is a kludge, a monument to tenacity. Someone, or many someones, who were never meant to heartweave, have found a way.

"It's glorious," Justine says softly, reaching out to touch it as she would a holy relic.

"My child is our expert," Raye says. "But the Watch have them locked up, who knows where. It's only right that it be used."

"Thank you," Justine wipes at her eyes. "I will do my best to honor them in their absence."

Raye smiles, clasps a hand to Justine's shoulder. "Everyone who works for the cause honors it."

It takes time to secure the weave to the loom, which lacks the extreme precision of the tertiary looms. On anything but a heartloom, resuming the project in this way would have been impossible, and even on a heartloom it requires many hours and great care. For once, Justine does not theorize about the arcane forces that govern the heartloom. Theory does not matter. What matters is the work, the patterns of her feet on the treadles, the shuttles gliding across the shed. The harness Justine wears is a bit small for her, uncomfortable, and even now the thread will not always come. When it will not, she wanders, turns to greet them, and shakes Justine's hand. Her grip is firm, her hands calloused, her smile inviting as cool water.

"Mina told me what they did to your project," she says. "I'm so sorry. My name's Raye."

"Justine. It was going to happen sooner or later. Thank you for having me."

Raye clicks her tongue. "There's no need to thank me. This space is for mutual aid."

As Justine's eyes adjust to the darkness of the expansive room, she can see what Raye means. It must have been a warehouse, once, its high ceiling lost in darkness, pools of lamplight marking various stations. In a nearby one, a pair of adolescents work to lay out a newspaper. Other stations seem to hold murals or images in progress. At one, an elderly person, stooped and alert, cuts lengths of cloth into bandages.

"It's amazing," she says. "I've never seen anything like it." Never even imagined it.

"You haven't seen anything, yet," Raye says, and takes her to the loom.

It is set off behind walls, unlike most of the other stations, to allow for the indirect lighting that is best for weaving. It has none of the majesty of the Grand Loom, nor even the straightforward functionality of the tertiaries. It is stranger than either and to Justine's eyes far more impressive. The word that springs to mind is *wild*. It shrines, some sense of them. She's refrained from making visual reference to the futures they would never have. No one needs such reminders. This was to be a tribute, not a funeral shroud.

She was saving Zara for last, but that will never come to pass, now.

"It's gorgeous," Mina says, very softly, wiping at her eyes.

"I'd meant to leave it near the shrines, for people to do with what they wanted," Justine says. "But then I thought it wasn't my right...and now it doesn't matter. I've lost access to my loom."

Mina pulls a tissue from her robes, blows her nose. "They kicked you out for this, didn't they?"

"Yes. I just thought...maybe you would know someone who might have some use for it." She rolls it back up carefully, and when she looks up, Mina pats the sofa beside her.

"I can do better than that," she says and reaches out to take Justine's hand.

———

They slip through a series of narrow alleyways, switching back and watching for any sign they are being followed. When Mina is certain they are not, she stands before a nondescript door, knocks twice, then thrice more. An older woman admits them and bolts the door before she

she had never walked those neighborhoods, never taken herself down streets where those who aren't welcome find means to survive.

She sets about making them tea again.

"My name is Mina."

"Justine." She responds without a thought, surprised at herself. Well, it would be ridiculous to carry on without names, and she couldn't very well share her project with a stranger. "I should have asked before, but I wasn't ready."

"It's nothing," Mina says, smiling. "There's no rush. Only what you're ready for." Justine feels suddenly warm.

They drink their tea and speak softly. Justine tells Mina a little about Zara, about the errand of kindness she was on when she died. She isn't ready to share the details, but she sees Mina understands. It's a comfort to have someone to share experiences with, but also tense, as though any wrong move could pressure an exposed nerve.

"Well," she says at last. "I meant to finish this, then figure out what to do with it. But now I know it won't be finished, and, um, it seemed right to show it to you."

She unfurls the half-completed weave, lays it down on the floor in front of Mina. The pair of faces, the victims of the Watch's weapons, are impressionistic; Justine's memory and technique weren't up to the challenge of composing realistic portraits from memory, but she thinks she captured something of their essences as displayed in the

After the meeting, she approaches Freckles, worried she is violating some unspoken taboo. But she needs to do this.

"Would you...would you be willing to stop by my flat sometime?" she asks. "I have something I'd like you to see."

To her surprise, Freckles nods at once. "Of course. I'll come tonight, if that's okay." Seeing Justine's worry, she adds quickly, "I, uh, acquired some papers after last time."

They make it to the flat without incident. Only when Justine brings up the lights does she realize her shadow isn't in the corner. She gasps. "It's gone."

"More likely it's still on its way. It followed you to our meeting. Did you know that?"

Surprised, Justine shakes her head. "It never has before, that I know of."

Freckles takes a seat on the couch, and sure enough the shadow passes through the wall and takes up its spot in the corner. "I visit mine occasionally," she says. "It's hard to communicate with them, but from what I can tell it works with new shadows, helps them get...situated, I suppose." She smiles. "They have their own places, their own means of mutual support."

Justine had never seen anything like that before the shrine. Then again, why would she? People with shadows would rather talk about anything than those without, and leave the room. One of the others, a younger man, flushes. The facilitator lifts her hands, palms down, as if doing so will calm everyone.

"They do what they will," she says. "Some do go join communities with other shadows, or stay with their people, if we'll let them. My own shadow visits me once, maybe twice a year."

Justine blinks, trying to make sense of this. "What does it want?" she asks at last, and the woman shrugs.

"They keep their own counsel. But I like to think it just wants to see how I am getting on." When Justine has nothing more to say, she continues. "They are no different than we are, getting by without us as best they can." She smiles at the young man who reacted so strongly to Justine's words. "Would you like to tell us about how it goes with your shadow?"

He nods, takes a deep breath. "It's splitting. Becoming two shadows." He pauses for a long time before continuing. "It's strange to feel it moving on without me. Like if I'd shed a limb, and it had grown a body, started its own family."

Justine came here hoping for answers, for reasons. Theorizing, as always. As though reasoning could change the fact that she'd lost Zara, then been sundered by grief. As though answers could heal her. Foolish.

beating loudly in her ears. When she finally summons the courage to speak, her voice sounds strange. It isn't, as before, as if she is looking at herself over her shoulder, but still she feels she does not fully know this person whose words she hears.

"My shadow stands in the corner of my flat." She pauses, expecting, what? Shock or surprise or disbelief. And she finds something like that on some faces, but by no means all. The leader—no, she realizes, the facilitator—only nods. "It had been watching my flat from across the street. I invited it in."

She falls silent, glad to have unburdened herself but not feeling the relief she hoped for.

"How do you feel about it?" the facilitator says after a few moments.

"I want to know what it wants." Justine hears in her own words something like petulance. There are a couple of nods, but the facilitator only quirks an eyebrow, as if waiting. Justine hasn't answered her question.

"I don't know how I feel. I was afraid of it, but now I just...wish it would tell me why it is here. Or go away and leave me in peace."

"Where would it go?" Freckles asks. The facilitator looks in her direction but doesn't interject.

"I don't know," Justine says. "Wherever it wants. To live with other shadows, maybe." She feels some of the air

She carefully folds away her project and tucks it under her arm. "Goodbye, Professor," she says.

Justine is almost out the door when he calls out to her. "Don't throw this all away, Justine," he says, breaking decorum by referring to her by her given name. When she turns back to him, incredulous, he meets her eyes for just a moment, then looks down. "Don't take this so personally."

"It's not personal at all. I see that now." She leaves him standing there. At the edge of campus, she hurls away her robe. It catches briefly in the wind, tumbles and snags on a hedgerow that marks the place where the university ends and the streets begin. She walks home in loose trousers and overshirt, only the half-finished wall hanging under her arm and the slip of paper in her pocket remaining as markers of the dream she leaves behind.

―――

Justine returns to the cellar, to Freckles and the others. If the group finds it odd that she has returned after her rushed exit from the last meeting, no one says so. Only Freckles raises an eyebrow, studying Justine's face for a moment, then looking behind her to the stairway, as if she expects someone else to enter. But Justine is the last, and they begin as they had before with the invocation of their rules.

Others speak occasionally in that room bound by silences, by absence. Justine does her best to listen, but her heart is

Such a tempting offer. How she craves continued access to a loom, the credential she's worked so hard to earn, the comfort and security of life behind a university's walls. The loss of her stipend means even her frugal lifestyle will exhaust her remaining funds before long, and then where will she be? Out on the streets? Begging her mother's estranged family for a place to sleep? Another jobless worker, and one without useful skills?

She stares at the vivid yellows pulled from her essence, the intricate images she has never previously managed. Of what use is the promise of someday completing her work if it can't serve its purpose now, when people are grieving? What use is her art if it cannot offer them even this small thing?

"If I can't do the work I need to do," she says, "then what's the use of this place?" She begins removing her work from the loom, carefully tying off ends, even though she knows she will never be able to finish it.

"The university does so much good," he says, even now unwilling to look at her. "It provides safety, stability, and essential funding to the city. There's no need to get...irrational. No need to burn everything down." A terrible choice of words: she is not interested in destruction, but in creating something new. And now she is certain that, whatever he once was, he is a functionary, a cog, driven to defend that thing which molded him to its needs. He has allowed himself to see his highest goal as protecting it. As though the ivy-bound walls were going anywhere, with or without his protection.

Pain flares through her, white-hot, the kind she has not felt since her early days of mourning. This is all she has left and now he is taking it away too.

"You do have a choice," she says, more sharply than she intends. "We all do."

He stares at the loom. Even half-finished, there is no denying the work's politics, and she wouldn't do so even if she could.

"It's lovely," he says, as though the aesthetics are what is at issue. "But the university will never allow it. It can't seem to be taking sides."

She should fight this, demand to finish her project unmolested. Champion her rights as an academic. But she suspects that he will put neither the university nor himself at risk. And without his support, she can never hope to finish, never hope to pursue a career here or at any other university. Even if she wins the argument, she loses everything.

"If you won't stand up for your students' right to make the art that calls to them—" she says, and hates herself for the generality. "If you won't defend me, then what use is any of this?"

He has never looked younger, standing with his mouth agape. "We can forget about this," he says at last. "Finish a more...practicum-appropriate project, earn your doctorate, and then you're free to pursue whatever projects you wish."

in the corner, makes no effort to approach her, to communicate. It only stands.

She goes onto campus repeatedly but can draw no essence for her work. Finally, she abandons her geometric exercise and begins sketching a new project.

The threads come fitfully, sometimes flowing like they once had, other times drying up completely, and most often a trickle that Justine hopes is more akin to priming a pump than a well on its dregs. She can think of nothing to do but keep at it, for at least she is working again. Nothing is repaired, but at least she is weaving again.

She is several days into her new project and not quite halfway through when Professor Morinth enters unannounced. He stares at her work on the loom, woven in gleaming yellow, with two somewhat abstracted faces. She doubts he has been to the shrine, doubts he knows these faces, but the meaning of the yellow weave is clear. It's the color hung from windows, left to dangle from clotheslines, the color adopted by the protesters. There is no mistaking her intent.

Of all the arts faculty, Morinth is the one who might have been sympathetic to this new direction, this rejection of the meaninglessness of art, and she can see in his eyes that he is. For all the good it does her.

"I have no choice but to report this," he says after a long silence. "You know it will bring an end to your studies here."

The shadow folds its arms across its chest.

"I can't help you! I can't help either of us!" She shouts and the shadow wavers, though whether through reluctance or under a gust of wind-blown rain, she cannot say. "If you won't show me what you want, then go. Just go. Please."

The shadow tilts its head, and that is all. So much time bracing herself to confront it, and she is no better off than she was before. No, that is not quite true. She is not afraid of it anymore, just bone-tired.

She turns her back on the shadow, rapidly crosses the street, her shoes sloshing with water. Her shaking hands struggle with the lock. When she finally opens the door, she hesitates, turns around.

"If you're not going to leave," she shouts across the street, "then I suppose you'd better come inside."

The shadow doesn't move, but by the time she ignites the lamps in her flat, it is there, standing in the corner by the sagging bookshelf. It does not move while she strips out of her wet robes, starts her kettle boiling, and waits to stop shivering. It is there when she goes to sleep, and still there in the morning.

―――

For the next few days, Justine worries she will wake with the shadow's hands around her throat, or with it trying to stitch itself to her skin, or some other horror. But it stays head where her hair will never truly cooperate, will frizz up at every opportunity. She realizes she's been hoping to be wrong, that it would be someone else's shadow, someone else's problem. No such luck.

The shadow, being a shadow, says nothing.

"I'm here," she says. "I know you've been waiting for me, and I'm here. What do you want?"

No sound but the rain, no movement save for a slight tilt of its head, a mannerism Zara teased her about, one that always meant she was struggling with a puzzle, a challenging weave or a difficult exam question.

"You shouldn't be here," Justine says, hating its silence, the staccato of her heart's pumping, the rain's drumbeat. "I never wanted to be without you, but I can't change things. They killed her, and you tore away and now..." Justine trails off. Now what? She cannot put things right. She once saw another student, furious with his own weave, take a pair of scissors to it. The heartweave had torn easily, as if in rebuke of the effort that had created it. All that remained were frayed threads on the ground. No going back.

"I can't do anything for you!" She realizes her voice is rising, becoming a scream. It feels like the sound comes from someone else's lips. She has found her rage, but still she is nothing but a passenger to it. "I don't know what you want, and I have nothing to give. It's over. Don't you understand?"

Justine wanders on. The fog turns to drizzle as she drifts among streets, through alleyways and unfamiliar districts. Desperate times make for desperate people, and it is unwise to walk alone through neighborhoods she does not know. She does not care, cannot imagine going to campus and her loom, and is not ready yet to turn towards home. When she realizes what she is waiting for, her fists clench, her spine tightens like a thread stretched too far, ready to snap.

She walks until it is full dark and raining in earnest. The wind has at last arrived, a gale blowing in from the harbor, pelting the streets with a nearly-horizontal downpour that brings in the autumn cold for the first time this season. Her teeth chatter. She pulls her arms around herself. Cold does not matter. Nothing does.

Time to face her shadow.

It waits for her, its body made somehow even less substantial by the wind passing through it in gusts. It shimmers like a reflection on a lake's surface. Justine thinks it turns to her as she approaches, but it is hard to be certain.

She trudges toward it. She can neither make herself hurry the confrontation nor run from it. When she reaches the edge of the pool of lamplight, she hesitates, her momentum at last failing her.

"You *are* mine," she says at last. There is no doubting it, the shape, the posture, even the blurred edges atop its

She steps closer. A chalk-drawn mural, its details lost now, charred beyond recognition.

So that was why the protests had gained renewed strength. Someone had tried to destroy this memorial. Very recently. Someone wished to erase the dead. Justine staggers, kneels before the shrines. The hollowness in her chest remains, but now it is not alone. It shares space with rage.

Some time later she finally forces herself to rise, feeling eyes on her from the dark facings of the buildings across the way. She turns to see movement around a small bonfire inside one of the damaged structures, its front wall collapsed, its beams charred and bent. There are people in its depths, watching her, their shadows—

—no, not only their shadows. Severed shadows are there too, moving on their own, with no people to cast them. Humans and independent shadows both, living in the wreckage. She has never seen anything like it, had no idea shadows gathered, or that there were people who might share space with them. Lives, even.

She yearns to go speak to them, to understand, to ask why her shadow is haunting her. But she hesitates. This is their home, and she is an outsider here. They have not approached her and have allowed her to pay her respects. She will not intrude. She wants to leave an offering at the shrine, but her pockets are empty save for her curfew pass. She has nothing to offer.

She arrives at a block like any other, some of its buildings standing, many partially burned and collapsed. One might miss it entirely, save for the twine with which the Watch cordoned it, the signs demanding everyone keep out. No one seems to be on guard, though, and the four small shrines are evidence people have been ignoring the command. Justine glances around, then slips under the barrier. Not really a barrier, just a line that is easy to cross, once you know you can.

The shrines are arranged in a semicircle. Artists' likenesses of the four victims stand in each shrine's center. Piles of tiny objects cluster around them: candles; small gifts; tear-stained notes; a series of small, smooth rocks stacked into piles; bundles of yellow wildflowers.

Justine cannot bring herself to look at Zara's picture and does not need to. She can bring Zara's face to mind as easy as breathing, but is not eager to invite that pain into herself. The others, though, she stares at. Strangers, all of them, two younger and one older. All protesters. She found she could no longer think of them as rioters. And even if they had been, it was the Watch who struck them down. Who murdered them, she at last let herself admit. The Watch, who left Zara bleeding on the street, when all she'd been trying to do was take food to her cousin. Yes, it was the Watch who did it. Not the protesters. Not the millworkers and the jobless, not students like Freckles.

That's when she notices: these shrines are new, as yet untouched by rain. They're piled atop ash, the same ash that darkens the brick wall behind them, effacing, what?

But that is a fiction, a veneer. It is the artist's job to observe keenly, to see past the surface. As a Heartweaver, she learned to look beneath her own surface, until that well went dry, and when she attempted to pull raw material from her depths, not even dregs emerged.

What is beneath this surface? Lowered heads and few offered greetings. Windows shuttered when they should be thrown open, ready to catch the harbor breeze that will disperse the fog. Everything is gray, the color leached from the world. The people in the distance, mere shadows. Appalled, she looks away, anywhere but at the people. Above her, the familiar face of the neighborhood, her home for years now. Few people even put out their laundry these days, as if it would be stolen or used for torches or—she does not know what. The few pieces that remain hang limp in the damp air, yellow towels and sheets the only splash of color in the near-monochrome morning.

The blocks pass under her feet. She moves with neither urgency nor direction, but when she realizes where her legs are taking her, it feels inevitable. The stone fronts of the student district give way to the newer neighborhoods abutting the mills—rickety timber buildings, occasionally reinforced with brick, that were thrown up when the mills opened, as people flooded in from the country for the jobs they offered. Now there are few jobs, worse wages, more hunger. Now there are burned-out buildings and violent confrontations with the Watch. Now there are loved ones dead in the streets.

She steps away, realizing she is blushing. She is just as inept at trying to signal that this isn't an approach as she ever was when actually trying to express interest.

The other woman looks at her curiously, as if trying to suss out what strings might be attached to the offer. "All right. But I'll take the sofa. I'm not going to kick you out of your own bed."

Justine winces. "I'd rather have the sofa," she says, and then, despite everything, it spills out. "I haven't been able to face the bed since, since…"

"I understand," Freckles says. "I'll take the bed. And be out of your way in the morning."

True to her word, she is up before dawn. Justine pretends to sleep as she slips out the door with first light.

———

Justine walks for hours. Down the narrow streets of the student district, as residents hurry to their classes, or congregate around carts selling pastries redolent of cardamom and squash. Here and there are shattered windows, iron gates slammed shut when before they would have opened to invite customers. Beggars, the ones willing to risk the Watch, ask for coin. She has none to give. Here and there, the Watch make their patrols, but without the urgency she saw last night. It is as though everyone has mutually agreed that during the day, things will carry on as if all is well.

Silence. Freckles stands, moves to the opposite wall, its dull stone face covered by a weave, just a simple thing, a two-color fractal in crimson and silver. Nothing more than an exercise, really, but Zara liked it.

"This is breathtaking," Freckles leans in to admire the detail. "I don't get to see many heartweaves up close. Your work?"

"Yes."

"Thank you for saving me back there," Freckles says. "Passion or not, without you I would have been doomed."

"If you hadn't helped me, you wouldn't have needed it."

"I had a twin, once." Freckles is framed by the weave, the dim lighting of the flat making her face an unreadable mask. "For a long time after, I couldn't...wouldn't reach out to anyone. I was terrified. Until I had to admit there were things I couldn't do alone."

Justine feels her awaiting a response, giving Justine space to form thoughts. But thoughts are the last thing she wants right now.

"I'll leave you be," her guest says. "Thank you for the tea."

Justine jumps up. In the tiny flat it only takes her a few steps to get to the door. "No," she says. "Don't go. Please." She is afraid she will be misunderstood, and more words rush out of her. "You can have the bed. I'll take the sofa. Too big a risk—to leave now."

required fewer hands, heard whispers of the diseases that ran rife among the crowded flats of the millworkers. She knows people are desperate, but at first she had been too immersed in her studies to give it much thought. And later, there was nothing but grief.

She tries to avoid thinking about that day, but it was not the protestors who killed Zara. It was the Watch. The Watch who formed the line, who fired their muskets.

A surge of nausea hits her. She cannot speak of that, nor think of it. An ugly thought rises in its place. "And *Facing It Together* is, what? Recruitment?"

The other woman stands suddenly as if the seat—or Justine—has burned her. "What? No. Absolutely not." Her eyes are wide, her jaw tight. "It's for people who've lost their shadows. I can be passionate about more than one thing."

Is there nothing Justine can do well? She buries her head in her hands. After a few moments she feels weight beside her, a hand on her shoulder.

"I'm so—" Freckles pauses. "I shouldn't snap at you. It wasn't an unreasonable conclusion. Just an incorrect one. I invited you to the group only because I thought…I thought it might be of use. Like it has been for me."

Justine cannot look at her. "I don't know how to be passionate, not anymore."

"I'm sorry," Freckles says, breaking another silence after nursing her tea for some time. Justine turns back from the window, from her shadow.

"Twice you've apologized to me, twice it wasn't your fault. It's nothing."

"You saved me. You don't even realize—"

The walls are thin enough that Justine drops her voice. "You're one of them. The rioters."

The other woman stares at her like she's just sprouted wings. "Rioters? You mean the protestors?"

Justine does not understand. She sits beside Freckles, leaving space. She does not want to impose.

"But yes, I am," the younger woman continues, very quietly. "Part of them, I mean. Trying to support them. Most of the workers have much more at risk than I do."

Justine had felt the tightness in her acquaintance's body with the warden, felt her episode shake the sofa. She was already risking so much.

When the riots—the protests—started, Justine paid them little mind. Though they spilled out occasionally from the mill district, though there were curfews and further spikes in food prices that strained her and Zara's modest means, she knows little about them. No, that is not it. She has seen the hungry and homeless on the streets begging for scraps, read about the great machines in the mills that

"Get her home," he huffs. "And don't let me catch you out after curfew again." Justine feels him watching as they walk on.

She's been dreading her street, meaning to send her escort away before they near the lamp across from her flat. But now there is nothing to do but go forward. If wishing made things so, the shadow would be gone, but it stands as it has the previous nights, silent and unflinching. She forces herself not to stare at it. "Come up," Justine says, half offer, half insistence. She can feel the other demurring. "The warden will be on the lookout for you."

That convinces her, and they stumble up the stairs to Justine's second storey flat. Freckles guides her to the sofa, and both sit heavily, their ragged breaths not enough to fill the silence.

Finally, Justine gets up to make tea, and when she returns, Freckles is shaking. Justine sits beside her, wraps her arm around the younger woman.

"I'll be all right," the other woman says, clasping her shaking hands together. She rests her head on Justine's shoulder, takes deep, shuddering breaths.

Then it is over. Not all at once, but like a spring shower. You could not say when it stopped raining, precisely, but there comes a point when it clearly has. Freckles sits up, takes up the cup of tea Justine had placed before her.

understand it. She might face a fine, but has nothing more to fear—

Oh.

The warden looks up, first to Justine, then the other woman. "Curfew pass," he demands. Freckles' body is drawn taut as a warp. She stutters, reaching for words she doesn't have.

"She doesn't have them," Justine offers, though she has never been quick on her feet. Her escort's nails dig into her shoulder. "It's my fault, sir. I grew ill on campus, and she offered to help me get home. If she hadn't helped me out, she'd be home by now." Justine knows she should be afraid, lying to a warden, getting mixed up in who-knows-what. Her heart doesn't flutter. Earlier the flatness deserted her, and now here it is, returned for no reason she can name.

The warden's eyes move between them, then down to the sick on the front of Justine's robes. He sniffs the air, twists his face up like she is a refuse pile. "Where do you live?" he demands, and Justine gives him her address, two blocks away.

"And you?" Justine is certain Freckles will stumble again under his question, but she has gathered herself and gives him an address roughly halfway between Uni and Justine's flat.

"If your episodes are anything like mine, it will pass soon," the younger woman says. They still have not given each other their names, and Justine has no desire to. "I'm studying physiology. It's your body's reaction to stress. Like when you're already nervous and then a cat jumps out of the alleyway."

"I've been feeling like that since—" Justine stops herself, furious that she's nearly volunteered something no one else has a right to know.

They walk on in the unnatural stillness of the evening. "Yes," Freckles says. "Me too. Maybe—"

"Present your curfew passes," demands a voice from behind them. Both women tense and turn. A warden of the Watch, though he looks barely old enough to be out of his parents' house. Justine fishes her pass from her robe's pocket. She has not heard the nine bells, is almost certain they have not chimed. They are not out after curfew. A year ago, she might have made a fuss, but a year ago there had been no curfew, no riots, no Zara dead.

"Here you are, sir," she says, glad for once that her voice sounds tired, flat, not angry or despairing or any of a hundred other things. It sounds like nothing.

He examines it as though it is in code. Freckles still hasn't produced any documents. Belatedly, Justine realizes why. The other woman is an undergraduate and wouldn't have them. Tension radiates from her, but Justine does not does she realize someone is holding her hair back from her face.

Justine wipes her lips on the back of her hand and turns to see Freckles crouching beside her, her face pinched with worry.

"Are you all right?" she asks, one arm around Justine as though she might collapse, even though the weaver is on her knees and has one hand bracing herself, even though there isn't much further to fall.

"Yes," Justine manages. "I just needed air…"

"Let me help you home."

"No, I can…" Justine doesn't finish the sentence. The struggle to get to her feet requires intense focus. When she finally manages it, she realizes the other woman is supporting nearly all her weight.

"I have these episodes too," Freckles says, and adds firmly, "Now, point me in the right direction."

She is insistent and Justine's legs feel like their bones have deserted them, so she does not object.

"I'm sorry," Freckles says after a while. "I wish I'd warned you it can be… intense. I've never figured out what to say. How to say it." She sighs.

"Not your fault. I can't…" Justine lets the sentence trail away. She cannot even talk about not talking about it.

her mother immediately apologized to the other girl and pulled Justine away. *We don't ask such questions*, her mother said, and would say no more.

As an adolescent she'd heard people whispering about it, snickering behind the backs of fellow students unlucky enough to have parents without shadows, and she even joined in occasionally, the breaking of the taboo the point in itself. Everyone knows about the shadowless, but most have the good grace not to speak of it.

This, though—it makes her skin crawl. When someone speaks, all eyes turn toward them. Everyone knows what sort of things happen to someone to strip them of their shadow, that only the worst emotional wounds can cause it. To be known for it, to have everyone wondering about the source, certain only that it was terrible—

Justine realizes she is shaking. She pulls her legs up under her chin, grits her teeth. No, no, this is the last thing she needs. The others' voices are far away as if they echo from far down a tunnel.

"...I just want to know it is okay," someone says. "The thought of it out there, alone, hurting..."

Justine climbs to her feet, her body like a distant automaton, out of her control. "I'm sorry," she hears herself stammer, and then she is up the cellar stairs, on her knees, emptying her stomach onto the alleyway. She retches long after there is anything to lose, and only then

"All are welcome to share or stay silent, as they wish," the woman says. She does not give her name, nor do any of the others who speak after her.

"In my dreams, my shadow is still attached," a young man in student robes says. "I used to have dreams where I was falling or flying. Now I have just this one. It's sunset. I'm walking down a quiet lane. I look back, and there it is."

A murmur of sympathy, then a silence. "Would you share with us how the dreams make you feel?" the woman asks. Justine sees her as their de facto leader. She is younger than Justine had first thought, but her back is bent, her forehead creased with worry.

"Joyous," the man says. "Like I was whole again. And then I wake up, it hits me all over again."

"If we aren't what we once were, that doesn't mean we aren't whole," Freckles says, and Justine feels a tension in the room, a site of dispute.

The sharing moves on slowly. At first it seems others are reluctant to speak, but it isn't that. They carefully wait until whoever is speaking has truly finished, and Justine is certain some of them won't utter a word until they figure out exactly what they wish to say.

There is something perverse in hearing others talk about their missing shadows. One of Justine's earliest memories is of playing with another child on a stoop. As it grew dark, she realized the other child didn't have a shadow. She asked about it with the directness of childhood, and flame-light directed inward by curving brass backdrops. The room is dark, but the circle is bright as day. Brighter. Taking her position amidst the others, Justine sees the reason for the arrangement: with so many light sources, there are no true shadows. No temptation to see if everyone here was truly shadowless, or if some merely have wounded shadows or are con artists.

Justine half expects a con. Why else would the shadowless gather? Why would anyone volunteer their own incompleteness? It feels like picking at a scab, only much worse. Why, then, is she here? *Because it is something other than being home*, she tells herself, but knows that is not the full truth.

There are eight of them in the circle, the youngest an adolescent still in their school clothes, the oldest a man whose weather-beaten face looks as ancient and hostile as a blighted mountainside. Some are students, a couple have the calloused hands and hungry frames of millworkers. One bears herself like an aristocrat, and the silk clothes she wears suggest it is no affectation.

"We are gathered to create a space of honesty and mutual support." Justine notices the silence only when words break it. The speaker is one of the mill workers, maybe a decade older than Justine. "Even when those goals are in tension, we must honor both of them as best we can." There are nods from the group, murmurs of agreement. Justine suspects she is the only newcomer.

She reaches the doorway to her building, fumbles with the keys. It is coming for her. She can sense it, its weightless bulk closing on her until—

And then she is inside. She slams the heavy door, the building's foyer echoing with its sound. She can't resist looking through the peephole. Her shadow stands where she left it, waiting.

Later, awake on the couch, in the unnatural stillness of the curfew-silenced night, she wonders if it will ever stop waiting, and if she will ever be able to weave again. And then a terrible thought: is it even possible to heartweave without one's shadow? No one has told her otherwise, but then, who would?

In her grief after Zara's death, she lost her shadow. If she has lost her craft, too, there is nothing left.

———

Whatever Justine expected from 'Facing It Together', it was not this vast, low-ceilinged cellar with dirt floors and rock walls. People sit in a circle in the center of the room. She knows none of their names, though she recognizes the freckled woman and one or two others, perhaps from passing them on the street, sharing a classroom with them, or some other tenuous connection.

The room is clearly used for storage most of the time, with sagging boxes and haphazardly stacked clutter making vague outlines against the dark walls. Around the gathered group, braziers burn, a dozen of them, their wish to draw attention to their condition, to lay open their wound for all to see? The thought is stomach-turning. Horrific.

When she heads back to her flat, night's veil is drawn over the world, and she can almost forget about shadows. Until each pool of lamplight reminds her, every bench and garbage bin throwing their own darkness, until Justine feels as though she's a soap bubble about to pop.

The night is unnaturally still. The Watch have announced another round of curfews. It hurts too much to focus on such things, and she has no need to. She has special dispensation, documents from the university that state she is a doctoral candidate and so allowed to be on the street after curfew, such is the university's clout and wealth. Even so, most candidates won't venture out after dark. The consensus is that it is safer that way.

ot safe enough. Zara bled out on the pavement in broad daylight, as did the others who had been felled by the barrage of musket fire.

Lost in those thoughts, she has almost forgotten about what awaits her until she turns the corner onto her block, and there it stands, a dark translucence in the light. No eyes, no mouth, nothing but the outline of Justine, yet she is certain it sensed her coming, has turned its full attention to her.

The woman pulls a thread of red hair from a freckle-dusted face. "I hope we can help each other," she says and glances around, as if worried she will be sanctioned for disturbing Justine's stillness. She holds out a sliver of paper, which Justine studies for a moment, then takes from her. She expects the woman to say something, to clarify, or perhaps even to apologize. But the undergraduate just nods and walks away without looking back.

When she is out of sight, Justine unfolds the paper.

Facing It Together, the paper reads, along with an address on the edge of the student district, near the mills. *Every Thirdday evening, seven bells.*

It makes no sense. It is as if she's been invited to a secret society in the most awkward possible way. And there is something else, something wrong with interaction, that she struggles to identify.

She retreats to the library, unwilling to walk home while the sun sinks low in the sky, and only then does she realize why she hadn't noticed the woman's approach: she too had cast no shadow.

———

Justine waits for full dark to return home, looking through the library's stacks for information on detached shadows, but there is next to nothing. Unsurprising. Those with shadows typically want nothing to do with those whose have been severed, and what shadowless person would weave without the constant need to intellectualize, to explain, to develop grand theories about how to produce from her own essence the colors and textures of thread she seeks.

But the thread she has on hand runs low, and no more emerges from within her. The loom whirs on with the comforting sounds of the thread unspooling, the shuttles passing through the shed. The pattern unfolds itself as though she is unnecessary to the process, but the spools waiting to be filled with her essence remain empty. The weave comes to a stop, half-finished, its resources depleted, its creator barren.

———

Justine doesn't notice the stranger approach. No surprise, since she sits with her head in her hands, staring at the manicured lawn, shining green under the sunlight. In mid-afternoon, the quad is too busy, and she's not ready to return to her empty flat. She's chosen instead the stillness of the grounds around the reflecting pool, which are rarely crowded, and even when others are present their voices don't rise above whispers.

A gentle cough startles her. Above her stands a young woman, wearing the unadorned robes of an undergraduate. It is a minor violation of etiquette for her to approach a doctoral candidate unbidden, but Justine has no use for such rules.

"Can I help you?" Justine whispers.

Traditional weaving requires precision and planning, intricately preparing the warp in advance. Heartweaving, pulling as it does from oneself, is a very different skill. It allows one to create the warp's essence as one works, allowing for greater control and improvisation, while also requiring great focus and precision. Such is the price of creating a weave out of nothing but oneself. Or perhaps the heartloom's function is very different. Some theorists claim it simply holds space onto which the True Warp is created.

There are many debates about heartweaving, including over the best way to induce the desired threads to emerge, but Justine has never found a better technique than to weave a pattern that's as easy to her as breathing, pulling in more complex elements as threads emerge from her chest as they sprout like spring flowers, which are then guided by the arcane harness down her arms and then fed into the loom that incorporates them into the warp.

Her hands and feet move on without the need for thought. The threads are thin as spiderweb, reds and purples, blues so dark they are almost black, bluewhites like lightning that hurt to stare at directly, ochre and pearl and a green like the last flash of daylight, all laid down in a geometric pattern, one of the first she mastered, its shape and rules better known to her than her own body. A weave she can produce without thought, an elegant expression of the perfect, glorious uselessness of her art, conveying no meaning, only beauty, a pattern she can accomplish on a machine like that, one that was capable of working with the finest threads of one's essence. She'd been so sure, then, of her talent, the trajectory of her career.

And Zara had been her eager audience through it all, her belief in Justine's greatness outstripping even the artist's own. Even at their lowest, when Justine had let herself fall back into an ex's destructive orbit and Zara had nearly left her, that faith in Justine's skill had never wavered.

And now Zara was gone. Just a few wrong steps, a moment's inattention on an errand, and she'd been caught between the Watch and the food rioters. And that had been that.

The tertiary looms are much less impressive than the Grand Loom, but even so they are valuable beyond words, for only at such a true heartloom can one weave from their own essence. Perhaps a handful are in private ownership, and rumors place one at the Lord Mayor's residence. Aside from those, there are no heartlooms in the city but those at the university. Standing before her assigned loom, its functional but uninspiring lines taking almost every available inch of space in the cramped studio, Justine can't imagine how she ever had the confidence to use it, the control and technique to draw from herself what was needed, to pull threads from her mind as easily as singers draw melodies from their lungs. She prepares the loom with what remains of the thread she pulled from herself when Zara was still alive. A simple pattern, one she's long used as an exercise.

she is looking over her own shoulder, observing herself from a distance, though there is no such vantage point in this cramped office. "Soon."

Morinth doesn't believe her and she can't blame him. She's only telling him what she's expected to. There's no conviction in her voice, nor panic, nor even pain. Beaten flat. Not even the knowledge that, without her stipend, the funds she inherited from her mother won't last long.

"See that you do," Morinth says. She is almost at the door when he speaks again. "Ms. Revel." He still won't look at her. "I will not be able to hold a loom for you forever."

There it is, her years of studies nearing an ignominious end. No degree, no more heartweaving. Nothing. She feels as if she should cry, as if another person who finds herself in such a position *would* cry. She leaves his office without a word.

———

Doctoral Candidates in Heartweaving are allotted one of the tertiary looms. Only those craftspeople who have attained the rank of Doctor of the Holy Arts and maintained an official relationship with the university have use of the Grand Loom. For years, Justine has dreamed of someday working with it, will never forget the first time she saw it, large as a room, its brass filigree almost glowing against the dim, recessed lighting that allowed the threads' own light to illuminate the project. She'd lain awake nights planning what she could university, the trees shedding leaves, even the undergraduates going about their days, their shadows trailing from them as though it were the most natural thing in the world. She keeps looking behind her, half-expecting to see her shadow following her, but there is no sign of it.

She has a meeting with Professor Morinth, one she has been putting off until sensing she could no longer reschedule it. She must face him.

"I have sympathy for your situation," Morinth tells her, sitting behind his oiled oak desk, "but there are deadlines to consider." The youngest member of the department of visual art, his face is unlined under a thin beard that does little to make him look older. He won't look directly at her, as though losing one's shadow is catching. At least he still speaks to her. When strangers notice her lack, they either force smiles through gritted teeth or ignore her entirely.

She knows what he's going to say before he says it. She must make progress if she wishes to remain a part of the program. The small stipend she receives is dependent upon making progress. But the work won't come. She lacks the focus even to read, can't handle the analytical side at which she's always excelled, much less the practicum, the heartweaving itself, which is to be the core of her dissertation.

"I will have work to show you, Professor," she says, her own voice sounding distant to her. It seems for a moment

Shadows of the Hungry, the Broken, the Transformed

When she finally turns from the window to dump her cold tea into the sink, she looks down out of old habit, as though she'll find her shadow once again attached. As though what has been torn apart could ever be reassembled.

Four months now since she lost her shadow. How many nights has it been out there, waiting for her, keeping vigil? And what does it want? She picks up a book, Faulen's *On the Joyous Uselessness of Heartweaving: A Reflection on Craft and Purpose*, and flips a few pages before she admits she's absorbing nothing, sets it aside.

She could confront her shadow, ask what it wants. Demand it go away. Beg, threaten. To what end? She doesn't know. It is still there when she closes the drapes. She lies sleepless on the sofa, unable to face the vastness of her bed.

––––

When Justine steps onto the street the next morning, she's met with the smell of smoke, of ash. The food riots must have resumed, though the Watch had just last week assured the university they had everything under control. Whenever she thinks of the riots, the agony of grief washes over her anew, and it is all she can do to push those thoughts away, unable to bear them.

It's an uncharacteristically sunny day for autumn, with shadows everywhere, thrown by the old stone buildings in the student district, the stately ivy-lined walls of the

Shadows of the Hungry, the Broken, the Transformed

Izzy Wasserstein

Justine's shadow watches her. It stands under the lamp post across from her flat, her smoky semblance, flickering and shifting under the gaslight. She's at her window, tea cooling in her hands. Though the shadow has no eyes, Justine is certain that it stares at her, just as she is certain it is hers. She would know it anywhere.

© 2022 Kit Harding

Fantasy - 4197 words

About the Author

Kit Harding is a writer, librarian, and maker who belongs to the trees and sea of New England. Her work has previously appeared in the Zombies Need Brains anthology *Derelict*. You can find her online at https://writerkit.dreamwidth.org/

gorge beside the village, willing myself to jump in. Originally, when I'd set out, it hadn't been to kill the gods; it had been to find a way to get him back. Bringing back the dead was impossible. But stopping the cycle wasn't. If it had vengeance alongside it, that was simply a nice bonus.

"Fine," she said. "Abandon us again. Disappear into the night. Refuse to take responsibility for your actions. But one thing's certain: you aren't the person Eric loved anymore." She left. I did not turn to watch her go.

I remained at the window for a long time, but then went to my cedar chest, pulled out the spear, and laid it on the table. I didn't think Clara was right about that. Eric had always forgiven me for my difficulties with the world. I thought he'd forgive the path I was walking now as well. But even if she was right, I'd gone too far down this road to turn back. The spear was almost finished. After that, I'd die killing a god. Eventually, enough others would walk in my footsteps that all the gods would die, and people could manage themselves. This cycle had to end.

There were no other options.

"They don't need to know everything you've been."

"You would have me leave Eric unavenged?"

"You think you're the only person who lost someone? I lost him and you that day. I raised two children on my own. And at least with him I knew he was dead. I could grieve for what we could have had and go on. You just disappeared one night and I never knew what happened!"

"You would have stopped me," I said, my voice heavy. "I couldn't let that happen. Don't you see? It *has* to end. The gods are petty nightmares who use children as pawns. If I have to sacrifice myself for the greater good then so be it."

"You walked out on your responsibilities!"

"To fulfill a higher one!"

"Tell that to Darian. It's his son you killed today. He doesn't remember you at all. But he does remember crying for you, for years, wanting to know if it was his fault you went away. He'd just lost his father, and then you left him too."

I turned away from Clara and walked to the window. "I did what I had to do."

"You can't even look at me. You can't even show me your face."

I didn't reply, but remained staring out the window. I hadn't had other choices. Eric had been the other half of my soul. After he'd died, I had gone out every night to the attention to me and thus did not see the child slip a bundle of papers off the shelf near the door on her way out. I was grateful the mask hid my amusement. She'd gotten, completely at random, some of my notes on the legends that hinted at weaknesses the gods had, ones I had collected in my travels. She would, at least, find stories that were strange to her within the pages.

The hidden meanings in those stories would have to wait until she was older. For a brief moment, I was almost sorry I wouldn't be able to guide her through them. The feeling was quickly subsumed by a fresh wave of anger. The life I should have had, the one where I traveled and returned with new stories just to share them, where I would teach her stories just because she liked them, had been stolen from me by the gods.

"Did she tell you her name?" asked Clara.

"No."

"Elica."

I could not keep the sudden pain from my face, though again the mask concealed it. They had combined my name and a feminized version of Eric's—a name that had to have come from Clara, as Elica's mother would have scarcely any memory of me.

"It's not too late, you know," said Clara. "We've lost time, but you could still come home."

"After everything I've been?"

"You think I care about that? You think my life has been worth *anything* since Eric died? I died too, that day."

"And yet you lived long enough to kill others." Clara did not shout. Her voice remained level. "You killed one of Eric's grandsons. You. Not the gods. You think he would have wanted to see you do that?"

"I defended myself from an attack by the gods. His death is another to avenge. He chose to obey, just like Eric did. And he died for it, like Eric did. I was no threat to the village and they chose to send teenagers after me anyway. They always choose to send people who can't possibly accomplish the tasks, and the tasks aren't even important! What kind of gods are those?"

"They're like teachers," said the child. "They make you do things you aren't good at for no reason."

I snorted. "Except your teachers won't kill you and the gods will."

"Do you have a spear like Kylien had? Can I see it?"

"*You* are going to go straight home," said Clara. "Right now. You will wait for me there. If you go somewhere else I will know, and you will not like the consequences."

"But I want to see the spear!"

"Now."

The child pouted, but reluctantly slid off Clara's lap and started for the door. Clara immediately returned her

her granddaughter into her lap, looking suddenly very old. I felt no triumph, only exhaustion of my own. My mask felt less like a shield than a child's hiding place.

"What are you planning, then?" Clara asked. "What's worth killing this many innocents?"

"The gods killed those innocents, not me," I snapped. "And I intend to return the favor."

Clara paled. "It's impossible to kill the gods."

"But you have a story about it!" said the child in Clara's lap. We both stared at her. I'd forgotten how much children *listen*—I'd assumed we were having an argument over her head, and some of it certainly was, but apparently she'd been able to follow enough of it to make it worth paying attention to.

"What story?" asked Clara.

"The one about Kylien Deathseeker."

I laughed at Clara's affronted expression. "Very good. That's the story that started me on what I'm doing too. It's not just a legend, you know. She really did it. I found out how. I'm making a weapon. I wrote everything down, and scattered copies of my notes in my travels so the next one to lose someone to the gods will have more to go on than I did."

"You'll die in the process," said Clara.

"Because she ran away when your mother was young." She looked at me. "What *exactly* did you do?"

"In my defense, I thought she was another one of your hero-children coming to kill me. And I did give her a potion for it; in another half-hour or so it'll be like it never happened."

There was a long pause.

"You haven't changed at all, have you," said Clara. "The rest of us grew up and grew older."

"Not everyone grew older," I snapped back.

"And some of us moved on. You do that, when someone dies."

"If you want to let the gods mindlessly run your life, sure! You grow up, you tell yourself you're skilled and heroic because you survived or not good enough because their eyes never fell on you, and you let the next generation go on."

"It's better than freezing in place and turning into a bitter shadow. You think angry, friendless, and refusing to even show me your face is what Eric would have wanted for you?"

"I think he didn't get a chance to want things for me because he was killed in a petty power struggle!"

There was another long silence, and then Clara slumped a little, and sank down into the room's sole chair. She lifted

"You never came down and told us you were here. You never introduced yourself."

"And this merits sending people to *kill* me?"

"The gods sent people to kill you."

"The gods sent Eric to best a sphinx for no other reason than petty point-scoring. Have you forgotten so quickly that the gods see us as toys? Or are you so determined to infuse his death with meaning that you've convinced yourself their pettiness matters?"

That scored a hit; Clara stiffened slightly and her face took on a fierce cast. I turned and swept back into the cottage. The child was, a bit surprisingly, exactly where I had left her. This became less surprising when I saw the way she was looking at the edge of the table; apparently it was too tall for her to feel she could jump off it safely.

"Grandmama!" she exclaimed as I entered, and I realized Clara had followed behind me. "I was captured by the witch!" She sounded as though she considered this a grand adventure. "And she's that lady from your painting!"

Clara gave the child an exasperated look and walked over to the table. "Her name is Eleanor and she's your mother's godsmother."

"Why don't I know her, then?"

speech in town today made it obvious to anyone who knew you then. Or would, if everyone else weren't so convinced you're the offspring of a demon or other such nonsense. And if you'd known Edmond's lineage, you wouldn't have killed him. If I'd known who you were before he came here, I'd have made sure you knew." The grief was heavy in her voice. "You killed my grandson today, Eleanor. You left me to raise my children on my own when you were their godsmother. At least take off the mask and let me see your face."

I stood, in silence, but made no move to remove the mask. I had left Eleanor behind long ago.

After a time, Clara sighed. "You still go silent, when you don't want to answer the question. I never understood how Eric managed to wait you out."

"Why are you here?" I asked.

"To get my granddaughter."

"You didn't know she was up here until I told you. Try again."

"Because you've apparently been living up here for ten years pretending to be the witch in the fairy tale and killing anyone who got close to you, and once upon a time you were my husband's closest friend."

"I never pretended to be anything. You heard me, when I spoke today. I built a cottage on unclaimed lands, I kept a small herd, and I never bothered anyone."

I was saved from having to answer by a shout from outside the cottage.

"Eleanor! My hands are open and they are empty; I come to speak and not to fight."

The voice was older, but definitely Clara's. I felt a wave of dizziness as memories washed over me. The last time I'd seen Clara she had been shouting at me about how I wasn't the only one who'd lost someone.

I quickly grabbed the dropped mask and tied it on. Conversing with a child with my face exposed was one thing; Clara was another matter.

"Stay there," I whispered to the girl and then moved to the doorway.

Clara was standing in front of my cottage, her hands extended palms-up in front of her.

"I have your granddaughter," I said, attempting to speak in as booming and ominous a voice as possible.

"And you're not going to do anything to Eric's granddaughter when you know that's who she is," she said, her voice infuriatingly calm. "You don't need the mask thing; I know who you are."

"Assumptions lead to death," I said. "I've already killed one of Eric's grandsons today."

She rolled her eyes. "Your voice hasn't changed *that* much since the last time I saw you, and even if it had, that

"I should think everyone went white when I talked. Aren't you all supposed to be terrified of me? That's why the heroes keep coming to kill me."

"Different from everyone else. She didn't talk at all after. She went into the trunk where she keeps Grandpapa's things and pulled out the painting and sat staring at it for a while."

"I bet she didn't show it to you, though."

The child gave me a conspiratorial look. "I was spying."

I managed to maintain a straight face, but it was not easy. Spiritually, she sounded more like she ought to have been my grandchild than Eric's.

"Spying has negative consequences," I informed her.

"I didn't get *hurt*, though. And you helped me after." She paused. "Why didn't you help Edmond, after you blasted him?"

"Is Edmond the boy who was here earlier?"

She nodded. "He's my favorite cousin."

I froze. Clara had had twin children when I'd left. Even if she'd remarried, had other children, there were reasonable odds that I had killed Eric's grandson today.

The gods would *pay* for this.

I wondered what she had been expecting to see. The inside of my cottage was kept neat and clean, with herbs drying from the ceiling and rows of bottles and books on the shelves that lined the room. In the corner opposite the front door was my bed; beside it were two doors, one leading to the pantry and the other to the privy. At the food of the bed was a cedar chest, beside it an armoire. Apart from the house containing far more books than any normal villager owned, it looked like any reasonably neat wisewoman's cottage. Which was more or less what I *was*, gods' enmity notwithstanding, but who knew what stories this child had heard or invented about me? Certainly those stories were terrifying enough that this was the first time I'd ever had problems with children trying to peek at the scary witch, in a decade of living here.

"Grandmama has a painting of you," said the child, breaking into my thoughts. "A little one."

I raised my eyebrows. So this was Clara's granddaughter, then. And possibly Eric's, as well, depending on which of Clara's children she had descended from. If Clara had had other children—she hadn't remarried when I'd left, but who knew what forty years could bring?

"You couldn't have seen my face enough to recognize me in the village, not through the mask from a painting that's fifty years old." I had been in my mid-teens when Eric had painted that portrait. He'd said it was for practice, and so he would always have something of me with him.

"Grandmama went white when you talked."

this new being that had appeared in their midst. I slipped through my small herd and knelt beside her. She was conscious, looking back at me with some interest, but her eyes were unfocused. Definitely a concussion of some form—likely not a severe one; I had pulled my magical blow hard once I'd realized who I was aiming at. It was unlikely she'd be able to walk down to the village for a bit, and I didn't want to go back down there carrying a semiconscious child; *that* was a sure way to get the whole torches-and-pitchforks mob after me rather than just would-be heroes, and while that wouldn't be a complete disaster it would delay my plans and require me to move. So I lifted her into my arms, carried her into the house, and laid her down on the table.

It was the first time I'd had a *living* person laid out on the table. I'd had training in healing—every witch does—and if the priests hadn't singled me out as evil I'd have had live children in my cottage multiple times a week as they brought me their injuries. I always kept all the tinctures ready for most types of injury, knowing that if there had ever been a disaster in the village I would not have been able to resist helping. Now I was glad of my forethought, as it meant I could just pull a bottle off the shelf and carefully drip liquid from it into her mouth, without having to lose time mixing it. She sputtered at first, then swallowed convulsively. After a few minutes I was rewarded as her pupils returned to normal and she began to look around the room with interest.

find them. Eventually the gods would learn better, or they would fall and leave us to govern ourselves.

Once inside, though, I found I could not face another session of working my blood through the metal of the spear. The intentionality it required was, in that moment, beyond me. Instead, I tore off the mask and flung it away, then collapsed into the sole chair and sat exhausted. I hadn't tried to argue with them since before I'd become a witch. They hadn't listened then, to a destroyed young girl who'd lost the only person who'd ever mattered to her. Now they didn't listen to a terrifying masked figure who wielded powers beyond their comprehension. They were nothing if not consistent.

A gasp from the doorway startled me, and I was instantly on my feet in a fighting stance. Sending two would-be heroes in the same day wasn't something the village had ever done before, but I couldn't take chances. I sent my magic lashing out towards whatever had gasped before I saw just *who* was in my doorway: a little girl, no more than seven, who had been peeping in the open door of my cottage. Frantically I pulled on the magic, trying to bring it back. The spell rebounded and exploded in all directions, sending a painful magic-burn through my mental pathways. The force knocked the child out into the garden. I rose, swaying a bit with dizziness from the magic-burn, and headed into the garden.

The child was lying flat on the ground, unmoving. The alpacas, being used to strange explosions, were gathering around her with some interest, leaning down to nudge

"By your own laws, it's not murder if it's self-defense," I said. "You're the one who keeps sending children to kill me!"

"Because you have angered the gods!"

"If I've angered the gods so much, perhaps they should send someone who has a hope of killing me!" I saw him draw himself up as if to go on a tirade and raised my hand to forestall him. "Fine. Follow your gods to your doom and back. Let them call me a monster. Keep trying to kill me. What's a lost son, or five? You can always order the women to make more." Suddenly exhausted, I turned and left the village to trudge back up the hill. Stupid sanctimonious priests, always going on about bowing to the will of the gods. What gods worth following cared so little for the lives of their people? Bow to the will of the gods and wind up dead every time!

I kept myself in good shape, but I was in my sixties and living a fair distance above the village. By the time I reached my cottage my anger had died down to the ever-present background hum I had always experienced. I was nearly finished—had nearly completed the forging of a weapon that could kill a god. Probably not more than one god, but I had lost the things that made life worth living long ago. If I could at least demonstrate that it was possible, it wouldn't matter if I died in the doing. The next young girl who woke up and realized she was meant to be something more than a god's sheep would have my example to know it was possible, and I had left copies of my work scattered through the world where she could

Options

I trudged down the mountain slowly. There would be few people on the village streets this time of day, as many would be in the fields, but they would have known the boy had come to kill me, and the shepherds on the hills knew what it meant when I came down to the village with a body floating behind me. Normally I accompanied this procession with lightning strikes and other intimidating displays to discourage them from all attacking me in a rush of bodies, but this time I was just too tired. This boy had been too young, his death too unnecessary. I had to complete my plans before this could get any worse.

By the time I reached the village square some of the braver ones had gathered around the edges. Children whispered and pointed. I reached the center of the square and slowly lowered the boy's body to lay it down.

Normally I did not speak to them, but this *had* to end.

"I've killed every one you've sent," I said harshly. Those who had gathered jerked back, startled. "I've killed *only* the ones you've sent. I have never brought ill luck onto the village. I have never stolen your livestock. I have never taken your children. So if you have any brains left in your heads, you might consider what sort of gods still feel the need to keep you sacrificing children like this."

"The gods keep us safe," snapped a man in the long red robes of a priest of Zarkanen. "You dare to question that, vile witch?"

His presence was a sign the gods were growing increasingly desperate. They sent children, yes, but it used to be older children. A furious anger filled me as I washed the body. The villagers thought I was showing my contempt for them by returning the bodies so carefully cared for, but that had never had anything to do with it. I respected the children and hurt for them. They usually knew they were hopelessly outclassed in fighting me, and yet they came anyway, chosen by the gods, bolstered with promises of protection that were half lies, never once asking themselves why anything that called itself a god needed to work through a mortal vessel in the first place.

With the blood cleaned away and preservation magics laid, the boy looked as though he was merely sleeping on that table. The sight broke my heart. He should be out thinking about an apprenticeship or working his father's farm, not coming at a witch using a sword. But he'd fallen prey to the gods' blandishments and now here he was. I wrapped myself in my cloak, donned a mask, and set out for the village, levitating the boy's body behind me. The mask was probably unnecessary, but I didn't want to take a chance that there were still some in the village who might remember me. None of the would-be heroic adolescents who'd come after me had ever shown any sign of recognition on seeing my face, but they were of a younger generation.

My fall had come forty years ago and more, when I was still a teen myself.

most of them, it was the only unconditional validation they had ever received.

"You fought so well," I said instead.

He smiled, and closed his eyes. I held his hand as the breath left his body, and only then did I let the tears fall. The heroes were always so young. Vulnerable to the siren call of a god's promises and the resulting gifts of speed or strength or smarts. I had wondered for years why they always chose teenagers. Maybe they just couldn't be assured anyone older wouldn't see through the relationship offered and recognize how one-sided it was.

Either way, my job was now clear. I lifted his body into my arms, using a bit of magic to help with the weight, and carried him into my house.

I don't have minions, or any sort of elaborate castle hideout. I live alone in a small cottage high on a mountain above a village that produces far too many heroes. At the center of the room sat a large stone slab which served as a workspace, and it was on this slab that I laid his body. Then I began to wash the blood from his wounds. This one had been younger than any of the others to come for me. He looked barely sixteen, if that. He was handsome and wearing armor that had once been fine. He had fought well, attacking me so fiercely that I had been forced to kill him. But he had been no match for my powers.

Options

Kit Harding

"It's okay," I murmured, dropping to my knees beside the fallen hero. "You did well. You did so well."

"Supposed to defeat you." He didn't have the strength for more than a whisper.

"I know," I said. "You're still a child. They should never have sent you to fight me."

He bridled at that, for a moment looking fierce despite the terrible injuries to his body. "I had to save them."

"I know." This was not the moment to say that I had never been going to threaten his village. I had knelt over innumerable dying teenagers over the years. It was better to give them some semblance of peace, and validation. For

community and what is the latest trend occupying the martian kids now.

Salt and Flowers sees the return of Jessica Lévai, author of *Starter Culture* from Issue 4, with a couple who are protecting a child from the monsters that live in the woods around their house. But, as always, not everything is as it seems. Julio Angel Ortiz's *Sombra* is a temporal agent who is investigating a case with deeper ties to his past than he realizes. In *The Blackbirds in My Sister's Chest* by Katherine Westermann Alma's sister and best friend is gripped by a mysterious wasting illness. The family reacts with fear, confusion and ultimately denial. Alma is left alone to struggle with the painful realities of helping her sister. And finally *The Last Good Day* is another fantastic story by JL George, who gave us *Osteography* from issue 5. Trapped in her home as the world falls apart outside, Dani tries to remember the last good day she had. It's harder than she expects.

The end of this pandemic is slowly creeping closer, quicker in some places than others. As I write this the small-o variant is threatening to not be affected by our current vaccines. Vaccines are needed for the whole world, not just us rich nations. Stay safe until I see you all again in **April** for Issue 8.

— Paul Campbell *Dundee, Scotland, November 2021*

I am also proud to be able to say that we are now an official sponsor of FIYAH. They are a quarterly speculative fiction magazine that features stories by and about Black people in the African Diaspora. They do so much more to help underrepresented authors than I will ever be able to, so I am happy, and humbled, to be able to help them to do that.

This brings us to 2022 and our shift from three issues a year to four. The next issue will be out in April 2022. It's a small change, shortening the time between each issue by a month. Interestingly, becoming an at-least-quarterly magazine brings us into the semi-pro zine category. Should anyone feel that we should deserve a nomination... *hint-hint*

On to our stories for this issue. We open with *Options* by Kit Harding. A witch defeats an unprepared and misguided hero and is forced to face her past and the choices she has made. In Izzy Wasserstein's *Shadows of the Hungry, the Broken, the Transformed* Justine is haunted by her own severed shadow and the loss of her girlfriend, while civil unrest escalates around her. *Normalization* by Xauri'EL Zwaan follows after a terrible accident that kills most of a collective, a member of this hive-mind races to the side of the one other surviving member, who has gone silent. Juliet Kemp's *Opening Doors* looks at death, justice, community and redemption on a Martian colony as Erin faces her own mortality, what considerations can be taken for a murderer in a small

Editorial

Welcome to the seventh issue of *Cossmass Infinities* and the start of our third year. When I started the magazine back in October 2019, and the first submissions started to come flooding in, I had some doubts that I could manage all the reading that was required. I had a little panic and closed the submissions after only a week. A lot sooner that I had originally planned. The panic passed and I was able to find the eight gems I wanted to create that first issue.

I managed it once, I could do it again. I started work on the second issue and opened up for more submissions.

After about six months I found a routine that I could maintain, with a regular submissions window at the start of every month. Not long after, while watching the *#BlackLivesMatter* protests over in America, and learning more of the history of short story genre publishing, I resolved to improve how *Cossmass Infinites* was able to represent Black, Asian, Latin, LGBTQ+, and other under-represented authors. I didn't want to make a one-off submissions call, then forget to do it again. So, I baked it into my schedule. Every other month, the submission window is exclusively for those authors whose voices had been ignored for too long.

185 The Blackbirds in My Sister's Chest
Katherine Westermann
Fantasy - 6059 words

213 The Last Good Day
JL George
Science Fiction - 4896 words

Contents

11 Options
Kit Harding
Fantasy - 4197 words

31 Shadows of the Hungry, the Broken, the Transformed
Izzy Wasserstein
Fantasy - 9495 words

73 Normalization
Xauri'EL Zwaan
Science Fiction - 4947 words

93 Opening Doors
Juliet Kemp
Science Fiction - 3508 words

111 Salt and Flowers
Jessica Lévai
Fantasy - 5244 words

133 Sombra
Julio Angel Ortiz
Science Fiction - 9443 words

https://www.cossmass.com/

Cossmass Infinities Issue 7 ©2022 by Paul Campbell

ISBN 9798772219201

Cover Art by Grandfailure

Title Font "Snowslider" designed by Samy Halim

Options ©2022 by Kit Harding
Shadows of the Hungry, the Broken, the Transformed ©2022 by Izzy Wasserstein
Normalization ©2022 by Xauri'EL Zwaan
Opening Doors ©2022 by Juliet Kemp
Salt and Flowers ©2022 by Jessica Lévai
Sombra ©2022 by Julio Angel Ortiz
The Blackbirds in My Sister's Chest ©2022 by Katherine Westermann
The Last Good Day ©2022 by JL George

The right of the individual authors to be identified as the authors of this work has been asserted in accordance with the Copyright, Designs and Patents Act 1988.

All rights reserved. No part of this publication may be reproduced, stored in a retrieval system, or transmitted, in any form or by any means, electronic, mechanical, photocopying, recording or otherwise, without prior permission of the copyright owners.

Cossmass Infinities

Issue 7

January 2022

Magazine of Science Fiction and Fantasy Stories

Edited by Paul Campbell

https://www.cossmass.com/

Cossmass Infinities

Issue 7

ONE

A young woman's raw screams tore through the icy fabric of the mid-winter dawn. Marielle's chest tightened at the sound, and she forgot about the sleepless night she'd spent, and the thrumming pain behind her eyes. Tea sloshed all over the table and spilled onto her lap, scalding her hands and legs as she slammed her mug down and jumped up.

She jammed her feet into her leather boots and sprinted out the back door before her father even had his coat on.

"You're sick! Stay in the house, stupid girl!" he yelled after her, but she was already running for the barn.

The right segment of the heavy double-winged door stood quarter of the way open. The screaming stopped.

No warmth on her face when she reached for the latch. No shuffling of hooves or flapping of wings. No bleating, and no happy snorts and panting as she stepped inside. Only the stench of excrements and fear.

Her insides heaved. The byre was a mess of blood and entrails. It took her a mere second to fully understand what had happened here, and she retched into the straw.

A goat's leg lay to the left of the small window, another by the haybox, and the animal's head was

1

inside the manger, dull eyes bulging and tongue drooping from its half-open mouth. Its hide sprawled beside the door, as if someone had spread it out there and meant to take it later but forgotten.

The carcass of the Reindl family's cow hung suspended from one of the rafters, carelessly stripped of its flesh. The two geese were gone, save for their heads, and someone had sliced open old Charlotte's belly.

Marielle had grown up with that dog — she'd gotten her as a puppy, and the old lady should have been in the house last night, but Michel had forbidden Marielle to take her inside. Charlotte had lost most of her sight and control of her bladder over the past few weeks, and Barbara, who'd never liked her, had been complaining about the puddles in the kitchen.

The maid was still wailing and kneading her sweaty hands as she ran from one end of the barn to the other, hair pasted to her skull, and calling on all the saints. Marielle couldn't bring herself to go to her and comfort her. Right now, it was all she could do not to hate her.

"Damn gypsies," Michel muttered from behind Marielle, shoving her aside.

He grabbed Barbara by the shoulders and shook her. "Get a grip, woman!"

The young maid howled even louder, and Michel slapped her across the face several times before she fell silent. Michel scowled at her, forcing her to look at him, and she probably decided that she had more to fear from her employer than she did from the remains of the dead animals, because she stayed quiet. He finally let go of her and pushed her at Marielle.

To Marielle's horror, Barbara's clammy, hot palm closed around her hand, and she pressed her feverish face against her shoulder. Marielle didn't feel like offering reassurance and crudely shrugged her off. More sobbing, and silent tears spilled down the front of Barbara's dress.

Michel hunkered down to inspect the straw beneath the cow's carcass, as though the congealed blood could tell him what, exactly, had happened here. He rubbed a few smears of it between his fingers and Marielle suspected he was trying to guess at what point during the night the animals had been slaughtered.

Next, his gaze wandered up to the roof, where the storm had wrenched loose a number of shingles, leaving a rectangular hole and a clear view of the sky in one place.

Marielle wanted to kneel beside him to stroke Charlotte's clotted fur, but she dared not. His face was white as a church wall, and she didn't know what he would do.

She became aware of the scuffle of feet outside and spun around, half expecting to see some kind of monster, troll, or devil, but it was only her mother, closely followed by little Susi. She quickly turned, barring their way, but then Barbara almost bowled them all over, vomiting as she ran from the barn.

Johanna's eyes widened as she took in the carnage. She pushed her youngest daughter behind her, one hand clamped over her eyes.

"No need for Susi to be here," she told Marielle in a trembling voice, and sent them both out into the yard. Then she faced her husband. "What's going on?"

"Damn gypsies," he mumbled, "that's what's going on."

"You don't know that," Marielle's mother hissed and added something so softly Marielle couldn't hear.

"Shut up!" Michel picked up a handful of soiled straw, rose, and flung it at the wall right beside Johanna's head. "I paid that debt a long time ago. And what do you think we're going to live off in the spring, or eat next winter? *Gratitude*?"

Johanna hurried to close the door, but it jammed on a loose brick or a clump of dirt. "We don't need the cow or the geese."

"The cow and the geese are bad enough!" Michel gesticulated at the empty stall where their Wallach, Gustav, should have been. "But those gypsy-vermin took the *horse* that plows our fields."

"We don't know it was the travelers," Johanna repeated quietly.

Michel rubbed a hand over his brow, jaw clenched, and then formed a fist. For a second, Marielle thought he was going to hit her mother, but he didn't.

"They stole the Habermanns' hens last week," he said as if he were speaking to a dimwit who was trying his patience. "No tracks at the Habermanns' place, no tracks here. Not a single footprint." He motioned out the door, ignoring the girls.

Marielle's glance wandered across the yard and the almost immaculate blanket of snow on the cobblestone pavement. Her father was right. The only tracks here were their own. If anyone had been here last night and taken all that meat, they would have needed a cart, at least, or eight strong men to carry the load on their backs. There should have been *lots* of footprints and tracks inside the yard because Michel had cleared the snow that had fallen all through the previous day with his shovel before he'd gone to bed.

"Habermann told me he found one of his birds running around the woods near their camp," he continued. "That was the day before yesterday. Voigt and his clever councilmen still haven't done anything about it. But they will now, mark my words."

Johanna didn't challenge him, and he stomped past her, yelling at Barbara on his way to the house. "Stop your whining, you useless wench, and help my wife and daughter clean up that mess!"

Then he grabbed Susi's arm and marched her back toward the house, muttering, "And you, young lady, are going to stay inside and do your chores until your mama tells you it's all right to come back out."

"I didn't tell the woman our names," Susi said out of the blue.

Michel stopped dead. "What woman?"

Susi's glance darted back and forth between her sister and her father. Her lips quivered.

Marielle didn't want Michel to make her answer. "One of the gypsy women came to sell trinkets last week," she said, "and to ask if we had pots that needed mending. But we didn't let her in."

In her grandmother's day, they would have. No one mended pots or kettles better or cheaper than the tinkers, the old lady had once told her. They came through these parts every year, and every year since grandma's death they'd turned them away at the door, though Marielle thought that the gypsies who had set up camp near Grainau a week ago were a different family than those who'd been there the previous years.

"There you have it," Michel said, glaring at Johanna. "They were getting a good look around while one of them was distracting the girls. And where were *you* while all this was going on?"

"It was only an elderly woman," Marielle said, irritated. "Charlotte would have let me know if—"

"That mutt was deaf!" he told her, eyes blazing.

"I didn't tell the gypsy woman our names," Susi said again. Tears welled from her eyes.

Michel looked down at her sternly, but this was Susi, and some of his anger melted away. He could never stay mad at her for long.

"This isn't your fault," he said. "It doesn't matter whether or not you told her your name or anyone else's. They do magic with names, but they don't need a name to steal livestock and ruin good, honest Christian people. Now get back into the house, child."

He gave her a little push that told her he meant it, but she cast Marielle a questioning glance over her shoulder, sobbing. Michel's lips narrowed to a thin line, and Marielle could tell that it bothered him, but he said nothing.

"Go on," she mouthed to the girl.

She didn't want to undermine her father any further than she already had, and this disaster wasn't something a girl her age should have to look at too closely. This wasn't something *any* of them should have to deal with, but here they were.

The knacker who was responsible for Breitenau and the other villages surrounding Garmisch was obliged to come for the carcasses if they sent for him, but Herbert Mandl was known to take his time, and it wouldn't do to leave the cadavers here for very long. They had to handle this themselves as quickly as possible, and put up with Mandl's tantrum afterward.

He'd charge them for the transport anyway, whether he came for the remains or not, and they would have to pay him, even if he'd never set foot on their property. It was his right. Michel wouldn't be happy about it, but he couldn't be *much* more unhappy than he was now anyway, could he?

Marielle watched him march off down the lane without looking back, pulling his coat tighter around him against the icy wind. He was a proud man who'd

seen a lot of setbacks over these past hard years, and he liked to pretend it was him alone against the world.

Johanna finally managed to dislodge the door. She opened it all the way, then pushed the other segment back on its hinges, and took a handkerchief from her sleeve.

"Poor Bella," she said, dabbing at her pale lips and eyes. "That milk would have been good to have."

Marielle nodded, watching Michel plod off down the lane, but she wouldn't miss the milk and butter as much as she'd miss Charlotte. She swiped at a tear of her own and sniffed. Her headache was ten times as bad as it had been when she'd dragged herself out of bed this morning, and she was almost numb from the cold, but the work would busy her hands and warm her up.

TWO

It took them a good part of the early morning to scrub the blood off the walls and get the tools and troughs, fodder boxes, and anything else that may have been soiled out of the barn to clean them. They loaded the blood-soaked straw onto the cart, and Barbara fetched the neighbor's aging nag to pull the little wagon out onto one of the nearby fields so they could burn the spoiled straw.

Some tinder and a few oil-drenched rags got a good fire going. Marielle gazed into the blaze for a time, losing herself in the colors of the heat; the flecks of ultramarine and lighter shades of blue wavering at the center of the orange and red flames, and the yellow fleeting sparks that danced above them. She stayed until the ashes blew across the snowy meadow, streaking it black.

Around noon, Oliver Wasl sent his son, Caspar, along to help them with Belle's remains, since Michel hadn't returned yet. Marielle supposed her father would be drinking at one of the taverns after he'd talked to Voigt. She could only hope he wasn't getting everyone there riled up.

Caspar heaved Bella's and the goat's carcasses onto the cart and helped her scoop the remaining entrails into some old flour sacks. Finally, only Charlotte's body was left.

"Can't we bury her?" Marielle asked him, swallowing the lump in her throat, but she knew she wasn't being fair.

Pity glinted in the corner of his eyes, and she was sure he might have said yes any other time of the year, but it was generally against the law to bury anything larger than a rat near the village. Charlotte was too big, and right now the topsoil was frozen solid beneath the snow. Voigt would have them both in the stocks if he found out. This wasn't Caspar's mess, and she had no business asking him. He was already doing more than enough for her family.

"I'm sorry," Caspar said. "I'd put her in the vault if animals were allowed."

Marielle nodded quietly. Their village had a receiving vault, but it was for the human casualties of the dark season, not for pets. There was no place in warm rooms for sick dogs, and there was no place in cold ones for dead dogs.

He laid Charlotte on the wagon with all the gentleness of someone who understood the loss of a friend, and Johanna covered her with a blanket.

"It *couldn't* have been the gypsies," Marielle told her softly while Caspar was busy hitching his father's old horse up.

Johanna tilted her head. "They're travelers who move from place to place, and they take what they want along the way."

Marielle could tell her mother wasn't convinced. She wouldn't have fought her father on the issue if she was. He needed someone to blame, and her mother dared not disagree with him twice in one day. Michel wasn't a cruel man, but he made use of his rights in his house, and Johanna tried hard to please him.

"They're poor, not stupid," Marielle said.

"Voigt might disagree with that in light of what's been going on here," Johanna said firmly, studying Marielle. "If it wasn't the travelers, people might say it was witches, and if the council sends for the witch-finder, then God help us all, so mind you keep your opinions to yourself."

The witch-finder… God help us all.

Marielle knew what the hangmen and witch-finders Joerg Abriel and Christian of Biberach had done here not so long ago. She also knew that some families in the village struggled more than others nowadays, and the winters here were long. But that didn't make it right, of course.

Michel would make sure that the Garmisch burgomaster would have the bailiff and his deputies arrest at least two or three of the gypsy men and have them tortured until they confessed to anything they were accused of. Then he would have them hanged to frighten the rest of the travelers off.

If they were lucky, no one else's hens or geese would go missing once they were gone. But who could say where this would end?

The bishop of Freising didn't care what went on as long as the earldom in his charge kept filling his

pockets. He dined well on their venison, and the marble his miners dug out of the earth in Werdenfels adorned churches and cathedrals all over the Holy Roman Empire. His philosophy was that any kind of trouble was best dealt with swiftly so his laborers could get on with their work.

The bishop's representative hadn't set foot in Garmisch in all his life. He made no secret of the fact that he didn't like the area and would never take up residence in the deteriorating stronghold that guarded the main trade road. Last they'd heard from his clerk, he was currently on his way to some island in the Mediterranean to tend to his delicate health. No help could be expected from him either.

Marielle felt sorry for the travelers, but ultimately, she had to admit to herself that her mother was right – the Reindls had other worries. Getting through the cold season without their meagre livestock would be manageable, but the cow would be difficult to replace in spring, if they could afford it at all. The goat had been their luxury, and not *that* important, but losing their Wallach was a fiasco.

Seeing Charlotte on the back of the cart was only Marielle's personal disaster. She almost felt guilty for grieving for her dog, but she'd loved her.

She understood why someone who was possibly watching their family starve would steal their geese and butcher their cow, and she could even imagine why they would take their horse – stupid move though it was, since Gustav had a star-shaped white patch on his back that would identify him anywhere in these parts – but why would anyone kill a sick old mutt like that? They could have just cut her throat or throttled her. Instead, some evil soul had made her suffer, and the shrieking wind had covered up her howls of pain. A bitter mixture of helplessness and anger boiled inside her, and she fought to swallow it down.

"Change out of those dirty clothes and give them to me before you leave," Johanna told her. "I've got some washing to do while you're gone anyway."

She faced Caspar. "I'll leave you a clean shirt and a pair of my husband's pants in the barn for when you get back. I'd like to wash your things as well. I don't want your mother to have to do it. You can give me your coat before you go home. I don't have a spare one that'll fit you, but I'll give you a blanket to get you there. I'll wash everything and dry it by the fire tonight, so you'll have your clothes back in the morning."

She'd already filled the stone basin in the yard with water from the well, and some of Barbara's things were soaking in the icy water.

"I bet it was the gypsies. There are some pretty shady characters out at that camp, if you ask me," Caspar said, wiping his hands on a rag after he'd washed them. "Just think about it. Your mother's right. If you talk like that and ask too many questions, people will think you're accusing one of them, and then they'll start accusing each other."

Marielle avoided looking at him. "I see."

There was no sense in arguing with him even if she didn't agree. But she had to admit that it would have taken no less than magic to pull this off – or so it would seem. And this aspect was what her father would be propagating down at the tavern. Plenty of the regulars he drank with were superstitious old fools who would believe him.

Still, she had the strange notion that this was different than what had happened at the Habermanns' farm. The Habermanns' hens had disappeared, not a feather left in the coop, but no one had touched the rabbits they kept in hutches right next to their hen house. Their dog and cat were alive, and Sebastian's cows were both still there as well.

Maybe the culprits were not one and the same, or surely they would have taken those cottontails. Rabbits were so much easier to steal than hens. Less ruckus – less risk of being caught.

Marielle was lost in thought and heartache as she and Caspar led the horse into the woods with Barbara slowly plodding along behind the cart as their involuntary chaperone.

In summer, Caspar had asked Michel for permission to court Marielle, but her father had turned him down, and he hadn't let Marielle out of the house without someone to look out for her virtue since. Most of the time this was Barbara, and Marielle knew she hated it. They both did.

Not that she had any intention of running off with Caspar Wasl, of all people. He wasn't hard on the eyes, and he'd always been friendly to her, but the Wasls were broke. Between the dry summers and the harsh winters of the past few years, they'd had to sell most of their land, and the only thing Caspar and she had in common was their birthday.

She rather liked the idea of marrying someone like Harald Habermann next year, if her father approved. Michel thought highly of the Habermanns, and he and Harald got along well. Granted, Harald was a beer-drinker and hated the wine her father loved, but unlike Caspar, he didn't skip out on his chores on the farm, nor did he run off into the mountains whenever he was supposed to help on the fields. He'd often come to help on theirs as well over the past summer and autumn, and Michel acknowledged that.

Marielle had spent more time with him recently than anyone was aware of. He was better at sneaking around and keeping secrets than Caspar. They'd even managed to meet in the barn alone a few nights ago before she'd gotten ill.

They'd shared a piece of his mother's apple pie and talked about this and that, and then they'd kissed. He'd made her compliments and told her how beautiful she was. It had been wonderful right up until Barbara had ruined it for them. She'd burst in and started making a scene just when he'd confessed his love and things had gotten heated. But she hadn't told on them.

Marielle had a feeling that their maid had a thing for Harald, too, and as much as she'd have enjoyed getting Marielle in trouble, she didn't want Harald to think badly of her. Heaven knew, Barbara didn't have a hope in hell where Harald was concerned. For as long as she could remember, he'd called her *Crabby Barbie*, and made fun of her big nose.

Along the way to the knacker's yard, *Crabby Barbie* kept falling farther and farther behind her and Caspar, alternately complaining, muttering prayers under her breath and calling to them, making them wait for her. Marielle wished she would just shut up and go back home. At one point, they lost sight of her entirely.

Caspar had enough sense to let it go and be quiet, content to look out for birds, like he often did when he was out and about. He was likely the only boy in the entire area who could tell you the name of *any* feathered thing you pointed out to them without having to think about it.

As they trudged on, his gaze often wandered to the sky. A magnificent bird of prey was circling, perhaps a red kite. Its feathers reflected the rare sunbeams in a way Marielle had never seen before. It seemed to be searching for quarry. Nature was dazzling out here, and Caspar had an eye for it, but he was a dreamer who'd never make ends meet.

The new snow made for a difficult few miles through the forest. In places, they had trouble guiding the horse around the drifts. Marielle felt feverish, her head pounded, and her sweat-drenched underclothes clung to her beneath her dress and coat. The icy spurs of the previous night's storm had her shivering, and she just wanted this wretched day over with.

A little way beyond the forest and well outside the Breitenau village boundaries, Herbert Mandl's house nestled between two tall pines and a crooked old oak tree. His property was in the middle of a wind-swept meadow where nothing grew in summer, and snow turned gray in winter, long since abandoned by the farmer who'd once tended it.

The main building had started out as a one-room hovel when Mandl's great grandfather first settled in the area. It had been added to with each generation since, and to Marielle, it looked like a child's drawing of a house rather than a proper home. Perhaps it hadn't been one in a long time. Mandl's wife had left him many years ago, and she'd taken their child with her. Heartbroken, he'd never married again and barely managed on his own.

Behind the house, several more equally unplanned-looking buildings huddled together around a messy yard: a tumbledown barn, a large L-shaped shed, a crooked building Mandl called his *workshop*, the stable where his horses sheltered in winter, and a large kennel. Several dogs were chained to a post in the yard most of the day, and they barked viciously whenever someone ventured too close to the property.

The sickly-sweet smell of decay and foul eggs hung in the air and grew more intense the closer

Marielle and Caspar came to the knacker's house. Bitter bile rose in her throat when they passed one of the pits on the field where Mandl buried the remains he couldn't burn or sell. She felt ill before they even reached the wattle fence surrounding his herb garden, and the sound of Caspar's voice calling her name was nothing but a distant whisper over the din of the wail in her ears. She doubled over and vomited, and she couldn't seem to recover.

Caspar hurried to help her, but he was too slow and couldn't catch her before she fell headlong into the snow, world spinning out of control. The last thing she saw before losing consciousness was a burst of flames, even though there was no fire alight anywhere nearby.

THREE

She woke up on a hard dirt floor with the taste of smoke and ashes in her mouth, and a strange play of light and darkness all around her. The damp, icy air churned in front of her as she coughed. Her head throbbed, and her arms and legs hurt. Her skin felt too tight one second, crushing her, and too loose the next. Then it started tingling, and she realized she was naked.

Her teeth chattered. Slowly, she got up off the floor. Where was she and how on earth had she gotten here?

Her eyes gradually adjusted, and her surroundings took on shape. She recognized the curved form of the wooden supports that held the gables, and the panels that separated – *had* separated – Gustav from Bella and the geese.

There was a new, huge hole in the roof above her right next to the one where the storm had damaged the wooden shingles the night before. Its ragged edges were burning despite the snow dripping down from them, and the beams next to it were smoldering.

Noise and shouting penetrated the walls. Her father's frantic voice boomed, and someone answered. A child screamed, then fell silent.

The threadbare coat her mother had worn while they were clearing out the carcasses in the morning

hung from a nail on one of the supports. Marielle hurriedly slipped it on and made her way to the door. It jammed, like it had in the morning. She shook and rattled it, pitched herself against it, and howled in frustration, but it wouldn't budge, and no one seemed to hear her.

The barn's only window was located high up in the wall. She found a pail to step on so she could reach it and battered the shutters with her fists until the hinges tore loose. They fell down the other side, and she hoisted herself up and squeezed through the empty frame. She managed to turn inside the opening so she wouldn't topple out head-first onto the cobblestone pavement, but she didn't land gently all the same, and her knees and shins lost a lot of skin.

The air in the yard was heavy with smoke, and a surreal scene unfolded in front of her. Flurries of black and silver flakes swirled everywhere, dancing like dark fairies and ghosts around a bonfire, but the *bonfire* was where her father's house and their woodshed should have been, and the flakes weren't snowflakes – they were soot and embers.

Her neighbors and other people she couldn't identify were trying to combat the flames, but the fire had already peeled away the roof of her family's home. It was gnawing at the building's half-timbered walls with its searing-sharp teeth, hissing, spitting out bits left and right, and roaring like a wild animal with the pure pleasure of it. Only the stone chimney defied the monster's rage, standing tall amid the blaze.

Not far from the well and the stone basin in the yard lay a crumpled figure, barely moving in the dirty snow. At first, Marielle believed it was her dog, but then she remembered Charlotte was dead. She took a cautious step forward. Her heart missed a beat when she identified her sister, and she broke into a run, sliding on the slippery cobblestones.

Clumps of partly frozen slush cut into the soles of her feet and ripped at her knees as she went down on them beside the whimpering form. The stink of charcoal and sulfur mixed in with the wood smoke. It told Marielle that at least portions of the child's skin and hair were burned.

She rolled Susi over and stroked back strands of matted hair from her filthy face. On impulse, the child groped at the angry red and black patches on her forehead and right cheek, yelping with pain.

"Susi!" Marielle called, not knowing where to touch her. "Can you hear me?"

Susi looked at her from tear-filled eyes. For a moment, Marielle thought her sister would try to sit up and throw her arms around her, but instead, she screamed.

"Papa!" the child wailed, scurrying backward and away from Marielle. "Papa, help me!"

Marielle tumbled on her backside. She didn't know what to say. What was going on here? Was the girl hurt so badly that she was out of her mind and imagining things?

"Susi, no, listen, it's *me*, Marielle…"

In an aching need to comfort her sister, she got up on her knees and tried to reach out to Susi, but her hands wouldn't obey her. She wanted to tell her sister everything was going to be all right, but the truth was, she didn't know if it would be. Susi was terrified of something, perhaps of *her*. But why?

"You set fire to everything!" Susi cried again.

What did the child mean by that? Marielle's heart pounded as though it were about to burst, and she pressed her fists against her temples as Susi's keening rose in pitch and volume. Relief flooded her veins when, from the corner of her eye, she saw Michel running toward them. Then she realized he was wielding a pitchfork and getting ready to use it.

"Get away from her!" he bellowed, voice distorted, face a grotesque mask of hate laced with a thin thread of fear. "Get *away*!"

Marielle barely recognized him. "Papa!" she called. "It's me, Marielle!"

"I'll kill you!" he shouted at her. "I swear, I'm going to kill you!"

Was he drunk? Had he gone mad? He was a good father, and she couldn't believe what was going on when he jabbed at her with the fork. He really meant to murder her.

"Damn you, demon!" he screamed over the roar of the fire, thrusting the fork at her again and again with all his strength.

She managed to keep moving and steer clear of its prongs. The metal clanged against the cobblestones, bending every time he missed. Eventually several of the prongs broke off and the wood splintered, but that didn't stop him. He kept after her.

Marielle had to get out of this place, but she couldn't gather her legs under her well enough to get up out of the slippery slush and avoid being stabbed at the same time. She begged him to stop but the only sounds her lips could form drowned in the bedlam.

"Now I've got you!" he yelled, backing her against the cart that lay on its side in the middle of the yard. He towered over her and took aim. "To hell with you!"

There was nowhere left to go. She drew her knees against her chest and wrapped her arms around her head, for all the good it would do her. She tried to picture her mother and pretended Johanna was holding her. The next time Michel brought what was left of his fork down, rusty metal and splintered wood would plunge her into an ocean of pain, and then it would be over. This was the night she was going to die.

Michel thrust the fork at her. Its remaining crooked prongs sliced through the air toward her arms and head – but they never met their mark.

A pinpoint of golden light exploded behind Marielle's eyes and bloomed out into a supernova brighter than the sun. The energy radiated out from her and threw Michel back like a ragdoll. The

pulsating pain in her head ceased, and she regained control of her legs. She didn't think she could run, but she got up, and her vantage point shifted so abruptly and without her willful control, it stopped the breath in her lungs. She wasn't just on her feet, she was rising up into the sky. Her mother's coat disintegrated and fell to the ground in a rain of dust and ashes. An instant later, she saw Susi and her father from above.

Michel stared up at her, jaw unhinged, and time seemed to stand still for the space of a few heartbeats. Then he dropped the pitchfork and pulled his youngest daughter up off the ground, crushing her to his chest as he bolted for the woods.

Some of the neighbors who'd been trying to save the farmhouse had been watching them, keeping their distance. Seeing Michel run, two of the Wasl brothers abandoned all hope of putting the fire out. They followed him into the forest like frightened rabbits, trying to drag Caspar along, but he stood rooted to the ground, just staring in morbid fascination. Strangely, she thought she might be the first feathered thing he couldn't name.

The Habermann boys felt braver. All of them but Harald were there. They launched stones at her, and anything else they could find. A large rock hit her square on the belly, but it bounced straight off and back to the lad who'd pitched it – only red-hot and hissing. It set fire to his coat. He shrieked, flinging himself into the snow.

Thomas Habermann, the eldest of the Habermann boys, hurtled a hunting knife at her, and it barely missed her face. She had to flee, but she didn't know how, or where to go. Caught in the mayhem of the worst nightmare she'd ever had – this *had* to be a nightmare – she twisted and turned haplessly in the air until something finally gave, and she gained a minimum of control over herself. An outrageous surge of power coursed through her, and she rocketed upward and out of harm's way.

An idea formed in her mind: she would head for the river. When they were children, she and half the young men down there had played along the banks of the Loisach, like most Breitenau children, watching the raftsmen, trying to catch a few fish, and exploring the woods. She knew all the landings and all the storage and weather shelters. Something told her that no one would follow her there tonight. Not in the dark.

She moved at a breathtaking speed and circled the barn once to get her bearings. Then she dipped, scattering the Habermann brothers like hens, and soared through the flames that were consuming the house where she'd been born. They rose to meet her, lapping at her body, but their heat did not sear her. Like a salve on a sore, it felt pleasant on her skin.

She surged toward the woods, unaware of the trail of sparks she was leaving in her wake. They lit up the darkness, fell to the earth, and drew patterns into the snow, melting it, boiling it, and cooking the dead

grass and moss beneath. The Habermann brothers did not give chase.

Blind with sorrow and confusion, she entrusted herself to the howling wind, and whatever other forces were taking her away from her burning home and the people she loved – the people who were supposed to be her family and friends, neighbors and childhood playmates. She could never harm them, but a wild, strange instinct told her that if she stayed, more of them would suffer.

FOUR

Swathed in darkness and mist, more than a dozen caravans crowded a clearing in the woods near the banks of the river Loisach just outside of Breitenau. Horses snorted somewhere close by, and hooves scuffed at the frozen ground.

Marielle hadn't made it as far as she'd hoped. Covered in bleeding scratches and bruises, she found herself stumbling toward one of the firepits that still held some of the previous night's glowing embers beneath the ashes.

Shivering, she hunkered down as close as possible to the circle of smooth river stones and carefully put her hands on one of them. She couldn't decide whether they were merely warm or much too hot. Her fingers and feet were numb with the cold, and she was going to freeze to death if she didn't find some way of warming up and covering herself.

A huge mongrel slunk out from under one of the wagons, startling her, but it didn't growl or bark, and Marielle wasn't afraid of big dogs. Cautiously, the animal moved closer until it was right next to her, head down, tail wagging, as if to greet an old friend. It sniffed her arms, licked her face, and buried its nose in her hair.

Thankful, Marielle leaned into it, relishing its soft fur and glad for the extra warmth. Through its panting

and snuffling next to her, she didn't hear that someone else had noticed her arrival and was approaching from behind.

"Here, girl," a woman's soft voice said.

Marielle felt a nudge, and a blanket was draped around her shoulders. Her stomach lurched. She couldn't bring herself to look up, and the blanket slipped off her as she edged away, awkwardly trying to conceal her breasts and privates with her hands and arms.

"Don't be afraid," the woman said, allowing Marielle to put some distance between them. "No one will harm you here."

Clouds concealed the moon, and Marielle couldn't see much beyond the shifting shadows by the firepit, but shades of gray painted the outline of a crone into the night, frail and bent, and nowhere near as tall as her.

An odd sense of familiarity overcame her, and her gut told her that the old woman didn't pose a threat any more than the dog did. She looked around and listened for movement, but no one else seemed to be awake, and the camp remained quiet.

The woman offered her the blanket again. Marielle felt her dark eyes studying her.

"Silly child," the crone mumbled, teasing her, and speaking in a heavy accent that belonged nowhere Marielle had ever been. "Go on. Take it so you won't freeze. Then you can stay and say thank you, or run off back into the woods. It's all the same to me, but I won't have you dying on my doorstep."

Marielle hesitated for a moment, but in the end she took the blanket and tried to cover as much of herself with it as possible. The dog took this as a cue and pressed against her once more.

"Good," the woman said. "Now, what will it be? Will you stay and come inside my caravan with me, because I'm certainly not going to stand out here all night, or will you leave and go back to wherever it is you came from?"

Marielle took too long to think about it. Her mind felt as numb as her legs did. The old woman turned to leave.

"Wait," Marielle said. "Wait for me. Give me shelter for the night if you can."

The woman glanced back over her shoulder at her and nodded, motioning Marielle to follow her.

The caravan was warm inside, and it smelled of chicken soup. The old gypsy lit an oil lamp, limiting the airflow straightaway so it wouldn't give off too much light. Marielle immediately saw why: at the front of the caravan, farthest from the door and the little stove in the corner, several children slept beneath a pile of furs and a patchwork quilt on a wide bed. Above them, a picture of the ocean.

A cabinet with floral patterns on its painted doors stood next to one of the windows, and an ornately carved barrel-lid trunk beneath the other one opposite.

In the middle of the room, a table and a rocking chair huddled together on a soft woven rug.

One of the children stirred in the bed, eyes only half open. "Puridaia?"

"Hush. Go back to sleep, little one," the old woman said, and the child's head sank back into the pillow.

She turned to Marielle, and for the first time, Marielle saw her creased face clearly. She was the traveler-woman who'd come to her family's house the previous week, asking if they needed anything repaired, but she'd looked so much younger then. Maybe it was only the artificial light drawing lines and furrows in much darker colors than the sunlight would. Or perhaps Marielle simply hadn't been paying attention.

The old woman smiled and knelt to rummage around in the trunk. "What do they call you?" she asked.

Marielle sat down beside the stove. If she could have, she would have crawled inside. She was still considering whether it was wise to tell a gypsy her name when the woman handed her woolen socks and undergarments.

"You're Puridaia?" Marielle asked, ignoring her question.

The old woman laughed. "To them I am." She gestured to the children. "Though I no longer have sons and daughters of my own to give me grandbabies. If you like, you can call me Puridaia, too."

Marielle nodded. She had initially assumed *Puridaia* was a name, though now she rather thought it must be a word in the gypsy language. It seemed impolite to ask, however, since she wasn't going to reveal her own name.

She stared at the stockings and underwear. "I can't take these. I have nothing to give you in return."

Puridaia sighed. "What are you going to do? Stay naked?"

What *was* she going to do? "You don't understand." She was whispering now. "I can't repay you."

She knew she shouldn't be here. The heat from the stove felt so good, but it was making her drowsy. She wanted to go home. Susi was hurt, and she had to find out what had happened to her mother, but her father had tried to kill her, and she couldn't figure out why. What had she done to make him so mad at her, and why had everyone started throwing stones at her? With things as they were, she didn't have a home to go back to. She had nothing left in all the world.

"You're wrong," the old woman said, pushing the clothes at her. "You have more than you think. You have a name. Now, which one did your mother give you?"

Marielle looked at her feet. She didn't truly believe she had anything to lose by telling the woman, but Johanna had made her promise she wouldn't tell her name to *any* gypsy who came to their door. She would not break her promise now.

Puridaia sighed as though she understood. "All right then. I will call you Aurica – Golden One." She took hold of Marielle's hand. "I saw you earlier. Your aura is golden, child, did you know that?"

Marielle gave a little laugh. There was nothing *golden* about her. Especially not after what had happened tonight. Something had gone so wrong that she would never be able to put it right again. Her mother had named her after the Virgin Mary, but she had never felt more distant to the Holy Mother than now.

"It's important to have a name that has meaning," Puridaia said, and piled more wood into the stove. "We all need meaning in our lives, and it's good to know your destiny."

She poured some chicken broth from a skillet on the hob into a tin cup and handed it to Marielle.

"When you're done, try to get some sleep," she said, and got two more blankets out of the trunk for her. "We'll find you a dress in the morning. I know someone about your size."

The old woman pulled some furs from the storage space beneath the bunkbed, arranged them on the floor, and curled up on them like a cat. She was snoring softly before Marielle had finished her broth.

Marielle was so tired, she just bundled herself up in the extra blankets and went to sleep leaning against the wall beside the stove.

FIVE

Her nose tingled, and she woke up. Marielle opened her eyes and a little girl jumped back from her, giggling, holding a long straw and looking pleased with herself.

"My Puridaia says you should wash yourself and try on the dress my cousin Theresa is giving you," the child said, revealing a big gap in her baby teeth as she smiled the same smile that lit up the old woman's face. "It's a gift because you're a cousin now too, *Aurica.*"

"The Golden One," Marielle mumbled, rubbing her eyes. "But I'm not a cousin."

The child laughed. "You're very pretty, though – for a *not-a-cousin*."

Marielle frowned, but the girl was out the door before she could ask any questions.

A copper basin sat on the table and next to it a tiny piece of soap, a washcloth, and a towel. An opulent green dress with a long wide skirt and golden trimmings, and a silky woolen shawl lay draped over the rocking chair. This was something she'd never have dreamed of wearing, but it didn't seem like she had another option.

Marielle hurried to clean herself up, glad that the water was warm, and put on every piece of clothing she'd been given. She found a pair of wooden shoes

by the door and left the caravan in time to see several of the travelers' wagons pull out of the clearing.

Most of the caravans had been made ready to move on despite the uncertain weather. No one was paying her much attention as she scanned the campsite – they were all busy packing their possessions. The tinkers were leaving.

"Feeling better?" Puridaia asked her.

She had a way of appearing out of nowhere. She was carrying a crock, and the huge dog that had kept them company the previous night was happy to see her.

Marielle nodded. She was bruised in a lot of places, but other than that, she felt fine, physically.

"I can't thank you enough for taking me in," she said, scratching the dog's ear.

Puridaia tilted her head. "I'm glad you found your way last night."

Marielle bit her lip. All she remembered was that she'd wanted to hide in one of the rafters' shelters down by the river. She'd been ever so cold once she'd reached it and found that it must have fallen down during the storm.

"What are you going to do now, *Golden One*?" Puridaia asked.

Marielle tried to avoid the old woman's gaze, irritated. "I don't know."

Puridaia set down the crock and took her hands in her own, giving them a little squeeze. Marielle gasped at how warm the old woman's gnarled fingers were.

She looked up into her eyes and for an instant, Puridaia's deep brown pupils turned to a rich, deep blue.

Marielle freed her hands and retreated from her, heart hammering. "What *are* you?"

"The question is, what are *you*? And what do you *want* to be?"

Another wagon pulled out of the clearing, and the man on the driver's seat waved to Puridaia.

The child next to him blew Marielle a kiss. "Farewell, not-a-cousin!"

"Puridaia, you should make haste," the man said. "They'll be here soon. They're searching for thieves, arsonists, demons, and witches again, as always." He wiggled his bushy eyebrows at Marielle.

Puridaia chuckled and waved a dismissive hand at him. "The entire ensemble, huh? Don't worry, I won't be long."

"They think I burned down my family's house," Marielle said. "And they think *your* people stole livestock in the village."

"But are they right? *Did* you burn down your family's house?"

Marielle truly didn't know what she'd done in between passing out at the knacker's yard and waking up in her barn, but her father had called her a monster, and she didn't even want to think about the panicked look in her sister's eyes when Susi had retreated from her. But why on earth would she have done such a thing?

Defiantly, she folded her arms across her chest. "Are they right about *your* people stealing hens and geese, and butchering our cow?"

Puridaia shrugged. Her mischievous smile revealed as many gaps in her teeth as the child's had earlier. "Hens are birds. They go where they please if you don't close the coop." The smile disappeared, and her expression turned serious. "Cows not so much."

She carried the crock up the steps that led to her door and put it inside. Marielle helped gather up some odds and ends from around the firepit, while the old woman untied a clothesline from two nearby trees, and secured some of her furniture with it inside the wagon.

One of the last young men remaining on the campsite lent a hand and harnessed the brown Wallach that pulled her wagon. He hitched it up as she folded back the little wooden treads to her door at the rear end of the caravan and fastened them in place. Finally, she was ready to go, the last wagon on the campsite.

The old woman scrambled onto the driver's seat. Then she fastened the ends of her embroidered headscarf, and tucked a few loose strands of hair in, as if she was heading off to church, rather than fleeing from an angry mob.

"Can I come with you?" Marielle heard herself asking. It seemed like a good idea, for now. Anything was better than staying behind here.

Puridaia shook her head, tugging down her sleeves and smoothing a blanket over her knees.

"Everyone feels the cold in winter, child. I only take those in who can't fend for themselves, or those who can't conquer the shadows. But I see you're well able to look after yourself, and that makes me glad. I gave you to your mother seventeen years ago and wished you a good and long life. I wish you that still. *Try* for it, Golden One."

Marielle's throat closed up. "What are you talking about?"

The old woman sighed, thought for a moment, and then leaned down to her. "When my family last made halt here, your mother was without child after five years of marriage. She came to me for a potion. A few other women from the village did, too. I gave them what they asked me for, and I warned them about the consequences. All I requested in return was that they give you the names I chose for you. I'm so sorry none but one did. Whatever happens now is out of my hands."

This couldn't be. Babies didn't come about by drinking potions. Drinking the concoctions the Garmisch barber surgeon sold for sore throats and boils on the bum never had any consequences beyond a bellyache and an empty purse. This had to be the height of superstitious mumbo-jumbo, if not heresy.

"It's the truth," Puridaia said, studying Marielle's face with amusement.

"But even if I did believe you, what kind of payment is a name for a potion? And what does that have to do with anything?"

First names weren't important. She knew four Hermanns and three boys named Thomas. Her aunt Liesl was one of five Liesls in Grainau alone, and Marielle knew of at least two other girls with her name in Partenkirchen and Garmisch. Only family or house names really mattered in Werdenfels now. They determined a person's credibility and reputation.

"You're wrong. First names *are* important," Puridaia said, observing her closely. "They bring you closer to your own destiny – and they also protect you against human weakness, and the weaknesses of your family. You're stuck with your people, and you'll never change them, but you can change yourself, and your name is your own, not anyone else's, so a name is a very valuable thing. My people believe in giving children a good start in life. It's hard enough as it is."

Marielle didn't know what to think. The old woman had to be crazy.

Puridaia chortled, perhaps snatching up this thought from her mind as she had the last one.

"Times are tough, *Aurica*," she said. "The weather is growing colder and colder, and there are years of hardship to come for this valley. In times of trouble, human souls are more flawed than in times of plenty. Your father was weak and impatient, as many men are, so your mother tried to take control over something she did not understand, as many women do."

Marielle couldn't follow. This woman was talking in riddles, more so than the village priest. She needed clear answers.

"What happened last night? Am I a witch?"

Puridaia laughed. "No, dear. You certainly aren't. You weren't meant to be on this earth, but sometimes, with a little effort, you can turn ashes to gold, and a barren field will bloom. You were a gift to a desperate woman many years ago, and a healthy baby is as godly as it gets, don't you agree?"

Now she'd lost her completely.

The word *gift* implied good things that were freely given and benefited someone, but nothing even remotely good was going on here. The old woman had probably profited from her deal in some material way, even if she denied it. Getting to choose a name for a few village brats she might never see again seemed too cheap a price even for a phony potion, and too selfless for someone who lived on the edge of poverty without a place to call home.

"Ask your mother and find the others so you'll know I'm telling the truth," Puridaia said, reading her thoughts once more. "You're *not* a witch."

"Then what am I? And *what* others?"

Puridaia had obviously decided they were finished and ignored her. She clicked her tongue, jiggled the reins, and the brown Wallach got moving, slowly at first, then faster and faster. The wagon's wheels moved through the snow with ease, as though it wasn't there at all.

Marielle followed alongside for a little while, trying to persuade the old woman to tell her more, but soon, she couldn't keep up anymore. She fell hopelessly behind and pressed her hands to her stinging sides. Her dress was soaked to the knees, and her feet slid around inside her wooden shoes. She had no idea what to do next.

Shouting alerted her to the presence of riders in the woods. It came from the direction of the clearing less than half a mile behind her.

Jesus, they only had to follow the tracks... She spun around to look at the snow-covered trail behind her, but all she could see was her own footprints.

SIX

The more she tried to hide her tracks, the worse things got. The forest offered next to no cover. Only a few young beeches had stubbornly held on to their dead foliage. The river was close by, but it wasn't frozen over yet, and she was cut off from the caves where she'd played as a child.

"Up ahead," someone yelled.

She could see movement in the trees. There had to be at least a dozen men, and they were spreading out. There was nowhere to go.

Nowhere but up, a small voice inside her mind told her. *Up, Golden One, up and away.* But she didn't know how.

She looked at the sky through the bare, black branches, and there was the red kite again, the one Caspar had thought so fascinating just one day ago, when her biggest worry had been her dead dog. The bird's feathers shimmered in the sunlight, and she wondered how far up it really was when it cried out, but in a way she'd never heard a bird cry out.

The earsplitting, high-pitched sound brought her to her knees. She covered her ears with her hands, but that didn't mute the sound. Her head pounded like it had the day she'd been to the knacker's place with Caspar.

Somewhere between the trees, a horse reared and threw its rider off. Several others bolted, and a gray rouncey dragged Thomas Habermann behind it. The young man's foot hung caught in one of the stirrups, and his leg jutted out at a strange angle to his battered body.

A panicked ambler charged past her, almost knocking her down, and two of the Wasl brothers were blindly stumbling through the undergrowth, blood pouring out of their ears. She was glad Caspar wasn't with them.

An indefinable muddle of screams and shouts echoed through the forest, but the screech of the bird almost drowned them out.

Just when Marielle didn't think she'd survive this, its shriek grew softer, changed pitch, and turned into a song. The melody sounded vaguely familiar, and she found that she could take her hands off her ears, but glancing around, the others weren't recovering as quickly as she was. She was going to get a second chance, and she hurried to turn and make a break for it.

Strong arms grabbed her. Georg Strolz, a furrier from whom her father had bought a pretty pair of gloves for Johanna last Christmas, had been right behind her. He held her in an iron grip, breathing heavily as he crushed her against his huge belly. She squirmed and wriggled, kicked, and scratched, but he was a half a foot taller than she and double her weight.

"I've got one of them," he yelled. "Help me, someone!"

No one came. She didn't know if Strolz recognized her or merely saw a woman in a fancy gypsy dress and assumed she was one of the tinkers. He'd probably never looked at her too closely when he'd seen her out on the street or at church with her family. But all the worse if he *did* know who she was.

She struggled for a mere half inch of space, veered around, and rammed her elbow into his gut. Winded, he loosened his hold for a second. She scratched his face and tried to free herself, but again, he pitched all his weight against her.

"Do that one more time, and I'll throttle you," he said, and shoved her up against the nearest tree, twisting her arm. "I'll put you down like a rabid dog, you dirty gypsy whore!"

She'd never have believed anyone could say such a thing. Not sober. Then again, her own father had tried to kill her last night.

She gathered all her remaining strength, stretched her back, and attempted to lever herself off the tree, but he, a man of his word, wrapped his hands around her neck and squeezed, closing off her windpipe.

That little voice in her mind spoke up again: *Up, Golden One. There's only one way out, and that's up.*

Stars cluttered her vision, and a bright flare of golden light engulfed her. In an instant, she was free of the furrier and hurtling up through the branches toward the sky. Bits of burning fabric and ashes rained down from her, and Strolz was in flames. He collapsed into the snow, thrashing. Marielle felt no sense of guilt – only relief.

Up, the voice had said, but she was more than just up. She was flying.

Golden wings unfurled to either side of her, and she filled her lungs with air. Her chest expanded, and she let out a cry that scattered the wildlife and horses and men in the forest once again, but it was all the same to her. She had escaped. She had no idea how she'd done it, but she had gotten away.

She circled the clearing where the gypsy caravans had stood and followed the river back toward the village a little way until she could see the knacker's place. Right above the field, a movement in the sky caught her eye, and she realized she'd been mistaken earlier. The bird she'd seen wasn't a red kite but something else entirely.

A strange winged being the size of an eagle swooped down toward her. She was wary, but not afraid. Her gut feeling told her that it wouldn't hurt her.

Its plumage shimmered golden in the sun as it glided closer, and its long tail weaved tendrils of fire through the air. A crest of blood-red and yellow feathers crowned its head, and it studied her from sapphire-blue eyes before it banked left, eddying toward the edge of the forest. There, it tore through the branches and dead foliage, and vanished.

Marielle briefly considered her options and decided to follow it. She plunged through the same opening in the trees where she'd watched the wonderful bird disappear, but it was nowhere to be seen. Instead, a young man knelt on the ground near the edge of the field, naked and shivering. It was Caspar.

The moment her feet touched the ground next to him, she became human again: skin, flesh, and bone, and she was freezing.

"Christ almighty," a gruff voice said from behind her before she had the chance to do anything further. "Now I have *two* of you to deal with."

SEVEN

For all the filth in and around his yard, the knacker's house was clean and much more comfortable inside than Marielle would have guessed. He owned good solid furniture, and he'd spent a lot of money on the tall tile stove in his living room. The floor in front of it was covered with well-tended soft furs, and Marielle felt safe and warm here.

"Drink this," Mandl told her, and handed one of two steaming mugs down to her.

Without hesitating, she curled her fingers around it and drank. The strong, spicy wine burned her lips and made her light-headed, but she was glad to have it.

Caspar sat across from her. He took a small sip and coughed, almost spilling his wine over the shirt Mandl had loaned him. The knacker thumped him on the back and laughed.

"Son, you need to toughen up," he told Caspar, and pointed at Marielle. "That tiny little woman over there will drink you under the table."

The big man broke chunks of bread off a loaf and offered one each to Caspar and Marielle. Caspar just looked at his while Marielle ate in silence. When she was finished, she cast Caspar a glance that made him squirm.

"Why were you in the forest?" she asked, but she already knew the answer.

There was something wrong with both of them.

"Why were *you* there?" he said pointedly.

Mandl drew air and was about to speak, but loud knocking at the front door interrupted him.

"Knacker, are you there?" Sebastian Habermann called. "We want to talk to you!" The knocking turned to hammering.

Marielle's heart pounded. Mandl had taken them in – she hadn't even had time to ask him why – but what would he do when he found out that everyone in the village was probably looking for her?

"You two – into the basement," he told them in a low voice, "and don't make a sound."

Caspar surprised her by grabbing her arm and dragging her to her feet.

"Come on," he said.

He pulled her into the central corridor of the house and around the staircase to a narrow, oddly shaped door that had been fitted to accommodate a broom closet, or so Marielle would have assumed.

"Hold your horses," Mandl called to the men outside when he was sure Marielle and Caspar had shut the door under the stairs behind them.

He was back to his usual unfriendly tone, sounding as though someone had just pried him away from his favorite meal of the day.

"What do you want?" Marielle heard him asking after another moment.

"We can't stay here," Caspar whispered to her. His breath trembled. "I know my way round, and I can get us out of the house."

"Why do you know your way around the knacker's place?" she whispered back. "And why did *he* help us?"

"Because he *knows*, and I found out."

He took her by the hand and guided her to the back of the closet, where he pressed an elbow against the false rear wall. It swung away from them, and he ushered her down the narrow steps behind it, into the low-ceilinged basement.

Easily, as though he'd been here a hundred times, he steered her through the musty-smelling, cluttered cellar, and led her to a room on the back end of the house, where Mandl apparently stored his ready-chopped wood for the winter, and several dozen crates of homemade schnaps that would have made the Abbot of Ettal green with envy. So this was how he was able to afford his nice tile stove.

The knacker had piled short logs man-high against the walls on three sides of the room, while the crates were stacked in rows halfway up against the outside wall. Above them, near the ceiling, an opening in the wall funneled upward straight to a hatch at the base of the building on the yard side of the house. Light and cold air streamed in through the cracks around the edges of the hatch.

Caspar carefully scaled the crates, testing if they were solid enough to hold their weight. When he was satisfied, he helped Marielle up, and then pressed the hatch up just far enough for them to get a look out into the yard.

Mandl's dogs were barking fiercely and yanking at their chains. One of Caspar's younger brothers was poking around the workshop, and two men Marielle knew as her father's drinking buddies were searching the shed.

The floorboards creaked and groaned under the weight of hurried footfalls in the rooms above. Some of Habermann's cronies were inside the house now, and Marielle didn't doubt they'd also want to search the basement.

Caspar must have been thinking the same thing, and they both climbed back down from the hatch, frantically searching for something to block off the woodstore's entrance.

An empty, battered cabinet that was missing one of its doors leaned against the wall out in the main corridor. It was so heavy they could hardly carry it, but they somehow managed to haul it back to the woodstore without making a sound, and maneuvered it in front of the frameless opening. They left just enough room for them to squeeze past one after the other to get back inside.

The huge old thing scraped sharply across the floor when Caspar pulled and tugged at it from inside, hoping to cover the whole of the entrance well enough to hide it. Marielle held her breath, but with all the trampling and moving of furniture upstairs, and the dogs barking non-stop, no one seemed to have heard.

"You must have seen *something*," Sebastian Habermann shouted at Mandl in the yard then.

He sounded so close, she clambered back onto the crates and pushed the hatch up again just a finger's breadth to see what was going on. Habermann and Mandl were arguing.

"What the devil do you think I do out here?" Mandl snarled, poking a finger at Habermann. "I'm just a dishonorable knacker. I spend most of my days burying, burning, and boiling your waste, and most of my nights shoveling your *fine* neighbors' shit from the streets, and you're here, accusing me of – well, *what*? Just *what* are you accusing me of?"

"I'm not accusing you of anything, man," Habermann said. "Not yet. Unless, of course, we find evidence that you're helping *them*."

"You're stealing my time, that's what you're doing!" Mandl replied, growling. "And where the hell is Voigt? I don't answer to *you*."

Habermann was constantly shifting his weight from one foot to the other, boots squelching in the mushy snow.

"He's nervous as hell," Caspar whispered.

"No wonder," Marielle said. "After what happened in the woods."

Caspar nodded slowly. "I think you *killed* Strolz."

She didn't understand how, but she knew she might well have. That made her a murderess, on top of everything else, and she had never meant any harm. Not to anyone.

Habermann spat on the ground. "You'll answer to *anyone* who comes here," he told Mandl, more condescending than she'd ever heard him speak to anyone but his own sons.

"You're as worthless as the shit you shovel," he went on. "God knows why, but old Voigt's father must have taken a liking to you, allowing you to shack up with one of *them*," he said. "But to me, that means you probably know where they are, and you know what spells they use to bewitch the wildlife and get around without leaving tracks."

"There's no such thing as spells and magic except in your imagination, you old fool."

"Adding blasphemy to your crimes?" Habermann asked.

Just then, Caspar lost his footing. Instinctively, he tried to steady himself by clutching at Marielle. Surprised, she let go of the hatch. It slammed into place, and she caught Caspar, but one of them knocked against several of the crates so hard, the glass bottles clanged.

"What was that?" Habermann said, shuffling around.

"That was probably your boys laying waste to my house," Mandl said sharply. "I'll have you pay for *anything* and *everything* they break in there."

Marielle let out a breath of relief and closed her eyes for a few seconds.

"Look here, Habermann," the knacker continued, "I have no idea who or what you're looking for, but

my wife left this place sixteen years ago because she couldn't stand the hypocrisy of all you pious apes. Her people are not related to the clan you're looking for. They never came back, and that's the end of it."

"So you've been telling us. But the truth is, she just left you to do her whoring elsewhere. A knacker such as yourself was beneath even the likes of her. Isn't that so?"

"Good God," Caspar said, fists clenched.

"Get off my property," Mandl said in a low, almost unhuman voice. "And take your riffraff with you, or I'll break every bone in your body just to see you suffer, no matter what they do to me afterward."

Even down in the basement, Marielle sensed the explosive tension above them. She felt sorry for Mandl. Habermann wasn't going to stand for this, and with the Garmisch burgomaster so undecided, he'd probably send a messenger to the Werdenfels governor's clerk, demanding that he send for the hangman. But maybe if she surrendered herself to them now, she'd be the only one they'd put on trial.

"I'm going up there," she whispered to Caspar. "They'll have him whipped if he does anything to Habermann."

He seized her arm. "No."

"I have to."

Caspar refused to let go of her. "*Wait.*"

Above them, Habermann fell silent for a time. Then he called to his sons and the others. Apparently, he had decided to take Mandl at his word and live to fight another day.

To the knacker, he said, "This isn't over."

EIGHT

Mandl was sitting in his upturned kitchen, nursing a cup of the mulled wine he'd warmed for them earlier on the stove. Miraculously, the pot he'd filled had survived the search, but several cups and shattered crockery lay scattered on the wet, muddy floor. He made no effort to offer them any more of the wine. Marielle was sure they'd outstayed their welcome.

"Thank you," she said simply.

She wouldn't be able to repay him for what he'd done for her, but the knacker never did anything for free. Why should he? No one did, dishonorable or otherwise.

"How much did you hear when Habermann and I were talking?" Mandl said, sounding tired.

Caspar leaned against the wall. "Most of it. We were hiding in the woodstore."

"So I heard from up in the yard. You're lucky Habermann didn't."

"We thought they might come down and find the door to the basement."

"Sebastian's boys are so dense they couldn't find their own feet if they looked down."

Marielle almost disagreed with him. She didn't know about the other Habermann boys, but she knew Harald better than the knacker did, and she liked to think he'd refused to take part in the search because he was a good, clever man and because he didn't want to believe she was guilty of any of the crimes they might be accusing her of. But she understood why Mandl was angry.

"Thomas probably broke his leg falling off his horse in the woods," she said in a small voice. "And I think I hurt Georg Strolz pretty badly."

"Habermann said something along those lines. Strolz might go blind, but they'll both live, if that's what you want to know."

That was a relief, despite everything. "Do either of you have any idea how my family's doing?"

Caspar and Mandl exchanged a glance.

Caspar answered. "Susi and your mom got hurt in the fire, but nothing serious. I think your father took them to your aunt's place in Grainau."

Good. They were safe.

"That's what I wanted to tell you when I came looking for you this morning," he went on. "And… and Susi was wrong, you know."

Marielle's brow creased.

He gave her half a smile. "Just in case you were wondering, I don't think you set fire to the house."

A tear spilled over her cheek and she wiped it away. Had he been close enough to hear last night? She was glad to have him on her side.

"I don't know what to believe, but my family obviously thinks I did it. Why would they, if it wasn't so?" She fixed her gaze first to Caspar's and then to Mandl's.

Mandl drank deeply from his cup before he spoke. "You have a gift, and they're understandably overwhelmed."

"Well, this is some *gift*." She scoffed. "It has things catching fire around me, and all of a sudden I can fly – and so can *he*, by the way." She gesticulated at Caspar, but Mandl seemed no more surprised than he had been when he'd found them both stark naked in the woods.

"Master Mandl, I'm deeply indebted to you, but I have to ask: what in God's name is going on?"

Mandl set down his cup and folded his hands across his lap. "You're a shapechanger, love. A phoenix." He looked directly into her eyes.

Her breath hitched. This couldn't be. Being a shapechanger was probably worse than being a witch, though she couldn't remember this being mentioned anywhere specifically in the Bible. And she'd had no idea a shapechanger could turn into a phoenix. Not that she really believed in the existence of such a creature. Beings of this sort only existed in the stories people told their children to frighten them – didn't they?

Still, she clearly remembered the beautiful golden bird she'd stared at in awe above the forest that morning before she'd found Caspar. *Above the forest...* She'd been flying at the time, and humans didn't fly, of course. She'd flown the previous night too, only she'd been so deeply shaken she hadn't wanted to think about it. Now, she had no choice.

Ask a question and you'll get your answer, the ever-present, unnerving voice inside her said, *even if it isn't the one you'd like to hear.*

She had to sit down. "Is this a sickness for which there is a cure, or a curse we're stuck with?" she said. She felt hot again, and her temples throbbed.

Caspar pulled another chair up. "Neither." He put a hand over hers. "Now calm down and don't get all upset again."

Mandl leaned forward, careful not to invade her space, but serious about demonstrating his presence. "The boy's right. Take deep breaths and stay with us here, or you'll shift, and I don't want you to do that in this house. Not with Habermann close by. Do you hear me?"

"Shift?" Marielle asked.

Right on cue, delicate golden veins formed on Caspar's hand. They emanated an unnatural heat, and she snatched back her hand.

Caspar chuckled. "We can change at will if we learn to control it. I did, and so can you."

Tiny flames sparked on the now entirely golden skin of his hands, twisting up his fingers, and his eyes changed from brown to blue and back again. The flames around his hands flared up for an instant, flickered, and died as quickly as he'd made them appear.

Marielle felt the color drain from her face. "Habermann was telling right," she said. "The travelers bewitched us, didn't they?"

This couldn't be the side effect of some weird potion, even if she did accept what Puridaia had told her.

Mandl gave a small laugh. "Once and for all: this is not a curse. A curse is something evil you can't live with."

"Call it what you want. I was at the tinkers' camp last night. The old woman – Puridaia – she said she gave my mother some kind of fertility potion. My mother, and a few other women from the area. Just assuming she was telling the truth, either that potion did something to us, or those travelers put a spell on us afterward. It's devilry."

Mandl straightened his back and his eyes narrowed. "Watch what you call *devilry*. Your mother just wanted a healthy baby, and she had one." He cast Caspar a glance. "As did Josephine Wasl after two stillborn children, and… and my wife, a few other women as well."

"It's not natural," Marielle said, "and people are suffering because of it – because of *me*."

"You're right. People *are* suffering. But not because of a potion your mother decided to take, and not because of you," Mandl said. "I don't believe that. Whenever something goes this badly, it's never just one thing that went wrong. It's a chain of events with a whole line of individual mistakes that don't seem like a big deal each by itself, but they all add up in the end."

Caspar tilted his head, listening, but not actively participating in the conversation. Marielle wished he'd say something too. This was as much about him as it was about her, and she couldn't grasp how he could seem so unruffled. Then again, he'd never been easily upset.

Mandl sighed and waggled his cup at them. "Listen. Wine will warm you, and it will calm you. If it's strong and you're not used to it, you wake up with a headache the next day, and you may not remember too much from the night before. But you were probably warned about it. That's not a curse. It's the price you pay for warmth and calming, and for not heeding those warnings."

A grin played around Caspar's lips now, as though he knew what the knacker was getting at, and it occurred to Marielle that she'd underestimated him. She seemed to have misjudged quite a few people in her life.

"The old woman mixed a potion for your mothers," Mandl continued, "and she gave them instructions. They didn't follow them, and now you children are the ones to wake up with the headache."

"Is there a way to reverse this?" she asked, realizing the accuracy of his words. She had been having headaches for weeks now.

"No, but you can change how you deal with it and live your life, and you can prevent further harm. What did Puridaia talk to you about? And what did she tell you to do?"

Marielle tried to remember. "She said something about names being important when I wouldn't tell her mine, and she called me *Aurica*."

"She gave you your name. The one your mother should have given you to protect you and keep you from changing shape until you're ready and can make your own choices. It was a part of the deal Johanna made with the old woman because it describes the nature of your gift – and thus gives you more control over it."

Caspar nodded. "The old woman told me mine, too, the day she went from door to door in Breitenau. Everything has gotten easier since, but I already knew I was different."

"Since when?" Marielle asked.

"Summer."

She frowned, casting him a questioning glance. How had he kept his secret this long, and why was he so utterly at ease with it and in control, while she'd failed so miserably and probably burned down her own home?

"I had Mandl to help me before the gypsies came back. He found me behind his workshop after my first transformation. I didn't remember what happened either. All I know is that I'd been sick and upset over something. But I didn't set fire to anything... I don't *think* I did."

"What else did the old gypsy woman tell you?" Mandl asked Marielle.

"She said to go and find the others." Her gaze wandered between Caspar and the knacker. "How many *others* are there besides us?"

"Many," Mandl said. "But here, there is only one left, as far as I know. I don't know who that is, but he or she isn't like you two. It's likely they don't have the golden glow, because I don't think *you* burned down your own house either, and tinkers don't slaughter cows and old dogs like that. Someone else did. That's the one you have to find if you want to know what really happened."

Caspar frowned. "I think I've actually seen that one. But how do we find them?"

Mandl shrugged. "I can't help you there. Leanabel never told me who the other women were, but there are at least two people you can ask who might know."

Marielle couldn't imagine what good finding the other one would do them. "But even if we learn who it is, what then?"

"Try telling them their name," the knacker said simply, rising from his chair. "We all have a right to know who we are so we can make educated decisions."

NINE

Marielle's coat had once belonged to Leanabel Mandl. The sweet scent of summer flowers still lingered in its fur lining. She pulled it tightly around herself, tied her scarf, and drew the hood over her head.

Her boots were too big for her feet, but that didn't bother her. They, too, had belonged to Leanabel. The years hadn't dried them out or cracked the leather; Mandl had kept them well-greased, and this told Marielle just as much about the love two adults could share as the soft, much-too-expensive gloves her father had given Johanna for Christmas one year. It gave her another angle on the knacker and confirmed yet again what a bad judge of character she had been.

She took her leave of Mandl, and Caspar and she headed for the Loisach. They split up on the riverbank. Caspar plodded off in the direction of Breitenau, while Marielle made her way to Grainau.

The local farmers kept the road between the villages well maintained throughout the year, but she was afraid of running into anyone who might recognize her, so she decided to walk cross country over the fields and the knoll that overlooked Grainau.

From the crest of the knoll, despite the hazy weather, she saw the bent topmost part of the Zugspitze directly opposite, towering over the other jagged mountains behind the village. She'd heard that a young lad had climbed all the way to its summit last summer, and she'd been envious. What a view he must have had from up there.

Dusk descended and bathed Grainau in shadows. She took shelter in one of the half-empty *stadls* that dotted the meadows around the village and waited for dark. By and by, soft yellow lights came on in the windows of the houses.

When she was certain that no one else would be about, she cautiously made her way to her aunt's home. The kitchen was at the front of the house, and she hunkered down beneath the window and listened. Aunt Liesl was telling one of her older daughters off for falling asleep over her sewing, and Marielle's twin cousins Emilie and Franz were bickering over a honey cake. Between the snippets of conversation, eventually she caught her mother's voice, telling Susi to mind herself on the stairs going up to bed.

Just hearing her made Marielle feel less lost and lonely, and she was content to stay where she was for a while, drinking in the familiar family routines she missed so badly. She'd never been separated from her mother and sister for more than a day.

Michel didn't seem to be there. At least she couldn't hear him. A quick peek in the window verified his absence. Perhaps he was in the stable, helping her uncle.

Carefully, she made her way around the building for a look, but the animals had already been seen to.

She was about to return to the house, trying to work out a way of getting Johanna's attention without upsetting her, and without alarming everyone else, when she heard a small sound near the back door. The light of a lantern sparked to life and illuminated her mother's face.

After everything they'd been through these past days, Marielle almost expected her to scream or call for help, but Johanna just clasped a bandaged hand to her mouth and stifled a sob.

"Come here, child," she said softly, and opened her arms.

Marielle hesitated before she slowly moved toward Johanna, afraid to misinterpret, or that the situation might yet turn sour. Nothing of the sort happened and before she knew it, she found herself wrapped in her mother's embrace for one precious moment that seemed to pass by much too quickly.

Johanna motioned her to be quiet and pulled her into the shed, limping badly. She closed the door behind them and hung the lantern from a hook in one of the beams.

"Mari, what have you done?" she whispered.

Marielle looked at her feet. "I'd love to tell you I'm innocent, but I can't promise that I didn't burn down our farm. I just don't remember."

Johanna lifted her chin and looked her firmly in the eyes. "It's going to be all right. We'll sort this out."

Nothing was ever going to be all right again, but the love in those words meant forgiveness. Marielle hadn't counted on being forgiven, but she'd hoped for it.

"I never meant for anyone to get hurt, least of all you or Susi."

"I know," Johanna said, gently stroking back her hair. "We'll be fine. Susi will heal. None of us wanted this to happen."

"But you knew it *could*." She hadn't come here to let her mother share any of the blame she alone had to carry, but she needed to know the truth.

Johanna's face froze up.

"I didn't believe it," she said. "Neither did any of the others. No one except Leanabel." She turned away, too ashamed to face Marielle. "But you already know that. You're wearing her coat, so I assume you went to see Mandl."

Marielle hadn't realized Johanna might recognize the coat. The fact that she did spoke volumes: her mother had known the knacker's wife well enough to remember a piece of her clothing.

"He's a strange man."

"He is. But he was good to Leanabel."

"Tell me about her. It didn't seem appropriate to ask him."

"She came from one of the travelers' families that passed through every year. The Roses, I think. She had the most wonderful singing voice you can imagine, and Mandl fell in love with her. She left her family for him, and they married."

This sounded like a fairytale to Marielle.

"But we treated her like dirt," Johanna continued.

"All the women in the villages shunned her and laughed at her. When her baby came, one day after you were born, she gave it the strange gypsy name she'd been told, but people gossiped. Some even claimed the child wasn't Mandl's. And then she just couldn't take it anymore. No one saw her leave. No one ever saw her again, and Mandl wasn't the same."

Marielle could well imagine what the young woman had gone through. As the wife of a dishonorable knacker *and* a woman from a gypsy family, Leanabel Rose would have been one of the least welcome people in all of Werdenfels. Had she known what she was getting into when she'd married Mandl? Maybe not.

Decent farmers' wives and other women from families with honorable professions would have crossed themselves whenever they saw her approaching, and they'd have walked on the other side of the street. They'd have spat on the ground and called her names behind her back – or to her face. These things might be tolerable if you lived within a dishonorable community and knew you were moving on soon, but living with them indefinitely and in isolation, away from your own people, was bound to be another matter entirely.

"We got what we wanted from the traveler-woman, but by the time you were born – all within days of each other – we had managed to convince ourselves that it wasn't the potions, but just a coincidence. We thought we had it all figured out, and we didn't listen to Leanabel. She was beautiful, and she was smart, but she was a gypsy. We laughed at her and refused to speak to her anymore because she wouldn't stop talking about her fears."

As a child, Marielle had never seen Johanna go back on her word, even in matters of little consequence, and she hadn't thought her mother capable of treating anyone with disdain. Not Johanna, who always had a kind word for the linen weavers and even the miller's wife. To Marielle, her mother had always seemed infallible.

"But you *knew* what could happen to us if you didn't keep your end of the bargain. The names were meant to be our protection."

Johanna nodded. "We were warned. We didn't listen because we honestly didn't believe it was true. You have to believe me."

"But as children, we were forbidden to tell strangers our names. You always said they'd have to make do with our house name."

"We thought the Wintersteins might curse you if they found out we hadn't given you the names the old woman told us, or come and take you away one day."

"But the names the old woman gave you were supposed to protect us."

"I know that now."

"We would have been warned," Marielle said, "and we might have been able to control it."

Johanna nodded. "I'm so sorry."

Marielle wiped a tear from her cheek. "I am, too."

She paused. "I met Puridaia Winterstein. She told me the name you were supposed to give me."

Johanna took her hand. "Aurica. I didn't forget."

"The Golden One." Marielle remembered laughing at the thought because she hadn't been able to appreciate the real meaning of those words at the time. "She said I have a golden aura."

Johanna's eyes widened, glistening with a mixture of joy and relief. "Then it's *not* you. It can't be. It's *got* to be one of the others. I think that's what she came to find out."

Mandl had already guessed as much, but it was so good to have certainty. A great weight lifted off Marielle's shoulders.

"Who is it?" she asked.

It couldn't be Mandl's daughter. She wasn't even here, if the knacker hadn't outright lied to them.

"We swore we'd never tell anyone after Leanabel left." Johanna kneaded her hands. "We just wanted the gossiping to stop, and it did."

"But that's not the problem now. The problem is finding the one who's responsible for the fire and killing the animals. They did it once, and they could strike again. Tell me who the fourth child is."

Johanna's shoulders sagged. "I promised I wouldn't."

"You gave Puridaia a promise too. You didn't keep it, and look what happened. Now's the time to put things right, Mama, before someone else loses their home."

Johanna looked so torn, Marielle felt her sorrow, but she didn't pity her. It took a whole line of mistakes to form the chain of events that led to a catastrophe, Mandl had said, and her mother was the first link.

Johanna wiped a trembling hand over her eyes. "You're right. I never thought it would come to this," she said after a moment. "Wait here."

She left the shed and returned a short while later, carrying a small, rusty tin box with a battered lid. She handed it to Marielle. It held several small scraps of vellum, each with two names written on them. The first one she pulled from the tin read *Marielle – Aurica*. There were two other scraps beneath the first. She studied each in turn.

"You children grew up together. I'm so sorry."

TEN

With her father and uncle likely to come home drunk and unpredictable from the tavern, Marielle declined her mother's offer to hide at her aunt's farm for the night. As tempting as a good night's rest in the warm hay loft sounded, she didn't believe she'd go unnoticed. She wouldn't sleep much anyway.

Besides, getting back to the knacker's place would be easiest during the night. She could use the road without being seen, and wouldn't have to go back across the fields. No one in their right mind would be out there.

Leanabel's boots were soaked, and Johanna brought her a pair of Liesl's. After a quick meal of bread and cheese, she set off.

The clear sky promised a bitterly cold night, and the freezing air seeped in through her clothes and boots right to her bones. She walked as fast as she could, boots crunching on the frosty crust of the snow-covered road, trying to keep warm, and at the same time outrun the endless loops of thoughts that churned in her mind.

A coppice lay between the road and the barren field that surrounded the knacker's yard. The sky beyond the trees glowed orange, and columns of smoke rose above it. Exhausted as she was, she ran most of the way through the little wood, but Mandl's house was lost.

The fire had already destroyed the main building, and the two pines beside it had collapsed into the flames. The roofs of the workshop and the barn were ablaze, and burning embers dripped from their gutters.

Marielle found the knacker behind a pile of rubbish on the rear side of his workshop. He lay in the mud with his dead hounds at his side. His clothes and skin were a blackened, vulcanized mass on his raw flesh, but he was somehow still alive. She didn't want to imagine his pain, and fell to her knees beside him, hoping death would come quickly.

"Mandl?" she whispered, bending over him and unsure if he could hear her. "What can I do? Tell me how I can help you."

He couldn't seem to see her and groped around, disoriented, clutching a knife in one hand and a blood-soaked bouquet of golden and black feathers in the other. She caught the hand with the knife in hers, wincing at the touch of his raw flesh, and gently pried the blade from his burned fingers.

"I made a mistake," he said, barely audible. "I know who it is now."

She nodded, biting her lip. "Me too. But we'll put it right."

"I hurt the dark firebird, but I couldn't kill it."

Marielle wasn't sure if a phoenix *could* be killed, and even if so, she doubted she'd be able to do it.

"You were very brave."

"The whole village will burn..."

Helpless tears spilled down her cheeks. She couldn't control them.

"No, it won't. We'll put things right," she said, clueless how she was going to keep her word on that.

She'd never felt so inadequate and powerless in all her life as she had over the past few days, but this *had to* stop.

Mandl attempted to half-turn over and gestured at the dog closest to him. "Take care of her," he whispered. "She's all I've got left."

She glanced over her shoulder, though she already knew the animal was dead. She didn't have the heart to tell him. "I will."

He seemed relieved and lay back. "You're a good girl."

She didn't think so. She was afraid. His labored breathing stopped. Marielle rocked back on her calves and said a silent prayer for him.

The fire was now spreading rapidly throughout the outbuildings. Groaning, the roofs of the workshop and the shed caved in. Windows burst, and the half-timbered walls seemed to evaporate in the heat. She couldn't carry the big man, nor drag him far enough away from the workshop and the now smoldering garbage pile to salvage his body. She had no choice but to leave him.

She was about to get to her feet when she felt something nudging her leg. A tiny puppy had crawled out from under its mother, eyes barely open and not old enough to walk. She picked it up and inspected the shivering little creature by the light of the blazing building.

"He meant *you*, didn't he?"

Miraculously, it was unscathed. She flipped its mother on her back to look for her other young, but of the four she'd saved, only this one had survived.

"What now?" she asked the tiny pup.

She knew she'd be blamed for its master's death and everything else if she couldn't come up with something fast. She'd hoped Mandl would know what to do. With him gone, she had no one to turn to now.

Johanna had already tried to explain everything to Michel, but he hadn't believed her. He'd known about the deal her mother had made with the gypsy woman, but Johanna hadn't told him about the others at the time. She'd kept their secret all these years.

When she'd been sure she was pregnant, he'd taken his life's savings to the camp and told the clan never to come back. He'd thought a few silver coins would buy their way out of the promise Johanna had given.

Even if he came round, he'd never let Marielle near him or Susi again. He was convinced she'd turned into a demon – his and Johanna's punishment for their dealings with a witch. To him, his eldest daughter was dead, replaced by a monster he had to protect his remaining child from.

The pup squealed. Marielle kissed its nose, opened her coat, and tucked it into the vest beneath the bodice of her dress to keep it warm. It nestled against her skin and fell asleep as she set off for Breitenau.

ELEVEN

The Habermanns' farm hands didn't sleep in the house. They had to make do with the loft above the horse stable. Two maids occupied one corner, separated from the rest of the loft by a few blankets draped over a clothesline, while an aging laborer snored in another, bundled up against the cold with a bottle of schnaps beside him.

By the light of the moon, Marielle discovered Barbara awake and sniveling softly on her makeshift bed almost right beside the hatch.

"Please don't scream!" she whispered, peering through the opening.

She steeled herself for the worst-case scenario that had been playing in her mind since she'd left the knacker's yard. If Barbara decided to raise hell, she had to be ready to jump and run for it.

Barbara's head bobbed up and she gave a small gasp. "What are you doing here? I thought you'd be in Munich by now!"

"Shush! You'll wake everyone."

"Oh no, we're all right. *He's* deaf as a doornail." She pointed at the sleeping laborer. "The other two won't come out of there again until the morning. You wouldn't believe the things that go on under this roof with Sebastian's boys getting them drunk every night and doing as they please with them up here." She made the sign of the cross.

Marielle's jaw fell and her heart sank. She couldn't be serious.

"Don't look so shocked," Barbara said, obviously enjoying the expression on Marielle's face. "Didn't you know what kind of fellow your precious Harald is? But Thomas probably won't be up here again for a while now. The barber surgeon says he may never walk again, never mind climb a ladder. That's on you, by the way, isn't it?"

This was just too much information Marielle couldn't digest and didn't want to right now. "Just stop," she said raising a hand in a defensive motion. "I don't want to hear this. Can you please just put on a coat and come down with me? It's important."

Barbara tilted her head and scoffed. "You don't tell me *anything*," she hissed. "In case you haven't caught on: I don't work for your family anymore."

Marielle drew a deep breath. "Listen, this isn't about my family. It's about *all* of us. This entire village is in danger."

Barbara suppressed a hiccup. "I don't want anything to do with you anymore. You were always mean to me."

Marielle couldn't deny that. Perhaps she hadn't been outright mean, but she'd never been friendly to Barbara either. Now was not the time to quibble, so she chose to be honest.

"I'll say it like it is: we've known each other all our lives, since your parents died and mine took you in, and we've never gotten on. I don't like you, and you don't like me, but we're both in trouble–"

"*You're* in trouble," Barbara cut her off, bristling. "I don't have anything to do with the mess you've gotten yourself into, so just go away. As soon as I have enough money saved up, I'm leaving this wretched place, too."

The maid turned from her, ending the conversation. She was about to pull her blanket over her head, but Marielle grabbed her arm. Wispy golden threads curled up the back of her hand and around her fingers. Barbara trembled all over until Marielle pulled back.

"Going away won't solve the problem. Not yours and not mine."

"*I* don't *have* a problem!" Barbara replied from between clenched teeth.

Marielle fixed her gaze to Barbara's, eyes a gleaming ocean of blue. At first, Barbara's eyes only reflected Marielle's, but then the glow became her own.

"Your name is Aurelie," Marielle whispered. "You know what you are. What *we* are. And if we don't put an end to this and anyone else gets hurt or loses their home, it'll be our fault."

Barbara's voice hitched. "How did you find out?"

"My mother."

A strange silence stood between them. Finally, Barbara broke off their connection. Defeated, she threw back her blanket.

"I'm coming down. Wait for me outside."

The puppy in Marielle's vest moved, giving off a tiny whimper. It would need something to eat soon, or it would die. She descended the ladder and looked around the stable. One of the stalls was empty except for an old fodder box, and Marielle opened it, meaning to deposit the pup inside with a little straw to keep it safe until she could think of something.

The lid was broken, and when she pushed it all the way to one side, she realized that a cat had built a little nest inside. She'd just had a litter of kittens and was too busy and exhausted licking them clean to bother with Marielle.

Maybe, just *maybe* this would work.

Marielle took some of the soiled straw from the bottom of the box and rubbed the pup with it. Then she put the tiny squirming creature in with the kittens and pulled the lid back the way she'd found it.

"You'll be fine here," she mumbled, hoping someone would find her there in the morning and have pity on her if the cat didn't let her drink.

It was even colder out in the yard than it had been when she'd first arrived at the farm. She shifted her weight from one foot to the other and puffed warm air into her fists until Barbara stepped out of the stable behind her.

The maid pulled a woolen cap down over her ears, and Marielle studied her. She didn't look like someone who'd been stabbed with a knife just hours ago. Marielle forced a smile and embraced her firmly, just to make sure. She let her hands glide down the other woman's back and shoulders. Barbara startled, but she didn't react the way someone who was in pain might have.

"All right," the maid said softly when Marielle let her go. "What do you want from me?"

"The truth. Who burned down my parents' farm?"

Barbara hung her head. "I did."

This, Marielle hadn't expected, and it came like a blow in the gut. Barbara had grown up on that farm, eaten at their table, and witnessed Susi's birth.

"Why?"

The maid raised her gaze to Marielle's. "I didn't mean to. You have to believe that I never meant to harm anyone. Your family was always good to me, and I love Susi as if she were my own sister."

"But you *did* hurt her, and my mother. They could have been killed."

Marielle only wanted to understand. After what had happened in the woods the previous morning, she knew all about wielding a power you couldn't control, but why the farm?

"I was so mad at you after you and Caspar left me behind in the woods. I turned back, and I meant to go home, but I was *so* angry. I shifted to my phoenix. I flew over the woods, circled over the mountains, and

then I came back to Breitenau. It was getting dark, and I hid behind the woodshed to change back to my human form, but your mother saw me. She screamed. She didn't recognize me, and I couldn't find the clothes I always kept there. Someone must have discovered them, maybe Susi, or your mother."

Marielle recalled the extra-large pile of laundry in the stone basin before they'd set off for the knacker's yard.

"Your father heard her screaming, and he came running. I panicked, and I shifted back without intention. He didn't know it was me. He only saw my phoenix, and he yelled and shouted. He threw chunks of wood at me. I tried to fly away, but I ended up crashing into a pile of flour sacks that we'd left under the roof overhang. You know, the ones from the barn that we were going to wash."

The ones they would have soaked in the stone basin by the well if her mother hadn't already had all those other clothes of Barbara's in it.

Barbara shrugged, helpless, and Marielle could imagine how fast the dry linen sacks must have caught, and how quickly the flames would have spread to the wood shavings under the chopping block, from there to the shed, and on to the house. One thing didn't make sense, though.

"Why did my father think it was *me* who set the woodshed on fire?"

"All your parents saw was a firebird. You changed on the knacker's field. It was your first time. Caspar told me you were airborne before he could try to help you. He said he looked for you, but he couldn't find you, and he assumed that you crashed into the barn later. Your father must have seen you – or someone else did."

Perhaps Caspar had. He'd been there, along with everyone else, fully dressed – in her father's shirt and pants. He wouldn't have needed them unless he'd shifted and flown, and he had to have gotten them from the barn.

He must have arrived at her parents' farm either along with her or a little later, so he must have known she was there, and he'd jammed the door and left her inside to burn. She could only hope Barbara hadn't had a part in it.

"Tell me the truth." She took Barbara's hands in her own. "Did Caspar slaughter the animals the night before?"

Again, Barbara nodded. "I think so."

"But are you *sure*?"

"Look, no one knows what really happened here," Barbara said. Tears streamed down her face. "You just have to leave. Things will settle down again if you do. Everyone's blaming the gypsies anyway, and the Habermanns are telling people you went away with them–"

"Change of plans, dear," a clear voice interrupted her from the shadows near the house. "I think it would be quite appropriate if she stayed after all."

Caspar's wings unfurled and illuminated the entire yard. He looked like an angel of vengeance as he sauntered toward them.

"I'm disappointed in you, Barbara," he said as though he was talking to a misbehaving child. "You promised you'd keep our little secret. I knew I shouldn't have trusted you. You just can't keep your mouth shut. You'll probably tell anyone who'll listen."

TWELVE

Marielle's headache was back, and the pain behind her eyes hit her like a stone. Whatever happened now, it was bound to end in catastrophe.

"Caspar," Barbara said, "don't."

"Don't *what*?" he asked. "*You* said you were sick and tired of her."

He flapped the fingers of his left hand dismissively in Marielle's direction. His right arm dangled uselessly by his side. Dried blood covered much of his chest where Mandl had wounded him, and he was naked except for a pair of pants that he'd probably stolen somewhere.

Marielle smelled smoke, but before she could say anything, one of the first-floor windows in the house burst, and shards spewed outward. Within seconds, another bang followed, and a tornado of flames began spreading unhindered throughout the building.

The backdoor was kicked open, and two people stumbled out, coughing and spluttering. A young man with his leg in a splint, probably Thomas, flung himself into the snow and lay where he fell. The other ran back inside, perhaps to save more of his siblings.

The explosions brought the dairymaids from the barn out into the yard. They took one look at Caspar and fled. Caspar ignored them, the fire, and the shouting from the house.

"*You* were *always* complaining to *me* about how badly Marielle was treating you," he continued quietly, still moving toward them, "and how you wished the plague upon her. You wanted her gone from here at any price. Are you pretending to be her friend now, and giving her advice?"

Marielle darted her gaze from the house that stood in flames to Barbara and back. Sweat beaded on her brow, and she retreated from the sobbing maid.

"Don't listen to him," Barbara wailed.

"That's right," Caspar said, not taking his eyes off Marielle. "She was in on it."

His smile turned to a vicious grin, and he fixed his stare to Barbara's, while all hell broke loose behind him and someone jumped from the burning second-floor balcony. The man looked up, and one after the other, the younger children were tossed down to him. He caught them, and they all immediately started shoveling snow into the fire.

"Go on, tell her how you begged me to put that stupid dog out of its misery because you had to clean up after it every day."

Barbara rocked back and forth on her heels, arms clamped tightly around herself. "But I didn't *mean* it! It was just *talk*!"

"It wasn't just talk, *Crabby Barbie*!" His eyes gleamed, but not gold. They were pure black when he glared back at Marielle. "She wanted you gone, and she would have done anything to make it happen."

"Why did you slaughter the animals?" Marielle asked him, disregarding Barbara, who was pleading with her now inarticulately. "And why Mandl?"

"Do you know how much the butcher in Mittenwald will give you for a pound of beef nowadays, even from an old cow? And are you aware of how long you can feed a family of six on the cabbage that money will buy?"

Had the Wasls been starving? Why hadn't she known this?

Another of the older Habermann boys jumped from the blazing balcony. He joined the others in scooping snow into the inferno.

"That's why you needed Gustav," she said more to herself than to Caspar. "How did you get him off the farm without leaving tracks?"

"I had help from your dairymaid earlier in the evening," he said, looking at Barbara. She covered her face with her hands.

"You could have asked for *our* help," Marielle said.

"Who? *Yours*?"

He laughed, but the sound turned into a cough, and he touched the right side of his chest with his good hand and winced, spitting blood into the snow at his feet. His wings faltered and their fire died.

"While you were rolling around in the hay with Harald Habermann?" he went on then. "You selfish bitch! Have you ever spent even a minute of your life thinking about other people? You, who's always getting others to clean up her mess? Or should I have begged your arrogant father?" He paused. "He accused me of being a gold-digger when I asked him to let me court you!"

The pain in his voice spilled over onto his skin, turning it to gold. She expected him to shift to his phoenix and prepared to let her own instincts take over, whatever they would have her do. But instead, black patches appeared on his body.

At first, Marielle thought the dark stains that were spreading on his gold were a deception caused by a cloud moving across the moonlit sky, but then she realized he wasn't turning into a phoenix. This was something else, and the shock on his face told her he knew it.

She signaled to Barbara without letting him out of her sight. "Run to the Bergers and tell them the Habermanns' house is burning. Your family needs help."

Barbara didn't waste one second.

Cioara, the little voice in her head whispered. *Tell him.*

The third scrap of vellum had that name written on it, but her mother couldn't tell her what it meant.

Everyone has a right to know who they are.

"You're Cioara," she said loudly, putting two and two together. "*The Crow.*"

He stood in the middle of the yard for a few heartbeats like an unfinished statue, and raised his good hand to inspect it. He turned it this way and that in front of his face and let out a mad laugh.

"You didn't know, did you?" she said.

She was sure he'd lied when he'd told Mandl and her about meeting Puridaia. He'd never heard his name spoken out loud – or hadn't *wanted* to hear it.

"Mandl found out that you lied. Is that why he had to die?"

Caspar's hands changed to claws. Black feathers sprouted all over his body and he shrank. He glared at her full of hate, wanting to speak, but instead of words, all that came out of his mouth was a caw, and an instant later, a huge crow sat where Caspar had stood. It tried to flap its wings, but one of them wouldn't obey, and it couldn't leave the ground.

Marielle felt the tension leave her body, and her head stopped hurting. It had been him all along. Caspar was the one without the aura, and without the help he would have needed to make the kind of decisions that would have kept him golden.

The laborer who'd been sleeping in the hay loft appeared next to Marielle. Strangely unimpressed, he looked around. Then he pushed his fingers between his lips and whistled. A gypsy caravan rounded the rampant hazel scrub that grew on one side of the barn. It stopped, and Marielle thought she recognized the driver with the bushy eyebrows and the child beside him.

"Gathering waifs tonight?" the laborer shouted to the gypsy.

He picked up the crow that had been Caspar just a

few minutes ago. It tried to peck him, but he turned it on its back, and it quieted straightaway.

"Yes," the driver shouted back. "If you have one that can't conquer the storm."

"We certainly do," the old man replied, and carried the bird to the caravan.

He handed the crow up to the gypsy, and the man with the bushy eyebrows carefully inserted it into a burlap sack. He closed it with a piece of cord and passed it on to the child next to him. The child sat it on her lap, smiled, and waved to Marielle. Marielle blew her a kiss.

"Any more out there who can't withstand?" the driver asked.

The old field hand looked over his shoulder at Marielle. She nodded.

"I think there might be." She pointed in the direction Barbara had gone.

"Can you tell me her name?"

She bit her lip and thought about it. "She knows it, and she might tell you herself," she finally said.

The man grinned crookedly, shrugging. "She is the master of her own fate."

Then he clicked his tongue and juggled the reins, and the caravan drew away as silently as it had come.

The laborer returned to Marielle and watched it leave. He pulled a flask from the pocket of his coat and uncorked it. Without a word, he offered it to her. She accepted and took a big swallow, and then another. The brandy slid down her throat like honey and warmed her all the way to her feet.

"Let's get a little farther back and out of the way," the old man said when the flames reached the roof of the farmhouse, and he led her out of the yard and onto the road.

There, they sipped the remainder of the brandy and watched as the Habermanns and the Bergers continued to try to save the building with the stubborn determination that was so typical of the people here. A true Breitenauer always battled on against nature and the elements, no matter how lost the cause. Eventually, however, there was so little of the house left to save, they had to give up, and they then concentrated on not letting the blaze spread to the barn and the other outbuildings.

Toward morning, Thomas and some of the smaller children had been accommodated in the stable loft and in the barn, while their parents and the other siblings were sitting in the yard, passing around a few flasks of their own.

THIRTEEN

A few days after the Habermanns' house burned down, head councilman Arthur Voigt received a letter from Barbara Weissenbacher. In it, she claimed responsibility for the fire at the Habermann farm as well as the one that had destroyed the Reindl family's home. She explained that she'd acted out of jealousy over a young man, attempting to drive Marielle away by spreading false information.

After he'd discussed the matter with the other Garmisch councilmen, Voigt visited the Reindls and the Habermanns. He read the letter to them. Since no one would openly admit to seeing something so unbelievable and preposterous as a firebird on the nights their houses had burned down, the bailiff was called upon to form a search party and find Barbara. They combed the woods of Werdenfels for over a week but had no success in finding her. Neither she nor Caspar were ever seen again.

Marielle had a feeling they were both well on their way south with the Wintersteins despite the new snow in the alpine passes. The travelers would get wherever it was they were going, in time.

She briefly wondered if Caspar would remain a crow for the rest of his days, and found herself wishing he would not return to his human form. How she – and everyone else in this place – had managed to overlook his capacity for cruelty, she'd never fathom. Gentle, understanding Caspar, of all people. Her father had called him *soft*.

She couldn't quite picture Barbara living her life on the road, but there wasn't a doubt in her mind that Puridaia had instilled the fear of God in the maid. Barbara would otherwise never have written that letter, for all the good it would do Marielle. Michel knew the truth, and there wasn't a chance in hell they'd be a family again.

The Reindls didn't object when the gypsies were blamed for the missing and slaughtered livestock. Who else could it have been? Certainly not one of their neighbors, and the Habermanns shared that opinion. After all, Thomas had been attacked by one of them, trying to bring them to justice. Innocent people didn't hide in the woods and then run away, and they didn't go attacking deputies. Georg Strolz had gone blind, and he swore that the man he'd fought with in the woods had been a huge, bear-like giant with a torch, probably a Firestarter, so this case, too, was soon closed.

Harald Habermann had been on a drinking splurge at the Abbey of Ettal when the Reindl family's house burned down. He'd heard the news the very next day but decided against returning to Breitenau.

Michel's misfortune was Thomas' misfortune, and Marielle guessed she just hadn't been pretty enough for him to rush to her rescue and marry her anyway.

Not now that her dowry had turned to ashes, along with the farm he'd hoped to take over from her father when the time came. The dreams of a second son had gone up in smoke, and although she bore no grudges, she did regret having kissed him.

Sometimes, ashes could turn to gold, though, as Marielle knew, and apparently so could hops. She was happy to hear a number of years later that Harald acquired new dreams and lived them to the fullest. He found God, took his vows, and joined the Abbey. Not only did Padre Benedictus, as he called himself, have a greater love for beer than he could ever have felt for a woman, he also had a knack for the fine art of beer-brewing. Within months of taking over from the aged master brewer, he doubled the Abbey's turnover, and kept increasing it every year from there on in as long as he lived, making Ettal's beer famous all over the empire.

Michel rebuilt the Reindls' house, but Marielle never came back to Breitenau to live with her parents and little sister. She, too, had other goals now. There were mountains to climb and oceans to discover.

She often thought of the Mediterranean seaside painting in Puridaia's caravan. Good thing she was free to find out which one it depicted – free as a bird, just like the young man who'd climbed the Zugspitze despite everyone telling him he couldn't. She couldn't help thinking about him, and admired his courage. One day in spring, she plucked up enough of her own to seek him out.

He lived on the Tyrol side of the mountain, and she smiled when he told her his name: Aurelius. His parents had fond memories of Puridaia and her family, and they welcomed Marielle with open arms.

They owned a little tavern that catered to merchants and travelers who had many strange and wonderful tales to tell. Marielle worked there for food and lodgings for herself and her dog, Charlie, the shaggy St. Bernard Mandl had left to her.

That summer, Aurelius taught her how to climb, and she taught him how to fly. In autumn, they married. Together they saw many a mountaintop from the Alps to the Madoni mountains in Sicily, and acquired wonderful, golden tales of their own to tell to their children and grandchildren.

AMBERFLAME

Willa's feet were freezing beneath her blanket, but it wasn't the cold that kept her awake. She'd been feeding the flames in the hearth like her life depended on it, just to give herself something to do while everyone else in the tiny one-room cottage slept – or at least pretended to.

The little ones deserved to be warm at night. Heaven knew there was a hard winter ahead. The past few days had already given them a proper taste of it, along with a high fever and a persistent cough. She made sure both children were snug beneath their covers and swung her legs out of the bed just as a polar gust cracked the rickety shutter of the window across from her.

Swiftly, she covered the five paces to the window and glanced out. When she didn't see what she'd been hoping for, she pulled the shutter back toward the frame – but not all the way.

Closing the window might have helped keep the heat inside the cottage and saved them some wood, but it was out of the question. She needed to be able to see outside from her side of the bed, and as long as her father couldn't afford glass for the windows, this particular shutter would just have to stay open at night over the next weeks.

At the other end of the room, Bertram stirred in his sleep, flipped over on his back, and snored like a boar

digging for chestnuts in the thicket. She wondered how her mother put up with him. He was a good man, but he liked his liquor and often drank too much. He'd had nearly a whole bottle of elderberry blossom schnapps after their evening meal, and he'd done a lot of tone-deaf singing, yelling, and ranting before he'd finally started snoring.

Love had a way of making you deaf to things you didn't want to hear, and blind to things you didn't want to see, Willa supposed. When she was sure her mother had stopped crying and also gone to sleep, she crossed the creaking floorboards to the north-facing window once more to scan the forest on the opposite hillside.

Again, nothing.

Her heart sank, and she laid another log on the fire. A few parched pine sprigs that had lost most of their needles wilted away in a vase on the mantlepiece. Next to it, a winged angel roughly the size of a dove prayed silently. Her grandfather had carved the wooden statue for her when Willa had been little, trying to instill some Advent cheer in the house. She missed him every time she saw it.

Eventually, she decided to call it quits and shut the window all the way. It was getting too late, and she had to walk to work in the morning so they could afford the ham her mother had ordered for Christmas Day. It would be a long, cold trudge to Silverberg through the icy forest if she took the short route, and an even longer, colder one if she walked along the main road.

One more moment, she told herself twice or three times as she stood watching the pale moon journeying across the night sky. Then, just as she was about to latch the shutter, the three lights she'd been waiting for flickered to life one after the other in the window of the hunting cabin on the other side of the narrow valley. Willa smiled, forgetting her weariness.

She didn't hear Thomas leave his bed and startled when the little boy pushed up against her from behind, snaking his thin arms around her leg. His cheeks were too warm, and his nose was runny. She bent to pick him up, wiped his face with a damp rag, and put him back under the covers without waking his twin, Emma.

"Go back to sleep and get well," she whispered.

"You go away every night," Thomas mumbled, already half asleep again.

"Not true," she said softly, wishing it was, and instantly feeling guilty for it. She kissed his forehead. "I need to fetch some more wood for the fire. I'll be back soon enough."

He seemed satisfied and nestled into his pillow, sticking his thumb in his mouth. He was too old to be sucking his fingers, but she let him be. Their father scolded him for it too often, not realizing he was only augmenting Thomas' need for his soother every time he did.

She pulled on her clothes, grabbed her shoes, and slipped outside without looking back. Her skin tingled from the icy air and anticipation, and her breath misted in front of her, forming ghostly shapes in the night as she tugged on her winter coat and pulled the hood up over her face. Then she hurried down the hill, cutting through a sparse hazel grove instead of taking the road that led past her father's house to the village in the valley.

The shortcut brought her to Aliment Lot, a field that bordered on the low, crumbling cemetery wall just outside Aldabach. She hesitated before stepping out into the open, scanning the area and trying to calm her breathing so she could listen for any sign of movement. There was no cover here, nowhere to hide, and the place itself gave her the creeps.

Her biggest worry was the watchman up in the church belfry. On a moon-lit night like this, Frank Bogner would have clear sight of Aliment Lot. The field and the cemetery wouldn't be his main focus of attention, but the monotony of observing the same part of the sky due south and the endless hours until dawn would have him looking for distraction – if he was there and awake. Also, he was getting on in years, and he loved his schnapps as much as Bertram did.

Willa watched the belfry for a while. When she didn't see any movement, she decided to risk it and scurried across the rime-white meadow, avoiding the pole in the middle and taking care not to step on the unmarked graves on her side of the wall.

The souls of sinners slept beneath the unconsecrated, frozen soil here. They had to wait for their day of judgement, or so the pastor would have the *decent* people of Aldabach believe, just as he would tell them that everyone's fate was measured and written.

Among the sinners on Aliment Lot was a widow whose two young children Willa had watched from time to time. The woman had hung herself after they died of the fever two years ago. In the grave beside hers lay an adulteress whose husband had five children out of wedlock. He'd thrown her out of the house with nothing but the clothes on her back on a cold day last January. They'd discovered her body in the woods a week later.

Willa put wild roses, daisies, or forget-me-nots on both graves whenever she came by on summer nights, but nothing bloomed right now except for the frost on the windowpanes at the hunting cabin, so tonight she had no flowers to leave.

She climbed over the wall to where the God-fearing people laid their dead to rest, hoping the gate at the other end of the yard wouldn't be locked again as it had the last time she'd been here. The wall on the village side was higher than it was toward the field and the woods, as though the living didn't like to be reminded of the deceased too often, even if the deceased happened to be *decent* people.

When she reached the iron gate, she pulled so firmly on its frost-crusted handle, she almost landed on her behind when it swung back. The screeching sound of corroded metal sent a shiver down her spine, and she was sure she'd woken half the village. She darted toward the nearest cluster of half-timbered buildings, and ducked back into the shadows of a cluttered alleyway.

Aldabach had a population of three hundred and thirty souls, and when the nights grew longer and the days colder, people liked to talk. She could imagine what they'd be saying about her the next morning if someone saw her sneaking around at this hour. She waited for a moment, listening, observing, and then continued on her way.

All was remarkably quiet, even at *The Boar*, the village tavern. The woodcutters sometimes drank late into the night here, and the stench of urine and feces from the mid-street gutter was overwhelming. She held her breath, trying not to step in anything as she went by.

Three buildings down from the alehouse, someone opened an upper-floor window, and Willa dipped behind a rainwater barrel. Swearing loudly, Matilda Cordwainer emptied a chamber pot out onto the street. A window in the house opposite opened, and a woman with a frilly nightcap appeared in the frame. It was Anna Potter, one of the chattiest women in the Vales.

"People are trying to sleep," Anna said, irritated.

"Child's coming," Matilda's said, "and it's probably a bit on the heavy side."

"Well, *you're* a bit on the heavy side, dear. What do you expect?"

Willa chuckled, and immediately clasped a hand to her mouth, hoping she hadn't been heard.

"You're a great help," Matilda muttered.

Anna huffed. "Want me to come over?" she asked without much enthusiasm.

"Not yet. I'll need Ingunde if it isn't here by dawn."

"As you please," Anna said, "but wake that lazy husband of yours to fetch her. I have bread to bake in the morning."

Anna shut her window, and Matilda retreated into the house, still swearing like a sailor. When she felt it was safe, Willa scurried past, heading for the shallow river that dissected Aldabach.

The village church was on the other side of the stream. She cast another wary glance up at the belfry but still couldn't see anyone. Bogner would probably doze through a war, she thought, edging toward the arched bridge.

Ice coated the worn flagstone pavement and glinted in the moonlight. She held on to the parapet, but her feet kept sliding out from under her, and she was glad when she was back on the frozen dirt road beyond. Passing the church, she heard Bogner mumbling in his sleep and quietly wished him sweet dreams that lasted until she was back in her own bed.

A dog lay on the stoop in front of the carpenter's house. It looked up at her, wagging its tail when she approached, and she patted its head. The hound licked her fingers and gladly took the bite-sized bit of sausage she'd brought for it.

The village bakehouse still smelled of the spelt loaves that had been in the big oven the day before.

Its brick chimney was warm, and no frost had settled on the shingles of its roof. Her mother would be relighting the fire in the oven the next morning, and ten more women would take their turn at baking the bread they'd need for their families' meals over Christmas.

A little farther up the road, a dim light shone in the midwife's ramshackle cottage, but there was hardly a way around it unless she cut straight through the brush, so Willa stayed on the road. Ingunde had already seen her anyway. The old woman crouched in her doorway, softly talking to a cat that slunk around her legs.

Willa briefly considered turning around, but then decided she had nothing to fear. Ingunde was ancient, and she didn't waste her time spreading rumors, though by way of her profession, she was probably the best-informed person in the twelve villages.

"You're up late, Willa Goodfellow," the midwife said, straightening, and pulling her woolen shawl tightly around herself.

"So I am," Willa replied, flashing her a bright smile. "And I have no excuse." There was no point in lying. Ingunde wasn't stupid.

The old woman seemed baffled at her brashness but didn't follow up. She could probably guess where Willa was going. The midwife might have seen her come by this way after dark before. God knew she'd been up and down to the hunting cabin at least once a week since summer.

"Matilda's baby is coming," she offered, breaking the awkward silence. "She might send for you in the morning."

"Good to know," Ingunde said. "I'll go and see her first thing." She smiled at Willa kindly. "You take care now."

Then she turned and went back inside with not one, but three cats on her heels. People around here thought she was crazy for feeding them and letting them into the house. Cats were said to be bad luck, and most folks in Aldabach killed any strays they found wandering around the woods. Willa didn't much care for that particular practice. Animals couldn't be good or bad, or sway fortune in either direction. They were what they were.

Shivering, she continued on her way. The hunting cabin perched on a natural terrace near the top of the hill, and by the time she got there, her feet were numb, but she was giddy as a child.

It was balmy inside the little cabin. Aberlin had lit a crackling fire and sat cross-legged by the open hearth, absently stoking the flames when she quietly slipped inside. He only became aware of her when she dropped to her knees beside him. The radiant smile on his face never ceased to make her heart miss a beat, and the world outside the cabin was forgotten.

Without a word, he enveloped her in his warmth and kissed her lips. Life was good. She let him undress her and lead her to the bed – the bed with the beautifully carved headboard and the fragrant

embroidered sheets where she'd decided in summer that he would be her first and only man.

Aberlin had been her best friend, and now he was her lover. Whenever they were together, she felt like a queen. He was gentle and giving, and she never doubted him when he whispered that he loved her more than his life. He touched her as though she was precious and breakable, and he treated her with more respect than anyone else had ever done.

Sometimes, after dark, they went walking together in the woods behind the cabin, and he told her of his hopes and dreams. At least those he had for the villages over which his father's castle held vigil. He asked for her opinion on matters that were important to him and listened to what she had to say.

He made her laugh with his silly stories about the padre who'd tried to teach him Latin up until last year, the cook's antics in the castle kitchen, or Wildflower, his favorite horse. He didn't speak unkindly of others, and she adored his incorrigible optimism.

The one thing they didn't talk about was their relationship. She was only part of his life by night while the Vales slept. He would never ask her to marry him, and she wouldn't lead him to believe she wanted him to. Marriage hadn't been a likely option at the best of times, and then, two things had happened.

The first of them was that Aberlin's elder brother had gotten himself killed. Jacob's death had crushed her tentative girl's fantasy of a future with Aberlin because it meant that he was now his father's sole heir. Any night she spent with him could be their last, depending on how quickly his mother managed to find a good match for him.

Despite the crushing effect Jacob's death had on her, Lady Gerlinde had retained her soft-spoken manner and compassion for the needy. She no longer left the castle quite as often as she used to, but Lord Immanuel valued her advice, and her cleverness and foresight commanded respect in the Vales. Any girl of noble birth might gladly consent to the connection with Aberlin, knowing this was part of the prize.

Willa's only consolation was her certainty that Gerlinde wouldn't let just anyone have him. He was her last living child, and she would want someone for him who would eventually shoulder her burden, run the castle, and have his back without question or complaint. Someone who would give him children to bear his name and inherit the lands Gerlinde's forefathers had fought and died for. Someone whose hands were never chaffed when she stroked his beautiful face, and whose feet were never cold. Willa hoped Lady Gerlinde would choose someone kind and loving.

The moon moved across the clear sky like a rider on a mission, and she knew they didn't have much time left before dawn would awaken the little village and her parents would find her gone. The three tallow candles in the window had burned to tiny stumps because they'd been short to begin with, and the fire in the hearth had died.

She turned in Aberlin's arms and found him studying her.

"We should run off," he said unexpectedly.

Her spine tingled. *And then what?*

"*I* should run off," she said out loud instead of just thinking it.

"Are you sorry you met me?"

She wasn't, but she didn't want this conversation. Not tonight. It would make her heart heavy, and she had no use for a heavy heart.

"Of course I am," she told him, dead serious. "Look at me, naked and freezing after being ravished by the Vales' tyrant-lord in the woods. How will I ever get over this and lead a normal life again?"

His face went blank, and she burst out laughing, hoping he'd laugh along with her and save her – save them both. It took him half a heartbeat to comprehend that she was pulling his leg, or trying to. For one horrible moment she thought he would be mad at her. Finally, he ventured a grin, but he was a bad actor, and it was the saddest grin she'd ever seen.

"I'm sorry," she said, and coaxed him to roll over, pinning him down beneath her.

She brushed a stray strand of golden hair from his brow and fixed her gaze to his. He was all warmth and hard muscles, nothing like she'd expected a blue-blooded second son to feel like before she'd felt his body on hers for the first time. The scent of fresh hay and apples clung to his skin, and memories of an azure summer sky danced in his eyes whenever he laughed. Oh, how she wished he'd just followed her lead and laughed at her bad joke now, but she should have known him better. He'd been a part of her life for over two years, and she still didn't know what to expect from him.

"I'm sorry," she repeated, caressing his cheek. "I love you." That had to be enough. She couldn't give him anything more, and she couldn't take anything from him either. She had no right to him.

His fingers traced the line of her jawbone, and he pulled her to him. His lips tasted of honey on pine sprigs, and she ached from longing for him. He could have left the bed and the cabin instead of kissing her, but he was still here, and it was almost unfair. Life was never fair in the Vales, and yet they were together. For now.

She stroked and kissed every inch of him, and they made love again, but his words kept reverberating in her mind, and the sad look in his eyes would not give her peace. Things would be different between them next time they saw each other. If there was a next time.

She watched him sleeping for as long as she dared to stay afterward, wishing she had nowhere to be in a few hours, and took care not to wake him when she got dressed and pulled on her shoes. The stars were already waning, and a gray, hungry dawn lurked just beyond the horizon in the east.

A heavy weight bore down on her shoulders, slowing her as she made her way back toward the village. For the first time in her life, she felt a little sorry for herself. Shivering, she bent to stroke one of Ingunde's cats when she reached the midwife's house, and a dark shadow passed directly overhead. Her heart stopped.

Amberflame!

Bogner was likely still asleep – who'd raise the alarm? Who'd warn everyone?

Silently gliding down from the hill, the crimson dragon was so close, its mighty horn-tipped wings whispered against the treetops. It was a wonder the beast didn't see Willa on the narrow road below.

Ingunde's cat disappeared into the undergrowth, and Willa froze, unable to move, unable to breathe as she listened to the hoarse sound of Amberflame filling her lungs with air as she slowed her advance. Then, a bellowing roar shattered the night, and the sky lit up as the dragon's first firebolt hit the church belfry, killing the slumbering guard.

The little steeple exploded in a red-hot blast, and burning debris rained down on the bridge. A molten clump of iron – the remains of the bell – came down in the river with a thud, smashing the ice on the water's surface.

At last, Willa came to her senses and bolted, arms up to protect her head. She took cover behind the woodpile Ingunde kept beside her cottage. Why was this happening? Why tonight?

The dragon rose, doubled back, and dipped once again, spewing another gush of flaming bile at the church. The force of the flare took what remained of the roof clean off, and the whole building was ablaze.

Amberflame ascended and circled, and moments later, another explosion ripped through the air, but Willa couldn't see where. There was too much smoke, and it bit into her lungs. Something touched her shoulder, and she screamed, realizing a second later that it was only Ingunde. Deathly pale, barefoot, and in her nightgown, the old woman looked like an apparition.

"Come on!" the midwife yelled, dragging her to her feet. "We have to get away from the house!"

Willa knew she was right, but at the same time, doing so probably played straight into the dragon's strategy: Amberflame destroyed buildings to draw as many people as possible out into the open, where they would either become easy targets or get to watch the carnage.

Willa moved through the trees, following Ingunde as though in a dream, running for her life without feeling the soles of her feet touching the ground. The sensation only wore off when they reached a rocky alcove some way into the forest and she regained some sense of direction.

The alcove was protected from three sides, and a cluster of too-densely grown young beeches and bare hazel bushes provided cover near the opening. The narrow cavity in the hillside had once served as one

of two entrances to a silver mine that had collapsed over a century ago.

It had been blocked so children wouldn't wander inside, but the honeycombed earth was always shifting here with the autumn rains and the winter storms. A gap in the wall had widened sufficiently to allow the two women to crawl inside one after the other just as the dragon's next blast of fire hit.

For a second, golden shafts of light speared into the mine's entrance, illuminating the claustrophobic space around them. They both knew the monster had aimed for Ingunde's house. The only other building this far up on the hillside was the hunting cabin near the top. Willa's stomach lurched.

"No," she whimpered. She was about to turn and inch back out the way she'd come, but Ingunde grabbed her around the waist.

"Don't!" the midwife hissed. "Stay here!"

"Let me go!" Willa's eyes filled with tears.

The cabin wasn't far, and she had to warn him. She'd be there in no time if she scampered straight up the slope instead of taking the path, but Ingunde didn't have to tell her that this would be suicide.

Five years ago, the dragon had destroyed one of the farmhouses on the other side of the village, and everyone in the building had died either in the fire, or in the moments afterward. A maid had tried to escape into the woods. Amberflame had picked the girl up like a ragdoll and torn her to pieces. The farmer's youngest son made it to the river, badly burned, only to drown because no one dared come to his aid. They'd found him face-down in the water along with three other bodies after the beast had gone.

Several people died during the attack that night, but the dragon had not eaten even one of them. Amberflame only fed when she was hungry, and she certainly had been hungry – but she liked to taunt them and play with them if one of the Vales' communities refused to give her what she wanted. She always made *them* choose.

Tonight, the dragon should not have been anywhere near here. Not if she'd gotten her Aliment in Tannenberg the previous night.

Something must have gone wrong. Perhaps Tannenberg's designated sacrifice had absconded at the last moment, or they'd just refused to send someone's daughter, mother, or sister to the field where the dragon would devour her, and now Aldabach would have to pay the price.

Willa's heart thumped madly in her chest, and all the warmth and goodness she'd taken with her from the cabin evaporated in the icy air. How many would Amberflame kill tonight? Whose mutilated bodies would they find strewn around the valley in the morning?

Aberlin would have been safer at the castle. Had it not been for her, he'd have been asleep in his own bed. He'd have been out of harm's way.

She made another attempt to reach the opening, and again Ingunde held her back. "Don't be stupid,"

the midwife said. "You don't have a chance."

"You don't understand!"

Ingunde pressed her against the rock wall with all her strength. "I understand better than you think."

Willa shook her head and struggled, but Ingunde didn't let go of her.

"I know Aberlin is up there," she said. "I care about him, too."

Willa found this strange. It stood to logic that the old biddy was aware of his presence in the cabin, and she had to assume that he and Willa were lovers, but why should she know him well enough to care about him?

No one in the Vales *cared* about the people who lived up at the castle on the next hill. Many of them blamed the nobles for the misfortune that had befallen the villages. Those who had seen the battlefields and fought side by side with their lord in their king's last war understood the price of their artificial safe haven – those who remained at home had no idea.

Willa struggled. "What do you know of Aberlin?"

"He was born on a night exactly like this, and I nursed him and his brother when Lady Gerlinde couldn't. Jacob and he both drank from my breast for nearly two years, so don't go assuming you are more entitled to a concern for his safety than I."

Ingunde sounded so upset, Willa didn't doubt she was telling the truth. Only she wouldn't have thought Ingunde could still have nursed a child eighteen years ago. She looked much too old to have cared for an infant even forty years ago, but Willa realized she knew very little about Ingunde.

"Look," the midwife continued, cautiously letting go of Willa, "neither of us can help him now. He's smart. He will have left the cabin as soon as he grasped what was going on, and it won't do to put yourself in danger. Calling to him would bring him out into the open, looking for you. You'd *both* be in danger then. We're going to stay put until this is over. It's the best we can do."

And they did. Three more explosions shattered the early hours of December 23rd, and the screams they heard made Willa want to cover her ears. She didn't think she recognized any of the shrill, desperate voices, and prayed that none of them belonged to one of her parents, or the twins.

With Bertram drunk, it would have been up to her mother to get everyone out of the house. She should have been there to help her bring the children to safety. Perhaps this was her punishment for all the times she'd lied to and deceived her family – her punishment for loving the wrong man.

Eventually, day came. The screaming stopped, and the dragon was gone.

Willa crawled outside and glanced around, joints stiff, mouth dry. The smell of foul eggs and scorched meat hung in the air. She bent over, retching until she was able to steady herself well enough to make a decision.

"Go and look for Aberlin," she told Ingunde. "I have to see if my family is unharmed."

She ran all the way, past the smoking ruin of Ingunde's home, the ashen remains of the bakehouse and the church, and through the village center of Aldabach, where *The Boar* and the two houses on either side of the inn had burned almost to the ground within less than an hour.

People were dousing the smoldering skeletal frameworks with water from the river, as well as the walls and roofs of the neighboring buildings to make sure the remaining heat didn't set them on fire. Hot embers still carried on the wind, fluttering like cherry petals in May, only they were black instead of white.

Six hastily covered bodies lay lined up along the street. Willa was astonished there were so few. She hesitated for a moment, staring at a charred foot peeking out from under a quilt, and then grabbed someone by the arm.

"Tell me, do you know who that is?" she pointed at the body, but couldn't look the man in the eye.

He shook her, and his face came into focus. She recognized her mother's older brother. Arthur Theis was one of the village elders, and he was helping to carry the buckets from the river.

"Where have you been, girl?" he shouted. "Angela's half crazy. They're searching the woods for you."

She nodded at him and pointed at the burned remains again. The man's size matched Aberlin.

"It's Christian Potter. Anna and the children are safe. The beast got Harold and Josepha Bricklayer, Agnes Hofmeier, Frank Bogner, and Alexander, the boy who was helping Johann Ackermann on the farm down on the Silverberg Road. No one knows why he was out here."

Maybe visiting his beloved, Willa thought, and crossed herself. Mouthing a thank you, she headed for the cemetery. Her family had survived, and Aberlin probably had, too.

Somewhere, a newborn baby cried. Matilda's child. The sound eased the hot knot in her stomach.

She found her parents' cottage untouched, and the twins inside, sleeping. A neighbor helped her call off the search in the woods, and when her parents returned, they had a lot of questions. Most of them were difficult to answer.

Around noon, Theis' eldest son came to inform them about a meeting in the village center. A small paved area there served as a market square twice a year. Everyone was expected to attend. The dragon would return after dark, and there were decisions to be made. Willa knew what that meant.

They bundled up the children, sat them in a hand cart, and immediately headed for the village to hear what the elders would have to say.

Many of the people who came had to stand on the muddy street because the square would not accommodate them all. The voices of men and women, young and old, the freshly bereft, and those who'd already learned to live with their losses over the years blended into a hum that steadily rose until the elders arrived. Lord Immanuel was with them, and he'd brought Aberlin.

Relief washed over Willa. It must have shown on her face, because she suddenly felt her mother's arm around her shoulder.

"I'm glad he's unhurt," Angela whispered.

"Quiet, please!" Theis called. "We have much to discuss!" Soot still clung to his coat, and his hands and face were filthy. He looked as tired as Willa felt.

"Lord Immanuel!" Bertram said before Theis could welcome them. "I hope you're here to help, and not just to make pretty speeches again."

Both Theis and Immanuel cast him an irritated glance.

"I know you've all had a lot to contend with these past years," Immanuel said, looking at him directly, "but we can find a way to resolve this situation."

"*Resolve this situation?*" a man who'd just joined them said, taking his place among the elders. It was Zacharias Hofmeier. "We lost our friends, neighbors, and relatives last night. We want to know what happened."

Immanuel patted his back. "I sent my steward to Tannenberg this morning. He confirmed what the honorable Theis told me most of you already suspected. There was trouble two nights ago, and no Aliment was offered."

"And so *we* pay, and pay, and pay again," Robert Cordwainer shouted. "We have six deaths to mourn, and ten are injured!"

For the umpteenth time, Willa wondered what kind of trouble the people of Tannenberg had run into. Had their Aliment fled, or had someone decided to fight back… like Jacob had?

Doubtful they'd hear the whole truth from Immanuel today, she looked at Aberlin and found him staring straight back at her. She couldn't read what she saw in his eyes, but it wasn't any kind of accusation or anger. Perhaps she would have a chance to speak to him later, though her father probably wouldn't let her out of his sight again today.

"Let Tannenberg send someone!" Matilda called, getting ahead of Theis. She stood next to her husband, holding her new baby in her arms.

With five children in the house now, Willa was sure the cobbler's wife was scared to death her husband or she might be chosen next. One more baby, and the elders would take them both out of the pool. Children under the age of fourteen and parents of six or more children were exempted, though Willa had no idea whose not-so-clever mind had come up with that number. Five orphaned children were just as apt to starve as six, when their remaining guardian's means were exhausted.

"And we also demand reparations for the families of the victims," Theis said.

Immanuel turned to him. "I'll make sure they receive them."

"But that won't solve the bigger problem," Hofmeier said.

A murmur went through the crowd. The elders seldom spoke up against their lord, but Hofmeier had everyone's sympathy. His grief was almost choking him.

Immanuel looked taken aback, but Willa didn't think he was truly surprised. The trust had been broken – *again*. Five years ago, Millbach had failed them, and last night, Tannenberg had done it again.

Although he couldn't protect the twelve villages against the demands of the dragon, a lot of people believed Immanuel should at least protect them against each other and punish those who broke the rules of their arrangement, if their shortcomings harmed the other villages.

But Willa knew this wasn't how it worked. Immanuel had to uphold his end of the pact to the letter, or his days as lord of the Vales were counted.

"I said I'd never get involved in the choosing process, and I won't," Immanuel declared. "No *von Aldabach* ever did, and I won't start."

"You said a lot of things," a young man who'd been friendly with Alexander shouted, rising above the other voices.

"What is it you demand of me?" Immanuel said then.

If he sent soldiers to make sure the Aliments were on location in the Vales' villages every full moon night when the dragon came, it wouldn't be long before people would fear *him*, and not the dragon.

"Why doesn't *he* ever provide an Aliment?" Matilda's eldest daughter muttered.

Willa turned to her. She and Ruth had played together as children.

"They lost a son last year."

Ruth cast her a derogatory glance. "But it's not like they *sacrificed* him."

"He died trying to kill it—"

Frank Bogner's grandson cut in. "The beast is loyal to the lords of the Vales," he told Willa, as though he was speaking to an ignorant child from anywhere but here. "Immanuel could just order it to stop killing us. He doesn't because it's his way of keeping us in line, if you ask me."

Willa decided not to argue because you couldn't win an argument with an idiot, but Bertram had overheard what the lad said and clipped him on the ear.

"Young fool! You know nothing!"

Bertram had no great love for the family whose ancestor gave this village its name, but he'd fought alongside Lord Immanuel against the last great army that had tried to overrun the kingdom. He'd told Willa what the dragon could do on the battlefield, but he'd also told her that Amberflame wasn't allegiant to Immanuel's family in the way that someone who hadn't seen her in action might assume.

Amberflame was a killing machine a hundred times more effective than the black powder the king imported from Asia nowadays, but she killed for two reasons only: to protect her territory, and to feed. The Vales were her territory, and had it not been for the dragon, the twelve villages that were right in the path of the Eastern Empire's mercenaries would have been razed to the ground during the war.

Immanuel raised his hands to command attention, and most of the talking ceased.

"I will say it again: I won't involve myself in the choosing process. That is the duty of your elders. It always was. But I will make sure Tannenberg sends the Aliment before sundown, by force if necessary – this *one time*."

"We're grateful for that, Milord, but it's your duty to keep the peace in the Vales," Hofmeier insisted, casting Theis a sideways look. "And we must ask you to continue to do so now that we've had not one, but *two* breaches of the agreement in the past years. *Both* times, *our* village has paid the price, and we want *real* compensation."

Immanuel's stare became as icy as the air. "I do appreciate that Aldabach has been unduly burdened, and I assure you, I will see to it that the people of Tannenberg will live up to their responsibility. I don't know what more I can do."

A few Aldabachers nodded, apparently satisfied, but most remained silent, waiting to hear how Theis or Hofmeier would respond.

The twins fussed, and Willa gave them a piece of hard bread each to busy them.

Theis shifted his weight from one foot to the other and rubbed his stubbly chin. His gaze briefly met Willa's before he spoke. "We want more. Our next Aliment would be due in January. We want Tannenberg to provide a replacement so our village can recover without suffering yet another loss so soon after this disaster."

This time, shouts of agreement rang out.

Again, Theis glanced at Willa. Her stomach clenched, and her expression derailed for an instant. Aberlin's eyes widened when he saw the exchange between them, and he said something into his father's ear. Immanuel took Theis aside, and he, Theis, and Aberlin spoke quietly. Their words were drowned out by the excited chatter all around.

"Would they choose a new Aliment for November then, or would it still be whoever was picked for January?" Ruth mumbled, not aiming the question at anyone in particular, but the boy next to her suspected that the person would remain the same.

"Once you're chosen, your days are numbered," he said. "But Theis never tells. Only he and Hofmeier know."

"I wonder who it is," Angela whispered to Willa. "Poor soul hasn't said a word to anyone."

Willa dared not look at her. It didn't feel safe. She didn't think she could look at anyone right now.

Theis had broken the news to her in spring so she could make peace, say her goodbyes, and live life deeply until then, as he'd put it.

He'd been devastated, but there would be no special treatment for the family members of an elder in Aldabach, or anywhere else in the Vales. She was his favorite niece, and the best advice he had for her was not to squander the months that remained of her life, and prepare herself.

She *had* prepared throughout the summer, in a way, working hard and enjoying the sunshine whenever she didn't have to work. She'd taken Thomas and Emma to the lake on warm days, and she'd walked in the woods with Aberlin – and allowed their friendship to become more. Loving him had been *living life deeply*.

But she had only planned on telling her parents after Christmas. She didn't want them to suffer longer than necessary. Bertram had cried for days when they'd buried two of her siblings, children born before the twins and sick with dysentery before they were strong enough to survive the illness. That was when his drinking had gotten really bad.

Parents shouldn't have to bury their children. It wasn't fair. To no one.

Willa's gaze wandered to Aberlin once again. He looked distraught and seemed to be arguing with his father. Had Theis told them? Panic churned in her bowels.

Hofmeier carried out the thankless task of drawing the names of the Aliments from the village's church register, and her uncle had the duty to witness it. Both were sworn to secrecy for as long as the Aliment chose to keep it that way. Some Aliments made one big celebration of their last months, while others sank into depression and stopped living before they actually died. Either way, the whole village partook in their fate, and Willa had decided this was not for her. Her fate was her business, and no one else's.

She'd made Theis and Hofmeier promise to keep their mouths shut until she was ready. She wanted to be the one to tell Bertram and Angela, and she wanted to choose the day and time, but the anguish on Aberlin's face told her Theis had broken both his oath to the people of Aldabach as well as his promise to her.

What was he playing at? He would lose his standing in the village if he tried to wiggle her out of this. *Of course* she wanted to live, even if it was only for another few months more, but not at someone else's expense. Time was precious. For everyone.

The Tannenbergers had done them wrong, yes, but no one should have to die in her stead. Not a father or mother of five.

Immanuel beckoned for silence. "People of Aldabach," he called out, "there is no *good* solution to this problem. I will do as I promised, and the Tannenbergers' Aliment *will* be here to still the beast's hunger tonight. The victims of this tragedy will receive full compensation, but my decision is final: we will not change the course we're on." He paused to let this sink in, then added, "God willing, everything will go back to normal soon."

Then, he turned and mounted the horse his squire held ready, followed by Aberlin. Aberlin glanced back at Willa twice, and twice she felt her heart breaking into a thousand pieces because she was sure he was going to do something stupid.

"Let's go home," Bertram said, picking up the little cart's tow bar.

Willa held Angela back to give him a few strides head start as the crowd slowly dispersed.

"Mother, there's something I need to do," she said.

Angela was about to protest, but Willa had already decided she wasn't going to let anything stop her. She needed to go after Aberlin, and she wasn't above lying to Angela. If only her parents knew him, and if he had been anyone but Immanuel's son, they would never have objected.

"Ingunde's house was destroyed last night, and she asked me to help her find her cats. They were scared and ran off into the forest."

Angela frowned, scrutinizing her, but then slowly nodded. "All right. But hurry home. I don't want you out after dark."

"I'll hurry," Willa said, hugging her. "I love you."

Angela stared at her for a moment, bewildered, and Willa immediately regretted her words. When was the last time she'd told her mother that she loved her? A year ago? Two?

Bertram had already turned back, but Angela snagged him by the arm and hustled him up the street, telling him God-knew-what. Willa didn't care, as long as she was free to go, and so she ran, despite the egg-sized lump in her throat.

She hurried over the bridge and headed uphill. The shortest way to the castle was through the woods behind the hunting cabin. Ingunde was going in the same direction, calling to her cats.

"Stop!" she cried when she spotted Willa.

"No time," Willa replied, rushing by, but Ingunde broke into a sprint and grabbed her.

"Willa, *please*!"

"He's going after it," Willa told the old woman. Bone-weary and upset, she could barely see because the smoke still stung in her eyes.

Ingunde pulled her into an embrace. "Hush, child. Why would he do such a thing?"

Willa allowed herself to catch her breath, and then wiped her tears away, stepping back from the old woman.

"He knows I'm the next Aliment."

Ingunde's jaw worked. "I'm so sorry. Are you sure?"

Willa nodded, and resumed her uphill march. "He thinks he can protect me. I have to stop him."

Ingunde struggled to keep up. "You're right," she said. "But you're going to need help."

Willa didn't know how the old woman would assume to help her. She suspected Ingunde was just playing for time, so she walked faster, but Ingunde managed to keep up until they reached the hunting lodge.

There wasn't much left of the building, but somehow the stable behind it had survived. Its walls were scorched, but the structure and roof were still intact.

The double-winged doors stood wide open. Aberlin must have either set Wildflower free before the dragon had torched the place, or escaped the inferno on her back, risking that the beast would perceive the mare's movement between the trees.

"Please wait," Ingunde begged, grabbing her arm. "There's something I have to show you." She gestured at the stable.

"I don't have time!" What was the old bat thinking?

"You need to come with me and *look*! I really *can* help you – not just to find Aberlin, but to kill the dragon."

The tone of the midwife's voice made Willa halt. Maybe Aberlin kept something in his father's stable besides his horse. Weapons that could pierce Amberflame's scales? Armor? *Magic*?

Hope lit up like a candle in her heart. But then – wouldn't Aberlin have long since made use of anything that could kill a dragon if he were in possession of it? Wouldn't his brother have?

Jacob had died fighting Amberflame, and Aberlin would too, if she didn't stop him. He'd ride out and look for the dragon's lair, and Willa had no idea where he'd begin, so she had to catch him while he was still at the castle.

"What are you talking about?" she asked Ingunde. "Dragons can't be killed."

"True," the midwife said, "but humans *can*."

"Which is why I have to stop Aberlin."

Ingunde threw her head back in dismay. "Willa, if you want to save him, you're going to *have to* kill Amberflame. And you *can* because she is human by day, and on nights when the moon isn't full."

Willa spun around. "You're crazy!"

Ingunde didn't know what she was saying. Dragons were dragons, not *human by day*. They slept in caves and came out at night to do whatever it was they did when they weren't terrorizing villages and feeding on humans.

"*Please*," the midwife begged.

Willa shuddered. What if Ingunde was right? "Whatever it is you want to show me, do it quickly."

She cast one last glance up at the path that would have led her to the castle within half an hour if she managed to hold her speed, and then followed the midwife.

The stable wasn't very large. It had a window at the back, barred to keep out anything bigger than a rat. A pile of straw occupied the space below. Ingunde retrieved a fork and started pitching the bedding to one side. Willa couldn't bear to watch the old woman toiling, and fetched another fork to help her. When they had cleared most of the pile away, Ingunde went to her knees and pulled aside a tarp that

had been spread out on the floor underneath, revealing a sturdy trap door.

"What is this?" Willa asked.

"A shortcut to the castle." Ingunde smirked. "Aberlin's not the first ruler of the Vales to bring a lover here."

She cleared the dust off the ring and twisted it, pulling at the same time. The hatch was too heavy for Ingunde, and Willa lifted it for her. Its rusty hinges moaned. It hadn't been opened in a long time, and something told her Aberlin couldn't have known of its existence. Beneath it, a stairway led into the darkness.

Willa remembered seeing an oil lamp hanging on a nail by the door. She fetched it and frantically searched for something to light it with, but before she could do anything further, the lamp lit up by itself. All at once, her mouth felt dry. So there *was* magic here.

"Stands to reason, doesn't it?" Ingunde said softly, as if she could read Willa's mind.

Willa retreated from her.

"Don't be afraid. I'm on your side. I want to help you, and I want to help Aberlin. Please let me."

"I don't know you anymore," Willa said.

"That's all right. I know you, and I know you want Aberlin to live. You were ready to die for us all, and I can't think of anyone who's braver than you, so be brave one more time and trust me."

Trust was a fragile commodity, and it always came with a price if it was broken. Generations of people from the Vales had been brave before she had even been born, Willa thought. Brave for their people, so the dragon would protect them in times of war. The fact that Amberflame fed on them in times of peace had never seemed negotiable. Not since one of the beasts that had gone before Amberflame had destroyed the Vales' thirteenth village over a hundred years ago when they'd tried to trap and kill her.

"Why should I?" Willa said.

"Because I know who Amberflame is by day and where she is now, and I'm willing to share that knowledge so you can kill her. But you must swear one thing to me."

Willa shook her head. "If what you say is true and you know her identity – her weakness – why haven't you told anyone and put a stop to this madness?"

Ingunde's brow furrowed, and sorrow settled into the lines around her eyes. "I made a promise many, many years ago..." She paused, fidgeting. "To my brother."

"And what's making you go back on it now?"

The old woman dabbed at her eyes with the back of her hand. "He knew the truth about the woman he loved, and he accepted it, kept it a secret. But he wouldn't have wanted this. Jacob is dead, and Aberlin will be too, if Amberflame isn't stopped. I couldn't live with myself."

Willa made up her mind to riddle the midwife again later. If there was a *later*.

"All right. What is it you want me to swear?"

"I want you to swear you'll kill the beast, and never reveal her true identity to Aberlin or any other living soul."

Willa was willing to kill *any* kind of beast for Aberlin, but even if she knew the monster's human face and where to find her, no one could kill a dragon. Least of all she. Or could she? She didn't even have a sword. At best, she'd make it to the castle by use of the hidden passageway Ingunde was showing her, and keep Aberlin from trying to go after Amberflame.

If she could accomplish this, she'd walk out on Aliment Lot with her head held high when the time came. It was the best she could hope for, but she decided to play along, praying that the old woman couldn't *really* read her thoughts.

"I won't tell anyone."

That seemed good enough for Ingunde. "Follow me," the old woman said, and descended the narrow stairway.

Willa lost count of the steps they went down into the earth, and she could merely guess the distance they covered in the underground tunnel with the flickering lamp as their only guiding light. She guessed this must have been part of the network of silver mines that had once made the Vales so valuable to the king.

Countless times, the passageway forked, and she lost track of the left and right turns they took before they came to a vertical shaft. Inside, one ladder above the other was fastened to the rock wall leading upward. It rose up so high, Willa couldn't see its end.

"I don't think I can make it up there," Ingunde said, and Willa held the lamp to her face. It was a miracle she'd gotten this far. The midwife didn't look like she could even make it back to Aldabach.

"Where exactly does this go?" Willa asked.

"You'll know when you get to the top." Ingunde rummaged in the pockets of her coat and produced a small dagger. Its hilt was made of gold, but it didn't look very sharp. "Remember your promise."

"I can't kill a dragon with that!" Willa said, horrified.

"Yes, you can," Ingunde said. "Trust me. My brother was a blacksmith and an armorer by profession. He made this as a failsafe, but never used it. Its magic will reveal itself when you need it."

"What about Aberlin?" Who was going to save him, if she was going up that ladder to tickle Amberflame with a blunt butter knife and get herself killed?

"He'll be there, and he'll need you."

Willa shook her head in disbelief and tried to hand the dagger back to Ingunde, furious with herself for having let the old woman talk her into this.

Ingunde refused the blade. "Jacob is dead because he didn't have this."

"You knew Jacob was going after Amberflame?"

"No. I should have guessed he would at some stage, but it's hard to tell someone you love the truth when you know it's going to cause them a world of pain."

This, Willa could relate to. She'd been lying to *everyone* she loved since summer. But she needed to know what to expect.

"Let's assume I agree to go up this ladder. What will I find up there?"

"The answer to all your questions and to our mutual problem."

Willa lowered the lamp and closed her eyes for a moment, considering her options. When she opened them again, Ingunde was gone.

She had two choices now. She could go up the ladder, armed with a short, blunt blade and either talk Aberlin out of going after the dragon, or attempt to find and kill Amberflame with it, depending on what was up there. Or she could go back the way she'd come and try to extract more information from Ingunde, but what good would that do? The woman had obviously gone mad.

The flame in the oil lamp flared up one last time and then died, leaving Willa in total blackness. She shook the decrepit metal vessel, as if to confirm to herself that the oil was all used up, and when she didn't hear a single splash, she set it down. For lack of anywhere else to put the dagger, she tucked the useless thing into her sleeve. Then she felt around for the ladder, trying to tell herself that it wasn't a terribly difficult climb.

She grabbed hold and started putting one foot above the other, one rung at a time, very carefully at first, and then increasingly quicker. Halfway up, a wooden tread broke beneath her foot. Her cold, slippery hands barely found purchase and she almost plummeted, but managed to haul herself up again and continue climbing. It seemed like the ladder would go on forever, and she was so exhausted by the time she reached the ledge at the top, she trembled like a leaf.

Gasping for air, she lay there flat on her stomach for a moment, until a thin sliver of light caught her eye just a few feet ahead. It was almost too good to be true. She moved toward it on all fours and discovered that it came from a gap at the bottom of a door. *A way out.*

Cautiously, she stood and searched for a knob or a handle. There didn't seem to be one, but there was a soft murmur of voices on the other side. She pressed her ear to the wooden panel. Two people were talking. They were moving around, and she could only hear them when they were close to the wall.

"… looking for you… What are you doing up here?" a man's voice asked.

The other voice replied, but Willa didn't understand what it was saying.

"I have to do this," the man said, and Willa recognized him as Aberlin.

"No. I forbid it," the other voice said, rising in pitch. "You don't know what you're doing!" It was a woman.

"I'm not stupid. I know what killing Amberflame would mean for the Vales – both sides of it. But it has to be done."

"... no way you can win. You can't kill a dragon. Not without magic!"

"I may not have magic, but I do have a good sword."

"... not going to lose you too."

"But I'm not *Jacob*. I'm not keeping this from you... not doing it because I want to go down in history as a dragon slayer. The woman I love is going to die if I don't kill the beast."

"You don't know what love is!"

"I know that your own grandfather was a commoner from Aldabach, so you of all people should understand."

There was another silence, and then the woman said something Willa couldn't hear.

Furious, Aberlin replied, "I know where Amberflame is going to be tonight, and I will kill her to save Willa."

"Don't do this!" the female voice implored him, distraught. "You'll die, and everyone in Aldabach will pay the price – your Willa included!"

Once again, Willa frantically searched the panel for a latch of some kind, anything to open its lock.

"They've already paid enough. We all have. Please give me your blessing, Mother."

But the woman couldn't bring herself to. A door slammed, and Lady Gerlinde sobbed.

Willa launched herself at the panel that was keeping her from Aberlin and tried to force it, pitting every last bit of strength she had left against it. She had to talk to him before he left the grounds, and tell him she didn't want him to take on the monster. Not for her.

Her feet started slipping on the sandy gravel that covered the ledge, and she groped around for something to hold on to. Her fingers wrapped around a short wooden lever that protruded from the wall left of the door. It snapped down, releasing the lock as she stumbled forward, headlong out of the shaft's exit.

"Who's there?" Gerlinde cried out, spinning around, but Willa was already back on her feet and blinking at the sudden onslaught of daylight in her eyes, even if there was precious little left of it.

Angry leaden clouds coursed across the open sky above them, and Willa realized she wasn't at Aldabach Castle at all, but at the siege castle just across from the stronghold. It had been built during a war at a time when there had been no dragon to protect the Vales. The smaller structure had mostly fallen to ruin over the centuries, but the keep still stood, and here she was, face to face on its rooftop with Lady Gerlinde.

"What are you doing here?" the older woman asked, aghast. "No one knows about the passageway!"

"Never mind," Willa said, carelessly brushing strands of matted hair from her face. "I have to talk to Aberlin!"

She ran the length of the battlements, looking down, trying to locate him. He couldn't have gotten too far yet. She called out to him but didn't think he'd hear. Not with the fierce wind that howled around the parapets and the rain that was setting in. The sun sank relentlessly toward the horizon, and it got darker by the second.

Gerlinde seized her arm. "You're Willa!"

Willa looked straight at the woman who'd given Aberlin life, and really *saw* her for the first time. Then she understood. Within one second, Gerlinde's eyes flashed from deep blue to emerald green and back. There was a wild, uncontrollable fire in them, something ancient and fascinating that could easily spread, and Willa recoiled as the irises shifted back and forth between a perfect round shape and a serpentine slit.

Gerlinde's face also began changing – at first, only on the surface. Soft, human skin sprouted delicate red scales around her nose and eyes. After a moment, the bone structure beneath began shifting. The transition seemed to be causing her pain, and she released Willa. Clasping her hands over her face, she turned away, but Willa saw that her slender fingers had become long, gnarly claws.

"Go!" Gerlinde yelled, her voice hoarse and desperate. "I won't recognize *him*. I won't recognize *anyone*."

Willa felt like she was suspended in time as the beautiful woman she knew as the Lady of Aldabach slowly but surely turned into the Monster of the Vales, growing in size and unfurling wings that ripped through the back of her already tattered dress. Gerlinde was Amberflame. Ingunde had told her the truth. She was human by day. But even so, how was she supposed to kill her?

"Go!" Gerlinde screamed again, putting as much distance as possible between herself and Willa. "Run!"

Panicked, Willa bolted for the door that led downward into the keep, but when she opened it, Aberlin came charging out, nearly bowling her over. At the same time, the dagger Ingunde had given her slipped from her sleeve and clattered to the floor.

He *had* heard her.

Emerald eyes wide, the form-changer spun around and stared first at her son, and then at the dagger.

Harried and confused, Aberlin put himself between Willa and the beast. "Stay behind me," he yelled.

There was no trace left of Gerlinde in the dragon's eyes, and she roared and struck out at him, tearing into his chest. Blood spurted from the wound, and he staggered backward, crashing into Willa.

All Willa could do for him was break his fall and let him slide gently to the floor. The wound in his chest was deep, and she knew he wouldn't be able to stand up. He was in shock, and he probably wouldn't know what she was saying, but she bent to his ear anyway.

"Hold on, my love," she whispered, and retrieved the dagger from the ground beside him. It was better than nothing, and she wouldn't die or let Aberlin die without a fight.

A sudden break in the clouds seemed to loosen the dragon's hold over the soul that dwelled in the beast's body. The extra light slowed the change to a halt, trapping her between phases. Blue eyes fixed on the bleeding body on the ground, the monster howled, throwing its head back in human anguish.

The metal hilt of the dagger felt warm in Willa's hands, and she nearly dropped it when it began to quiver and glow. An almost liquid luminescence emitted from the golden grip, sheathing the useless iron blade in a transparent silvery substance that extended it to a good four feet in length.

She waved it several times, testing it, though she hardly had any idea what to do with it. It felt so light, she doubted it would cause the creature before her much damage, but she had as little knowledge of magic as she did of sword-fighting, and there was clearly some sort of sorcery at work here, so she had nothing to lose. Her instincts told her to go with it.

Without another thought, she lunged at the form-changer who was neither completely dragon nor woman anymore. Amberflame did not see her coming. In one swift motion, Willa thrust the glowing silver blade upward, deep into the underside of her chin. The howling instantly stopped, and the form-changer stilled. Willa tugged the blade free, and Amberflame's dead weight fell backward over the battlements, crashing to the ground below.

Willa didn't have to see the lifeless body to know the monster was dead. She dropped the sword. It stopped buzzing the second she let go of it and reverted back to a useless dagger.

Aberlin lay where she'd left him. She fell to her knees beside him in a puddle of rainwater and blood, bent over him, and cupped his face in her hands, silently begging him to still be alive. His eyelids fluttered open, but he looked right through her.

"Don't leave me," she said, caressing his cheeks. "We're free – the dragon is dead. We can leave this place and be together."

Aberlin's eyes cleared, and he seemed to focus. She smiled. He raised a blood-smeared hand to her face and awkwardly stroked her skin. His fingers were cold.

"I was such a fool," he said with great effort. "I didn't see what was right in front of me."

"It's not your fault, you couldn't have known." Heavy rain pelted down on them, and she briefly wondered if Immanuel had been aware. How could he not have been, when Ingunde had? The crone's brother had been Gerlinde's grandfather.

"We were happy," he said between shallow breaths, and suddenly she understood that love didn't just make you blind and deaf. It could render you completely helpless. She couldn't justify what Immanuel had risked and sacrificed, or the secret Ingunde had kept, but she understood.

"We were," she said, not daring to move. She kept her gaze fixed to his, holding their connection until the light in his eyes faded and died. Then she shattered, and she cried.

That night, the people of Tannenberg sent a small party to accompany a frightened, gangly boy of seventeen to Aliment Lot. When the dragon didn't come, they took him home again, leaving half a pig, five hares, two baskets of parsnips, a large hamper of freshly baked bread, and a pile of warm blankets. Arthur Theis distributed the goods among the survivors of the attack and the families who took them in.

Ingunde suffered a fatal stroke in the early hours of Christmas Day, and in January, a new midwife took up residence in Aldabach.

In the spring, Tannenberg sent ten men to help rebuilt the houses that had been destroyed. It took them all summer, and by the time they finished the hunting cabin, Willa's baby had been born.

Immanuel came by to see the child only once, asking if it was a girl. Willa was sure he would have taken her back to the castle with him if it had been. Perhaps he would have raised her as his own. Perhaps he'd have drowned her instead. But it was a boy, and he seemed greatly relieved. He gifted the cottage in the woods to her, and she never saw him again.

The years went by, and Immanuel passed away, leaving the castle to abandonment without a legitimate heir. The king no longer had an interest in its upkeep, and wind and weather wore away at the structure until the glass in the windows broke, the roofs collapsed, and weeds and brambles took over the Great Hall.

Eventually, even the dragon was forgotten by most, but every year in December for as long as she lived, Willa lit three candles in the window of her home so she would remember her time with Aberlin.

When Willa, too, passed away, the little cottage stood empty for a long, long time. Every night in the weeks before Christmas, her great-granddaughter, the first girl to be born in her family for ninety years, would look out across the valley from her parents' house and see three lights in its window, and her deep blue eyes would shine emerald green just for a fraction of a second.

AMÉLIE

ONE

The boom of the cannons stopped Amélie in her tracks. She couldn't breathe as she listened for the blast and crack of metal colliding with stone.

Then, merciful silence. No upheaval. No screaming. The wall held.

She rubbed a trembling blood-smeared hand across her mouth and counted to five, telling herself to get moving, but for the moment, it was all she could do to stand there, gripping the handrail.

The cannoneers on the hillside were probably reloading, despite the fog and the darkness. They hadn't stopped bombarding them since midday, when they'd apparently received replenishments after a week of throwing rocks at them. They could only have gotten those supplies if the last of her father's regiments outside the blockade had either perished or abandoned them.

This meant the people of Castle Thiersburg were alone now, and they knew it. Amélie had felt a lot of questioning eyes on her this afternoon, but she hadn't been able to give them any answers.

The south wall had taken so many hits over the past hours, it was a miracle the outer fortifications were still standing. If the Swedish general with the Saxon name and the French gold broke through tonight and got as far as the inner protective walls,

he'd take the castle within another day or two. She didn't want to think about what would happen then.

"Are you all right?"

Amélie startled and looked around. A little girl stood next to her, perhaps five or six years old. The child's face was filthy, and her threadbare clothes didn't fit her tiny form. Probably one of the orphans.

Amélie bent down to her. "Yes. I'm all right. Are you?"

The girl stuck her thumb in her mouth and nodded, though Amélie saw that she wasn't.

"Hungry?" Amélie asked.

Hesitantly, the child nodded.

Amélie pulled a small linen-wrapped package from a pocket in her apron. She'd been saving her day's ration for later, but she wasn't hungry now, so she unwrapped the stale biscuit and crumbly cheese, and offered both to the girl.

"Don't squirrel it away," she told the child. "Best eat it here and now."

Wide-eyed, the little one stared at her for a few seconds but then seemed to understand, and sat down on the steps. Huddled against the wall, she gobbled her food as if she hadn't eaten in days.

"God bless," Amélie whispered, stroking the child's hair, but the girl was so busy gnawing at the rusk, she didn't look up again.

Steeling herself, Amélie took a deep breath and continued up the narrow tower steps to the donjon's topmost floor, where her mother's room lay. She dreaded opening the door, and immediately felt guilty for it.

A cold, wet summer had sped along Romilda's illness at an alarming rate. The Lady of Thiersburg had been coughing up blood for weeks, and by the time she'd taken to her bed in August, heartbroken after Amélie's father had been killed, the war had already consumed a large part of their homeland.

Amélie loved her mother, but deep down, she hoped Romilda would be asleep. All she wanted to do was just sit with her without having to talk. Maybe she could even doze for a few hours in the upholstered chair by her bedside, and pretend she wasn't needed elsewhere.

She didn't want to tell her about the horrors she'd seen in the makeshift infirmary today. A soldier who'd seemed to be recovering well from a relatively small wound had taken a terrible turn. He'd suffered spasms, and they'd had to tie him to his cot so he wouldn't hurt himself. A few hours ago, his jaw had locked in a terrible grin, and his seizures had gotten so bad, he'd broken his back and died.

Another man had succumbed to gangrene, and there would be many more like him. The smell of infection was everywhere, and they had no surgeon to amputate diseased limbs.

But Romilda had horrors of her own to deal with, and there was no physician to mix a medicine to help her through. Amélie wished her uncle had been able to stave the enemy off for just another few days.

Then, at least, her mother's troubles would have been over.

As things stood, Romilda didn't know how close Thiersburg was to defeat, and Aunt Eleonore had made the family and servants promise not to tell her. Hope was sometimes better than any elixir, but the Lady of Thiersburg was no fool, and Amélie didn't think she had the strength to lie to her mother if she asked outright.

She slipped inside the bedchamber as quietly as she could and shut the door behind her, shivering. The room seemed colder than the rest of the castle, but the scent of rosewater and new linen lingered in the air. One of the maids had been here to change the sheets and Romilda's nightdress, and Amélie was grateful.

Uncle Theobald had ordered all lights out after dark, so the little room was as gloomy as the stairwell. She stubbed her toe on a foot bench that hadn't been there earlier, and sent it scraping across the floor.

Romilda stirred. "Amélie? Is that you?"

Amélie nodded and hummed, dropping into the chair. She didn't trust herself to speak as she took her mother's hand in her own, feeling every bone beneath the parched skin.

"Where's Martin?" the older woman asked.

Amélie shrugged. "Somewhere in the castle." She couldn't actually remember when she'd last seen her twin.

Just then, two more people entered the stillness of the room.

"I'm here," Martin said.

He didn't approach the bed. Instead, he stood in the corner by the door. The pressure and the fear of the past weeks had changed him, shaken him, and Amélie knew he couldn't deal with another loss, or anyone else's troubles right now.

Today was their seventeenth birthday, but there would be no celebration, no candles, and no gifts this year. Amélie felt ancient, and she supposed he did, too.

The other man who limped in behind Martin was Uncle Theobald. He'd taken a bullet in the leg trying and failing to save her father's life. The lid of the wooden storage trunk by the window moaned as he seated himself on it.

"I don't hear them firing their cannons anymore," Romilda said.

Martin folded his arms across his chest. "They're probably out of ammunition again."

"They might be packing in for the night," Theobald said. "They can't possibly see a thing out there in the dark, and with all the smoke."

"How long can we hold out?" Romilda asked.

Theobald hesitated. "We have supplies."

Amélie couldn't think where. She'd taken stock a few days ago, and they were running low on the most essential things, even with strict rationing. They were fifty-one days into the blockade, and they just had too many mouths to feed.

"How long?" Romilda asked again.

Silence. Theobald covered his eyes with one hand. Amélie's heart went out to him.

If she had to make an estimate, she'd say they'd lost over two thousand soldiers on the battlefield beyond Thierstal, and that number again of peasant recruits. That left around five hundred men-at-arms protecting the castle, and all the helpless and injured they'd taken in from the surrounding villages.

Right now, over fifty men lay wounded or dying in the banqueting hall and in the outbuildings. They had around thirty elderly and children sick with a fever, and diarrhea was making the rounds, especially affecting the youngest of the children.

How long before they either starved or died of some disease, provided the Saxon didn't find a way in first? Amélie's best guess was a week, at most.

"Thiersburg will not be conquered, and we will not give up," Theobald said.

Amélie wondered at the confidence in his voice, but she also admired him for it. He and their father had been a lot alike. Thiersburg was their home, and the two had sworn to defend it until their last breath.

"Gerome was right not to surrender," Theobald continued. "Kattenburg will send reinforcements soon."

Martin scoffed and leaned back against the wall. "If they can afford to."

Kattenburg hadn't answered to Gerome's plea for

help. The messenger he'd sent had returned with nothing but a note from Alexander, saying he needed time to consider. They'd run out of time a few days later, when Gerome had died in battle, and they'd had to close the castle gates.

Amélie felt sorry for Martin. He would have been married to Sir Alexander's daughter in spring. He loved the pretty girl with the deep brown eyes, and Amélie believed Anna loved him just as much, but love couldn't stop the war machines, and it didn't feed the people. The girl's father wouldn't put Kattenburg at risk for a lost cause.

Castle Thiersburg perched on the hillside overlooking both of the main trading routes that pulsed through the country like arteries, conveying wares from all corners of the continent and as far away as India and China. This was the stronghold the Saxon needed in order to conquer and control the small strip of land between the Black Forest and the Vosges.

Kattenburg was nothing more than a plague-ridden crumbling ruin in the sticks, and if old Alexander was smart, he'd stay out of this and raise the white flag if he so much as saw one of the Swedish general's mercenaries on the road. If and when Thiersburg fell, Alexander would have no choice but to bargain with the Saxon. Then, one day, he'd marry pretty little Anna off to someone who could give her a good life and keep her safe, and perhaps rebuild the family estate. Amélie couldn't blame him one little bit for that.

Theobald was only telling their mother what he thought she needed to hear, but Amélie suspected he also wanted to give Martin hope. Martin should have been the next Lord of Thiersburg, and he had so many dreams. Her brother had always talked about the things he would do, and all the improvements he would make once he had taken Gerome's place and was lord over both Thiersburg and Kattenburg.

Romilda released a shaky breath. "I wish your father was here. He'd know what to do."

Theobald leaned forward. "He'd tell us to have faith, dearest. God is on our side."

Again, Martin scoffed. Amélie supposed it was the best thing Theobald could have said, but she didn't believe they'd be saved from defeat just by *having faith* any more than her brother did.

Where had God been when her father was slain? Gerome had always been a good Christian. He'd been kind, generous, and forgiving, but that hadn't helped him against the Protestants' steel, and the Saxon wasn't even willing to return his body to them for a decent burial. Thus, the Lord of Thiersburg lay in a pit with the rest of this war's dead, not a prayer said over his remains.

Amélie wiped a tear from her cheek, and Romilda squeezed her arm, as if reading her thoughts.

"It's all the same whether we have faith or not,"

Romilda said, "as long as we remember that we are not helpless."

Amélie had never felt more helpless in her life, but she also knew things could change in a matter of days, whether for better or for worse, and Gerome had taught his children that there was a lesson in everything. No cloud crossed the sky without watering the land. Still, Amélie had trouble seeing the reasoning behind this war.

Another round of cannon shots shattered the night, followed by a deep rumble and screams. The south wall was falling.

Theobald rose. "I think I'm needed," he said, bending over Romilda to kiss her cheek.

"No," she said, her voice surprisingly determined. "Let Gunther and Rothenbach handle this. They're probably down there now. I need you here with me. It's time."

Harried, he momentarily balked, but then nodded.

Romilda couldn't know Rothenbach was dead, but Amélie had a feeling it didn't really matter. They'd run out of strategies, and Thiersburg's guards would have no choice but to retreat to the inner fortifications. They simply didn't have enough men to defend the hole through which the Saxon's troops would now be spilling into the outer baily, while at the same time manning the walls in all the other places that were under attack.

Romilda beckoned to Martin. "Fetch me a light. They know where we are anyway."

Martin hurried down the stairs, and he was back with a burning tallow candle so fast, Amélie was sure he'd grabbed it out of someone's hand. He used it to light the oil lamp on the little table beside the bed.

Amélie needed time to adjust to the sudden brightness, and she startled when she saw her mother's sunken cheeks and the dark hollows around her eyes. Romilda must have noticed, and she smiled at her. It was a smile Amélie hadn't seen in a year, and she tried to relax and hide her embarrassment.

Theobald helped Romilda to sit up and tucked an extra pillow behind her back.

"There's a small wooden box with a fox on it in the storage trunk," she told Amélie, breathless. "Get it for me, please."

Amélie pushed past Theobald. He didn't say anything, but she sensed his inner conflict. He was torn between his sense of duty to his men, and his dying sister's request for him to stay by her side. Rationally considering, none of them could say how things would go from here on in, but he stayed because he was a family man first and foremost, just as Gerome had been.

She was glad she didn't have to rummage around for the box. It sat right on top of the silken dress Romilda had worn on her wedding day. Amélie had tried on that very dress not so long ago, but the box hadn't been inside the chest then. She would have remembered the beautiful artwork carved into the lid.

She passed it to Romilda, and the older woman opened it with trembling hands. Two amulets sat on a velvet cushion inside. Each had the size and shape of a small hazelnut and was mounted in a golden claw-shaped setting that was attached to a delicate chain. In the dim light, they seemed identical at first, but upon closer inspection, one shimmered blue and the other a dark shade of lilac.

Romilda appeared to struggle with the decision of which of the amulets to give to whom, but she finally passed the blue one to Amélie, and the lilac-colored one to Martin.

From the corner of her eye, Amélie could tell Theobald wasn't happy about this. Frowning, he started to say Romilda's name, but she cut him off.

"It's *my* decision, brother. Our grandmother left them to *me*, and these are *my* children, whose father *you* couldn't bring back to us."

Amélie saw the oceans of hurt and remorse in her uncle's eyes. He wasn't to blame for Gerome's death, and they all knew it, but grief and desperation made good people say ugly things. Death was a rider who stole not just one life, but months or years from those who remained behind to deal with the loss.

Theobald backed down, defeated, and Romilda returned her attention to Amélie and Martin. "Listen, and listen well," she told them. "These amulets have been in my family for over two thousand years."

Martin groaned in disbelief, and Amélie cast him an annoyed glance.

Romilda continued, as if she hadn't perceived the exchange. "I'm giving them to you now because my time in this world is up."

"Oh, Mother, no," Amélie said, but Romilda shook her head.

"Let me have my say. Worn directly on the skin close to your heart, these stones have an ancient magic that will unfold when you're most in need of it. My grandmother told me they were crafted by Druids to give their owners powers that would save their lives in times of peril."

Amélie tilted her head. "Like a protective charm?"

Romilda nodded. "Only better."

"Superstitious nonsense," Martin muttered.

Romilda closed her eyes for a few seconds, exhausted, and Amélie guessed it was not just from her illness and the pains that swept over her. She worried about Martin. She'd *always* worried about Martin because he was the one who was quick to judge and never listened, or even observed well enough to catch the important things, the things that set mechanisms in motion, or people's minds at ease. This was why Gerome had not taken him along into battle.

Amélie slipped the gold chain over her head and was about to drop the pendant down inside the front of her dress.

"Remember – not on your skin unless you're in danger," Romilda said.

Smiling, Amélie deposited the stone in between her bodice and the vest she was wearing beneath. She saw no harm in humoring her.

"There," she said. "Safe."

Romilda nodded weakly.

"A keepsake is best kept where it'll keep – in a box," Martin mumbled, studying his amulet with displeasure before tucking it into the pocket of his doublet.

Amélie was sure he'd hoped their mother might give them something more valuable than a pendant that so obviously wasn't a ruby or an emerald. If she had to guess, she'd say these two stones weren't any kind of gem at all. By the feel of them, they were simple, colored glass, though oddly cool to the touch. To Martin, they were worthless, but to Amélie, anything their mother gave them now was priceless.

"You have to rest," she told Romilda. "Sleep."

But Romilda clutched her arm like a woman about to drown. "You have to promise me you won't wear it more than three times."

Amélie nodded. There was no harm in it. "Only three times."

She took a damp washcloth from the basin on the nearby dresser and gently wiped perspiration from her mother's face.

"Yes, only three times," Romilda repeated, slurring the words. "The spell won't lift if it touches your heart again after that. You'd never be human again. Promise me you'll remember."

Amélie adjusted the pillow and kissed her mother's forehead. "I will."

Theobald moved to stand by her side and touched her shoulder. "I'd like you and Martin to look for Eleonore for me. Tell her to come up to see your mother. Then wait for me at the stables."

"What?" Amélie said, panicking. "Why at the stables?"

"Do as your uncle says," Romilda said softly. "Please."

"No," Amélie said firmly. Her mother couldn't possibly travel, and she wasn't leaving her here. What was Theobald thinking?

Romilda looked directly at Martin. "I love you both, but you must go now. You and your sister *must* live. You should have left this place days ago."

"No," Amélie said again, louder this time, but Martin wouldn't accept her protest and hustled her out the door.

Theobald shut it firmly behind the two and turned the key. Amélie wanted to bang her fists against the panel, but Martin gripped her by the arm.

"What is it you wish me to do?" she heard her uncle say, but she didn't catch her mother's reply as Martin forced her down the stairs.

"We can't just leave her here," she told him. "Let go of me. She's sick, she's confused, and she needs us."

"She has Eleonore and Theobald."

"This isn't right!"

"She's dying," he said, as though he was speaking to a child. "Don't you see? The Devil's at the gates, and there's nothing either of us can do for her right now, except take our fate into our own hands so she won't have to worry about us."

"She needs to be taken care of," Amélie said.

Martin paid her no heed.

Eleonore was already at the bottom of the stairs when they got there. The light of the oil lamp she carried painted livid shadows on the brickwork of the walls as she moved, heading up as Martin ushered Amélie down into the corridor that separated the tower stairwell from the main building's ground level.

"Uncle Theobald is with her," Martin told Eleonore, barely looking at her.

Eleonore briefly hesitated, but then nodded.

"God be with us all," she said, caressing Amélie's arm, and hurried on her way.

"Wait!" Amélie called out, but her aunt didn't hear her.

"What if I told you I choose to stay?" she told Martin, fighting him every step of the way as he pulled her toward the kitchen.

"I'd ignore you," he said simply, twisting her wrist to keep her moving.

She barely recognized him anymore. He was her twin, and she loved him even if they didn't always see eye to eye, but she'd always assumed their family meant as much to him as it did to her. It had when they were younger.

"How can you be so cold?" she said.

He stopped, spun her around to face him, and shook her.

"Do you want us *all* to die here? Do you want *me* to die? Because that's what'll happen – after they rape and kill you. I'm the Lord of Thiersburg now, and the Saxon will place a bounty on my head. He'll have me torn limb from limb to make sure that the peasants who survive this siege will serve and obey him and feed his army until he moves on."

"What about Mother? What about Aunt Eleonore?"

"Eleonore will follow as soon as she's said her goodbyes. There's *nothing* we can do for Mother."

Amélie's mouth opened and closed. She felt tears streaming down her face. Hell was a place on earth, and the Devil at their gates was bringing everyone's demons forth.

In her heart, she knew Martin was right. They had to save themselves, because staying here would be insane, but the family and the friends they left behind had just as much of a right to live as they did. How could she live with herself if she left now, knowing their people would be doomed?

"Don't!" Martin said, reading her. "It's one thing if three or four of us try to make it through the blockade, but it's going to be impossible to get any more of us to safety. It'll be a miracle if we make it at all now that the outer wall has been breached." His face was inches from hers.

"I have to talk to Eleonore," she said, pushing him away, but he had a firm hold on her, and when she stomped on his foot, he lifted her up and carried her.

"Everything's been said."

Amélie felt bile rising in her throat. They'd made this decision days ago – Mother, Theobald, Eleonore, and Martin – and they'd made it without her.

The cook and the maids had deserted the kitchen. Everyone who couldn't fight and still had relatives at the castle was probably with the people they loved right now, praying and waiting.

A few embers still glowed in the hearth, defying abandonment. Martin sat her down on a chair by the fireplace, motioning her to stay put. She heard shouting, crying, and orders being barked. Shots rang out. Metal clanged.

The Saxon had so many soldiers, they would be coming at them from all sides and in shifts, and Thiersburg's depleted forces would be so worn out by dawn, they wouldn't know which way was up. By morning, the enemy would be moving the heavy artillery into position to blast the inner fortifications off layer by layer, just as they'd done with the outer walls.

The stronghold was built on the crest of a steep hill, surrounded by mighty curtain walls, but those walls were from a time when gun powder had been hard to come by and cannons hadn't been invented yet. In those days, the Saxon wouldn't have stood a

chance. Now it was the people of Thiersburg who didn't have a hope.

"I'm sorry," Theobald said quietly to Amélie when he entered the kitchen soon after them, "but there's just no other way."

He pulled two sashes from a bag. They had the Saxon's colors, and he flung one of them at Martin.

"Put that on, my boy," he said. "It'll help keep you alive out there."

"Where are we going?" Amélie asked, watching Theobald trying to fasten his sash around his middle.

"Basel. To your father's relatives. There's nothing left for you here." He struggled with the knot. "It's what he would have wanted, and it's what your mother wants."

"What about Kattenburg?" Martin asked, pulling his amulet from his pocket and carelessly tossing it on the table before tying his own band.

"Alexander didn't ask for time to consider." Theobald patted Martin's shoulder. "He outright refused to help Thiersburg."

Amélie's heart sank for her brother. She snatched his pendant from the table.

Martin scowled. "Father refused to bargain with Alexander while there was still time. He should have given him what he asked for. Things would have gone very differently if he had."

Amélie couldn't believe what she was hearing, nor process the anger in her brother's voice.

Theobald stared at his nephew for a moment, eyes blazing. "We'll talk about this again later. We have to leave now."

"We have to wait for Eleonore," Amélie said, clutching Martin's stone so hard it hurt.

"She'll follow."

"But—"

Theobald took a deep breath and unbuttoned his cloak at the collar. "Look, I promised your mother I'd get you out of here and bring you to safety. We only have a small window of time because we must make it across the outer baily before it's completely overrun. We're taking the Baron's Tunnel."

He draped the cloak around her shoulders. It seemed much too heavy for her, but the woolen cloth and satin lining would warm her more effectively against the chill outside than the thin fabric of her own dress could.

"Come now. Aunt Eleonore will follow as soon as she's said her goodbyes."

Amélie didn't want to go, but staying would be madness. Staying would mean certain death.

TWO

The Baron's Tunnel was a secret passageway one of Gerome's masons had discovered while reinforcing the stronghold's protections. It led from the north wall to an old mining shaft in the lower third of the hill upon which the castle stood.

Local lore claimed it was older than the castle itself, but that it was haunted. It had collapsed several times while it was in operation, trapping dozens of poor souls deep inside the hill's belly. People claimed the dead could still be heard calling for help on cold winters' nights.

A hundred and seventy years ago, a robber baron had brought a small army of miners in from the Black Forest, allegedly to dig for precious metal near the collapsed mine. Instead of driving a new shaft into the ground, though, they'd reopened the original dig and extended the tunnel to connect it with the castle grounds so that the baron and his men could come and go unseen.

The legend said that when the miners had finished their work, the baron invited them to a feast at the castle, but instead of paying them for their labor, he'd poisoned their food and had his men kill any survivors to keep them from talking about the secret passageway and betraying its whereabouts.

Gerome had seen the war coming. He'd known Thiersburg would be right in the beast's path, and he'd told no one outside of the family about the rediscovery of the tunnel. He'd sworn Martin and Amélie to secrecy, but Amélie hadn't believed they'd ever actually need to use it. The Saxon hadn't been part of their reality then, and she hadn't understood the nature of the beast.

Tonight, she supposed she had to be grateful to the scoundrel who'd killed fifty miners and terrorized the neighboring fiefdoms until the Habsburgs had put a stop to his exploits. Without the baron's legacy, she and her brother would be lost.

The winding passageway was narrow and damp, and it seemed to go on forever. Theobald walked ahead of her and Martin. He carried a lantern, but kept its light so low, it was no great help to Amélie. Despite her uncle's bad leg, she soon fell behind, and every time he and Martin rounded a corner, she found herself in complete darkness. At one point, the tunnel forked, and she had to chance a decision so she wouldn't lose them altogether.

She kept looking back, hoping to catch sight of Eleonore somewhere behind them, but there was still no sign of her aunt by the time they reached the mine's exit.

Loose rubble and bushes concealed the opening. Theobald put out the lantern, and together, they cleared the rocks and brambles to one side as quietly as possible.

The narrow trail that led down into the valley proved even more difficult to navigate than the tunnel. Amélie slipped on the gravel, stumbled on roots, and lost all sense of direction in the pitch-black night. Nonetheless, she forced herself to put one foot in front of the other until they reached the bottom of the hill.

There, one of Gerome's elder stable boys awaited them with four horses. Amélie hadn't laid eyes on the lad in weeks at the castle, but she hadn't speculated about his absence. There had been too much coming and going before the siege, and then no more coming and going at all.

The young man trembled, and his hands were sweaty as he offered her the reins to an ancient nag that looked like he'd stolen it from the knacker.

"You took your time, sir," he said to Theobald. "It isn't safe here."

Theobald ignored the comment and tossed a purse to the young man. The stable boy weighed it in his hand, and the coins inside made a sated, clanging sound, not the kind of jingle Amélie would have expected from copper money. A whole wagonload of copper money wouldn't have been enough to buy anyone's loyalty out here tonight.

"Are there only three of you?" the lad asked.

"Wait until Lady Eleonore is here before you take off, and you'll get another one of these from her," Theobald said, pointing at the purse.

The lad fidgeted. "But it isn't *safe*. I keep seeing lights, sir. My family–"

Theobald thumped him as though they were friends. "Come on, man. You know your family will be glad to have that silver to start over in France."

"And all *we* got is a keepsake for the trip," Martin muttered to Amélie, only half-joking as he hastily helped her into her saddle.

"Shut up, boy," Theobald snapped, bringing his mare up beside Martin. "I don't want to hear any more of your whining. Your parents provided well for you, and the gift your mother made you is worth more than you could imagine."

Martin looked around uneasily, surveying the darkness. Amélie felt both his anxiety and a whole lot of what she thought was pent-up frustration.

Her parents hadn't been poor, but the war had drained Thiersburg's reserves. Foolhardy Martin probably hadn't realized up until tonight that there was nothing left. If Theobald had any more silver on him, they'd probably need it for bribes to reach Basel, and when they got to their father's relatives, they'd be beggars. Her family name would no longer guarantee them credit anywhere.

"Things are what they are," she said to him. "Pray for Aunt Eleonore, and that we'll all get to Basel safely."

"Shame I lost my amulet up at the castle. I could have used it to conjure us a flying carpet," he

whispered back, hoisting himself up into his saddle. "Or we could have traded it in for proper horses, at least."

Amélie reached out for his hand. "Don't," she said. She placed his amulet in his palm and gently closed his fingers around it. "It's hard enough as it is."

Somewhere close by, the uncut grass rustled. Shadows rose from the darkness on both sides of the hill. Heavy boots shuffled. Armor and weapons clanked, and not just a few.

Martin groped for his reins, and the stone slipped through his fingers, sliding to the ground.

They were no longer alone, and Amélie understood that the Saxon's men weren't as stupid as her uncle had thought.

"*You!*" Theobald barked at the stable boy.

"No!" The lad retreated from them, gesticulating. "No, sir, I swear it wasn't me!"

A spark flashed in the darkness. The crack of a musket sounded. The fourth horse galloped off into the night, and the stable boy fell face first into the dirt.

"No!" Martin yelled. "Don't shoot!"

Men emerged from the blackness, some of them impossibly quick. Amélie's stomach clenched.

"Where's the gold?" someone shouted.

"There's no gold to be had here," Theobald yelled, unsheathing his musket.

A split second later, more shots rang out, and the weapon dropped from his hand. His mouth fell open, and he slumped forward, toppling from his horse's back, but his right foot caught in the stirrup as the mare bolted. The animal raced toward the forest, dragging him along. Amélie screamed his name, but he was gone from sight so quickly, she couldn't follow. Her heart pounded, and she didn't know which way to turn.

More sparks exploded, and more bullets hissed through the air. The sharp smell of gun powder burned in Amélie's nose and throat. She spun around, laboring to keep her mount steady, trying to locate the gunmen.

Martin took a hit and moaned, but Amélie couldn't tell how badly he was hurt. Another bullet lodged in his horse's neck. The animal screamed, reared, and threw him off.

Torches flared up, one igniting the other. They formed an uneven flaming line that drew steadily closer.

Martin got back on his feet. Amélie observed six or seven thugs coming at him, brandishing partisans.

"I'm Martin of Thiersburg!" he bellowed, awkwardly drawing his rapier. "Martin of Thiersburg, do you understand?"

"We know who you are," someone called to him, sounding unimpressed.

"Go!" Martin shouted to Amélie. "Save yourself!"

She estimated a dozen more soldiers approaching her out of the darkness. Panic gripped her, and she didn't have so much as a dagger to defend herself with, but still she tried to steer the animal toward Martin. She couldn't leave him here.

"No, Amélie, flee!" Martin repeated, launching himself at one of the mercenaries. "Let my sister go! Do you hear me? Leave her alone!"

He slashed at the air in front of the man like a five-year-old with a hazel switch, and the mercenary laughed at him, while his comrades circled around.

"Please take that knife off him already, boys," someone said in a local accent. "And don't kill him. We might still get a good price for him somewhere."

"Amélie, *ride!*" Martin shouted again, but a bearded fellow had already caught hold of her horse's bridle, and a second man who stank of manure and beer was trying to pull her out of the saddle. She kicked out at him.

"Oh, don't worry about your sister," the man with the local accent said. "We're all perfect gentlemen here. We'll take good care of her." There was cruel laughter.

The man she'd kicked out at finally succeeded in pulling her off, and she landed on top of him in the dirt, momentarily winding him. She jumped up and made a break for it.

Hands reached for her, pulling and tugging. From the corner of her eye, she saw one of the mercenaries disarm Martin and land a punch to his stomach. He doubled over, groaning.

Someone grabbed at Amélie from behind but only got hold of her cloak. She yanked at the collar, ripping the buttons and a part of the lining off. It fell away from her, releasing a rain of coins on the ground. The sound of them and their glint in the scant torchlight was enough to distract the man and two of his friends, but everywhere she turned, more of their comrades came at her. She sprinted toward the forest, dodging them like a hare, but there were just too many of them.

They'd do terrible things to her if they caught her. They'd rape her, and they'd torture her. She'd heard and seen what this type of soldier did to any female they got their paws on. They weren't fighting for a cause – they fought for bounty, took what they wanted, and many of them had never seen anything but war all their lives.

Images of young girls came to mind, children hardly old enough to be called women. She'd seen their battered faces and broken bodies, damaged deep inside in every terrible way imaginable. Death would be a mercy by the time these men were finished with her.

They had completely surrounded her. There was nowhere left to run.

It was crazy, but suddenly she could think of only one thing: they must not find the amulet on her. Martin's already lay in the mud, but she couldn't lose hers as well. They'd take it from her, even if it was worthless, and they'd sell it or give it away for a mug of wine. But it was hers, and it was all she had left of her home and her mother. She would not surrender it without a fight.

Quickly, she shoved it into the top of her corset to conceal it, and it slid down into her undergarment. The coolness of the stone against her skin sent shivers down her spine.

Six bulky soldiers slowly closed in on her. One of them was laughing, and another was telling his comrades he'd get to go first because he was their captain.

Amélie's heart raced, and she wanted the sky to fall down on her and end this, but there would be no end to this tonight. Not until she was dead. She decided to make one last attempt to get away and tried to gage the gap between two of the men on her left. An odd thought crossed her mind just then: it would be so much easier if she were a fox, or some other fast little creature that could scuttle away into the undergrowth.

The amulet went from ice to fire, and for a fraction of a second, the glass felt as though it was burning right into her chest with an intensity that not only stifled the scream welling in her throat, but stopped her breath, her heart, and her rational thinking. The chain shrank and tightened around her neck, and the stone molded itself to her skin like liquid wax to paper. Her limbs ached and she felt pins and needles all over, as though she'd fallen into an anthill. Her legs went out from under her.

The next thing she knew, she was running for her life. The night's blackness dissolved into tones of blue and gray, and she saw every blade of grass, every pinecone and twig clearly in front of her. She became aware of a stream gurgling in the far distance, and the whispering wings of an owl swooping down on its prey. She perceived the shrew's wails as it was carried off into the crown of a tree, and she heard clambering, scuffling, and the mercenaries' curses. The men were so loud, she wanted to hide and cover her ears, but she knew she had to keep running if she wanted to shake them off.

The reek of the soldiers' unwashed bodies remained in her sensitive nose for a time, regardless of the distance she was putting between them and herself, but it was eventually cancelled out by the sharp scent of resin and fungi blooming on dead leaves, the pungent aroma of damp turf, and pine needles.

After a while, she caught a whiff of rain in the air, and soon a cool drizzle soaked her skin as she jumped over fallen branches and scurried between haphazard piles of foliage. Still, she dared not stop to seek cover.

When she couldn't go on anymore, the guilt of leaving Martin, her family, and her people behind hit her, and she collapsed behind the moss-covered trunk of a long-dead beech. She told herself to keep breathing, but she didn't want to breathe. She should have stayed at the castle with Eleonore and Romilda. She should have tried harder to help Martin.

It was difficult to tell how far she'd come. Perhaps the amulet had given her some form of protection after all. She couldn't explain to herself how she'd managed to evade capture, but she didn't deserve to escape. Not with what everyone else was facing.

She reached for the stone but couldn't grasp it in her hand. Strange. It had to be the shock, though she wasn't shivering. Soldiers in shock paled and trembled, but she didn't feel cold or sick. It was just that her fingers wouldn't obey her. She raised them to her face and let out a yelp. Claws and fur. Looking down at her belly and then at her legs, all she saw was red and white fur.

Hot bursts of breath misted in front of her face, and she tried to reconstruct the sequence of the night's events from her memory, but the harder she tried, the more confused she became. Eventually, she couldn't bear it anymore and curled up, burrowing into the soggy carpet of brown weeds and foliage in the hope that she wouldn't be discovered. Grief and sorrow took control of her, and she wept.

Had she lost her mind? How much could a person take before they went insane? She didn't know. Finally, fitful sleep overpowered her.

THREE

Dawn brought a burst of heavy rain, and Amélie awoke naked and freezing, but with fingers instead of claws, and smooth, human skin instead of fur. The amulet lay beside her. It had slipped off during the night, or she'd taken it off. She couldn't remember. What on earth had happened to her after those men had attacked them?

Trying not to directly touch the amulet, she dangled it in front of her face so she could inspect the stone. Cold, blue, and clear. No different from last night.

She considered burying it just to be rid of it, but she couldn't. It was her mother's parting gift. Telling herself not to be such a ninny, she looped the golden chain around her wrist like a bracelet. Her mind had played tricks on her last night, but she was certain the stone had a part in it. It had done *something* with her. But what?

She hugged herself, rubbing her arms and shoulders. It was only early September, but it felt like January. She needed clothes, or she'd get sick. The woods were probably crawling with the Saxon's soldiers, and since she had no means of defending herself, she had to make sure she didn't run into them, and that they didn't find her.

Closing her eyes, she listened for a moment. Rain dripped from the still-green canopy of leaves above. Crows cawed. The wind rustled through last autumn's deadfall. Nothing else. Gingerly, she pushed up on her knees and looked around, keeping her head low behind the fallen tree that had given her shelter.

Mighty oaks and thick beeches populated this part of the forest. It took her a few seconds to get her bearings, but an old woodcutter's mark on a nearby lime tree gave her an idea where she was.

Gerome had taken Martin and her hunting in the area all their lives. They'd been here just weeks before the Saxon had arrived to bring hell to their peaceful little world, so she was familiar with the lay of the land. But in all likelihood, so were the men who'd killed Theobald.

Their dialects – fragments of recollection came back to her, and her mind raced. Were they still looking for her? Had they killed Martin, or was he alive? One of the soldiers had mentioned getting a ransom for him. It stood to reason that they'd try to sell him to Alexander first, and if Alexander paid, there might be a chance she'd find him at Kattenburg.

Aching knots formed in her stomach. How many of the local men who'd been with the Saxon's mercenaries had known her uncle, and perhaps fought by his side? Did their families tend Thiersburg's or Kattenburg's fields, or their stables? If this was the case, she'd have to be careful who to trust. Was there anyone left she could trust?

One of her father's hunting cabins was within a few hours' walking distance. If she could make it to the little lodge without being seen, and if the Saxon's men hadn't gotten to it first, she'd find some clothes there. Her father had always kept a few things at his cabins; a shirt, some breeches, or a coat, at the very least.

Pity she hadn't been clever enough to head straight there under cover of darkness, but it was early yet. With any luck, the mercenaries would still be asleep. Trying to make herself as small as possible and listening again for any unnatural sound, she hurried off in the direction where she remembered the hut.

A frightened hare, the hoarse cries of a jay, and even the rustle of a blackbird digging for larvae and seeds under the bushes startled her along the way. She had to stop several times to get ahold of herself, but the cabin was closer than she remembered.

It lay well off from any of the paths people would take between one village and another, and there wasn't a farm, mine, or charcoal kiln for miles around. The seasoned structure nestled against a rocky scarp that rose almost vertically to a height of around thirty feet. Moss and leaves covered its roof, and elderberry bushes, ivy, and other creeping plants concealed both side walls and a part of its front.

The cabin blended in so well with the overgrown hillside, you wouldn't immediately see it if you didn't know it was there, but she had a feeling that the

Saxon's local aides would check for her here at some stage. They *did* know of its existence.

The stream that meandered through the narrow glade where the hut stood was swollen with the past days' rain. It had flooded a large section of the dell, turning it into a small, shallow lake. Its edges didn't appear to have been disturbed, and Amélie couldn't make out any tracks on the ground.

She glanced up at the roof and sniffed as she edged toward the building, approaching it from the side so she wouldn't have to wade through the water. No smoke, and no smell of smoke. She stuck a hand under the ivy curtain to feel the smooth limestones of the wide walled chimney. If someone had been here during the night, they'd have lit a fire in the hearth, but she couldn't feel any residual heat.

The cabin had two entrances: one in front, and one out back. She chose the one out back and quickly found the key her father kept in an oil-soaked rag underneath a large stone. Just to be certain she wasn't missing something vital, she pressed her ear against the door before inserting the key in the lock. Not a sound.

A few months' worth of rust obstructed the mechanism, and the key wouldn't turn right away, but when it did, the door swung back on its hinges, and Amélie breathed a sigh of relief. The windows were shuttered, but her eyes adjusted easily to the gloom, as though she'd retained some of the strange night vision she'd experienced during her escape from the Saxon's men.

Inside, the odor of straw, dust, cold ashes, and leather seemed more intense than they should have been, but in a good way. This was almost like coming home.

Everything was as she recalled it. Four bunk beds with straw mattresses leaned against the rear wall on either side of the door. A table and a few chairs occupied the middle of the room, and a basket of dry wood and kindling sat beside the fireplace. She longed for warmth but knew she couldn't risk a fire.

She found the chest with her father's extra clothing beneath one of the windows and groped around inside for something that might fit her. There was no shirt, but she pulled a musty overcoat from the untidy heap of flasks and hats, and wrapped it around herself, snuggling into the wool. Much better.

She set the hats and flasks aside and fished a pair of breeches out from under a set of cracked knee-high boots. They weren't a good size for her, but she found a belt to hold them in place, and stuffed the boots with a few rags before slipping her icy feet inside.

Close to the bottom, she discovered a dagger, and a long silken vest. The vest was probably Romilda's. She buried her face in the fabric for a moment, and then put it on underneath the coat, swallowing the lump in her throat. Crying wouldn't get her anywhere.

Rocking back on her knees, she tried to think. She had to find out what happened to her brother, though

she wasn't sure how to go about it. All she could do was head for Kattenburg and hope he was there, and that Alexander would remember his loyalties when she confronted him, but could she risk it during the day? She didn't think it was wise, but she couldn't stay at the cabin either.

An acrid taste in her mouth and a painful rumble in her stomach reminded her that she hadn't eaten since the morning before, but there was no food here.

She pocketed the two flasks, hid the amulet beneath her coat – careful not to let it touch her skin – and tucked her hair into the collar as best she could. There was no sheath for the dagger, but she managed to secure it between the belt and the breeches. Its hilt was so thick, it wasn't going anywhere.

When she'd donned the least battered looking of the broad-rimmed felt hats, she felt confident enough to leave the cabin to fill her flasks from the flooded dell. The water was cold but clear, and it tasted glorious. She gulped down several mouthfuls after she'd filled the first container. Her stomach protested, but it was worth it.

Just as she was filling the second flask, she heard horses and voices. The sounds came from above. Riders appeared on the hillside behind the ledge, coming her way, and she knew she was lost if they didn't change direction and pass by without looking down.

Painfully aware of the tracks she was leaving, she doubled back to the cabin, and pressed against the rear wall of the building. She didn't want to trap herself inside, but she also knew she wouldn't be safe *anywhere* around the building if they spotted it. If they did, they'd certainly come down for a look.

Seconds passed. Then she heard one of the voices say, "Jaspin, there's a house or something down there."

Her heart sank.

"Where?"

"Look. See it?"

She didn't catch the next part of the conversation, as if the riders were speaking in whispers. They probably were. They'd made plenty of noise getting here, but they were on their guard now.

Amélie carefully peeked around the corner of the hut and observed them rounding the edge of the scarp in close formation. One of the four was a redhead, and the blond man who rode beside him appeared to be very tall and broad-shouldered, looking like the image she had in her mind of a barbarian.

They all carried pikes, except for the tall blond. None of them was wearing the Saxon's colors, but she didn't think the mercenaries who'd attacked her last night had been either. You couldn't tell friend from enemy anymore.

She could try to make a break for it, but the men were on horseback and very close, and she was wearing boots that were too big for her. Still, surrender was not an option.

"It's just a run-down hovel. Looks abandoned," one of the riders said too loudly.

She ducked back behind the building. They'd seen her footprints. They *must* have.

"Might do for a place to lay low for a few days!" another answered, again almost shouting.

"If someone *was* here and they were to leave right now, they might live to see tomorrow," a third man yelled in a raspy voice that sounded as if he'd sustained some sort of throat injury.

What to do? She knew they'd get her either way.

Move, she told herself. *Walk. Don't run, just walk.*

And she did. She kept her head down and made sure not to look over her shoulder at the men as she walked away from them. They *must not* see her face. With her back turned to them, they wouldn't be able to tell she was a woman and probably mistake her for some poor soul dodging his duty on the battlefield. But even if they changed their minds and shot her, then at least it would be a quick death.

Ten paces. Her heart thumped so hard in her chest, she thought it would explode. Ten strides more.

"Thank you, good sir, for your cooperation," one of the men shouted after her.

There was laughter, but not the kind she'd heard the night before. Not the nasty, guffawing kind. Something told her these men weren't murderers. They were just soldiers, looking for a place to dodge their own duties for a while. She quickened her pace, nonetheless.

She hadn't gotten farther than another ten steps before she realized that the four behind her weren't the only riders in the glade. A small group of half a dozen more trotted straight toward her from the other side. Her luck had run out.

"What have we here?" the eldest of the men coming toward her asked.

She tried to get out of their way and slopped through the freezing water, but the riders spread out and the one who'd spoken to her blocked her path. She avoided looking at him and attempted to go around his mare.

"I asked you a question," he bellowed. "Being disrespectful to your liberators?"

Amélie recognized his voice, and her throat closed up.

"Look at me when I'm talking to you, man!"

The mercenary brought his horse around and kicked out at her. She managed to avoid the brunt of the blow but tumbled backward into the water and lost her hat. Her hair came free, and a cruel smile flashed across her assailant's pockmarked face.

"Look at that," he said. "I think we've found our little stray."

Amélie got to her feet, dripping wet, and drew her dagger from her belt. No way was she going to make it easy for these bastards.

"Is there a problem?" one of the riders behind her shouted. The four were heading toward her now, and she was trapped.

Ten to one. She couldn't stop shaking.

"No problem here, friend," Pockmark said, but his voiced didn't sound like he was speaking to a friend or a comrade. "This one got away from us last night, and we're happy to see her now."

He was talking down to the other man, and Amélie wasn't sure they were on the same side, despite being in the same army. The other man exchanged a quick glance with his companions.

"What was her crime?" Raspy Voice asked. "I mean, aside from dressing like a man?"

"She's Gerome of Thiersburg's daughter," one of the mercenaries with Pockmark answered.

Pockmark shot him a callous glance. "Shut up, you stupid shit!"

"How did she get here? I thought the castle was secured," Barbarian said.

Pockmark shifted in his saddle. His lips curved in disdain. "Escaped, obviously. What is it to you?"

The blond man turned his attention to Amélie. She felt her face flush.

"Put that dagger away," he told her. "Who are you, really, girl?"

Amélie considered for a moment, trying to decide whether he was mocking her. What would happen if she told the truth? What *could* happen if she didn't?

Finally, she lowered her dagger. "No one, sir."

She felt ashamed for denying who she was, but Barbarian didn't seem mean or unreasonable, and he was obviously in charge of his little troop of four.

"You may leave," he said.

Amélie's gaze wandered to Pockmark. His eyes blazed with hate.

"How dare you, *whelp*?" he shouted at Barbarian. "I have orders to execute her and her traitor of a brother before nightfall. For all the losses we have taken in this godforsaken forest, it is our *right* to–"

Barbarian approached Pockmark, and Amélie slowly retreated backward toward the cabin and out of harm's way. Martin was alive! But why had Pockmark called him a traitor?

"You're lying," Barbarian said. "Orders from whom?"

"The general himself," Pockmark snarled. "And we *will* have the girl!"

He motioned to his men, and they reached for their muskets, but Redhead, Raspy Voice, and their other comrade were faster. The three charged Pockmark's cut-throats with their pikes before any of them could discharge their weapons.

Barbarian pulled a falchion from his belt and disarmed the mercenary closest to him with one swift strike, severing his right hand with the heavy blade. Then he brought his horse around to finish the man off with a perfect blow to the neck.

Three shots rang out in the chaos. One of them went wide, one hit Barbarian's horse, and the third bullet grazed Amélie's shoulder. Warm blood trickled down her arm, but oddly there was no pain.

Rooted to the spot, she watched as Barbarian

leaped off his dying mount before it hit the ground. He pulled the fellow who'd shot at him off his own horse without much effort, and sank the cutting edge of his blade into the mercenary's face.

Raspy Voice and his friends took out one man after the other with their pikes until Pockmark was on his own. Barbarian's crew knew the art of killing.

With two pikes aimed at him and Redhead's hand resting on his horse's bridle, Pockmark dropped his useless musket and surrendered his dagger. Redhead forced him off the horse and kept his weapon trained on him until his companions had dismounted.

"Just out of curiosity," Barbarian asked, wiping blood off his cheek and chin as he approached Pockmark, "where is Martin of Thiersburg now, if you are indeed holding him prisoner?"

"Why should I tell *you*, boy?"

Barbarian snorted. "I know all of the general's men of rank, and all the local riffraff on his pay roll, but I don't know you. What's your stake in this?"

"It's how I earn my living." Pockmark spat at the younger man's feet. "Times are hard, and we all have hungry mouths to feed. Unless, of course, you were born with a silver spoon in yours. You might not know *me*, sonny, but it's just dawned on me who *you* are, and I understand now why the general doesn't trust you. You really *are* soft."

Barbarian raised his bloody sword to the older man's throat. "I will kill any nobleman in battle, but I won't bow to or abide by any kind of dishonorable butchery. Now, tell me – where is Martin of Thiersburg?"

Pockmark grunted a laugh. "Right where he belongs, *sir*. At the castle. They're probably getting ready to string him up as we speak."

To Amélie, Pockmark's statement worked like a slap in the face, and she started breathing again. The graze on her shoulder burned like fire, and the iciness of her sodden clothes had seeped into her bones, but the terror of losing Martin let her tap into a reserve of strength she wouldn't have believed she still had.

She had to get back to the castle and find a way to free her brother. She'd beg for his life, trade her own for his, do something, do *anything* to save him. She couldn't save the others, but she could save him.

One of the horses had wandered off in her direction, and she grabbed its reins. Pockmark's gaze followed her. He was the only one who seemed to notice.

"She really *is* his sister, you know," the mercenary told Barbarian in a casual tone. "And she's pretty! We could have had so much fun with her."

Barbarian turned just in time to see her dragging herself up into the saddle. She pressed her knees into the animal's flanks, but the mare wouldn't budge. Eventually, Redhead gave a shrill whistle. The horse looked in his direction and leisurely ambled toward him. With horror, Amélie realized she had no control over the creature, and jumped.

Redhead and Raspy Voice were already on their way by the time she picked herself up out of the mud, shoulder throbbing. She saw only one option for herself: the amulet.

Whatever it had done for her the previous night, it might work again. Perhaps wishful thinking and blind panic had simply given her speed, and darkness had provided enough cover for her to escape, but maybe it really did have magic powers. More wishful thinking, she supposed, but this was all she had.

"Mother, help me," she muttered, and produced the amulet from under her coat. She slipped it back through the collar and down between her breasts beneath the vest, thinking, *Fast! I must be fast! A deer is fast. It can outrun a horse, and it can go where no horse can follow.*

Instantly, she felt the pins and needles. Redhead and Raspy Voice stopped in their tracks, gaping at her. Behind them, Pockmark grabbed the third man's dagger from his belt and stabbed him in the belly. Barbarian turned and flung himself at Pockmark. Redhead and Raspy Voice raced back to help him.

A strange kind of loftiness overcame Amélie as the golden chain tightened around her neck and the stone attached itself to her skin, but she had no time to worry about it now that everyone was distracted. Her shoulder hardly bothered her anymore, and she bolted.

Nimble and determined, she knew she could cut straight through the undergrowth without losing her way. Her legs would carry her uphill and down again without faltering. Her senses soaked up the sounds and smells of the early autumn forest, just as they had the previous night, but this time, she was completely unafraid. She knew where she was going, and she was sure she could get there in time.

Shafts of light filtered through the clouds, sharp and bright, and moments later, the heavens released a downpour, but she sped onward, led by instincts she wasn't aware of any more than she was of the rider following her.

Calls echoed through the valley, a mix of voices she did not know, and a name carried on the wind: *Jaspin.*

She didn't know anyone named Jaspin, so she paid the voices no heed. They weren't important. Martin needed her.

She wished she had his amulet and could get it to him. Whatever the blue stone was doing for her, his lilac-colored charm would likely work in the same way. If one of Pockmark's mercenaries hadn't found it, chances were, it would still be lying in the weeds near where Uncle Theobald had died. All she had to do was find it and bring it to him. Once she got as far as the castle, she'd figure it out.

The one thing she couldn't wrap her human mind around was why Pockmark had called her brother a traitor. Martin would never have betrayed them. He was her twin. She would have known.

A shot rang out, and blood spurted from Amélie's side. She tumbled forward and plunged face first into a wet cluster of dead ferns. All day long, she'd been trying to work out how to save Martin, but it seemed she couldn't even save herself.

She briefly wondered why God had not made her a man, or at least a woman who could stay on her feet instead of falling down the livelong day, but the voices were coming closer, and not just those she'd heard earlier from behind.

"Leave her!" an angry man shouted. "I order you not to touch her!"

She held her breath. Another shot. Then blackness.

FOUR

When Amélie regained consciousness, she lay wrapped in a warm blanket on the lower of two bunk beds. A fire crackled in the hearth somewhere nearby, and the flames cast dancing shadows on the familiar walls and ceiling of the small room. The windows opposite were shuttered against the storm that raged in the darkness outside the cabin.

Someone had bandaged her wounds and put her into an oversized shirt. The same person had sat at her bedside, holding her hand, spooning water into her mouth, telling her she was safe, and that she would be all right, but she could not remember who. Reaching for her amulet, she discovered it missing.

This had to be a dream. Or everything else was, but the sting in her shoulder and the dull throb of the gash in her side were too real to support that kind of wishful thinking.

"Welcome back to the living," a deep, familiar voice said. Barbarian rose from the stool in the corner and stepped over to look at her. "You had me worried there for a few days."

"Why should my state of awareness be of any concern to you, sir?" she said, barely recognizing her own voice. Her throat felt as though she had swallowed gravel.

The man hesitated. He poured her a cup of water before answering. "I don't know. I just thought saving an injured maiden in the woods would be the noble thing to do."

He blushed and cast his eyes downward as he offered her the cup.

"Go away," she muttered, refusing the water and trying to get out of bed. Her legs failed her, but Barbarian caught her. He heaved her back on the mattress and gathered the shards of the cup up off the floor.

"Go slowly," he said. "I had a physician patch you up, but he says you need rest."

She fixed her gaze to his. "You know who I am."

Again, he hesitated before answering. "A woman I found in the forest, in need of help."

"And who are you to think you can help me?"

"My name is Jaspin," he said simply. "I already *have* helped you, and I will continue to do so, if you'll let me."

"What is it you want from me?" Her voice trembled.

She couldn't make sense of this. Why would a Lutheran soldier want to help his enemy's daughter, despite what he must have witnessed in the woods?

"I want nothing from you. I just want to do the decent thing amid all this madness. I'm not heartless."

"No. Animals are not as cruel as the soldiers fighting this war," she said, and he looked down at his feet.

How many had he killed? And had he taken pleasure in their suffering? Had he raped and pillaged like the rest of them? Probably. And yet he had saved her life.

"Is my brother still alive?" she asked.

Again, Jaspin hesitated, but then fixed his gaze to hers. "I'm sorry. I was too late."

"The mercenaries who were after me – they said they'd try to get a ransom for him."

Jaspin looked like he wanted to explain something to her, but then held off. "I think we should talk about your brother some other time, when you're feeling better."

Tears welled in her eyes. "What about my aunt? And my mother?"

Again, he shook his head. "I was told there were no survivors."

"Except me," she said softly, more to herself than to him.

How could she be the only one? Why had she left the castle? This wasn't right.

He reached into the pocket of his coat and produced her amulet. "I thought you might like this back," he said. "It lay near where I found you. The chain was torn. I repaired it." He placed it in her hand, much as she'd placed Martin's amulet in his hand the night they'd been separated.

"Did you shoot at me?" she asked, hoping he had, so she could loathe him even more than she did.

"No. It was a soldier out hunting."

She believed him, but she hated him all the same

because of who he was, and now she also hated him for saving her.

He rose. "Just rest, and we'll talk again later. I have to go now. There are two guards outside for your safety. You can trust them. If you need anything, speak to them." He studied her, but she couldn't look at him. "Neither door is locked."

That meant she was free to leave, but where would she go? She knew she was too weak, and he did, too. When she was sure he'd left, she buried her face in her father's pillow to stifle her sobs.

Eventually, dawn came. Jaspin returned with a physician, and the doctor changed her dressings. He commented on how well she was healing and told her she was lucky that there was no sign of infection.

She couldn't speak to either of the men, nor could she speak to Jaspin later that day when he brought her bread and made her soup. Days went by before she could bring herself to touch anything he made for her, and she barely spoke, but he didn't lose patience.

Every evening, he sat with her and told her the stories his mother had told him when he was a child. They weren't so different from the ones Romilda had told her and Martin on long winter evenings by the fire. *He* wasn't so different. He was kind, and he kept his word.

"Did your comrade survive?" she asked him one night out of curiosity. "The one who was stabbed?"

"No." He hung his head. "André was a good man. He had five children, and he would have gone home before Christmas. He'll be sorely missed."

She wondered if any of Pockmark's men had children, and if they would be missed. She didn't want to believe it, but if asked, their friends would probably say they'd been good men, too.

"What became of the captain who stabbed him?"

"He escaped. I wounded him, but he managed to get away. If we're lucky, he crawled under a rock and died."

She wondered if the Saxon general had felt the same about her uncle when he'd shot at him and Theobald had gotten away. There were two sides to every story.

"Tell me about your magic," Jaspin said then.

She shrugged. "I don't know much about it myself. You could say it was my mother's parting gift. I didn't believe in magic before. Not this kind of magic anyway."

He leaned his elbows on his knees and looked intently at her. "Is it good magic or black?"

She considered. "I haven't decided yet. It wasn't enough to save anyone but me when I used it, so it's a selfish kind of magic in any case."

He frowned. "I'm glad it did save you, though."

"You weren't afraid of it when you came after me. Why?"

"Because I knew you were a good person."

"Good people make bad choices and do bad things."

"Sometimes. And sometimes they either don't commit to making choices, which is just as bad, or they're not in any position to make decisions. But we must have faith, and trust in what our heart tells us, or we'll stop seeing the good things around us altogether."

"It's difficult to have faith in these times. There's little good left in the world."

He smiled, but she could see the sadness in his eyes. "That's why we have to be watchful. We have to look for it, and keep it safe, so that it doesn't become easier *not* to believe."

After Jaspin had bade her a good night, leaving her in the comfort of the cabin while he camped outside with his two remaining companions, she pulled her amulet out from under her pillow. Her faith might have gone, but the magic her mother had gifted her was still there. She hadn't imagined the fox or the deer – Jaspin had seen her change shape.

If she'd changed into a fox and a deer, what was to stop her from envisioning a bird next time she laid the amulet against the skin close to her heart?

A bird wouldn't remember what lay in the past, and its life wasn't very long. She'd fly away from this place and forget, and she'd never look back until death claimed her.

As a child, she'd always loved to watch the swallows that built their nests in the gables of her father's stables, and she considered this as she stared at the stone, but a swallow couldn't fly by night. An owl could. An owl would be a good choice.

The back door was unlocked, just as Jaspin had said it would be. She stepped outside and rounded the corner of the hut, peeking out far enough to make out the shadows of two men sitting on a log nearby, talking quietly between bites of food.

She slipped the chain around her neck and rubbed the pads of her thumb across the amulet. In her mind, she saw a snow-white barn owl, heart-shaped face the color of ashes, long, elegant wings, and feathers that would cut through the air without making a sound.

She was about to press the stone to her chest when a voice spoke up behind her.

"Don't go," Jaspin said.

"Why should I not?" she said. "There's nothing left for me here."

"You might not find what you're searching for out there."

"But then at least I'll have my freedom."

"You're free *now*," he said. "Tell me where you want to go, and I'll make sure you get there. You don't *need* that." He pointed at the amulet.

She shook her head. "I think I do. Go back to your people. Fight your war."

"It's not *my* war. I didn't choose it."

"I didn't, either. Yet, here we both are."

"Wait!" He raised both hands, palms forward, as if he was afraid. Surely not for her? "If you *must* leave now, please let me know in some way that you're safe when you get wherever it is you're going."

She didn't understand why he would want that. She'd been a burden to him since the day they'd met, and probably a dangerous one. Their people were enemies, and he knew who she was – yet he had not betrayed her, or harmed her. Perhaps she owed him this, since she owed him her life.

She nodded. "If I can."

"Then I'll be right here for as long as I can, so you'll know where to find me."

Without breaking their eye contact, she placed the blue stone inside her shirt, close to her heart. The change happened instantly. Feathers sprouted where skin had been, and her arms became wings. She shrank in size and shape, and her shirt and bandages slid to the ground.

The expression on Jaspin's face was neither one of shock nor disgust, and he watched her embrace the cool night air, filling her lungs as she took flight without having to think about it. Her wings felt as though they'd always been a part of her, and everything she did came naturally. The only thing that felt *un*natural was the weight of the human heart in her chest.

She rose as high as she dared, letting her instincts guide her as she circled the forest above the hut, weaving over and under branches and in between trees. She was free to go wherever she wanted, and she was sure she should have been heading away from this place as fast as she could, but something made her swoop down for another glance at the young man who still stood where she'd left him, observing her.

In a world of uncertainty, Jaspin was a mystery to her, but not a liability, it seemed. In a world where nothing would be the same again, he would be here for the next days, or even weeks, and maybe by then her grief would have dulled down far enough so she could speak to him about Martin. She had to find the courage to ask him what he knew and live with what she might learn.

She launched herself upward into the star-filled sky, dizzy and almost expecting her wings to fail her, but once she passed the treetops, she felt strong and safe, and she heard music. Each pinpoint of light in the endless black heavens seemed to give off a different tone. Together, they made up an enchanting melody that let her forget everything below the rustling tree crowns.

Simply gliding, she allowed herself to stop thinking, stop hurting, stop holding on to her blame, and once her mind had cleared, her human heart no longer felt like a stone inside her.

FIVE

She spent most of the first night exploring the darkness without straying too far from her father's cabin and the memories attached to it. Hunting and feeding came as naturally to her as flying, and she did not go hungry.

When the first rays of sunlight glinted on the horizon, she perched in an old oak tree and slept, for the first time in months untroubled by images of death and illness in the dark corridors and small courtyard of Thiersburg.

Wheat fields swaying in the breeze and the scent of the summer sun on the grass occupied her dreams as she rested. She was back on the bank of the small stream that branched off from the river near the village, looking down into the water at tiny fish scurrying about from one pebble fort to the next. Martin had loved the afternoons they whiled away wading through the warm water there with Peter and Johanna Rothenbach.

She dreamt of the day she'd caught her first trout in the river bend, more by accident than by skill. Martin had gutted it, but he'd forgotten to scale it before he roasted it on an open fire, and the four of them had ended up picking the scales out of their teeth. She'd been happy then, and so had Martin.

Her brother was at the forefront of her thoughts again on the eve of the second night, and she decided to try to retrieve his amulet. If she was going to see Jaspin again, she'd have to be human to speak to him, so she had to change one last time, and she wanted to get Martin's stone to a safe place before she did, in case she wouldn't remember him, or the stone, or anything else later.

She didn't know what exactly would happen to her after she shifted shape for the fourth and final time, but Romilda had said she'd never be human again. Perhaps her human soul would disappear, and she'd be an owl in both body and mind – an owl that would recall neither the lilac stone lost in the weeds, nor the young man it had belonged to.

As darkness descended, she left the cover of the slowly transforming forest and headed for Thiersburg hill. The mist above the village tasted of smoke and wet ashes, but as far as she could see, most of the houses were still there below her, and some of the windows were lit. It was too quiet, but perhaps the Saxon had already set his sights on other goals and moved at least a part of his troops on. No rest for the wicked.

At first glance, the fields to the south of the castle looked as though they had been plowed, but then Amélie recognized the shallow mounds of fresh earth for what they were. How many bodies did the damp soil cover? Did her loved ones lie in a tangled heap down there with the soldiers who'd died to defend

them? And how many other trusting souls had Thiersburg's walls failed to protect?

The stronghold itself stood like a gravestone upon the hill, dark and foreboding. She would have expected light and life about the place, and that the officers had taken up residence there, but the closer she got, the more obvious it became: the castle wasn't just dark – it was *black*. The Saxon had torched her family's home while she'd been sleeping, and eating, and listening to stories. He hadn't just wanted to conquer it; he'd wanted to destroy it.

The inner walls, the keep, and the other solid stone structures still stood, though cracked and wilted by the heat. The roofs and half-timbered parts of all the buildings had collapsed, and a light rain fell unhindered in through the openings, pooling in the empty, burned-out rooms below.

Nothing but piles of charred debris and soot remained of the outbuildings. The stables, the smithy, and even the two well houses were reduced to ashes.

The scorched shell of the donjon reached into the sky like a broken finger. Through the hollows where lead glass windows had once supplied warm, golden light to the rooms inside, she saw that all the wooden floors had fallen down. The chamber where her mother had spent the final weeks of her life was gone.

Everything was just gone. The castle had died along with its people.

Screeching and wailing, she coasted through the ruin until her strength was used up. Exhausted, she found shelter in a protected nook high up in the charred remains of the main gatehouse battlements. Sleep overcame her before daybreak despite her screaming heart. This time, her dreams took her back to the infirmary, but it was empty except for her and Gerome.

Her father stood by one of the windows, his back to the door. He turned when he became aware of Amélie. Young and unmarked by the bullets that had taken his life, he smiled at her and spread his arms, and Amélie rushed to embrace him.

"I love you, Papa," Amélie said, half-knowing this was a dream, but hoping it was more.

She didn't think she'd told him while he was alive, and she so badly wanted him to hear the words. In her mother's fairytales, the barriers between the worlds had always been thin, and since she knew magic did exist, many things seemed possible.

"Remember who you are," Gerome said, stroking her face. "Don't strive to forget. Make use of the lessons you were taught because there is always light in the world."

But Amélie couldn't see the light, and she wanted to forget the lessons of this past year. Every fiber of her being roared with the pain of loss and the injustice of it all. He kissed her forehead, and then he was gone.

Clear skies and a promise of the new season's first frost woke her at dusk, and she aimlessly drifted around the ruin for a while until darkness fell, and she felt safer. Enveloping herself in the endless fabrics of the star-sprinkled night, she sailed through the sky above the deserted villages and inspected the abandoned farmsteads. The ache in her chest beneath the blue stone throbbed, and she was no longer sure it would ever cease – not in this body, and not in any other.

Then she remembered Martin's amulet and made her way to the clearing where Theobald had been killed. She easily found the place where Martin had lost it because no one had cleared away his dead horse's remains. All she had to do was search the ground.

Digging through the weeds and the muck with her claws and beak, she found the lilac stone before long. Mud and loam had invaded the links of the gold chain, dulling it, but the stone gleamed in the moonlight as though it had been freshly polished. She stared at it for a while before picking the chain up in one of her talons. The best she could do right now was to find a hiding-place for it, and the castle seemed appropriate, so she headed back to the stronghold.

New smells wafted around the top of the hill, overriding the stink of the ashes that clung to the ruin's walls: fresh horse dung, leather, and roasting meat.

Circling over the inner courtyard, she observed a cloaked man kneeling by an iron fire bowl between the keep and the great hall, cooking a rabbit over the red-glowing embers. His hood was pulled down low into his face.

A large knapsack and a curved sword lay by his side. He'd unsaddled his horse and tethered her to a misshapen, melted handrailing that had once led up the steps to the main doors of the keep. It seemed as though he was meaning to spend the night.

She perched in one of the window frames, watching him for a time as he settled in. Eventually, she decided he wasn't a threat, but she took flight again nonetheless, deciding that the castle might not be such a good place to hide the amulet after all. She would find a better spot for it in the forest.

"It's you, isn't it?" the man shouted then, pushing back his hood.

She recognized Jaspin. Flapping her wings, she looked down at him and weighed her options. Finally, she decided to get it over with. Now was as good a time as any to talk.

She landed on the ground beside him, carefully setting down Martin's amulet before she plucked the blue stone from her chest with her beak, holding it away from her so that it wouldn't touch the skin close to her heart. Within seconds, she changed back to a young woman.

Jaspin blinked and released a deep breath. She realized she was naked.

"Give me your cloak," she said.

Without hesitation, he wrapped his fur-lined cape around her. Then he pulled several blankets from the knapsack and folded one of them over on itself a few times and laid it out on the ground near the cooking fire for her to sit on.

"Eat with me, please," he said.

This wasn't a demand or an order. It was a friendly request, and she didn't see the harm in it. She wasn't afraid of him and she had nothing to lose.

She took off the gold chain that held her amulet, and together with Martin's, she looped it around her wrist and settled in, pulling the second blanket Jaspin offered her around her shoulders.

"That's new," he said, noticing the lilac stone.

"It was my brother's." She held it out for him to inspect.

He hunkered down beside her. "Does it work the same kind of magic yours does?"

She bit down on her lip. She hadn't intended to tell him, but he was good at putting two and two together.

"I'm not sure."

For the first time, she really looked at him by the yellow glow of the embers in the fire bowl. Dark shadows rimmed his kind brown eyes, and he looked unwell.

"Are you ill?" she asked.

He shook his head and poured a small amount of brandy from his flask into a mug. "Just tired."

"Where are your friends?"

He passed her the cup. "Down in the village, waiting for me."

She took small sips of the brandy. Its sweet liquid heat spread quickly from her stomach outward to her limbs, and she held her cup out for more.

"Why are you here?"

"Waiting for you." He poured her another few drops of brandy, and then turned the spit that held the rabbit. Grease dripped onto the cinders, hissing.

"How did you know I'd come back to this place?"

"I didn't. I hoped you wouldn't."

She studied him. "This was my home."

"I know. I'm sorry."

"You should have let me die." She downed the last of her brandy in one swallow.

"And taken away your choice to live?"

A sound much like a bitter laugh escaped her lips. Her ordinary human life had been over the second she'd changed into the fox, but she knew she wasn't being fair. He had nothing to do with the events of that particular night. Not directly. He was a soldier who carried out orders – and put himself at risk by helping her.

"Thank you," she mumbled, remembering her upbringing, though she didn't feel entitled to the gift he'd given her.

The expression on his face told her he wasn't sure how she'd meant what she said, but after a moment, he rose and moved around a little, stretching his arms and back. Then, he folded another blanket and laid it on the cobblestones next to her.

"My father died yesterday," he said, plopping down so close to her, his warmth radiated out to her.

"I'm sorry to hear that." She genuinely was. "How did it happen?"

"He was injured in battle a few weeks ago."

She didn't know much about the Saxon's troops, but Jaspin wasn't older than twenty-five, so his father might have been an officer in his best years.

"Were you very close?"

"No. We didn't communicate well." He paused and flicked a tiny pebble across the yard. "He was a stubborn man, and I don't think he liked me very much. But he left me with a great responsibility."

Amélie tried to picture a large family; younger siblings and a mother somewhere in a farmhouse, grandparents, and a handful of laborers on the fields, but the images didn't quite fit the young man beside her. Jaspin wasn't a farmer's son.

He was a cook, a man who told stories, bandaged wounds, philosophized about life, respected death – and he wasn't afraid of magic. But he was also a well-trained killer, though not a murderer.

"Can you face them?" she asked.

"I think so." He stoked the embers and turned the spit. "But not the way he would have wanted me to."

They stared into the red heat in silence until the rabbit was done, and then ate. When they'd filled their bellies, Amélie drew her knees to her, hugging them to make herself as small as she could against the cold. Jaspin pulled an old doublet from his knapsack, draped it around her legs, and placed his last piece of wood in the fire bowl.

"You said you'd tell me why that mercenary – the one with the scars on his face – called my brother a traitor," she said when he'd settled down beside her again.

"Does it matter now?"

To her, it did. Pockmark had been spreading malicious lies, and Martin's good name deserved to be rehabilitated.

"Please," she said, placing a hand on his arm.

Jaspin laid his own hand over hers. "Martin bargained for his life."

"Of course he would have," she said softly. She didn't want to understand what he was saying. "My brother was wounded, and he was facing execution."

"*Before* you fled the castle."

"No, that's not possible." Or was it? After Gerome's death, Martin hadn't been ready to supervise Thiersburg's defense, and Romilda had chosen Theobald to take his place. Any bargaining done would have been organized by her uncle.

"It's how the mercenaries knew where to find you," Jaspin said.

She felt sick. "How…?"

"With defeat just days away, the general had nothing to gain from the bargain your brother suggested to him, so Martin sent a messenger to Alexander of Kattenburg, promising him gold he didn't have in return for safe passage to Kattenburg. He was just biding his time, knowing that someone would be waiting for him down at the foot of the bluff."

It took Amélie a few minutes to process this. Martin hadn't expected for the siege to end when it did, and he'd never intended to go to Basel with them.

"The man with the pockmarks – who was he?"

"The lord of Kattenburg sent him to meet Martin. He hadn't bargained for you and your uncle, just as your brother hadn't expected the south wall to fall when it did. A siege always seems to go on and on, and then suddenly it's over, and things move along very quickly from there. When Kattenburg's man realized there was no gold, he changed sides and decided to claim a bounty for your brother's head instead."

Amélie wiped a tear from the corner of her eye.

"I'm sorry," Jaspin said again, gently rubbing her back.

"You keep saying that." She tried to keep her voice steady. She wasn't going to cry in front of him now. "But it's all so hard to believe."

He gave her time. The fire died down to ashes.

"What are you going to do?" he asked eventually.

"Leave. What else *can* I do?"

"My offer still stands. Tell me where you want to go, and I'll make sure you get there safely."

She was beyond tired, and she rested her head against his shoulder. "Why?"

"I want to keep you safe."

"But I'm not sure I want you to. You were a part of…" She searched for words, couldn't form them, and motioned at the devastation around them. "*This.*"

"Not by choice. I was born into this war, raised on the battlefield, and expected to follow in my father's footsteps."

"You keep saying that, too."

"I have responsibilities." He talked like a little boy who'd been caught torturing insects.

She rose, joints stiff and sore, and Jaspin's doublet and extra blanket slid off her. "Yes. Of course you do. And so, you'll move on with your Swedish general next week or next month, and you'll take your war elsewhere, depending on who'll fund it. More men, women, and children who've done nothing to offend you will die, more houses will burn, and more crops will go unsown or unharvested."

He didn't look like a barbarian anymore. He looked small, but she wasn't finished yet. High horses were difficult to dismount.

"How can you say you're sorry and tell me this wasn't your choice when you deal in misery because your business is death? You do have a choice, because you *choose* to keep doing what you're doing."

He raked his hand through his hair and stood up. "It's all the same what you believe of me, but the general will not be moving on," he said evenly. "He'll be going home soon, and so will I."

"Yes," a familiar voice said from the entrance of the gatehouse. "In a coffin, both father and son. Just the thought of that warms my little heart."

Pockmark stepped out of the shadows, followed by a few of his cronies. An ugly, half-healed scar ran from his chin to his ear.

Amélie gasped, backing away from Jaspin in disbelief. He was the Saxon's son. How could he not have told her this, and how could she have trusted him?

Jaspin dipped to pick up his sword. "I thought I'd silenced that big mouth of yours," he said.

"You did me a favor, lad, the ladies love it!" Pockmark laughed, drawing closer. Amélie counted five men behind him. "But it's time we talked about the matter of the bounty you cost me. We can settle this like men." He drew his own blade. "Now that your buddies aren't here to coddle your blue-blooded arse."

"And *your* buddies are just going to stand around and watch me kill you?"

"They're here to witness that our business is settled fair and square," Pockmark said, baring his teeth to a wide grin. "You know, just in case anyone asks later, but I don't think the French will mourn your death. I hear Richelieu has already dispatched his own troops to reap the profits of your dear father's efforts here."

Jaspin put himself directly between Pockmark and Amélie, one hand behind his back like a duelist readying himself for the fight. In the pale moonlight, however, she saw that he was signaling her, pointing upward to the sky. He wanted her to flee. Why did everyone always want her to flee? Was that all they thought her capable of? Was she really *that* weak?

There would be no more fleeing. Jaspin had deceived her, but he'd also been good to her.

Observing Pockmark's comrades circling round, slowly edging toward her, she knew she didn't have a lot of time. Quickly, she untethered the amulets from her wrist behind her own back, not taking her eyes off the mercenaries closest to her. She fingered both chains and tried to compare them, then dropped the one that felt grimier, and brought the other one around to slip it over her head.

"Don't let her put that amulet on!" Pockmark yelled. "She's a witch!"

The man to her left was only ten feet away from her now, and he lunged at her at the same moment as Jaspin charged Pockmark.

She felt her assailant's iron grip, but he was too late to prevent the cool stone from touching her chest, and she pictured a huge white wolf with shaggy fur and eyes the color of her amulet. She changed in his arms the instant the amulet connected with her, turned, and ripped out the man's throat before he could even scream.

Meanwhile, Jaspin hacked and slashed at Pockmark, driving the older man back toward the gatehouse. Pockmark seemed unable to counter effectively, but he somehow managed to avoid serious injury from Jaspin's much heavier blade.

The other mercenaries saw what Amélie had done to their comrade, and two of them pulled muskets from their belts, while the other two retreated, drawing their swords but waiting to see what would happen.

Amélie leaped straight at one of the men who was taking aim at her, caught his gun hand between her massive jaws and severed it at the wrist. The man cried out. Bright red blood jetted from the stump, and he unintentionally spun right into the other mercenary's line of fire, shielding the wolf with his own body. The bullet intended for Amélie hit him in the back, puncturing his lung, and he sank to the ground. His comrade frantically tried to reload his weapon.

Jaspin was growing tired, and Pockmark started fighting back. He used every opening Jaspin left him, jabbed and sliced, and finally landed a hard blow to Jaspin's leg, drawing blood.

The white wolf sprang at the second gunman, and he toppled backward, losing his weapon, but quickly recovered and drew a dagger. Amélie tore his face off before he could use the blade on her. Then she turned her attention toward the remaining mercenaries. The two exchanged a quick glance and decided to run.

She chased one of them down and grabbed his neck in her massive jowls, snapping the bones as if they were brittle old sticks. She would have gone after the other one, but that was when Jaspin cried out.

Pockmark had cornered him, blood seeped from his doublet, and his falchion lay on the ground, several feet away. She charged at Pockmark, but Pockmark had already seen her and turned, bringing his blade around in one swift motion.

Jaspin called her name, simultaneously trying to reach his falchion, and a shot rang out. Pockmark froze. His face contorted, and his sword clattered on the cobblestones as he doubled over and fell forward.

Redhead stood in the gate, breathing hard, a smoking musket in his hand. He stared at the wolf, pale as a ghost, but seemed to comprehend who she was.

Amélie panted. Blood dripped from her mouth, and she had no idea what to do next.

"I'm glad you finally got one of those," Jaspin called out to Redhead, motioning at the gun. He leaned back against the wall and pressed a hand to his crimson-stained middle.

"You all right?" Redhead asked, not daring to move.

Jaspin loosened his doublet and looked down at his belly. "I'll live."

"Sure you don't need any help?" Redhead asked, gesturing at the wolf.

"I am. You've done enough. I thank you, my friend. Go back to the village. I'll be down in a bit."

Redhead pulled a face. "Try not to get yourself eaten," he muttered as he left.

Jaspin took a deep breath, and his glance met Amélie's. "Oh, love, what have you done?" he said softly, sliding down into a sitting position.

Amélie couldn't answer him, so she lay down next to him and let him stroke the soft fur on her shoulder. She had no regrets.

"You're going to leave me for good now, aren't you?" he whispered. "I wish you wouldn't." He wiped his nose on his sleeve, and she saw tears glistening in his eyes.

Her heart stopped. In another life, could she have chosen to stay with him? She wasn't sure, but she would have liked to find out. She'd lost everything, and she had wished for death more often than she could count these past weeks, longed to be anything but human, but if she had the choice now to become human just one more time, she might have decided to take a chance. *In another life.*

She pushed her muzzle into the palm of his hand for a moment, committing his scent and the warmth of his touch to her memory. Then, she got to her feet and padded to the place where she'd dropped Martin's amulet.

The stone was different. It shone with a light of its own, and it pulsed right along with her heartbeat. Fascinated, she barely noticed that Jaspin had followed her.

With great effort, he knelt and picked the amulet up. "What if I said I choose to come with you?" he asked. "Amélie, I'd give my life to be with you. I don't want to lose you. I love you."

She wanted to take the stone away from him and put a stop to his madness, but before she could do anything about it, he pressed it to his chest. Howling, she watched in horror as his eyes glowed purple for a second, and he smiled at her, but nothing further happened. He didn't change, but something inside her did.

When Jaspin became aware that the stone wasn't working for him, and that he couldn't shift shape like she had, his shoulders sagged, and he slumped down like an old man. Devastated, he fixed his wounded gaze to hers, powerless to alter the fate he'd been dealt, and the stone slipped from his hand. It shattered on the flagstones beneath him like brittle ice.

Staring at the tiny pieces, Amélie felt empty. An absurd flicker of hope had ignited deep inside her when Jaspin had told her he loved her, affecting her in the strangest, most unexpected manner, but that hope now lay in the dirt.

Perhaps she could have loved him back even in *this* life.

The realization hadn't quite settled yet when her skin began to tingle. Her heart felt like it would burst into flames, and the gold chain around her neck broke, releasing her stone. It, too, fell to the ground and went to pieces.

Everything about her came undone, and the mechanisms of time seemed to grind to a halt. She

heard a chorus of voices and thought she recognized them as her mother's, her grandmother's, and her great-grandmother's. They all whispered to her, urging her to make her choice.

She thought she'd already done that, but something had happened to change the framework of the amulet's magic: Jaspin. She looked at him, and she saw the renewed hope in his eyes. He couldn't help it – he believed in magic, and he believed in the light inside of her. In the most unlikely of times, he'd grown to love her, and love was the most powerful magic of all.

The fox, the deer, the owl, and the wolf inside her did not love as humans did, but they understood *hope*, and their answer to her unspoken question was unanimous.

She squeezed her eyes shut and allowed the transformation to sweep over her. It happened slower than it had before, but when she looked up again, she was human, and she reached out for Jaspin. He pulled her to him and cradled her in his arms. They stayed like that for a long time.

"And what now?" he asked eventually. "Where do we go from here?"

She didn't know, but she had faith in him, and she had faith in herself, and she trusted that they would find a new way to live.

ARTEMIS' WINGS

ONE

The wind called to the young man in the in-between hours, and he couldn't resist its beckons. He swallowed the foul-tasting powder his teacher had forbidden him to take when he wasn't there to protect him. Then – black feathers, hooked beak, talons as sharp as knives – he rose into the air, circling the islands in the lake, coursing through the sky as though the shape he'd taken on was the essence of his true being.

There were five islands in all, but only one was inhabited. The others had been abandoned thirteen years ago, when the monsters had first appeared in the black water. The people who lived in the castle on the one that was still inhabited weren't there by choice.

The island had once been King's Island, but the locals now called it Saint Jude's – Saint Jude being the patron saint of lost causes. To Raven, the island wasn't a lost cause. No more than the family who lived on it, and the young woman who loved to sit by the water, staring across at the other shore until her mother called her inside the very moment daylight began to fade.

The eldest of her brothers had been his playmates in childhood days, when the family had still resided on the mainland. Now they were captives here, and there was not much Raven or anyone could do, except remember them.

But his childhood friends weren't the only reason to come here. He had been flying over the surrounding woodland, the marshes, and the lake since his master had given him wings and awoken in him a taste – no, a *need* – for the forbidden freedom he felt every time he was airborne.

Getting to see the girl on the island was just the cream on the cake whenever he swooped down over Saint Jude's. She loosed a flurry of fireflies in his stomach that no girl in the village had ever provoked. Deep down, he knew this made *him* a lost cause.

In his dreams, he would sit next to her on the little pebble beach. She would smile at him, and he would find the courage to speak to her. In his reality, he could do no such thing because he was a coward.

More than once, his raven instincts had almost misled him to land on the island, but his human mind knew that the instant his spurred feet touched down on the rocks, the castle's parapets, the clay roof tiles, or even the branches of the trees, he would never again return to the mainland.

The curse that shrouded Saint Jude's would not let him leave again, and he would be damned to remain there for the rest of his days. That in and of itself might not have been the worst of fates, but who was to say he would transform back into his human shape if he decided to take that chance? A human life was long, and it could be a happy one with the girl on the pebble beach, but would a raven's? If he touched down on the island, and the curse prevented him from turning back into a human, would Raven even remember that he had once been a man?

The magic that held the island hostage was so strong, he could feel it in his bones, and he was afraid of it. Still, he came back every day, and every now and then he was tempted to land. What if something changed, and no one noticed?

Today, as he circled the modest castle's tower, the girl he so loved to watch wasn't at the beach, but he heard her before he could see her. She was chasing one of her brothers, the youngest of the seven. He was the one with the sad eyes and the most scars, but he was also the one she loved dearest, if Raven had to guess.

Quick as a weasel, the straw-blond lad sprinted across the vegetable garden between the castle and the forest of wind-bent pines, yew trees, and junipers that grew determinedly on the rocky side of the island. She pursued him and caught up without effort.

"You're it!" she shouted, playfully smacking his shoulder as she trampled a cabbage while darting past him.

She'd be in trouble with her mother for the cabbage. She was *always* in trouble with that eternally nagging woman, but right now, she didn't have a care in the world, and her laughter carried up to Raven like a song.

The boy froze for an instant, stunned as she passed him and dashed into the courtyard, but then he too laughed as if life was nothing but happy. They were like children whenever they were together, and Raven's gut told him that the straw-blond lad wouldn't be on this earth anymore if it wasn't for moments like these.

"I – I – I'm g – g – going to get you!" he called to his sister and took up the chase.

Their mother stepped out into the yard.

"Artemis!" she called to the girl, a mix of concern and anger in her voice. "You know you have to be inside now!" She glared at the lad though he'd done nothing wrong.

Artemis' shoulders sagged, and she slowed. Her brother's grin died on his lips as he caught up, almost slamming into her.

Raven felt the growing tension rising in the air between the three. The lad couldn't take it, and he turned and ran for the forest like the devil was after him. Raven watched him disappear between the weather-beaten trees, while the woman ushered the girl inside.

The water was calling to the boys. One after the other emerged from the castle. Most of them ran for the boathouse so they would not have to change shape out in the open. The eldest of them cast their clothes off on the island's steepest cliff, where they could dive straight into the deep water. They had made peace with their fate, unlike the others. In a way, Raven understood. They were as free in the water as he was in the air.

Then he remembered that it was past time to go.

TWO

"What are you doing?" Beatrice hissed. "You can't be out here this late!"

She grasped Artemis' arm so tightly it hurt, and pushed her along the hall and up the worn tower staircase.

"I was just coming in," Artemis said, disliking the whiney sound of her own voice.

Her mother manhandled her like a disobedient brat, and she was always talking down to her. Artemis hated it. The lads didn't have to put up with this. She doubted they'd stand for it.

Halfway up to her room, she dug her heels in and turned to Beatrice. "Let go of me! I can walk by myself."

The older woman closed her eyes for a few seconds. The harried expression on her face faded, and she stepped back from Artemis.

"This has to stop. We can't go on like this. You're always doing this – *every* single day." Beatrice raked a hand through her graying hair. "Look, I just don't want you to get hurt. Your *father* wouldn't have wanted you to get hurt. The island is *dangerous* at night, and if something happens to you, no one is going to come and help us."

Artemis bit her lip to stop the razor-sharp words that were forming on the tip of her tongue from toppling out and making a mess.

Your father wouldn't have wanted and *no one will help us* were part of a whole set of magic formulas in Beatrice's well-stocked cupboard of moral lectures and leverages. This kind of thing had worked well up until a certain point. Her father, despite his absence, had been a godlike entity in their lives, and no one dared question Beatrice when she conveyed something as being his will. *No one will come* was a fact they'd learned to appreciate when Chiron had lost his ear one night, and several fingers and toes the next.

Artemis cast her another dark look, and then continued up the remaining steps to the tower room where she whiled away the long hours between dusk and dawn. Banging the door shut behind her, she jammed the bolt into its keep, snagging a fold of skin between the barrel and the catch.

Swearing loudly enough for Beatrice to hear the unladylike language, she kicked at the door for good measure, only to regret it a second later. A clacking sound told her that her mother had engaged the lock from the outside and would be heading to the cliff or to the boathouse now, where she often sat until after midnight, watching the water and worrying about the sons she should be least concerned about.

Furious, Artemis sucked on her throbbing hand and limped to one of the chairs that stood at an untidy table in the middle of the room. A top-heavy pile of books sitting on the floor next to the table tipped over when she pulled the chair back, and she cursed again, not quite as enthusiastically this time.

She could take care of herself, and she didn't need to be sent up here and locked in like a little girl anymore. Today was her seventeenth birthday. She was practically an old woman, and it was time for new decisions. Everyone was unhappy, and the youngest of her brothers, Chiron, was scared to death. There had to be another solution for all of them, or they'd slowly go mad here.

Their troubles had begun with her father's death. Prince Ambrose had been the heir to the throne of their kingdom, but he'd been thrown off his horse and broken his neck before he'd even been crowned.

By then, Artemis' grandfather, the old king, had been weak and sickly. Castor, the eldest of Beatrice's children, was to be prepared for his duties, but he was too young, and he wouldn't be ready. Beatrice knew this, so she agreed to marry the old king's magician, Abaddon, who'd been in love with her long before she'd met Ambrose.

Love hadn't played any part in Beatrice's reasoning, of course. She'd been convinced that her eldest son needed a strong man in his life to look to for guidance – someone like Abaddon, whom Beatrice had at that time viewed as a man of principles with a capacity to handle power. The wedding was to take place on King's Island.

Artemis had liked Abaddon, and she believed her mother was content, at least, if not happy or in love.

But then, the night before the ceremony, Abaddon and she had argued, and Artemis heard her mother screeching at him to leave because she couldn't marry him after all.

Stomping out of the room, he'd discovered her hiding behind the door where she'd been listening. He'd bent down and stroked her cheek, brushing away her tears with his thumb. He'd always been kind to her and had never once raised his voice to the boys, so she wasn't afraid of him.

"Don't be sad," he'd said softly, a warm kindness in his voice that her mother did not possess. "I'll always be around. I'll send you birthday greetings."

She'd wrapped her arms around his neck, and he'd simply held her for a moment, another gesture her mother was incapable of.

The next morning, Beatrice had gone to the king and asked him to banish the magician from his court. Artemis was young, but not stupid: ending a relationship was one thing – but taking away someone's livelihood and home was another.

Sometimes she wondered if Beatrice had ever thought about this, but of course, it did not justify what had happened after that. Nothing did, but disaster never had just one architect – one of Beatrice's own clever sayings that she never tired of repeating when something went wrong.

A noise on the windowpane alerted her to a pigeon flapping its wings inches from the glass. The bird pecked at the frame, as if asking to be let in. Still sucking on her sore hand, she opened the window and plucked the creature from the ledge, turned it on its back, and fumbled with the cord on its leg, releasing the note attached. The pigeon flew off into the evening sky without dallying, and she smoothed out the tiny bit of paper with the neat handwriting.

Happy Birthday, it said, as it did on every November 26th, but there was more this time. *You will have a gift this year.*

He still remembered his promise, and she wondered why. Guilt? Some kind of calculation? Who knew? And a gift? From whom? From him? Fat chance. But she smiled anyway, and tucked the note between the pages of her diary.

Dusk was drawing close. Staring out across the lake, she watched the rippling water for a while and then scanned the opposite shore. She was late today, and she knew she might have missed what she was looking for, but after a moment, her gaze came to rest on the woodcutters working on the clearing near the narrow pier. She couldn't see them very well, so she dragged the tripod over to the south-facing window and efficiently set up her father's telescope. That was better.

The two men were sawing a log. Artemis knew them both. The older one was Benedict, and the younger man Elnathan.

They took care of the island's supply deliveries once a month, and they came several evenings in

November to cut firewood for Saint Jude's. They'd load the lumber onto a barge that was tethered to the very edge of the landing well before dark, and her brothers would row across the lake and fetch it in the morning.

When they'd been younger, Elnathan had always sat a few pinecone men and some figures pieced together from chestnuts in a makeshift box. He'd secured it in the wood pile so it wouldn't fall off. She thought the figures might have been for her, and she'd sent back the prettiest snail shells she could find on the island in the same box.

Eventually, he stopped sending the figurines, and the box had disappeared, but she had kept his pinecone men on the shelf above her bed until time had turned them to dust.

He would probably be courting a girl in the village by now, and that girl would be waiting for him on Sundays. Perhaps he would bring her some of those clever figurines, and she'd give him a kiss in return.

Today was Friday, though. The week wasn't over yet, and for a little while, Elnathan was still hers, because father and son seemed to be running just as late as Artemis this evening. The barge was still empty. But then it occurred to her how quickly the sun was setting. It wasn't safe. She wanted to shout at them to hurry up, but they'd never hear her, so she could only look on, warily eying the water's edge near the wooden pier as the two worked.

Apparently, it wasn't too cold out yet, because Elnathan stripped off his coat when they were done sawing, and he began splitting the logs to a roughly manageable size with his ax. Fascinated, Artemis watched him move with a kind of grace she'd never discovered in any of her brothers while they were chopping wedges. He was strong, and every blow of his ax accomplished what it was meant to.

The muscles of his chest and back strained against the fabric of his shirt in a way that made her wonder how they'd feel to the touch, and her cheeks burned up. Surely it had to be inappropriate to ogle the hardworking young man like this, but she couldn't very well go to him and ask if he minded. She couldn't even offer him a cup of wine for his thirst while he was chopping and slicing away. Who knew if she'd ever get to talk to him at all? Elnathan had never set foot on the island, and with things as they were, she would never set foot on the other shore again either.

When it had become so dark that working was impossible, he and his father began to load the logs, now cut to the length of a man's forearm and split down the middle, onto the barge. Just before they were done, the dark water of the lake stirred, and the two men jumped back, abandoning the rest of the wood. Swiftly, they gathered their things and faded back into the forest from where they'd come.

Artemis didn't like to imagine what had caused the tumult in the water near the barge, and she turned away, trying to think of nicer things – such as Elnathan. By God, he was handsome.

She also fantasized about the supply delivery her uncle's steward would commission for them next week. Probably the most exciting event of the month.

All of the island's deliveries came across the water via the barge – wood, flour, salt, wine, and whatever else the garden behind the castle couldn't provide. This time, they would have a side of beef and salted pork because Christmas was near, apples, and honey for baking sweets.

Her stomach growled at the thought of biscuits, and she realized she hadn't had anything to eat since breakfast. Too late now. She rummaged around the disorderly piles of books, papers, cups, and broken quills on the table in the middle of the room, and found a jar with some dried plums at the bottom. They'd have to do.

The scant light from the lamp on the hook near the stove flickered, and she wondered if she had enough oil to last her until she could sleep.

Hastily, she turned the flame down as far as she could without killing it, and rooted around in one of the small cabinets that lined the walls beneath the windows. More books, bottles of ink, and dust, but no lamp oil. Perhaps there wouldn't be any more downstairs either for the coming nights. It was the one staple they were always running low on.

She let out a groan of frustration and gnawed at her fingernails as she paced the floor. Enough oil to last from one month to the next couldn't be too much to ask for, could it?

She *needed* reliable light to read by and do her drawings before the night sky lit up, weather permitting, and she could observe the ever-changing starscape through her father's telescope. It was the only thing left to do, cooped up here after sundown during the dark season of the year.

Her father had spent a lot of time in this tower room and an almost identical one at Oak Castle because he'd loved to study the sky, apparently. She had practically no memories of him, but she'd discovered his journals and a few very disputable books in the cellar a few years ago – hundreds of pages of heretic knowledge in writings and sketches. They had captured her interest like nothing else ever had – aside from Elnathan – and she'd learned to direct that telescope of his at some of the phenomenal things he'd noted.

She poured herself a cup of weak wine, and moved the instrument to the other side of the room. There, she settled down on a threadbare upholstered chair. It was so old and worn, it had probably belonged to her grandfather, but it was comfortable, and she'd spent many a night in it instead of her bed.

This year's night sky was fascinating. Shooting stars enthralled her. They would dart out between the other pinpoints of light almost every night at this time of year, moving like the minnows near the lake's surface in early summer. She didn't believe in the legends connected with them, but she made a wish whenever she saw one anyway. It couldn't hurt.

Comets were next on her list, and much more scarce, but she had actually seen one a few minutes before dawn the previous morning, and she was pretty sure it would reappear tonight. Comets sometimes took weeks to pass by.

She'd read Aristotles' philosophical works on the stars and the sun being heavenly bodies within the earth's terrestrial atmosphere. She'd also read Brahe, who'd expanded on Ptolemy's theory that the stars orbited the earth, thus revolving around the stationary center of the universe.

But Copernicus had been convinced that the earth was a heavenly body moving around the sun along with other planets – along with the stars. That would mean a comet didn't just move across the sky, but through space, and who was to say how far it traveled over the centuries, or even millennia?

Watching the sky these past years, Artemis found Copernicus' conclusions the most reasonable. Yet Brahe's observations weren't without value, and she wondered if she'd ever discover new stars like the one he described in his work *De nova et nullius ævi memoria prius visa Stella*.

She'd been trying to get Beatrice to have her uncle or one of her father's friends send her newer books to read on the subject, but so far, Beatrice hadn't indulged her. Too expensive, her mother had said, and difficult to procure because the newer works were sacrilegious, of course. A relative of the king couldn't be found trying to obtain banned literature.

The comet that had appeared in the sky the previous night wasn't mentioned in any of the writings she'd studied so far, so chances were this was one no one had recorded before. Perhaps she would be the first, and could publish her observations about it, one day.

Unlikely anyone would ever want to read what she penned, though. She was a woman, for one thing, and women did not write books on science or philosophy, much less astronomy.

But the much bigger issue was this: people believed comets brought sickness and bad fortune. This made no sense to Artemis because she was sure that any comet they could see had to be nearly as far away as Venus, and how could any object that far away inflict disease or cause ill fate?

She tugged on the ratty old cloak she'd draped over the back of her grandfather's wingchair the night before, and rubbed her hands for warmth. The small stove near the door was cold, and she was about to relight it when she heard a commotion downstairs.

Yelling and whooping echoed through the halls, and voices drifted up to her, calling her name. She went rigid for a moment, not knowing what to make of this. She couldn't leave the room even if she wanted to, but curiosity niggled at her, so she pressed her ear to the door.

It flew open only a second later, nearly toppling her. Two of her brothers stormed in, dancing with joy. Chiron grabbed her by the hands and spun her around.

"W – w – w – we're free," he told her, eyes shining. "F – f – free!"

Bewildered, she looked from one of the young men to the other. "What? How?"

"Mother says it might be the comet!" Leo said, shrugging.

"The comet?" Her brows furrowed.

How could a piece of rock that was miles away in space have broken a magician's curse? Magic had to be done and undone by one and the same hand.

"Th – th – the people in the village have been t – t – talking about it," Chiron said, spluttering the words like a little boy. "E – E – Elnathan was at the pier when we picked up the first load of wood yesterday and told us."

Leo nodded, and continued for Chiron, taking the strain off his brother. "They're saying it's a bad omen and will bring war and famine, but Mother thinks it could be quite the opposite, because the water is quiet and safe tonight – and none of us have changed!"

She pressed her palm first to Chiron's chest and then to Leo's, trying to feel their heartbeat and the inner turmoil that was always present during the late hours of the day before the transformation. Then she let her gaze roam over Chiron's scarred face. There was no sorrow in his eyes. Her bewilderment turned to joy, but almost instantly shifted back to incredulity.

"You're not having me on, are you?"

Chiron vigorously shook his head, and Leo answered for him. "Would we be here if it wasn't true? Artemis, we can go back to the mainland!"

Her mind was all over the place, trying to find an explanation that didn't go against all reason.

"Maybe Abaddon decided to take it back," she whispered, thinking of the note.

You will have a gift this year.

"N – n – no," Chiron said, still shaking his head. "W – w – why should he? Th – the bastard didn't just suddenly g – grow a heart."

Her gaze caught on the side of his face, where a pink mark traced a path to his missing left ear, and she squeezed his hand – three fingers, and no thumb.

"L – l – look," he said, "I – I'm not sure i – if this is permanent or not, a – and I can't say how long this is going to last. Can't you just take Mother's word for it, and be happy for me? For *us*?"

She forced a smile, reached up and cupped his cheeks, hoping he would forgive her. "I *am* happy. How ever this came about, and whether it's for one night or for the rest of our lives."

He kissed her on the forehead and pulled her toward the door. "C – come on, let's go downstairs to the others and celebrate!"

She glanced back at the telescope, and the window beyond it. The comet had returned. It stood high in the night sky, glowing, dwarfing every other illuminated object near it. Something stirred inside

her, but she couldn't put her finger on it. A tear welled in the corner of her eye, and she hurried to wipe it away.

"W – what are you waiting for?"

She broke free from his grip. Quickly, she shut the mechanism that controlled the airflow to the oil lamp, killing the flame, and then followed her brothers down the stairs – for the first time in almost thirteen years *after* nightfall.

THREE

Dawn came, and Raven flew his rounds of the lake and the island.

He couldn't believe his eyes. Cas, Poll, Mercurius, and Leo were standing on the wooden pier, mainland-side of the lake, alive and human. Aries and Auri were rowing the boat across the water with Chiron and the women, heading for the shore as well.

The curse had lifted. When had this happened? He circled in closer, and he could have sworn the girl looked straight up at him and smiled, but that wasn't possible, was it? Girls did not smile at big, ugly birds. Still, things were about to get interesting.

He swooped in near the tower and set down on the roof. The shingles felt cold to the touch, rough with lichens. His heart hammered in his chest as he shifted his weight so he could follow the boat's progress for a while, and then he lifted off again, slowly coasting by the little vessel.

Snippets of conversation drifted up to him. He wanted to laugh for pure joy, but all that came out of his throat was a hoarse cackle. Then he realized that the smile on the girl's face wasn't genuine. It was fixed firmly in place to hide what she was really feeling. She was *torn*.

"What's the first thing you are going to do over there?" she asked Chiron, voice just above a whisper.

"I – I don't know if I am going to do anything s – special at all," he said quietly. "I – I don't remember if there's anything worthwhile over there." He grinned impassively and paused, and his hand wandered to his cheek and the ragged dent where his ear should have been. "A – a – and there's Abaddon to consider – you were right last night. W – w – we don't know how long this will last."

Raven grabbed hold of the thickest hazel branch he could find near the pier and waited.

"A – any plans of your own?" he heard Chiron say when everyone was on solid ground. "P – p – places you want to go? People you want to see? Secret lover to sh – sh – share kisses with?"

She blushed and thumped him, and he pretended to be in agony.

"N – n – no, but surely there's something you want to do?" he said, rubbing his arm.

She huffed to hide her embarrassment. Raven wondered if she remembered anything about the mainland at all. She'd been so young when she'd last set foot on it.

"A book," she finally said, voice a pitch above normal in a fresh attempt to sound happy. "I'd love to buy a new book."

Chiron tilted his head. "D – d – don't you ever tire of your decrepit tomes?" he asked.

"No." She pushed an unruly lock of hair from her face. "But that's because, unlike you, I can actually *read* them."

Then, the little party started off on their walk to the village. Raven supposed it would take them a good half hour. Did anyone know they were coming? Did Abaddon?

His stomach tingled, and he realized he was about to transform. Immediately, he let go of the branch and dipped down to the ground to find his clothes, hoping the islanders wouldn't accidentally stumble upon his horse. No one ever came here at this time of the day. Most people avoided the lake altogether, and he'd felt safe tethering the animal to a tree close to the path – but everything was going to change now. Life was about to get interesting.

FOUR

Wisps of smoke leaked from the chimneys of the half-timbered houses that clustered around the village's unpaved main street, only to fall back down to the ground and mingle with the mist that crawled between the walled pig sties and wattle fences.

Goats bleated. Geese complained. The smell of turf fires mixed with the reek of their muck and the night's fresh gutter dirt. It made Artemis' already giddy stomach spin, but she was too lost in thought to pay it much heed.

She'd longed for this day for most of her life, and now that it had come, it didn't feel right. She'd dressed in her nicest clothes and gotten ready for their trip long before dawn, hoping they would all go to the village together, but her mother had chosen to go straight to the king with the three eldest of the boys.

Shivering, she walked down the street in the chill of the early morning, trying not to step in anything, though it was impossible to tell where she was putting her feet. Aries made jokes about how nothing had changed here. Most of the others were silent. They looked as lost as she felt, piecing their own fragmented sets of memories back together.

A dozen wooden booths and stands, still empty and shuttered, dotted the tiny market square in front of the church, and several more were being set up.

The aroma of fresh bread wafted toward Artemis as they passed the village bakehouse.

The first loaves of the day had been set out to cool in a linen-covered basket on the table. One of the baker women was arranging raisin cakes on a platter, but she stopped when she saw Artemis and her brothers heading toward them. She nudged one of her friends, grabbing her chubby arm, and they both stared. Artemis had to suppress a giggle because the sight of them together was so comical. Hadn't anyone ever told them that it wasn't just impolite to stare, but that it also made you look funny?

"We're in luck," Aries told Artemis when he caught on to her bewilderment. "We couldn't have picked a better day to come. It's Christmas Market day."

Smiling courteously, he bade the women a good morning, rattling them to the core. The sturdier of them looked about ready to faint when he tossed a coin on the table and took one of the cakes off the platter for Artemis.

A farmer was unloading his cart next to the bakehouse, carrying crates of cabbage to his stand. He, too, stopped what he was doing and stared at them as though their presence was the most disquieting thing he'd experienced in a long time.

Artemis hadn't anticipated any kind of special welcome, but she hadn't expected to be gaped at like this either. Didn't these people realize who they were?

The raisin cake was warm and sticky in her hand. It had smelled godly half a minute ago, but she didn't know what to do with it now, and so she gave it to Chiron.

"Y – you sure you don't want this?" he asked.

She shook her head and took pleasure in seeing him scarf down the treat.

Noticing the exchange and how things were grinding to a halt all around them, Auri and Leo slowed their steps and waited for everyone else to catch up to them.

"Why is everyone staring at us?" Artemis asked Aries.

"Well, we haven't been around in quite a while, so some of them might be wondering who we are," her brother explained. "They're wise not to trust strangers."

"Others do know us, and they probably wonder how we got off the island," Auri said in a low voice. "They might be afraid we're a danger to them."

"But this is nothing to be worried about," Leo cut him off, sounding like a jovial fool. "We won't be here very long, will we? We'll all be going to the king's castle, once Mother has spoken to Uncle William, won't we?"

Aries studied him with a mixture of pity and wonder. "No, brother, we certainly won't. William might decide to take on Cas and Poll, and he'll know where to send Mercurius, if we're lucky, but beyond that? He has three sons of his own."

"But some of us will make a life for ourselves here," Leo said, all joy drained from his voice. "There will be land, won't there?"

"Look," Aries said softly, leaning in to him, "let's not discuss this right now. Not when we don't even know if we really *are* free. Let's just try to get through the next nights and be grateful if we do."

Leo glared at Aries.

Having learned to keep out of his brothers' disputes, Chiron wiped the crumbs from the corners of his mouth and took Artemis' arm, leading her away from the others. He motioned to a dark-haired man by the inn who was setting little carvings out on a square board balanced atop an empty rain barrel.

Her breath stopped, and she forgot about the hard reality of what Aries had tried to explain to his younger siblings for a moment. She was going to meet Elnathan.

The woodcutter had just begun arranging an impressive display of finger-sized angels on his makeshift table: some knelt, others clutched harps or trumpets to their chests, and some read from scrolls. Behind the angels, saints folded their hands in prayer or lifted them to the heavens.

Hauntingly lifelike miniature horses rose on their hind legs in mid-leap in the foremost row in front of the angels. A doe with her ears standing to alert scanned an imaginary forest for dangers, a fawn hiding behind her legs, and a family of boars filed through an invisible undergrowth, one after the other.

The beauty of the carvings captivated Artemis, and the prospect of seeing them up close made her brave.

Elnathan didn't notice her until she was right beside him.

"They're so lovely," she said.

His gaze met hers, and his eyes lit up in a way she wouldn't have thought possible. "Thank you."

She hadn't heard him speak before, and the warmth in his melodic voice stirred up a hurricane of butterflies inside of her. Suddenly embarrassed, she didn't know what to do with herself, so she just smiled.

"I still have a few of the figures you used to send across the lake," she said eventually, breaking the awkward silence.

His brow wrinkled, and he cleared his throat. "You... you do?"

She gave him a sideways glance. "No. I only said that because I wish I did." She watched his face freeze for an instant, grinned, and hurried to explain. "They don't last very long, you know."

His lips formed a perfect O, and the furrows on his brow deepened. "I'm sorry about that."

"No need to be. These are much prettier than the pinecone men."

His features relaxed.

"Thank you for the compliment," he said. "It took me a while to move on from pinecones and chestnuts, but I've learned a few things since."

He picked an elegant swan and handed it to her. She marveled at the detailing of the feathers on its wings. It must have taken him forever to carve.

"Don't you let him tempt you into spending your coins on a useless knickknack," Aries said, destroying the moment as he peeked over her shoulder.

Artemis heard the mischievous tone in his voice. Elnathan, caught completely off guard, did not.

"Oh no," he said immediately, "this is a gift."

"That's even more complicated," Aries replied, but then grinned and patted Elnathan's back.

Aries looked like he was about to start a conversation, but before he could do much more than ask how Elnathan had been, Auri pulled him away, wanting to show his brother an elegant hunting knife he had seen at the next stand.

Artemis tried to return the swan. "Thank you, but I couldn't–"

Elnathan refused it. "It's compensation for the years I neglected to send replacements for the flawed pinecone men."

There was that smile again. Her knees turned to jelly. She thanked him once more and hesitated for a second before Chiron took her hand and gently steered her away.

Over the next half hour, the streets filled with people from the surrounding villages. Crofters and craftsmen arrived, small merchants, and even a group of monks from the nearby monastery, and the islanders became less conspicuous. Artemis felt much

more at ease once she and her brothers ceased to be the center of attention.

She browsed the stands and Chiron used some of his money to buy them a small cup of wine each with honey and spices that she'd never tasted before. She wondered how Beatrice was faring with King William.

Beatrice hadn't seen her dead husband's brother in thirteen years. He might not know what to expect of his unannounced visitors. She'd never made a secret of the fact that she had been unhappy about signing away her sons' right to the throne after they'd been imprisoned on the island, but William had insisted that the land needed a ruler – a reliable *man* people would accept, and not a boy who changed shape by night on an island in the middle of a lake full of monsters.

Even knowing he was right, Beatrice had never lost her bitterness toward him. She'd called him a failure for not having succeeded at capturing and executing Abaddon. She'd gone as far as to doubt his willingness, and after that, the only communication they'd upheld in all these years had been through William's steward.

No, Artemis did not assume William would welcome his brother's widow and her eldest sons with open arms. Perhaps he would send them all away, but this was a bridge they'd cross when they got to it.

Carefully budgeting the coins she'd received from her mother for the outing, she acquired a new journal, but the only printed book she found was an ancient, dusty Bible. Mice or other vermin had chewed the corners of its cover. It was sitting in the middle of a wobbly table near the church, where an old woman with a huge bulge on her forehead guarded a few carved wooden crosses and some rosaries that looked so worn, they might have passed through more than one sinner's hands over the years – just like the Bible.

Artemis picked the tome up from between the strings of beads without asking, and the woman studied her with contempt.

"Put that down, dear. No use in pawing a book you can't read," she said.

"Oh, I *can* read," Artemis said, leafing through it. "But I don't think I want to buy it. There are pages missing."

She handed it back, and the woman snorted, wiping at the leather cover of the Holy Book as though Artemis' hands had left dirty marks on it. Then, she turned away, terminating their brief exchange.

Artemis wondered if the old biddy could read at all, never mind Latin, and decided the answer was probably no. The village didn't have a school. Truth be told, she couldn't see that the village had much of *anything* outside of today's market. She'd imagined the settlement to be bigger, and its houses in better repair, but the underlying stench of poverty in this place went far beyond the filthy gutters and the crumbling facades.

"Find anything interesting, child?" her mother asked, coming up behind her.

The old woman spun around, and her eyes widened at the sight of her king's sister-in-law. Red blotches spread on her cheeks as her gaze darted between mother and daughter, and she bowed reverently, finally putting two and two together.

Artemis ignored the crone and showed Beatrice her new journal, but her mother merely cast a fleeting glance at it. She knew Beatrice would have been happier if she had chosen a length of pretty fabric for a new dress from one of the cloth merchants down the street.

She hadn't expected her back from the castle so soon. Cas, Poll, and Mercurius weren't with her. So, William wasn't such an ass after all.

"The day is short," Beatrice said, taking her by the arm and leading her away. "The boys need some freedom, and I want us all to pay a visit to Oak Castle."

This was more than all right with Artemis. Oak Castle was the place where she was born. She had visited there at least twice a year as a child, but she had practically no memory of it. It would be wonderful to explore her family's ancestral home. But then something occurred to her, stopping her dead in her tracks.

"How far is it?" she asked.

Beatrice studied her. "If you're worried about the boys, don't be. We'll be back well before nightfall if we leave now."

Her brothers had been at the forefront of her mind, but she knew her mother would take no risks where they were concerned. There was something else though, and the guilt that weighed on her for her thoughts and feelings dragged her down like a stone: if she was honest with herself – honest as could be – she couldn't picture herself going back to the island with Beatrice tonight.

That part of her life was over, even if it meant leaving Chiron to his own devices. He was fragile and often lonely. Going to live somewhere else would be almost like abandoning him. It hurt. But if she was given a choice today…?

She looked her mother deep in the eyes and realized Beatrice was doing this for *her*. For the first time in her life, her mother was actually not just contemplating her eldest sons but considering her only daughter's future instead.

FIVE

Beatrice directed Artemis and her brothers through an alley that took them past the church and into the graveyard. Mercurius waited for them there with a young man Artemis recognized as a relative because he bore a noticeable resemblance to Aries. The two were guarding several horses.

"Hello, cousin," the man said. "You don't know me, but I remember you. I'm Jarlath."

Jarlath – he was the one who sometimes sent sweets to the island with their supply delivery. He was also the cousin who would sit on the throne one day instead of her brother, Cas.

Did the crown prince expect her to curtsey? If he did, she missed the moment, but he didn't seem to mind. He turned when half a dozen of William's soldiers in light armor appeared from behind the church, leading more horses. Much to her surprise, trailing along behind them was Elnathan.

The prince waved to the men, motioning them. "We haven't got all day, gentlemen!" he shouted good-naturedly.

"Close your mouth, dearest," Aries said quietly, leaning in to Artemis. "He's riding ahead to let old Alphard know we're coming. Alphard is his uncle, the caretaker."

She gave him her best scowl, and the crinkles around his eyes danced as he laughed. He mounted his white stallion, and she had already forgiven him when he reached down to lend her a hand up. She grabbed ahold and slid smoothly into the saddle in front of him, a move they'd rehearsed a hundred times for fun on a wooden practice horse in the island's empty stable.

She'd never ridden a real horse before, but she was more excited than afraid as she stroked the animal's neck and mane. Its warmth and the scent of hay and oats made her feel perfectly safe.

Jarlath handed Beatrice the reins to a chestnut-colored mare, and Artemis watched her hoist herself up into the saddle with more grace than she would have given her credit for. Beatrice looked years younger today than she had on the island last night, and she seemed almost relaxed.

Aries had noticed, too, and whispered, "Let's enjoy the day, little frog, *really* enjoy it."

Artemis nodded, and made sure the swan was still safely tucked away in the pocket of her coat. She hoped Elnathan would not just ride ahead to tell his uncle they were coming, but that he'd stay with them for a while.

Jarlath led them across a muddy pasture between the village and the forest, and then along the lakeshore. From there, they rode north and entered a sweeping, open river valley where none of the

drystone walls she'd seen all around the village segmented the landscape.

The valley meandered between a trio of expansive knolls. The gentle, grassy slopes rose and fell like a strange and haunting melody under the clear blue sky.

The group followed the road alongside the river for several miles before the dale opened up into a wider basin still. On their left, a sturdy stone bridge arched across the river. A newly built road reached far into the moors on its other side, and Artemis' breath hitched at the vastness of the land. Her own world had been so small, she never could have imagined this.

"There was nothing but marshes beyond when I was a child," Beatrice said, motioning to the bridge. "Your grandfather had the bogs drained and that new road built. I remember hundreds of men working here."

"Where does it lead?" Aries asked.

"To the same towns where the old trading road led. Just so much quicker and less dangerous for travelers and merchants with heavy wagons. Oak Castle was built to protect the old road because there were so many robbers and wolves in these woods. By the time I married your father, however, it was already obsolete. But Ambrose loved Oak Castle as much as I do."

"Father says he never understood why he chose to make it your family's home," Jarlath said. "As the crown prince, he should have been at Hill Castle."

Beatrice laughed. "Too many predators." Then she turned to Artemis. "And he always said he couldn't see the stars from there."

Jarlath scoffed. "Well, at least we have the thieves pretty much under control nowadays, but there are more wolves about than you would ever guess, and we've even had marauding bears here recently, trying to repossess a habitat they haven't been a part of in donkey's years, so to speak."

Beatrice's brows knitted, but he sped up his horse's pace, and guided them along the overgrown road to the right, away from the river and the grasslands that had once been marshes. A mile or so on, the road branched off into a forest where ancient linden trees flanked the mossy, neglected ditches. The trees grew so tall here, their stark gray branches seemed frozen in time as they reached for the sky, still and unmoving in the breeze. To Artemis, they looked like arms with long, spindly fingers, begging the heavens for stardust in the midst of winter.

Between the lindens' trunks, young beeches struggled for light, holding on to their dead foliage in protest of the cold, and a wild thicket of hazels, skeletal berry bushes, and dead weeds claimed the in-between spaces. Roots ran like veins across the mossy road, waiting to snag the horses' hooves. Here and there, abandoned cottages huddled between the trees, windows broken and roofs caved in.

Finally, the forest yielded to a clearing, and Artemis blinked at the castle in the bright sunlight. Surrounded by a moat and a wall with a round, stubby watch tower on each side of the barbican, the complex was about twice the size of the fortress on the island.

Creepers had conquered large sections of the outer defenses, and the moat had seen better days, but everything was fairly well intact. The drawbridge had been lowered, the double-winged gate opened, and the portcullis raised.

Elnathan awaited them on the other side of the bridge. The old man beside him bowed deeply to Jarlath.

"Welcome, my prince," the stranger said. Then he turned his gaze to Beatrice, eyes brimming. "Welcome *home*, Princess Beatrice."

Beatrice smiled at the aged caretaker. "Alphard," she said, "I'm so glad to see you here."

She reached out her hand to him. He clasped it in both of his and held it like a proud father might, and then led her horse in through the gate, as if she were a child and he afraid that she might lose control over the animal in the confined passageway.

There was nothing spectacular about the bailey, except for the ornamental fountain that rose from the center of the square. Adorned with sculptures of trout leaping from the water, it was a magnificent centerpiece for an otherwise merely functional courtyard.

The stronghold would have accommodated a sizable household, but all the buildings apart from the keep looked as though they had been added to the fortress rather hastily and haphazardly in the years following its original construction.

It didn't help that the smaller houses and workshops – a smithy, something resembling a canteen, and servants' quarters nestling along the west-facing wall – had fallen into disrepair during their many years of abandonment. The windows were either shuttered or boarded up, and ivy had seized hold of every crack and crevice in their facades.

Aries dismounted and helped Artemis down from the horse, throwing the reins at her before saving Chiron from a nasty tumble when his foot caught in one of the stirrups.

Elnathan took the reins from Artemis' hand and led the animals to the stable left of the barbican, while William's soldiers tethered their own mounts to the iron rings on the outside of the stable wall, and Alphard ushered the family to the keep.

A good blaze crackled in the huge fireplace of the Great Hall, and mugs of mulled wine stood ready for them on the banqueting table. The hot drinks and the smell of polish from the chunky, dark furniture drove away the chill Artemis had felt in the forest. She sank into an upholstered chair that looked exactly like the one in her tower room – only the stuffing and the fabric were so much less worn.

The warden seemed to take his job very seriously in those areas that one man alone could manage.

Without him, things would certainly have been very different. Artemis supposed the king paid him for his work here. Beatrice probably couldn't – not on her small appanage – the castle might not even be hers anymore.

They weren't poor, by definition, but Artemis knew their funds had always been limited. Ambrose's wealth had transferred to William along with the crown, but she wondered if that included this stronghold. If it had fallen to Ambrose with his marriage to Beatrice, this would actually be the case.

Following the same logic, they would be homeless if William wanted the castle on Saint Jude's back in his own possession now. Provided, of course, the creatures in the lake remained quiet, and her brothers didn't start changing again at night. The island would be no good to him with a monster infestation in the lake and on the shore, and the locals refusing to go anywhere near it.

All these worries made Artemis' head ache, and she lost patience with Alphard and her mother's reminiscing. While her brothers tucked into a meal of fresh bread and cheese, she emptied her cup, set it back on the table, and sneaked away to have a snoop around.

She was soon glad she did. Whether her mother still owned the castle or not, she realized wherein the real reward of this trip lay the moment she saw the paintings that decorated the large stairwell. Five portraits of her father hung along the wall of the wide wooden staircase leading up to the second floor. Five more had found their place in the corridor. She followed them like breadcrumbs.

There were no depictions of her father at the castle on Saint Jude's, and she'd always wondered why. Going by the sheer number of them here, she supposed her mother probably had them taken down on Saint Jude's and relocated to Oak Castle when she'd agreed to marry Abaddon on the island.

Open-mouthed, she gaped at the pictures, following every crease on her father's face that some painter had captured in the light of the various stages of Ambrose's life. The one he looked oldest on was probably the last he'd had done, and she tried to memorize the lines and the wrinkles, the shape of his nose, and the curve of his chin. His mischievous smile fascinated her. It reached right up into inquisitive eyes the color of Lough Locke.

She imagined how his laugh might have sounded – perhaps like Chiron's, since Chiron bore such a strong resemblance to him. They shared the exact same color of hair: fresh straw on a warm summer's day. All her brothers had blond hair. She was the only one of the siblings who had ended up with a dirty shade of last year's hazelnuts.

Absurdly happy and sad at the same time, she found herself missing a man she had as little recollection of as her childhood home.

Mechanically, she opened every door on the second floor, hoping to find more paintings, or some other object of her father's there, but the furniture in most of the rooms had been covered with linen dustsheets, and the walls were empty aside from the occasional crucifix above a bed.

Disappointed, she gave up, and was about to climb the stairs to the third floor when she heard steps on the wooden treads coming up from the Great Hall, and Elnathan peeked around the corner.

She fixed her gaze to his, and he smiled. "Looking for anything in particular? I could show you around, if you like," he said softly.

Her face burned. "That would be lovely," she said, almost whispering, and pretending this would be fine with Beatrice.

She grabbed his hand and rushed him up the next set of stairs before he knew what was happening. If he was surprised or offended by her behavior, he did not let on.

Most of the walls of the corridor on the third floor held portraits of stern or grumpy old men and women Artemis did not know, and a few landscapes. A dresser with a tainted mirror. A faded tapestry. More doors that led to bedrooms with dustsheets. But then, in between a mounted set of antlers and a tall candle-holder: a door unlike any other she'd ever seen.

Blackened iron hinges held its heavy oaken panel. Their ends branched out across the surface in a soft, winding floral pattern with oddly shaped blossoms at indiscriminate intervals.

From a distance, the design appeared merely decorative, but on closer inspection, Artemis recognized the Seven Sisters and their parents, Atlas and Pleione, fleeing from the Hunter. Her fingers traced the metal rods between the blossoms, awed at the smith's craftsmanship, and she smiled at Elnathan.

"I thought you might like it," he said, and she bit her lip, waiting for him to expand on that, but he simply unlocked the door with one of the big keys dangling from a ring he'd probably swiped from his uncle.

Had he ever looked up while he was chopping wood, and seen her in her tower window?

"Do you know a lot about the stars?" she probed.

"As much as anyone else, I suppose." He paused as they climbed the narrow wooden steps, and flashed her a smug glance. "But I know *you* do."

Again, she felt a rush of blood to her face, but she wasn't sure if she was hearing him right, and so she told herself to shut up and keep putting one foot ahead of the other.

From the outside, she would have assumed the little turret protruding from the keep's roof was a kind of belltower, but when they had reached the top of the stairs, they were standing in an open loft, almost identical in its layout to her father's study on Saint Jude's. A memory flashed up, an image she could barely grasp, but she knew she'd been here before. Only then, as a child, she hadn't really been paying attention.

Just like in the tower on the island, a table and two chairs stood in the center of the room. Low cabinets and bookshelves had been fitted to the walls beneath the windows, and a large telescope sat atop a tripod in front of the north-facing pane. To Artemis' astonishment, even the stove near the entranceway matched her own. The metal was warm to the touch – that meant it was in use.

"Alphard comes up here most days in winter to light the stove so the books won't get damp and moldy," Elnathan said before she could remark on it.

She bent to survey the titles in the open shelves. Some of them she recognized from Saint Jude's: Paracelsus, Cardano, Copernicus, but a few others were unfamiliar. Not all of them were about astronomy or philosophy, and they didn't have time for her to examine them more closely, so she decided to take a quick look at the telescope instead.

It was bigger and in better shape than her own. She felt her lips curving upward. If they didn't go back to the island, Alphard wouldn't need to light that stove anymore. She'd take care of it. There was more than enough room for a bed, too.

This place had been home to her family once, and, God and all the stars willing, it could be again.

"We should be getting back," Elnathan said gently. "I might be in trouble already."

She winced. He was right. She was being selfish. Beatrice might give her a hard time for disappearing, but she wouldn't let Elnathan off with a slap on the wrist – she could refute the arrangement she had with his father, and he'd never cut wood for her family again.

"Will you be heading back to the village now?" she asked Elnathan on the way back down. "With the Christmas Market going on and all?"

"My father is managing my stand. He's good at selling, so I'm not in a hurry."

He brushed past her so he could open the door for her. They stood together for a moment that seemed to go on and on, and she placed a hand on his arm.

"Thank you for this," she said.

He nodded, tilting his head at her in a way that melted her knees, but then he appeared to remember something, and the realization that hit him dimmed the spark in his eyes.

"I am your humble servant, Milady," he said slowly, pushing down the handle.

His words weren't meant to be unkind, but they struck her in the face like a gust of cold wind. He *was* her servant, and it became clear to her what that meant. Her heart bled as she stepped out into the corridor.

She was so muddled, she barely noticed the commotion downstairs. Not until Elnathan broke into a run and flew past her down the stairs.

The main door was open, and everyone was outside by the time she caught up to him. The horses in the bailey were rearing and tearing at their tethers, in danger of hurting themselves and each other. The soldiers were nowhere to be seen.

"What's going on here?" he asked no one in particular, face deathly pale.

Then his gaze fell on the mass of huge, writhing fish on the ground by the well, and Artemis saw them, too: not monstrous pikes like the creatures the boys turned into out in the lake, but trout, and all of them over five feet long. They thrashed on the flagstones, gasping for air. Eyes bulging and gills billowing out, they opened and closed their snouts as they struggled with death.

"Evil magic," Beatrice said, clutching the handrail with trembling fingers.

"We have to help them," shouted Aries, already down in the yard with Auri.

Artemis counted the fish, not wanting to believe this was true, but there were as many trout as there had been soldiers before. Their swords lay scattered around the steps leading up to the keep's entrance.
Had the magician known where to find the family, and had the soldiers been trying to fend him off?

Desperately, she tried to think of a way of saving them. They needed more than the few bucketsful of water from the fountain that Aries and Auri were splashing on their skin.

"Blankets," she yelled at Chiron. "Run to the stable and get horse blankets – as many as you can find!" Then, she followed Elnathan down to the fountain, where he and Leo were filling pails for Aries and Auri.

"We have to get them to the moat!" she shouted at him.

Elnathan immediately understood.

"Help your brothers," he told her. He pushed the pail at her, motioning toward Aries and Auri, who were pitching water at the gasping trout. "There's a cart in the stable. I'll be right back."

He raced to the stable, almost crashing into Chiron. Chiron had found a stack of blankets, and he sprinted to the fountain to soak them.

"Uncle, help me with the cart," Artemis heard Elnathan yell at Alphard.

The warden was just coming out of the kitchen building next to the keep, carrying a platter of fruit. He dropped the platter.

"Good God," he yelped, and followed Elnathan.

"I don't understand how he could have found out so quickly," Aries thought out loud, taking the next bucketful of water from Artemis' hands. "Who's informing him?"

Chiron wrapped the dripping blankets around the trout nearest to him. The one beside it had stopped writhing. Its fight was over, but Chiron didn't waste any time and moved on to the next.

Within minutes, Elnathan reemerged from the building, leading his horse, to which he'd hitched the cart. He'd tucked rags into the bridle over its eyes so it wouldn't spook like the soldiers' mounts. Alphard tried to calm the animals as Elnathan passed between

them, and then helped him get the vehicle into position to load up the fish.

"W – where's Jarlath?" Chiron asked Artemis.

She looked around. He was nowhere to be seen, but the gate stood wide open, and no one seemed to have noticed. No one except for Beatrice, but her mother's puzzled expression told Artemis that she didn't know anything about it.

The men hauled the five surviving trout onto the cart and made haste to get them over the drawbridge and into the moat. One of the beasts didn't recover in the murky water and floated belly up, but the remaining four pulled through and soon disappeared into the deeper regions of the trench.

"H – has anyone seen J – J – Jarlath?" Chiron repeated when they were all back in the yard.

"He ran off," a voice echoed through the bailey. "William raised a coward, I'd say."

The only sound was the gush of water in the fountain.

Artemis tried to locate the man who'd spoken, but she had been caught so off guard, he could have been standing in one of the doorways, and she wouldn't have seen him.

"Monster!" Beatrice shrieked, scanning the battlements. "Show yourself!"

But he didn't. The family drew closer together, shoulder to shoulder and back to back. The magician hadn't killed before, but now two men were dead.

Aries, Leo, Auri, and Elnathan drew their daggers. Chiron didn't own one.

Artemis frantically searched the windows of the keep. Most of them stood wide open. She nudged Elnathan, and his gaze followed hers, but then veered left.

"I'd think about what just happened here, love," the voice continued calmly, coming from everywhere at once.

Elnathan went rigid when he observed a movement near the stable, but he shook his head, cautioning her when he saw Artemis' questioning glance.

"Alphard is over there with the horses," he whispered in her ear.

"How can you be so cruel after all these years?" Beatrice shouted, scrutinizing the smithy and the canteen, but nothing moved there except for a blackbird on one of the roofs.

"Cruel?" the voice said, all sand and grit. "Look who's talking."

"Murderer!" Beatrice responded. "Fiend!"

"It was *friend*, once, and then *lover*," the voice said, full of sadness. "While it pleased you."

"We have to leave," Elnathan said quietly to Aries. "Uncle Alphard is getting the horses."

Aries nodded. "Take Chiron and help him."

"Yes, *do* hurry back to your island," the voice said, mocking them.

Artemis had no idea how the magician could possibly have heard the exchange when she barely

had, but it showed how vulnerable they really were.

"I wouldn't stick around *here* if I were you. The woods are full of robbers, and I don't think your king would pay a ransom. Besides, you only have until nightfall, unless you want to put your boys into the moat with the rotten trout – they're spoiled to the core, you know."

"Why are you doing this?" Artemis screamed. Tears tracked down her cheeks.

"For *you*, dear," the voice said, distant, and so softly and full of grief, Artemis might have believed him under any other circumstances but these.

The wind caught in the embrasures of the parapets, and the windows of the keep banged shut.

Elnathan and Chiron came back with Alphard and the horses. Together, they left, closing the main gate behind them. They drove their horses to the limit all the way back to the village, but no one followed them.

SIX

Elnathan stood on the wooden landing, watching the boat grow smaller. He'd wanted to tell Artemis goodbye, but who was he to speak to her at all? What *had* he been thinking when she'd appeared at his stand on the market, or when he'd shown her around Oak Castle?

Her face was blank, but her eyes betrayed her. So much sorrow. She was too young to be this burdened, and his heart broke for her.

The king had made excuses and refused to take her in. He had enough children of his own to worry about, so the *eternally nagging woman* had insisted Artemis return to Saint Jude's with her. She was a princess, by right, but she simply had nowhere to go, and the full extent of her tragedy twisted Elnathan's gut.

He wanted to wave to her when she stood on the little pebble beach, staring across the lake at him, but he didn't want to embarrass her and make things worse than they already were. Her brothers lingered around the shore and the boathouse, arguing until it was almost dusk.

Like clockwork, Beatrice reappeared on the scene, and shooed Artemis up the steep steps that led to the castle, while the boys went their separate ways. The strongest of them headed for the cliff, as usual. The others went into the boathouse – all but Chiron, who seemed remarkably calm. He'd been white as a sheet on the way back, and he hadn't said a word.

Elnathan didn't like it one bit. Quickly, he led his horse into the forest. Making sure he was alone, he tethered the animal to its usual tree by the path, where his father would find her should anything happen to him while he was airborne.

He foraged around in the saddle bag, spilling some of its contents, but soon found what he was looking for: the small envelope with the magic powder inside, a piece of parchment, and a quill. He tore off a strip of the parchment just large enough to write a note on, and then discovered he didn't have any ink.

He drew his dagger from his belt, nicked the pad of his finger, squeezed a big drop of blood from the wound, and dipped the tip of the quill in it.

Look out for Chiron! he wrote, dipped the quill again, and closed: *I am your humble servant.*

She would know that he had written the note, even if she might not assume that he would also be the creature who brought it to her.

When he was satisfied that the blood had dried, he rushed to the hollow tree stump where he always hid his clothes, stripped, and swallowed all the powder in the envelope instead of only a quarter of the amount, as he should have.

The transformation set in instantly. In less than half a minute, he rose up into the air with the note in his beak, Raven again.

Landing on the stone sill of her tower window was out of the question, but he was almost sure she'd be looking out. She did that every single evening, long into the night, so getting her attention wouldn't be a problem, he told himself – but then, all of a sudden, it was.

At first, he couldn't see her, and he flew around the tower repeatedly before he caught sight of her in the gloomy room, lying on her bed, crying. All the fight she'd had in her earlier that day when they'd saved those soldiers' lives had given way to exhausted misery, and he did not blame her. What a day she'd had.

He flapped his wings against one of the windowpanes, thrusting his beak at the glass over and over, and he cawed as loudly as he could without losing the note. He had no idea if she would have a way of helping Chiron. If she didn't, he'd have to figure something out – but he *would*.

She tried to ignore him and pulled the blanket over her head, but he kept at the pane stubbornly. It didn't matter if he broke it. The note he had written might save a life – or three.

Finally, she stomped over to the window and opened it, armed with a dustpan. She was ready to whack him with it, but he steered back, just far enough for her to observe him and see the note.

"Get away!" she yelled at him.

She was waving the dustpan so wildly, he was afraid she might throw it at him. Every instinct that

came naturally to the raven was screaming at him to flee, but the man inside the bird knew he couldn't.

Finally, she calmed down, and *really* looked at him.

"You're not exactly a pigeon," she said, frowning. "But you've got something for me, haven't you?"

He came slightly closer. She reached out her arm to him, stretching it out the window. Again, every instinct told him to fly away. Again, the man inside went against it.

She closed her eyes and turned her face away, protecting it with her other hand. He landed on her arm and smelled her fear of his beak and talons, so he stayed very still.

When she had gathered herself, she slowly pulled her arm inside a little way, and he admired her courage.

"You're not going to peck me if I take that note now, are you?" she said.

He moved his head from side to side.

"Did you just shake your head at me?" she said, holding her breath as she watched him.

He decided against any further exchange, and she plucked the note from his beak. The moment she had, he lifted off and flew away, careful not to flap his wings at her. Hurting her was the last thing he wanted to do.

Circling the tower once more, he watched her read the note, and then bang against the door, but it was locked from the outside, it seemed. He had not expected that. What now? His mind raced.

He had to find the boy.

Banking right, he dipped and flew over the yard and the vegetable garden, the small field, and dove into the twisted forest of crooked Scots pines and junipers. So close to nightfall, the raven wanted to grab one of the yew trees' branches, still his hunger on its bright red berries and hunt around for other things to eat or steal, and then find a good place to rest for the night. The man inside had to fight those instincts with every breath he took.

The last of the sunlight drained from the sky, and the world around Raven turned a dirty gray. His sight wasn't too good in the dark, and he would have to rely mostly on his hearing and his gut feeling from here on in. Soon, he would have to break off the search altogether and return to the mainland.

His time was almost up when he finally found Chiron. Naked and trembling like a leaf, the lad was lying next to a shallow rock pool in the stony cove on the west side of the island. It held just enough water to drown an infant if the child slipped and fell on its face, and Raven doubted that it could keep a five-foot-long pike alive. There were natural basins like this all over the islands that dotted the lake, but it hadn't rained much over the past few days, and the fierce wind easily dried them out.

Raven assumed this was where Chiron had gone to protect himself from the other creatures that ruled Lough Locke by night – the eels that grew to the size of sea serpents once daylight was gone, the enormous crayfish that wandered the islands' shores on warm summer nights and hid in the mud during winter, and his own brothers, who turned to pikes and lost their humanity and all memory of each other by the time dawn drew near.

In you go, Raven wanted to tell the boy, even if there wasn't really enough water.

In! he willed the lad, but Chiron curled up like a beaten dog when the transformation began. He had no intention of sliding in. Raven physically felt the lad's wish for death.

The shore was out of reach, and Raven was merely a bird, and not a man who could have carried him, as he'd done for William's soldiers that afternoon. His soul ached for the boy with the sad eyes, but he knew he had to resort to the only other means he had of saving him.

Cawing at the top of his voice, he flew at the woeful pile of skin and bones and beat his black wings against the convulsing body, forcing the pike's survival instincts to kick in and steer him toward the tiny pool. Raven pecked and tore at the wretched, defenseless boy, screeching at him until Chiron reached the basin's edge. There, the lad completed the change, and the thinnest, scrawniest pike Raven had ever seen slipped into the water, weak and bloodied. It lay on its side, barely covered, but probably safe in its puddle until morning, if it didn't move around too much.

Time to leave, Raven, the bird's human heart told him, *or you'll end up staying.*

SEVEN

Gray light leaked into the tower room through the frost-crusted panes. Dawn was barely more than a notion when the huge black bird returned. It kept flying at the window opposite Artemis' bed, cawing, and pecking at the glass.

She'd only slept for a few hours during the night, clutching the wooden swan Elnathan had given her on the Christmas Market. The noise from the racket at the window crept into the last of a string of restless dreams, and it took her a few seconds to wake up and disentangle herself from her blanket. Her hands hurt from pummeling the door, and her tongue stuck to the roof of her mouth as she hurried across the room. Stars danced in front of her eyes.

The raven thrust its beak at the glass with such force, she was afraid it might break – if the bird didn't kill itself first. She'd never seen or heard of a raven being used to carry messages, but this one was obviously an exception, and it was determined to deliver its note. Almost certain Elnathan had sent it, she took a deep breath before she opened the window and stepped back.

The bird hopped onto her arm without hesitation, and she took the strip of paper from its beak. It was longer than the last one. The creature didn't seem to be in a hurry. It went from her arm to her shoulder as she read.

Chiron is all right. Look for him in the rocky cove on the east side of the island. We have to talk. Wait by the window at dusk. –Your humble servant.

Relief knocked the wind out of her lungs. She wiped a hand across her face and sat down on her bed, bird and all.

"I hope your master is right," she thought out loud, croaking more than she was speaking.

Last night, she'd shouted her mother's name for hours while banging on the locked door, willing Beatrice to come back from the cliffs or the boathouse, or wherever she had been during this time, watching the water and feeling sorry for herself and the eldest of her sons.

Artemis was caught between loathing and pity for her mother. She tried to understand Beatrice's helplessness, but Beatrice wasn't helping *anyone* with her kind of crisis management. Moreover, she had prevented Artemis from searching for Chiron when he'd needed help.

A man on the other shore had known he was in some kind of trouble, but she, his own sister, had not. They had all helped several perfect strangers the previous day at Oak Castle, but Artemis had not been able to come to her own brother's aid because of her mother's stubbornness.

Oddly, the raven seemed to understand her inner conflicts. It stayed with her, holding on to her shoulder for a while, then cooed softly and took flight. It circled the tower several times, as if reluctant to leave her, and only headed for the mainland when the sun peeked over the horizon and painted the sky orange.

The lock on Artemis' door disengaged. Without saying a word, she shoved it open and pushed past Beatrice. The tray her mother was carrying clattered to the floor, spilling porridge, tea and shards all over the wooden planks. She sprinted down the stairs, pulled on two mismatched boots, and raced out of the building without bothering to explain herself.

On her way across the field behind the vegetable garden, she passed Cas and Poll. Bone weary, the two carried their torn shirts instead of wearing them. They might have waited too long to strip them off the previous evening.

Their shoulders sagged, and their hair dripped lake water. The wildness that was still raging in their eyes made her give them a wide berth. She knew better than to speak to them now. It would be another while before they were entirely themselves again.

Just as the note had promised, she found the youngest brother sitting beside a rock pool half-filled with water. Fresh scabs marked his temples, arms, and back. None of his wounds were serious, but it shattered her to see him like this.

"What happened?" she asked, sitting down beside him on a flat stone.

"Th – th – the usual," he said, absently rolling a blade of brown grass in his fingers. "N – nature doesn't l – like me."

His lips curved upward in a well-practiced, somewhat overused smile, looking exactly like one of the portraits she'd seen of Ambrose in his younger years. "O – o – or maybe it does," he went on, casting her a sideways glance, "a – and I'm j – just too e – entertaining to do away with."

She was now sure he'd spent the night in that puddle at the bottom of the shallow basin, and she couldn't imagine what this must have been like. He didn't need her pity, though. She'd often thought that if she'd pitied him less when they were younger, he might have learned to bite back when other creatures tried to make a meal of him. The elder brothers had learned – but Chiron didn't have the look about him that they did whenever they returned to the castle in the morning. He didn't have their furious reflexes or survival instincts to protect him, and even in face of certain death, he never would.

"Well, if we were on the mainland, you'd be the talk of the town for sure, sitting out here in the cold in your birthday suit," she said. "We'll get Leo and Aries to help you bring a few barrels of water here for tonight after you've slept, all right?"

He raised his eyebrows at her and a blush streaked his cheeks.

"Promise?" she repeated, fixing her gaze to his.

He blinked at her, and she knew she had him. He held out his hand to her, motioning at the pile of damp clothes next to her. "G – give me my p – pants, will you?"

The rest of the day passed so quietly, there was hardly any conversation in the castle, not even during the meals. Cas and Poll spent most of the day out at the boathouse, finally replacing the shingles that a storm had torn off the roof about a week ago.

Leo and Mercurius busied themselves cleaning the hen house and torching mites out from under the perches and the dark corners.

Artemis made sure Aries and Auri helped Chiron fill the rock basin with water from the lake. They hauled as many barrels to the pool as it took to make it overflow.

Beatrice felt more distant than ever to Artemis as they worked silently in the kitchen, mending clothes and preparing meals. Artemis couldn't tell whether the controlled expression on her face was meant to hide anger or sadness, but she suspected both.

"Don't ever lock my door again," she said. "I won't stand for it anymore, so help me God."

Her mother didn't so much as glance at her, but she nodded.

Late in the afternoon, she went to find Chiron. He was splitting wood, chopping at the pieces like a madman.

"You okay now?" she asked, setting down the basket she meant to fill for the tower room's stove.

He didn't look up. "We'll *all* just have to be, won't we?"

She didn't know how to reply, and silently gathered up the smaller wedges. She felt his hand on her arm when she turned to leave.

"I'm sorry," he said. "Y – you shouldn't be here at all, and I sh – shouldn't be making life harder for you."

She covered his hand with her own. "No one should be sorry but Abaddon. He put us here, and he's to blame. We won't give him the satisfaction of quarreling amongst ourselves and going crazy on this blasted island. Sooner or later, we'll find a solution to all this. Sooner or later, this *will* end, and we will lead normal lives. Don't you ever forget that."

He nodded, kissed her forehead, and went back to work – all without looking at her. Still, he'd let Aries and Leo help him with the water earlier, so she had hope he'd be all right. With temperatures still mild, it was improbable that the pool would freeze solid just yet, and they'd think of something over the next days for when that time came.

She lit the stove in her room and settled in by the south-facing window because it gave her the best view of the landing on the other shore. Elnathan and his father weren't there, and with all the heavy clouds in the sky, daylight was already fading. Her humble servant had abandoned her.

There would be no stargazing tonight, and she regretted that they hadn't thought to bring lamp oil with them from the mainland. Beatrice hadn't dared to lock her room tonight, so she went down to the kitchen and fetched a candle, as well as an apple and a cup of hot tea. She could read for a while, at least.

By the time she returned to her room, the raven was back and pounding at the window. Her heart leaped. Again, she let it in, and again, it sat on her arm. It carried a small envelope in its beak.

Put this in your tea and drink it all. Trust me, please. I am your humble servant.

The envelope held about half a spoonful of a reddish-brown powder that might have been dried clay. It smelled of mushrooms and rotten eggs. She grimaced and reread the words on the envelope.

The raven stretched its wings and cawed softly, as though she were testing its patience.

"I have no idea what this is," she mumbled, and tilted her head, glancing at the raven. "Do you? Or are you just teasing me?"

The raven mirrored what she was doing and inclined its head in the same direction.

Why should she put this in her tea? What would happen if she did? She dipped a finger into the powder. It tingled on her skin, but not unpleasantly. Maybe this was some sort of fungus. She didn't know much about fungi, but the reek of it was repulsive and definitely reminded her of mold.

Jarlath had included a pouch with several strange mushrooms in one of the supply deliveries a while ago. The accompanying note had declared it a birthday gift for the twins, Cas and Poll, and Cas had actually eaten one of the disgusting mushrooms.

He'd begun hallucinating soon afterward, so he might have at least *some* knowledge to help her out with her own little envelope, but she could hardly ask him now. Or in the morning, for that matter. He'd want to know where the sachet came from, and she wasn't going to lie to his face. She couldn't possibly tell him a raven had brought it to her window. He'd think she was hallucinating even without having eaten something she shouldn't have.

She regarded the bird with suspicion. Was it actually *grinning* at her? Impossible! And still, there was something uncanny about the creature. Birds did not behave like this – not even trained ones.

Trust me, the note read… This morning's message had said that he wanted to talk – how would mixing a powder into her tea help with that?

One thing was for sure: Elnathan would never harm her. He was a good man, and she was sure she could trust him with her life, but why the powder, and why the raven? Why not a pigeon, or a letter with the next provisions delivery?

Another uncertainty took up space in her tired mind: was the note really from Elnathan, or was this some sort of trick? An image of the magician wormed its way into her thoughts. It hadn't occurred to her this morning, but how on earth could Elnathan have known her brother was in trouble, or where to find him?

The raven hadn't told him, had he? She'd heard of parrots from Africa that could replicate the voices of their owners, and magpies that could whistle tunes, but never of a raven that could speak in whole sentences. On the other hand, what did *she* know of the world and all its forms of magic? She lived on an island in every respect.

"Who sent you?" she said to the creature eventually, studying it, willing it to answer in some way.

It wouldn't, of course, because it simply *couldn't*. But then it did: Carefully, it inched back over her arm and pecked at the miniature wooden swan lying on the sheets beside her.

For a second, Artemis doubted her own sanity. The raven stared at her, nudged the figure again, hopped onto her knee, and took off through the window as if to say *this is your choice now*.

The tea she'd made was still warm. She took a deep breath, inhaling the scent of mint and chamomile, and tipped the contents of the envelope into the cup. The powder hissed as it dissolved when she swished it around. It turned the tea into a rotten, repelling brew the color of filthy dishwater.

On a whim, she drank it anyway, watching the raven soar past her open window once again. What did she have to lose?

At first, she felt no different, though her stomach was struggling to keep the stuff down. Mere seconds later, the sickness passed, and she had other issues to worry about. Her vision blurred, her head spun, and she was sure the fungi were taking effect and that she was going to start fantasizing. Her clothes were suddenly too big for her. They fell off her like sheets

from a clothesline without pegs to hold them. The next thing she knew, she was airborne, and for some reason, ridiculously happy. There… she really was hallucinating – but then the raven called to her without speaking. She understood him as clearly as if he was standing next to her, and he was telling her to follow him, so she did.

An icy wind whispered through her ink-black feathers and carried her along without effort and without question.

Fly, it murmured in her ear. *You're free.*

To her surprise, she certainly was, because the tower lay behind her, and the island was merely a place in the lake beneath her.

The raven flew by her side, and she felt a strong sense of familiarity. His presence washed over her like spring's first warm breeze, and she became aware of a natural connection, as if they'd known each other all their lives not just by name. He was her partner.

Stay close, he said, and again, she heard the words in her head, but this time she recognized his voice.

Elnathan.

There was no time for questions, and no *room* for them inside her. She was much too keyed up and drunk on adrenaline to do anything but concentrate on her new limitless ability.

Swift as a shooting star, she flew loops around him and did somersaults in the air, swooped down, only to rise high as her wings would carry her again in a heartbeat. She wanted to laugh for joy.

We have to go, Elnathan told her, coming to her side again. *Our wings are borrowed, and daylight is almost gone. We don't see well in the dark.*

Almost disappointed, she trailed behind him in his slipstream until they reached the mainland. There, Elnathan guided her through the trees in the little forest beyond the pier. She landed beside him on a dead tree trunk, and he began to change shape mere seconds after his feet touched the mossy wood.

The sharp angles of the raven's skull softened, and nose and lips formed where his beak had been. Wings changed to arms, talons turned to feet, and feathers yielded to smooth skin. Observing him, she wondered if the transformation hurt, but he didn't make a sound.

Hunkered down between a tree stump and a scruffy bush, he just peered at her through wild eyes, breathless, and as though he needed something to anchor his mind so that he could reconnect with himself. She knew that look from her brothers.

Then, without warning, her own vantage point shifted. Pine needles and grit jabbed the soles of her feet, and an arctic drizzle hit her bare skin like a slap in the face. Shivering with cold, she rose, wrapping her arms around herself. Her heart hammered in her chest, but before she could say anything, Elnathan was there, enveloping her in his warmth.

"You're all right," he whispered, and held her close. "I've got you."

Impossible as the situation was, she felt a deep longing to kiss him. It seemed so natural to be with him like this. She pushed her hands through his hair, and pressed against him, feeling every part of his body against her own. He kissed her neck, her cheek, and her mouth, and left the taste of wild herbs and resin on her tongue when he slowly backed away from her.

"Wait here," he said. "You don't know it, but you're freezing. I'll be *right* back."

He searched around for something by the tree stump. Twigs broke, dead leaves rustled to her left, and she spun around, teeth chattering, and suddenly afraid, aware of her naked vulnerability here, embarrassed and shocked by her own behavior toward Elnathan.

He quickly found what he was looking for and didn't appear to give much thought to what had just happened between them. The soft woolen shirt he gently pulled over her head smelled of him. His arms brushed her skin and made her shudder all over again.

"These won't fit very well," he said, going down on one knee in front of her, "but I don't have anything that will." Like a father dressing his child, he held the leg of a pair of pants for her so she would be able to slip right in.

"That's fine," she said when she finally rediscovered her scratchy voice, and leaned on him so she wouldn't fall over. "Right now, I'd make do with a horse blanket."

He chuckled and then struggled with his own clothes for a moment before he went back to the tree stump and brought her a man's socks and a pair of boots.

"I wasn't sure you'd come."

"I trust you." She placed a hand on his arm. "But I *do* have questions."

He nodded. "Later. We have to get in out of the cold first."

"Where are we going?"

"To my house. We can talk there. My father is at Oak Castle with Alphard. He won't be back until tomorrow."

"Good God! Is that safe?"

Again, he nodded. "The magician was only there because of your family. He's never come there before, and my father and uncle don't believe he'll ever be back. Besides, someone had to bury those poor bastards we couldn't get to the moat in time."

He'd tethered his horse to a tree near the clearing where she'd so often watched him work with his father. From a bag attached to its saddle, he pulled a hooded cape and draped it around her shoulders. He didn't have one for himself, so she sat behind him on the saddle and tried to share its warmth by stretching the fabric around them both.

The horse carried them deep into the woods, where the freezing rain soon turned to sleet, and then snow. She noticed Elnathan was giving the village a wide berth to make sure no one would see them. Hardly anyone would be about at this hour and in this weather, but she was glad he was taking the long way around – for his own sake more than hers.

Elnathan's home looked too big to be a simple laborer's cottage, and Artemis wondered how a woodcutter could afford it. There was a large stable beside it for the family's working horses and equipment, and a roofed shelter where the woodcutters kept at least one wagon and a cart.

Inside the house, Artemis breathed in the scent of pine wood and smoke as she shed the cloak and hung it over a chair by the fireplace to dry.

Red embers glowed in the huge open hearth, giving off a balmy light. The main room was sparsely furnished, but not empty or cold. A solid wood parquet covered the floor, and glass panes glinted in the windows. Assorted tools that were probably decorative rather than functional hung on the walls around a painted plate rack and buffet with assorted crockery. A staircase to the right of the door led to the upper floor, and she guessed there were bedrooms up there rather than a hay store.

Elnathan stripped off his wet shirt and poked the embers in the hearth. He laid a few small wedges into the hot ashes, and then blew on them and poked some more. Tiny flames licked at the wood fibers. Quickly, he added more wood, and soon he had the blaze going again.

"Are you hungry?" he asked. "I have fresh bread."

Artemis shook her head, knelt, and settled against

him. He put his arm around her, and together, they stared into the fire.

"You have a nice home," she said, meaning it.

"My father built this house for the family he was going to have with my mother."

"You were born here?"

He slowly nodded. "But my mother died giving birth to me, and my father couldn't work in his old profession anymore."

"I'm sorry," she said, wishing she hadn't asked and prompted him in this direction. She hadn't intended to make him uncomfortable.

"I'd love to have gotten to know her. The way my father talks about her, she must have been a wonderful person. He never remarried because he still misses her."

Artemis realized life must have been more difficult for Elnathan than she'd assumed. She had only ever seen her own family's problems and pictured everyone else living as they pleased, envious of the freedoms they had.

Elnathan had grown up without a mother, and although she'd been aware of this, it hadn't occurred to her that he might have suffered because of it. Unlike her, he hadn't even had brothers or sisters. Granted, hers turned into monster-pikes at night, but at least she'd had Aries, Leo, and Chiron to play with by day, to talk to, and to teach her things her mother couldn't.

"You know how it is to miss someone you didn't even know," he said then, breaking the awkward silence between them. "I saw it in your face at Oak Castle when you were looking at the portraits of your father. What age were you when he died? Two? Three?"

"Three."

She liked to imagine she'd gotten to know her father just a little bit. Even without having talked to him about the important matters she might have needed his advice on, she'd felt his presence in his journals and the books up in his tower room – *her* tower room. They had opened her eyes for the things he saw when he gazed up at the stars. There was almost nothing private in those journals, and nothing about how he'd perceived his life with his family or friends, but his work had made up a large part of who he was. She was sure she knew many things about Ambrose that her older brothers did not.

She needed a change of subject, or they'd both be miserable by the end of the night.

"How did you know about Chiron?" she asked.

He hesitated. "I fly over the island, sometimes."

She tried to think if she might have seen him. There was no waterfowl on the lake and hardly anything bigger than a thrush on the island itself. While watching the stars by night, she hadn't been paying enough attention to the sky by day, apparently.

"I didn't know any such thing like the powder you sent me existed. I've only ever seen this kind of magic in the form of a curse."

He scoffed a laugh. "Did it feel like a *curse* when you were coursing through the sky tonight?"

"No, but–"

"And don't tell me you were afraid, because ravens aren't easily frightened. I *saw* you. I *felt* you."

She blushed, remembering that moment in the woods. He'd seen and felt *every part* of her, but *seeing* and *feeling* didn't just apply to that kiss, or the primal longing they'd both had for each other. It was the connection they'd shared while they were coursing through the air.

And still, admitting she'd been happy and more excited than ever before in her life seemed somehow inappropriate…

"It was good, wasn't it?" he asked, and she wasn't quite sure whether he meant being airborne or the kiss.

She pictured what would happen if her mother, Cas, or Poll found out she'd left the island tonight to be here with the woodcutter's son…

Elnathan shifted to face her. "Did I say something wrong?"

He blinked at her, and she couldn't bring herself to look away. A man wasn't supposed to be this beautiful. She stroked his cheek, and he tenderly kissed her hand, kissed her wrist, kissed her lips. She tasted honey in with the wild herbs and resin, and moved to sit on his lap.

She let him slip his hands underneath her shirt. They felt hot as he ran them over the skin of her back, and she allowed him to undress her, one piece of clothing after the other. All heat and throbbing and craving, she was willing to permit him to do anything that pleased them both, and she quivered under his touch.

Reckless, the flames in the fireplace murmured.

For a moment, she held back. True, she was being reckless. But no one would find out. This would be her secret – the first time she'd ever had something all to herself. She wanted him as much as she needed the air to breathe, and she had to have him. He was her partner in soaring through the sky, and if she held back now, she'd regret it for the rest of her life. Who knew what tomorrow would bring?

Again, she trusted him blindly."

EIGHT

"Where did you get the magic powder?" she asked him later that night, tangled in his embrace.

He traced the side of her face with his thumb, determined to distract her with kisses again, but she propped herself up on her elbow. She wanted answers. But how much could he tell her?

"You asked me to trust you," she said, "and I mixed that awful, stinking stuff in my tea and drank it without any idea what it would do just because you said so." She grinned down at him. "I think you can give me some credit for that."

He sat up and hugged his knees to his chest.

"It's a bit complicated. I'm learning another trade besides woodcutting and carving figures to sell for a penny at fairs and markets–"

"You mean sorcery."

She had a way of interrupting, and whenever she did, she inevitably scrambled his thoughts and made him forget all the wordy explanations he'd rehearsed for her.

Another thing he'd discovered about her was that she sure didn't believe in beating around the bush. He was glad she didn't generally dismiss or oppose his use of magic. If anyone, then she would have cause to. She'd been dealt pretty bad cards, and still… she *trusted*.

"I want to learn the art, yes. Every king used to have a sorcerer, and they would turn the fate of thousands in wars."

"Or get run out of the country for cursing the king's widow."

He wanted the earth to open up and swallow him. How was it that everything always came out wrong when he was with her? It was a wonder she was still here.

But then she grinned at him. "I was just making fun of you. Please go on."

He was going to put his foot in his mouth again if he did, so he pressed his lips together and desperately tried to think of a way of getting out of this, but Artemis' mien told him she wasn't going to let him off the hook. He owed her an explanation.

"I've *always* wanted to learn something that would be… *important*."

She hummed. "Something *important*? Do you not think that cutting wood and working with it as you do is important and exceedingly valuable?"

How did she continuously manage to baffle him? He kissed her temple simply because he couldn't resist.

"It is," he said. "I didn't phrase that well. People depend on me. I like what I do, and I could be content until the day I die – if I didn't know there was more. But I do, and there is so much to learn. Without magic, we wouldn't be together here right now. I could have carved figures and cut wood all my life, but that wouldn't have brought us together."

"Oh, but it did." She smiled. "Your pinecone men brought you to me for *years*."

He tilted his head at her much like the raven had done earlier. "Then they had at least *some* bit of magic for you over there on that island."

"You have no idea." She entwined her fingers with his. "Did you mix the powder yourself?"

She wasn't going to let this go, and she was right not to. He wouldn't have, if he'd been in her place.

"No."

"Who taught you?"

"I have a good teacher."

She rolled her eyes and sighed. "So I gather. But who is it?"

"He lives not far from here."

Her breath hitched so he could hear it, and he realized he was going to have to tell her *something* before she thought he was in league with the devil.

"Don't worry, it's not the magician who cursed you. I'm not stupid."

"I didn't say you were–"

He cupped her face in his hands and fixed his gaze to hers. "It's a relative of mine, and he doesn't want anyone to know he can do a few tricks. He could lose his livelihood. People don't take kindly to anyone who can do magic at the moment. Not since... Well, you know."

"Not since Abaddon cursed us."

Elnathan wasn't certain it was so much the curse as everything else that had been going on. Magic was a dying art, and caught right in the middle between the new tentative discussions about scientific discoveries and the dogma of religious teachings.

But there was something else, and it had to do with the realism of everyday life in poverty in these parts. He didn't believe that the commoners or peasants had grieved for the family on the lake as much as they'd missed the fish they'd relied on to feed their children, and the income their catch had generated to pay their rent and their taxes.

He'd heard stories about Artemis' grandfather and the two princes he raised – one a stargazing oddball, and the other a cold, selfish man with no empathy for the common folk.

"Abaddon's curse didn't just affect your family," he said. "A lot of poor people used to fish on that lake. You can imagine how it became a problem for them when they couldn't do that anymore."

Artemis nodded. "I remember another family living on the next island, and all the boats tied to the landings around the lakeshore."

"The king – your uncle – had everyone who couldn't pay their dues run off the land. There was a lot of bloodshed, and he wasn't interested in the fate of those who lost everything."

She went silent, and he regretted the words that had tumbled from his mouth so carelessly yet again.

"I'm sorry. He's your uncle. I shouldn't have spoken out of place."

"It's not that." She tugged their blanket tighter around them. "I often had nightmares during my first years over there, and I think I felt sorry for myself for a long time because I was only seeing my own problems. I shouldn't have been so selfish – I always had enough to eat, and I never had to suffer the way my brother does."

Had he heard right? Brother, singular, not plural?

"Chiron…" she said then. "That was you – wasn't it? You tormented him until he got into that pool, didn't you?"

He nodded, still ashamed of what he'd done, even if it had been to save the lad's life.

"I can't imagine what it's like being stuck on Saint Jude's. It's unfair either way, either side of the water."

They watched the fire burn low, and she snuggled up to him.

"Your relative," she said after a while. "You don't have to tell me who it is. But what is he teaching you, exactly?"

"Little things, mostly," he said, telling her nothing but the truth. "Things that don't attract attention and might come in handy one day."

Her eyes reflected the light of the glowing embers, and her brow crinkled. "Using a powder that can transform a human into a bird certainly isn't a *little thing*."

"You're right." He shifted to escape her scrutiny, but she cast him a look that told him this wouldn't be enough. "He doesn't exactly know I'm using it."

"What do you mean?"

He didn't answer, and she nudged him.

"Tell me, please?"

"I kind of... sort of... well, I stole it from him."

Not a pretty thing to have to admit to, but he didn't want to tell her an outright lie. He left things out, sometimes, but he didn't lie to the people he loved.

Loved...?

Was that right?

She still wasn't trying to run off, even after half a night of his excruciating blunderings and the sum of all his blatant honesty. He'd been stretching his luck, and he knew it, but she just gave a laugh.

"You *nicked* it?" she said. "I mean, won't he notice?"

"No, I don't think he will. I tested it for him, and that's how I know what it does – and where he keeps it. He didn't even make it himself. He told me he got it from a sailor who claimed he had it from a man he met on his travels to the east."

Elnathan wasn't sure he remembered this part of it correctly, but he recalled the words *sailor* and *traveler* from someplace he'd never heard of.

"How much of it is there?" she asked.

"A lot. And *very* little is necessary to change shape for a few minutes. He gave me way too much the first time I transformed, and I didn't change back until late the same night."

"That must have been frightening."

Her mien fell, and her mouth opened and closed, as if she meant to say more, but she didn't. She had to be comparing the magic that changed her brothers to the magic that had brought her here. Altering his position, he took her in his arms. She'd felt the joy of being airborne and the freedom of soaring through the sky the same way he did. Was what he would tell her next going to shock her?

"I was *terrified*, at first." He paused and pulled a face, but then decided to try to describe how the experience had moved him. "The thing is, the longer you remain a raven, the less human you are, and the less afraid you become. You aren't the same… um…" What was the word he was searching for? Person? Soul? Neither was altogether correct. "You're not the same as before."

She turned around, away from him, but pressed her back against his chest, spooning with him. "But you remember everything you do while you're a raven, don't you? Even if you take more of the powder?"

He didn't know an answer to that. "When your brothers come home in the morning, do they remember what they did during the night in the lake?" he asked. He'd always wondered, but doubted it. A whole night was a long time to be free of human thoughts, worries, and limitations.

"None but Chiron."

Elnathan hummed. Just as he'd thought. It was *brother*, singular.

"His heart is different." She sighed and wiggled free of him, sitting up. "I have to go back, you know."

He gave a tiny nod and sat up next to her. "But not just yet," he whispered, hoping to buy another hour or two. "Stay, a little while longer."

He couldn't stand the thought of taking her back to the lake like this. Not with all that sadness on her face and in her voice. Almost expecting her to push him away, he ran his fingers through her hair and gently down her shoulder before he kissed her neck and worked his way up to her lips, not quite knowing whether she'd welcome it, but she did.

She surprised him and nestled against him. Her touch made his whole body tingle, and he wished he could stop time. Every single moment with her humbled, awed, and fulfilled him, and he realized he had spent over a year's worth of evenings and nights sitting in this house, longing for his wings – but not tonight. He might never want them again if they could only be together somewhere far away from here. Anywhere would do, at least for him.

But who was he to make wishes or dream that big? He had nothing to offer her except for his love. Maybe that would be enough for now.

Slowly, he made love to her once more, watching all her beauty unfold on her face as she soared with him, and then fell the very moment he had taken her high enough into the sky on wings that were his own, and not borrowed. He had never thought he could be this happy.

A while later, she drifted off to sleep in his arms, but he dared not close his eyes. He didn't want to miss a single second of having her here, but he also knew there would be hell to pay if he didn't take her back to the island before dawn.

He woke her a good hour before sunrise. They barely spoke as he took her to the lake, keeping well back from the shore as she stripped off his shirt and pants and they kissed goodbye. He had just enough of the powder to send her back.

He wished he'd brought more with him from the castle, but the previous day, he hadn't imagined himself finding the courage to do what he'd done tonight – and not in his wildest dreams had he assumed she'd trust him enough to go through with it.

"I'm sorry I can't come with you," he told her, handing her the sachet. "I have to go back to Oak Castle to get more, but I can come to your window again tomorrow."

She looked up at him, shivering in the chill of earliest morning, and caressed his cheek. "Don't you dare let me wait."

Then she tipped the powder into her mouth dry because they hadn't thought to bring anything to dissolve it in, and a few seconds later, she took flight.

NINE

Froth bubbled on the little beach and turned to ice as the gray water lapped at the smooth stones and pebbles. A cold wind tugged at the hood of Artemis' coat and tousled her hair. She wiped her nose on a handkerchief, and when she turned to head back up to the castle, she bumped into Chiron and startled.

"I – I – it's freezing out here, little frog," he said. "W – what are you doing d – down here?"

"I just needed air."

"Well, you got that. Y – y – you've been gone forever. I haven't seen you since breakfast."

She gave him a weak smile. She hadn't noticed she'd spent so much time staring at the other shore.

"Y – y – you still pining for Elnathan?" he said, squinting across at the mainland and grinning. "He isn't over there, is he?"

She cuffed him and walked away, but he caught up within two or three strides. Earnest lines hardened his disfigured face.

"L – l – look, I just don't want you to be unhappy for the rest of your... you – you know..."

He fell silent. She raised an eyebrow and cast him an intentionally nasty look.

"I don't know where you're going with this, or why you're so concerned with me. Have I done something to offend you, brother?"

Hastily he shook his head. "I – I just thought I'd come down and keep you company, b – but it all went to hell when I opened my m – mouth, didn't it? I'm sorry. C – can we start again?"

"We're not fighting," she reminded him.

"A – all right," he said, jutting his chin. "I don't like fighting with you."

"That's because you always lose."

They would have laughed at this a few weeks ago, but neither of them felt like it now. She studied him. Misery had painted dark circles around his eyes.

"How are you feeling?" she asked.

He wiped his nose on his sleeve. "I – I wish we hadn't gone to the m – mainland."

"We would have missed out on a lot of things if we hadn't."

"Th – things w – we didn't miss before we had them." His lips twisted upward, but this time, he didn't manage his typical grin, and his expression derailed into a sad smirk.

She didn't know how to reply to that. Her conscience bothered her as she continued on up the slope to the precarious steps, hearing the crunch of his boots in the gravel behind her.

"I wonder what the king is doing to find Abaddon," she said after a moment, "with two of his soldiers dead, and four in the moat at Oak Castle."

Chiron scoffed. "Th – the king couldn't find him a – all these years. W – what makes you think he'll find him now? Maybe M – mother is right and he never really tried."

She stopped dead in her tracks. "He's our *uncle*!"

"Well, he – he wasn't very g – glad to see us back on the m – m – mainland."

She took the last dozen steps in twos. At the top, she turned to him again so she could see him properly.

"What do you mean?"

"M – Merc – told me he nearly had a stroke when they asked if he w – would take them on and have them trained. M – Mother and he had a huge a – argument, a – and, and–"

"Go on," she said, but instantly felt terrible for rushing him.

She had a feeling his stutter was getting worse, and she wasn't helping him with her impatience. He cast her a downtrodden glance as he tried to unclutter the words in his throat, and she held his hand the way she'd always done when they were children. Finally, he was able to continue.

"M – Merc said the only reason W – William agreed was b – because there were so many c – c – councilmen there who had been loyal to F – father, or he would probably have h – had them all put in the stocks for making demands."

Artemis had to think about this. William only had his throne in the first place because their mother had conceded it to him on behalf of her sons. All seven of them, to be exact. He would have been ninth in line if Ambrose hadn't fallen off his horse, and Abaddon hadn't cast that spell.

Not even her mother had ever suggested as much, but what if Abaddon had been on his payroll? What if he still was? She wanted to talk to Elnathan about this, but dusk was still so far off. On Saint Jude's Island, even time itself was cursed.

"Must have been a relief for William to see us go back," she mumbled, stepping through the gate into the courtyard.

Chiron nodded. "I b – bet. He must be having n – nightmares about the c – councilmen up – up – upturning that renunciation Mother signed for us in return for the a – appanage."

"But she would have gotten that anyway."

"N – no. We were c – *cursed*. H – he could have just t – taken the throne as if we no longer existed. To the world out there, we're just m – monsters." He gesticulated in the direction of the mainland.

"Don't say that." She tried to touch his arm, but he shrank away from her.

"Th – they're right. Y – you saw the way they looked at us in the village."

He had a point. "All right. But what happened to make him decide against doing that?"

"A – a few people spoke up for us."

"Those same councilmen who were there when the boys were?"

Chiron shrugged. "I sup – p – pose so."

The cold was starting to get to her. "Let's go inside," she said. "Warm up a bit before... before."

"B – before I go lie in my puddle, you mean," he said, and then looked at the sky. "I might get snowed in tonight."

Together, they slunk inside through a servants' entrance near the base of the tower. It led to the cellar beneath the kitchen, where they stored their wine and ale. A few dusty bottles of brandy sat on a shelf at the very back. Artemis poured them both some into cracked cups and they drank until Chiron had to go. She saw him off and went to her tower room to wait for Elnathan.

Lost in thought, she took a seat on the bed, but immediately jumped up again, plucking the swan from her blanket. Its neck had broken under her weight, slight as she was, and she felt like crying.

Her door opened a crack. She'd forgotten to engage the bolt.

"I wanted to wish you a good night," Beatrice said without coming in.

When Artemis didn't answer, her mother nudged the door inward a few more inches and peeked inside. Her glance immediately fell on the swan, but she didn't comment on it.

"We'll have snow tonight," she said instead, "and the lake will soon freeze over."

Artemis bowed her head. The lake and Chiron's rock pool. The lake never froze completely solid, but the pool would. Beatrice probably didn't even know about the pool. Her mother wouldn't understand that some boys weren't born to be hunters and heroes, so there was no point in discussing it with her.

"About time the king's steward sent our supply delivery," she just said. "We've run out of lamp oil again."

Beatrice offered a reassuring smile. "Should be here in two days," she said, and left the door ajar.

Artemis waited for a moment and then closed it all the way, locking it quietly. Behind her, the raven tapped on the glass pane.

He made a perfect landing on her outstretched arm. The tiny envelope in his beak contained more of the smooth granulate than there should have been. He'd written a short note.

Put half away for a rainy day.

Mindful of the fading light, she released the raven out the window, and tipped what she gaged as half the portion of the powder into an empty cup with a broken handle. Then she undressed, bracing herself for the foul taste of tonight's magic on her tongue, and swallowed the powder down without bothering to dissolve it in anything. The effect was instantaneous.

Again, Elnathan took the lead, and she followed. Thick clouds gathered in the sky, and daylight faded so quickly, she barely saw where they were going as they crossed the lake. Its restless black water churned, and she *felt* the shadows beneath the angry waves. She was glad when they were well clear of the island

and the monsters that guarded it, even if some of those monsters were members of her own family.

The happiness she'd felt last time didn't manifest itself while she was airborne even when they reached the mainland. Despite the near darkness, she felt watched. The notion intensified when they landed in the coppice where Elnathan had left their clothes. Twice, she thought she saw eyes glinting in the woods, only to have them disband in a thin flurry of snow, but the tingling in her bones wouldn't stop.

The mare felt it, too. The animal pulled at her tethers and stomped impatiently as the heavens opened and released gusts of sleet and snow down upon them.

Freezing, regardless of the thick cloak Elnathan had wrapped around her shoulders, Artemis put her arms around his middle and laid her cheek against his back. She didn't know where they were going, and she didn't care, just as long as it was far away from the lakeshore.

Many of the things she saw along the way were unfamiliar to her, but once they were clear of the village, she recognized the bridge they'd passed a few days earlier, and the ancient linden trees. They were en route to Oak Castle, but she didn't question him. She felt his heartbeat right through the layers of fabric between them. He knew what he was doing, and she wanted to trust him.

The drawbridge was down, but the gate and the portcullis were closed. They had to leave the horse alone for a few minutes to get inside the barbican. Elnathan had a key to the narrow secondary door in the double-winged gate that allowed one person at a time to pass through.

Once inside, Elnathan opened the gate long enough to fetch the mare. A postern allowed them to enter the gatehouse. From there, they were able to get into the bailey and raise the portcullis. Wet through and shivering, they led the mare to the stable. There, Elnathan lit a lamp and showed Artemis how to help him rub her down.

"Does your uncle know about us?" she asked, looking around for the old nag he'd used for the trip to the village, but it was gone.

Elnathan shook his head. "He's at the village. William summoned him, and I said I'd keep watch here tonight."

Why had William summoned the caretaker?

"Don't worry – it's safe," Elnathan assured her, throwing a blanket over the mare.

He made sure there was water in the stall, and then took Artemis by the hand and led her to the keep, lighting their way with the lamp. His massive keyring opened the door with a creak, and he locked it again behind them.

"I don't like being shut in," she mumbled.

He cast her a questioning glance.

"My mother always used to lock the door of my tower room so I wouldn't be tempted to wander off at night."

He immediately inserted the big key back into the lock and was about to turn it, but she stopped him and placed her hand over his.

"It should be safe enough to leave it open," he said, but she shook her head.

"Best if it's shut tight. Didn't you feel it too, back at the lake?"

He tilted his head and fixed his gaze to hers. "Like someone was there besides us?"

She nodded.

He stroked her cheek. "I think it was just something in the lake." Then he winked. "I get that feeling a lot over there."

He could be right. It had crossed her mind.

"We weren't followed in any case," he said firmly. "I would have known. I have…" He trailed off and paused, looking for words. "*Instincts*."

"Since you started using the powder to change shape?"

He raised a sassy eyebrow at her. "Do you still trust me? Despite my animal instincts?"

She huffed a laugh and wrapped her arms around him. She loved how he could take the sharp edges off this strange and dangerous world for her.

"It's chilly here," she said, feeling slightly better, if not warmer. "Got wood to light a fire?"

"Yes, but not down here, *Milady*." He grinned at her. "There's a room up on the second floor you haven't seen yet."

"Is there, now?" she said, playfully glaring at him.

"So much for trust!" He sniggered, and led her to a short corridor whose entrance was well concealed behind a tapestry in the Great Hall.

"Secret passage," he whispered, glancing over his shoulder, as though he suspected spies behind the curtains and was giving her information that could have either of them thrown in some deep, dark dungeon at any time. "Don't tell anyone."

Giggling, she climbed the steep, winding staircase behind him. At the top, Artemis found herself looking at another beautifully decorated arched doorway. The same craftsman who'd worked on the door leading up to the little tower had depicted Callisto here, hiding among the stars from Hera, and Actas with his back to her. Zeus, a silent silhouette worked into the door's lock, reached his hand upward to the others, as if trying to bring them all back to Olympus.

Elnathan unlocked it, and they entered a long, narrow room, illuminated by fragrant beeswax candles in silver holders on an impressive banqueting table. The table dominated the middle of the room, complete with ten high-backed chairs of exquisite quality.

Murals and family crests had been worked into the stucco that decorated the ceiling, and polished battle swords, blades pointing downward, hung at intervals along the wall across from the shuttered windows.

A huge green tile stove in the corner at the far end of the room lent it a pleasant warmth. To the left of the stove, a wide bench with cushions and a soft woolen carpet beneath seemed to call out to cold feet. She kicked off her boots by the door and went to stand on the carpet, while Elnathan shrugged out of his cloak and draped it across two of the chairs to dry.

The table was laid for two at Artemis' end, and a pot of stew sat on a ledge in the stove. She lifted the lid and sniffed. Glorious. How had Elnathan managed to cook a meal and light the candles before fetching her?

She looked across to him, baffled.

"I can't cook," he said immediately, closing the distance between them in a few strides. "I was here yesterday to pick up the powder, and I told Alphard I was bringing back company tonight."

"And he just made you stew and lit all those candles before he left?"

Another mischievous glint flared up in his eyes. "Half true. He did cook the stew because I asked him to. He can't wait to meet the girl I'm courting, by the way, and my father will be asking questions tomorrow no doubt. But the candles are my doing." He smiled and clasped her hand. "Watch, and don't be frightened."

All the candles went out for a moment. Artemis drew air. Then they relit by themselves. She'd been holding his hand, so he certainly hadn't gone round, blown them out, and then relit them.

"How did you do that?"

He laughed. "That's just one of the little things my teacher taught me."

She didn't know whether this qualified as *valuable* knowledge in the sense he'd explained when they'd last been together. Useful, maybe, and definitely a bit scary, but nothing that could decide the fate of mankind, and he seemed so happy, she didn't ask him to elaborate.

He gestured to her dripping cloak, and she handed it to him. Then he dragged back a chair for her, and she ran her fingers over the polished dark wood of the ornately carved top rail and spindles.

"My grandfather made these," he said. "And the table."

"Your grandfather was a wonderful carpenter," she said, and Elnathan smiled.

"He was the master of the guild, and my father was the master after him. My father even held a seat on the king's council."

She saw where Elnathan had gotten his talent from, and it struck her that their families had been connected for a long time. But if Benedict had been a member of the council, how had he fallen so far? What had he done to displease his guild, and the king?

Her mind wandered to Alphard, and the summons he'd received from William as she watched him ladle stew into her bowl.

"Did your uncle say nothing about why William wants to see him?" she asked after they'd eaten.

Elnathan had piled the cushions from the bench onto the thick carpet in front of the stove for them. He poured her another cup of wine and sat next to her, nipping at his own.

"He had *a lot* to say about it, actually."

She took a sip and set the cup down. It was rising to her head, and the stew had left an odd taste in her mouth. "Tell me?"

"He thinks William is getting ready to sell the castle because the land it's on has been reallocated. William is strapped for funds."

"It's not *his* to sell," she said, almost toppling the cup beside her when she shifted to face him.

"You're right. It isn't. That's why Uncle Alphard is so upset. He's getting too old to take care of the place on his own anyway, but he's devastated. He's been here forever, and he promised your mother."

Her mind spun. She'd have to talk to Beatrice. But what then? What could Beatrice do about it? What could *anyone* do if the king had reallocated land and made up his mind to sell an outdated castle that no one lived in anymore?

"I have to tell her in the morning," she said, and emptied the rest of her wine in one swig, feeling tipsy right afterward.

"Yes," Elnathan said, taking the cup from her hands. "I think she has a right to know."

"Is Alphard your teacher?" she asked.

The thought had been at the back of her mind ever since Elnathan had told her he was hiding the powder in the stable here. A trick like the one with the candles wasn't going to save her mother's inheritance, but maybe he had other things up his sleeve.

Elnathan read her. "He is. But nothing he can do will help your family with this problem, I'm afraid. He works with natural phenomena. He can read the stars and tell the future, and he really has a talent when it comes to working with animals, which is what interests me most, but he can't influence people's minds or anything like that. I've never seen him mix potions, remedies, or powders. He buys those from hedge witches and merchants and tests them on me." He grinned.

"He'll notice you're pinching that powder, one day."

"He won't." Elnathan tenderly pushed his fingers through her hair. "He's old as the mountains, in case you haven't noticed. He buys things, squirrels them away, and then forgets that he has them."

"You're disrespectful toward your elders, and you're a scoundrel," she said, giggling despite herself, and suddenly bone tired.

"Aye, Milady, I am," he said softly. "You're keeping company with riffraff."

Gently, he helped her to lie down. She felt him tuck a blanket around her before he settled in behind her, holding her, and she knew he would be watching over her as she slept.

TEN

The fire in the stove eventually died, and the room grew chilly. Elnathan woke with a start. He hadn't intended to go to sleep – he'd only wanted to doze for a short while, but through the cracks in the shutters, he saw that dawn was almost upon them now.

He opened one of the windows to check how much snow had fallen overnight. From what he could see, the forest was white, and an ankle-deep blanket covered the ground.

Artemis didn't react when he said her name, and he had to shake her lightly to wake her up. Then he scampered for his coat and boots, though he wouldn't be needing them for long. Taking Artemis to the lake on horseback was out of the question. They were running out of time fast.

He raced to the stable to check on the horse and fetch the powder they would need. When he returned, he found her still sitting on the carpet by the stove, hugging her knees and crying.

"Tell me how I can help you," he said, and sat down beside her for a moment.

She wiped her eyes and leaned against him, nestling into his arm. "You already are."

Life on Saint Jude's had to be a never-ending nightmare, but he didn't see how he could lift that burden from her shoulders right now. They didn't have a realistic alternative. At least not until he'd saved enough pennies and shillings from the fairs and the extra jobs he took on to get them *very* far away from this place – if she was willing to go.

He would marry her on the spot, but it was impossible. Who'd ever heard of a noblewoman marrying a woodcutter, and with a poor family repute to boot? Elnathan's grandfather had been banned from the carpenter's guild when he'd lost his seat in the king's council. Because of this, no one in Elnathan's family would be a member of any craftsman's guild ever again.

If he was honest, he hadn't planned beyond last night. Winter was only just beginning, and he had yet to figure out where they'd go next time he picked her up.

There would be a *next time* for as long as he had enough of the powder, but to make it last, he'd have to get as much of it to the island as he safely could whenever he went over to her. He'd take a double portion in each envelope he brought her from now on, and he'd give her another envelope to take back with her every time he sent her over on her own.

If she agreed to come to the mainland on her own once she was more confident with her new ability, he wouldn't have to waste a portion on himself whenever they met. This meant giving up his wings sooner than he'd expected, but he didn't care, as long as they were together – and it would afford him an extra few months to come up with a plan.

He couldn't ask Alphard for help. His uncle would kick him out on his ear if he knew what was going on. The old man might resent him until the end of days for breaking his word, even if Artemis would never tell his secret.

"We *really* have to go," he said, and helped her up.

"Can we come back, do you think?" she asked.

He nodded, though he wasn't sure.

Hurrying out into the corridor, she was right behind him as he fumbled with the keyring, but then she halted abruptly just inside the room instead of following him. They didn't have time for this, but he humored her anyway and doubled back to see what she was looking at.

Her gaze rested on the relief carving of an opulent blossom set in the center of the arch above the door. It had always reminded him of a primrose, though it was meant to be a much more precious, kingly flower.

"What's that?" she asked.

"You don't know anything, Milady, do you?" he said, giving her a conspirative look. "That's the Rose of Silence. It's there to remind visitors and residents alike that what is spoken or dealt with in this room will remain in this room, and that no hard feelings may leave it."

"Oh," she said simply.

He leaned in close to her. "No tattling on me to the king."

She gave him a playful shove. Laughing, he locked the door behind them, and they made a dash for the stable. He was afraid she wouldn't find her way back to the lake from here, so he measured out powder for them both, and they flew into a red dawn that lit the eastern sky on fire.

ELEVEN

Golden light flooded the cold tower room when Artemis crash landed on the plank floor. She grabbed the clothes she'd discarded the night before, pulled them on, and hurried to close the window against the icy breeze, but a draft banged it shut, rattling the frame, as the door behind her opened.

"Y – you're back," Chiron said. "W – where did you go with him last night?"

A combination of outrage and resentment darkened his face and severed the bond they'd shared up until then. He knew.

She wished she could have told him how happy Elnathan made her, but he wouldn't want to hear. He deserved happiness, too, but she doubted that he'd ever have a young woman waiting for him on the other shore. It was only human to want someone to love. *He* was only human, whatever else he became after the sun went down. Guilt colored her cheeks.

"Don't be angry at me," she said.

The indignation in his eyes stung as he stared at her and struggled with the words that wanted out but closed up his throat instead. If only he could yell at her, she'd gladly take the blows, but he just stood there, bitter and barely able to breathe. She went to him and reached for his hand. The gesture infuriated him, and he withdrew from her, shaking his head.

"Y – y – you don't know wh – what you're d – doing," he managed to say.

"Please don't tell anyone."

She was aware of how childish and irresponsible she must sound. She'd often said those words to him when she'd been disobedient toward her mother or the elder brothers. He never *had* betrayed her, but this was different, and they weren't children anymore.

He looked down at his feet, unable to meet her gaze. "It's n – n – not my place to."

"Don't judge me for something you don't understand."

Defiant tears leaked down her cheeks, and she knew this had come out all wrong. Her stutter wasn't physical. She made another attempt to touch his arm, but again, he recoiled.

"S – stop. And stop t – t – telling me what to think and what to d – do."

Defeated, she had to accept that he was in pain, and she could only make things worse every time she opened her mouth, so she fell silent, and watched him disappear the way he'd come.

She spent most of the day in her room, but when it was time to prepare their main meal of the day, she couldn't think of an excuse not to help Beatrice. She found her mother in the kitchen, cutting up onions for the soup, and quietly busied herself with a cabbage that looked like it had been stepped on, wondering how to begin the conversation they needed to have.

Telling her the whole truth was out of the question, but she had to let her know what was going on with Oak Castle. From what Elnathan had told her, decency didn't seem to be a thing with Uncle William, but Beatrice shouldn't have to find out after the fact.

"Alphard's nephew showed me around the castle when we were there," she said. "You know, before… before the trouble."

"Did he?" Beatrice peered at her through weary eyes, and then went back to her onions.

"He showed me Father's study, and the room with the big green stove and the Rose of Silence above the door."

The older woman hummed, and began dicing their last piece of salted ham to fry with the onions, but Artemis knew she was listening with more interest now.

"On our way back down, he mentioned William might be thinking of selling Oak Castle."

Beatrice stopped what she was doing in mid-movement – but only for a second.

"Can we prevent that?" Artemis asked, but then Aries and Auri walked in.

"Not a word to the boys," she hissed. "This is my problem, not yours."

Artemis was glad to be climbing the stairs of the tower an hour later. Auri, Aries, and Leo were still in the kitchen with Chiron, trying to persuade him to go to the boathouse with them at dusk. The rock pool had turned to a mass of snow sludge that would freeze solid during the night.

She stood at the top of the staircase and listened to the discussion turning into an argument, and the argument into a fight. Chiron's screams of frustration pierced her heart when they finally dragged him away against his will. She had to sit down on the stone tread for a moment, hands pressed to her face.

Eventually, she went back into her room and wrote her brother a letter to tell him goodbye. Elnathan would come for her soon, and she didn't think she wanted to return to the island after tonight. Selfish and childish as running away might be, she couldn't stomach this anymore. Not her mother's frigid disposition, not the older brothers' cool demeanor, and not the constant grinding of Chiron's death wish on her soul.

She folded and sealed the letter with some wax and a signet ring of their father's that they'd played with as children. Chiron shared a room with Leo, so she left her message under his pillow.

Back in her room, she sat in the armchair and waited, staring across at the little pier on the mainland. Someone had stacked a number of crates and kegs there, and covered them with a tarp while she'd been gone.

William's steward didn't always bother to come out to the lake and check if everything he commissioned was there, so the merchants he charged with the delivery often just left their wares a few yards back from the landing the day before Elnathan and his father came to load them onto the barge. Elnathan and Benedict were the only people who would do that job. No one else would even step out onto the wooden pier.

A consignment of wine had been stolen one night about twelve years ago, but the thieves had paid a high price. Apparently, a giant crayfish had tried to drag one of the men into the water, and another had lost a leg to one of the pikes trying to save his friend. No one had attempted to steal from them again after that, but no one had ever set foot near the shore of the lake again either, aside from the merchants who brought their goods during the day, armed to the teeth, and the woodcutters.

Elnathan and his father always came just after dawn on the day their supplies were due. They brought salted meat and other provisions that couldn't be left out in the cold overnight, and they would load everything onto the barge and push it out onto the lake as far as they dared. Then three of the boys would row across in their boat and tow the barge over to the island.

Since this would be the last delivery of the season, the boys wouldn't bring the barge back to the mainland but tug it into the boathouse for the winter. Normally, at least.

But tomorrow wouldn't be a normal day. Not for her, and maybe not for Elnathan, depending on what he would say or do when she told him she couldn't return to the island.

How he would react was anyone's guess, but she hoped his feelings for her went deep enough to justify the trust she placed in him. If things were ever going to change for her, then it was tonight – one way or the other, and with or without Elnathan, though she wanted to believe it would be *with* him.

Dusk slipped by, but the raven did not come. What was keeping him?

A clear sky left the earth defenseless to frost's icy breath as night descended and the comet returned, but its glow was dwarfed by the full moon that rose and reflected on the calm half-frozen surface of the lake. No ripples, no unrest, just eerie, old light. Her brothers would be in another deeper part of the lough.

She paced. Had he forgotten? What if he'd had an accident? Who'd know to look for him?

Her gaze fell on the cup with the broken handle on the table. She picked it up and swirled the rust-colored powder around in it.

Tempted to swallow her *rainy-day* ration, she opened the window. But where could she start searching for him? And how would she get back if she didn't find him?

Elnathan kept the powder at Oak Castle. She wouldn't make it much farther than the other shore on the amount in the cup, and the castle in the woods was much too far to walk. The castle on the hill above the village wasn't, but if she was to turn up there naked in the middle of the night, they'd think she was crazy and lock her up somewhere.

Irritated and annoyed with herself for her own cowardice, she rubbed a hand over her eyes. The longer she waited, the more she worried. Finally, she jammed a wedge in between the frame and the window so it wouldn't bang shut on her again, slipped out of her clothes, and swallowed the powder. The room around her went out of focus for an instant, and then she took flight.

Artemis stayed high above the water. She focused on the trees beyond the shore and concentrated on finding the spot where Elnathan had twice led her. She knew she shouldn't be doing this. It felt off, but there was no going back now.

From above, she could tell he wasn't in their usual place, but she hoped to find him somewhere nearby and circled higher to see if he was on the road beyond the path. Perhaps he just hadn't made it on time, but there was no sign of him, so she doubled back to the area around the shoreline, dipped down, and wove between the trees, scanning the snow for tracks, though she wasn't sure what she was looking for, or rather: *hoping* for.

Her heart sank when she felt the transformation coming on. She was almost right back where she'd started, and it was too late to land safely. Her wings failed as she took on her human shape once more, and she tumbled down through the bare branches of a willow from a height of six feet. Ribs aching, back scraped raw, and knees bleeding, she lay where she'd fallen for a moment.

She'd made a big mistake. Whatever had she been thinking?

The first thing she noticed when she finally caught her breath and sat up was the tracks all around her. They looked fresh. She hadn't seen them from above. Someone had definitely been here. It might have been the men who'd brought the provisions to the pier, but why would they take a detour through the trees instead of sticking to the path?

She crawled to the hollow tree stump. Shivering, she poked around inside the cavity for anything Elnathan might have forgotten there over the past few days. Nothing – not even a tinderbox.

An image of the tarp that protected the goods near the pier flashed across her mind, and she trotted to the shore. If only she could find something to cut the fabric with, she'd be at least somewhat warmer than she was now.

A clacking noise stopped her dead a few feet from the landing. Despite the freezing temperatures, a crayfish the size of a cow perched atop the tarp, and several more were leaving the water and stalking toward her. She yelped, pressing her hands to her mouth.

They never came out of the mud at this time of the year – how was this happening?

Then she saw the huge writhing bodies of a dozen eels slithering in diagonal movements across the icy lakeshore. Starlight reflected on their wet skins and in their black eyes. They were heading for the forest, maybe in search of the river, though Artemis couldn't even make a wild guess at what was driving them. They couldn't breathe air, could they?

She had to get to the village, or she wouldn't survive the night. Cautiously, she backed away in the general direction of the path, deciding she might as well head for the road. Who knew how many of the creatures were already crawling through the thicket, or what other nature of monsters she'd encounter in the woods? At least she could see where she was going if she stuck to the road.

Teeth chattering, hands and feet in flames, she hugged herself against the cold and ran, but no sooner had she found a steady pace than she saw the crimson stains off to the right of the path. They glinted in the moonlight like pools of rubies in the snow. Trickles and drips led from where she stood straight to the wagon trails near the shore. No doubt some poor creature – or human – had been badly injured and lost a lot of blood. Perhaps Elnathan? The thought sent her mind reeling.

There were also footmarks, and something had been dragged all the way here from the bushes farther back from the bank. She followed the trail until it ended behind a tangle of junipers. The mess in the undergrowth told of a desperate struggle.

On the edge of panic, she backtracked to the path, barely dodging one of the winding eels. The creature snapped blindly at her legs, and she sprinted for the road, unable to catch her breath. It was so cold, the ice-crusted snow cut like shards into the soles of her feet. Her toes caught on something, and she stumbled. Groaning, she fell to her knees.

At first, she thought she'd snagged a root, but then she discovered that she was sitting on a bundle of clothes. It was tied together in much the same way Elnathan rolled his shirt and pants into an overcoat to stow it away before he transformed. She buried her fingers and nose in the coarse fabric of the coat. She was sure it was his because it *smelled* of him.

Her stomach cramped. Clutching the bundle to her middle, she ducked down as far as she could, eyes wide as she searched the darkness.

Somewhere off to her right, snow crunched, and twigs broke.

"Best put those on, dear," a man's voice echoed through the trees. "You'll catch your death."

Artemis' heart leaped into her throat when she recognized the magician's voice. She made herself as small as she could. *Where was he?*

Her numb fingers couldn't work through the knot in the sleeves of the coat, and her face burned with shame as she struggled with it, while at the same time trying to pick out Abaddon's shape in the brush.

"Why are you here?" she shrieked, mercifully tugging a shirt free of the package.

"To save you," Abaddon said, as though this had to be clear to her.

Shaking almost convulsively, she yanked the shirt over her head, ripping it.

"Save me from your own doing? You've had your revenge! What *more* do you want?"

She had to keep him talking so she'd know he wasn't right behind her. A pair of man's pants came free of the bundle, and she pulled them on the wrong way around, trapping clumps of ice inside without realizing until it was too late.

"I never wanted revenge," the magician said. "I'm here because I made a promise to a little girl, and I don't break my promises."

He stepped out from behind a tree that seemed much too thin to hide him. For the first time in thirteen years, she saw the man who'd been sending her birthday greetings every year for almost as long as she could remember, as if to spite her family. He'd said he'd always be around, and here he certainly was. But didn't grief *ever* get old?

Artemis couldn't find a pair of shoes or boots, but the overcoat was a blessing after she'd finally untangled its sleeves.

"What have you done to Elnathan?" she asked, straightening, and trying desperately not to shake so hard.

"Why on *earth* would I do anything to harm that young man?"

Shadows distorted Abaddon's face as he slowly approached her, and she suddenly doubted her own perception. This wasn't the man she remembered – or was it? One moment, his nose and chin were sharp like a beak. The next, his features were those of a weary old codger whose back was bent and days were counted. Another second later, he was the magician again, the man who'd shown her silly tricks as a child, and who hadn't aged a day since then.

"You didn't think twice about harming my family either," she said, barely able to stand anymore.

He hummed. "I think it's time you learned the truth about that," he said, and tossed her a pair of soft leather boots that hadn't been there a minute ago. "Get those on and come with me."

"Why should I?" she said to his back, watching him walk off in the direction of the path.

He half-turned back to face her. "Because your lover will probably be dead in an hour if I don't get moving now, and he wouldn't forgive me if I left you behind in these woods tonight to deal with the wildlife on your own."

"That was his blood back there," she said, but she'd already known this.

"Indeed."

Impatiently, Abaddon motioned at the path with both hands, but her feet wouldn't obey her. What did Elnathan have to do with Abaddon?

"Suit yourself," he finally said, and continued on his way. "The sum of our choices put us in the places where we end up.".

TWELVE

"Don't be so late tonight," Benedict said. "Remember that we have to take these things to the lake first thing tomorrow before we start on the pines in the north sector beyond Coine Valley. It's a bit of a way there in this weather."

He pulled down hard on each of the straps that secured a load of supplies to their cart. They'd picked up the crates meant for Saint Jude's at the king's castle right after they'd completed their day's work so they would be at the pier just after dawn the next morning.

"Don't worry about me, Father," Elnathan said, doing the same on his side of the vehicle.

The path to the pier was in bad shape, and the snow and ice didn't make things better. Good thing the water wasn't frozen yet.

One of the wooden crates' lids cracked and dislodged. Elnathan undid the strap and pulled the box down from the cart, meaning to repair it, but it jammed.

"What's her name, by the way?" Benedict casually asked.

Elnathan's cheeks burned. "Can you hand me the crowbar?"

"Is she nice, at least?" Benedict said, handing him the tool. "Or are you going to bring home a two-headed dragon with someone else's brat in the oven after Christmas?"

"Didn't we agree that I'd get a few weeks to make up my mind whether she's a two-headed dragon or a banshee, before I waste *your* time on her as well as my own?"

Benedict laughed, and Elnathan yanked the lid free so he could reposition it. When he saw what was inside the crate, he hesitated.

"What's going on here?" he asked Benedict.

Bewildered, his father bent down to get a closer look. "What the hell...?"

Elnathan heaved another crate down from the cart and opened it, then a third, and a fourth. Smooth river stones bedded on straw – no salted ham, no cheese. None of the things they'd usually deliver to the pier for the islanders.

The two men exchanged glances. Elnathan didn't think Artemis' family could live on what they still had in their cellar for the next two or three months.

William's steward always had one of the merchants deliver lamp oil, ale, and miscellaneous other goods directly to the pier, but eight people wouldn't get through the winter on lamp oil and ale.

"I'll go to the steward in the morning," Elnathan said.

"You'll do no such thing." Benedict slapped the lid back on the first crate and nailed it shut. "They'll say you're lying and put you in the stocks."

"But–"

"No! Stay out of it. If they beat an old man, what do you think they'll do to you? And what do you believe your chances will be of marrying that girl of yours if we can't earn a living in this godforsaken place anymore at all? We can barely pay our way as it is."

William had finalized a deal with the warden under whose administration Coine Valley and the ancient forest had recently fallen to. He'd informed Alphard that his services would no longer be needed by telling him to gather his belongings and threatening the old man not to say a word about the trout in the moat.

Alphard had objected, and William had one of his guards punch him in the gut before hauling him out into the street. The priest's housekeeper had fetched Elnathan so he'd come and take Alphard home. In the afternoon, Elnathan and he had gone to Oak Castle to pick up his things – along with the magic powder Elnathan had hidden in the stable.

His uncle might not stick around after what had happened, but Elnathan did want to talk to him about the crates. Benedict wouldn't want to hear of it, but Alphard still knew some of the sitting council members, and he had many friends in the area and beyond who didn't like William any more than they did. Benedict had given up, but Alphard had nothing left to lose, and maybe he would think of something that could help them, or at least speak to someone who could talk sense into their king.

If this got around, surely even those in the council who supported William would have to speak out. Selling a disused, outdated castle that did nothing but cost money miles from the new trading road was one thing. Letting that family on Saint Jude's starve, cursed or not, was quite another. None of the councilmen were so young that they didn't all know Beatrice personally. Not many had spoken up for the fishers and crofters William had chased off the land and left to their fate, but this was different – Beatrice was the widow of a man they'd all have sworn fealty to.

Elnathan folded his arms across his chest, watching his father nail the crates shut again.

"There's got to be something we can do," he mumbled, trying for a reaction.

Benedict rose to his feet. "Use your brain. What do you think would happen even if, say, three hundred people in the village were to be outraged if you stood on the market square next Sunday before mass and told them what was happening? Would they storm the Hill Castle?"

The answer was no.

"Or would they all pitch in to feed those folks on their damned island when their king won't?"

The answer to that was also no. Most farmers and crofters in the area barely got by anymore. This place wasn't a vale of plenty, and they'd had two bad summers in a row.

That still didn't make it right, and he sure wasn't going to stand by and watch Artemis starve out there – or anyone else, for that matter.

He scoffed and left Benedict to deal with the remaining crates by himself.

At the cottage, Alphard sat by the fire, nursing a cup of watery ale as he stared into the flames. He didn't lift an eyebrow when Elnathan told him what they'd accidentally discovered.

"It had to happen sooner or later," the old man said softly, "but I'd hoped they'd have more time once they became visible again."

Elnathan pulled up a stool and seated himself opposite his uncle. "What are you talking about?"

Alphard emptied the cup he'd been holding on to and faced Elnathan. "Do me a favor," he said. "Would you please go to the pier and check what supplies have been left there?"

"They can't eat lamp oil."

"I still want to know if those crates are empty, too. If they aren't, then maybe our good steward was cheated. Everyone deserves the benefit of the doubt, my boy. You have to be very certain of the facts before you raise allegations like that against a king."

Elnathan nodded. "All right," he said, and cast a fleeting glance at Benedict, who'd just come through the door. "What if those crates really are empty, too?"

Alphard narrowed his eyes at him. "Then you come straight back and tell me. Do nothing on your own."

"You're going too far," Benedict said. "Leave my son out of this. We've lost enough to that family over the years."

Alphard stood up and studied Benedict. "You're right. We have. But do you think things will get better if we leave that woman and her children to their fate? Is it all right to just let it happen? I did that once before, and I'm not going there again."

Elnathan's gaze darted from Alphard to Benedict and back. "What is it you two are not telling me?"

"We all have our little secrets, don't we?" Alphard said with a sharp edge to his voice Elnathan hadn't thought him capable of.

The glint in his eyes made him wonder whether the old man knew about his relationship with Artemis, or if his words were aimed at Benedict.

Benedict huffed. "I think Uncle Alphard and I need to talk alone, son."

Elnathan hesitated for a moment, but when neither of the other men cared to elaborate, he took his coat and fetched his mare from the stable. He could make it to the pier and back with enough time to spare so he could still pick Artemis up and let her know what was going on.

One of the larger abandoned fisher huts in the woods near the northern shore of the lake still had a roof that was intact. Its windows were nailed shut, and the chimney had looked all right when he'd last been there. They could talk things through inside for a while, at least. He'd take along a hatchet and cut

some wood to keep them warm for a few hours, and they'd bring the horse in with them so it would be safe from the crayfish and the wolves.

With things as they were, he wasn't sure he wanted her to go back to the island in the morning. They had a lot to discuss.

New tracks in yesterday's snow snaked their way from the crossroads outside the village to the path that led to the lake. Only one set meant that the wagon hadn't returned yet, so Elnathan rode through the forest and tethered his horse in a thicket far enough from the pier not to be seen or heard.

Hidden by the unkempt undergrowth, he tried to get as close to the pier as he could, and spotted three men. He recognized one of them instantly.

Fur collar turned up against the cold, King William himself watched the other two unload several barrels and sacks, and a thick waxed tarp to cover them with. Since when did the king come to oversee any part of the supply delivery to the island himself?

Elnathan crept as close as he dared, hunkering down low behind an evergreen bush. The wagon driver and the peasant looked oddly familiar, too.

"Make sure that wine isn't stolen tonight," William said to the elder of the two men. "Stay awake."

"I'm not a fool."

"Yes, you are. You're a blundering idiot. We wouldn't be in this mess right now if you hadn't botched everything at Oak Castle."

Even from where he was, Elnathan saw the loathing on Jarlath's face.

"How were we supposed to guess Abaddon would show up? He hasn't been seen in thirteen years."

The king laughed. "If he hadn't put in an appearance, you would have found some other way of messing it up. It was a mistake to send *you* in the first place. I should have sent Brandon. You don't have the stomach for it."

"I would have gotten it done if it hadn't been for the magician."

"You never should have gone as far as the castle. I told you to do it in the woods. You had six strong, well-paid men at your command, and between the lot of you, you couldn't find a good time and place in that wretched forest to kill a woman, a girl, and a few unarmed, untrained boys who'd hardly ever sat on a horse before?"

"I'm telling you, we were being watched. We were never alone on that road."

"Well, you weren't alone at the castle either, apparently. I bet you pissed yourself and ran the moment you saw Abaddon."

"I didn't *see* him at all," Jarlath said in a small voice.

The king couldn't hide his disgust and slowly shook his head. "How the hell are you going to sit on my throne one day?"

"I *told* you, it was the ale the old man brought out. I didn't drink it, and I didn't turn into one of those…

those creatures. If I had, I'd be in that moat with them now, too."

"Alphard is a stupid old man. He's so loyal to your aunt, he'd kill himself before he'd aid Abaddon in any way. You were afraid, and you *ran*."

The younger of the princes had finished tying the tarp down over the goods they'd unloaded.

"Stay here *all night*, and stay awake," William told Jarlath again, tapping him on the chest. "And remember, not a drop from *any* of those wine kegs."

"Will it be a quick death, I wonder?" the younger of the princes said softly.

Without warning, William slapped him across the face. "I'm not a monster. But I'm not going to live with this anymore." He pointed at the island. "Those people over there are a danger to your rightful inheritance. They've been dead for *years*. They just don't know it. We're doing them a favor."

Elnathan couldn't believe what he was hearing.

"Oy, Brandon, we're done here!" Jarlath called into the forest then.

"Not quite," a voice said from behind Elnathan.

Elnathan turned, but all he saw before his world went dark was the blade flashing in the light of the late afternoon sun.

THIRTEEN

Artemis watched the magician go and stumbled forward, but she knew she didn't really have a choice. He was right. She couldn't stay here with the wildlife at large and without knowing if Elnathan was safe. What if he needed her? All that blood in the snow… She had *everything* to lose.

Her lungs were on fire. The snow in her pants turned to slush and spilled into her boots as she tried to run, but the magician moved ten paces away with every step she took until she screamed his name.

"Abaddon! Wait!"

For one instant, the world went out of focus. The sounds of the wind changed in her ears, whispering through her feathers, gathering under her wings. Soon, she was rocketing through the trees toward the star-sprinkled firmament, gaze fixed on the comet. The magician grinned up at her, and then changed shape to join her in the air.

I knew you had it in you, he said without speaking.

How is this possible?

How is it possible not *to fly once you've learned how? It's fear that keeps people in place, and it's hope and wonder that inspires them to change and to move.*

What are *you?* she replied, but he banked left, and all she could do was follow him.

The village came into view, and they were joined by other winged creatures who spoke to the magician in quiet tones, but all at the same time. Their voices layered one another, and she could only hear snippets of what was being said.

Did you convince her?

Is the boy alive?

Who is guarding the lake?

Several large barn owls, three long-necked night herons, and the biggest eagle owl she'd ever seen passed over the houses and the castle on the hill with them. The magician steered them toward a light in the sky above the beeches half a mile beyond the settlement, and Artemis smelled smoke.

The woodcutters' home was on fire. Jarlath stood forlorn in the yard. Deathly pale, he kept raking one hand through his hair as he watched the flames eating their way through the roof. A smoking torch lay at his feet. Two younger men were searching the barn and the immediate area around the house for something – or someone – but he looked unwilling to help them.

A wagon stood at a safe distance from the cottage. The burley driver had pulled his fur-lined coat tightly around his shoulders against the cold. Artemis didn't think she'd seen him before, but she knew who he was.

The others will be here soon, the magician told her. *I've called them all.*

Where is Elnathan? She prayed he wasn't still in the house.

Safe for the moment, but I have to go tend to him.

At that instant, a roar shattered the night. A bear came running out of the woods toward the wagon, followed by a pack of wolves. The driver saw them approaching and hollered at the horses, frantically flicking the reins to get them moving, but the animals smelled both the smoke and the predators. Panic-stricken, they veered off the path, crushing the wagon between two pines. The driver hurled himself off his seat just in time to avoid the collision and made a dash for the yard, closely followed by the bear and the wolves.

Strangely, none of the beasts really seemed to be in much of a hurry to catch up to him, or they would have done so long before he reached the young prince.

Jarlath pulled his sword and called to the other men. In a matter of seconds, the princes stood in the woodcutter's yard with their father much the same way as Artemis and her family had stood in the bailey at Oak Castle a few days earlier – shoulder to shoulder and back to back.

The bear and the wolves closed in on them, snarling as they circled them, while the birds flew low overhead, calling and screeching. William pressed his hands to his ears, but the cacophony only worsened when the giant crayfish arrived, clacking their claws. Artemis couldn't imagine how they'd gotten here, and how they could exist out in

the frost, but then she saw the eels, and she stopped trying to find an explanation.

Artemis had lost sight of the magician. A raven's eyes were all but useless by night, even with the moon and the comet illuminating the sky, and the fire below. She dipped down and searched the woods closer to the ground.

"Damn it, magician, come out and show yourself! I know you're here," William shouted. "Stop playing games with me!"

All at once, the animals in the yard began to change. Fur and claws turned to skin and arms, legs formed, and beaks remolded to human faces. Men and women rose and straightened their backs. Bundles of clothes appeared at their feet, and the shapeshifters tugged on shirts and caps and boots that defined them in their human standing.

One of the wolves was a fisher who'd often sold Beatrice a part of his catch when they'd first moved to Lough Locke. Most of the form changers present were fishermen and crofters, but there were also journeymen among them, farmers and soldiers, and the bear was a man Artemis recognized as their neighbor from the island next to Saint Jude's when she'd been a child.

"You're the one who's playing games," a young woman said. "You're burning down an honest man's house."

The king's jaw dropped.

Wagons and carts rumbled down the path that led to the house. People from the village had seen the flames and were arriving to help.

The bear-man stepped forward. "You had him killed, didn't you?"

"Who?" the king spluttered. "I had no one killed…"

Jarlath turned to him. "Father?"

"Your Highness!" one of the men from the newly arrived wagons called, beckoning him as he halted the vehicle at a distance to the yard and the blaze. "Come to safety!"

"Tell these good people about the day you murdered your own brother," the tall man whom Artemis recognized as the eagle owl form changer said.

"I did no such thing!" William yelled. "My brother fell off his own nag because he was a bad horseman!"

The princes exchanged glances, and the wagon driver went silent, uncertain what to do. Artemis stopped circling. She felt sick and perched on the roof of the stable.

"No – Prince Ambrose was an excellent rider. Tell everyone how you sabotaged the belt that held his saddle before you and he went hunting in the ancient forest," one of the wolf-soldiers said. "I was the guard you blackmailed to cover up the cut marks in the leather and destroy the evidence."

"Your Highness?" another wagon pulled in, and the king's steward stood up on his seat, trying to make sense of the situation.

"Magician!" William shouted again, breaking ranks with his sons. "Show your cowardly face, I know this – this *farce* is your doing!"

Abaddon stepped out from behind the stable. A raven sat on his shoulder. Artemis wasn't quite sure, but she believed it might be Elnathan. He was all right!

"William," the magician said, motioning at the new arrivals, "tell these people why you and your boys are burning down your former councilman's house."

"Seize him!" William shouted at his sons, but they seemed frozen in terror.

"Tell them how Benedict's son discovered that the wine you were going to send to your brother's widow was poisoned," the magician went on firmly.

"That's a lie!"

At that moment, Benedict carried one of the crates from the cart out of the barn and tossed it onto the ground at William's feet so that it burst open. Straw and stones spilled out over the ground.

"It's true!" Benedict said. "Our king wasn't even going to bother sending another sack of flour or bag of oats over there because he thought his nephews and niece would be dead in another week."

"All lies, you ungrateful bastard! You can't prove anything!"

William was about to hurl himself at Benedict, but Jarlath held him back, mindful of the crowbar in Benedict's hand. "Father, no!"

The crayfish-people were passing a keg through to the little group in the middle of the yard. It looked like the ones on the lakeshore under the tarp.

"We would never doubt your integrity, Highness!" the eagle owl man shouted, rolling the small barrel toward the king so that it came to a halt by William's feet. "Especially not in such substantial matters. No one here would take the word of a former councilman above your own. Please accept our heartfelt apologies. We've brought you a lovely keg of that excellent wine you yourself delivered to the pier of Lough Locke this evening to still your thirst and soothe your nerves, Sire."

Laughter erupted, and the eagle owl shifter mocked a bow to the king.

"Go on, Sire, you and your sons! To honor and truth!"

"And to Princess Beatrice's health," Abaddon said, turning to greet a hooded woman in a dark cloak who'd just arrived in a cart steered by Cas and Poll. The crowd parted for her.

"Yes, William," Beatrice said, "won't you drink to my health, and that of my children?"

"What's going on here?" the steward yelled again, wide eyed and shaking.

"The king wants to drink to Princess Beatrice's health," Benedict informed him again, as if he was speaking to an imbecile, and the form changers in the yard jeered.

"Drink! Drink! Drink!" the crayfish- and heron-people chanted, and some of the villagers joined in.

"Drink! Drink! Drink!"

Artemis could hardly believe what she was seeing. Without thinking, she hopped off the roof, and assumed human form half a second before she touched down lightly on her feet beside the stable. Another bundle of clothes lay in the snow there, as though the magician had known she would land in that exact spot.

This time, a dress had been folded into a warm cloak. Embroidered with threads of gold and silver, it resembled the one she would have worn to her mother's wedding as a child before everything had gone to pieces. It fit perfectly, but she knew it no longer suited her.

"Drink! Drink! Drink!" the crowd continued to chant.

"I shall do no such thing!" William shouted, and pushed the keg away with his foot. "There will be consequences to this! There's a price on that man's head." He pointed at Abaddon. "You're all aiding and abetting the evil sorcerer who's responsible for the misfortune of my poor dead brother's family!"

"If that wine isn't poisoned, why won't you drink it?" Beatrice asked, but William just stared at her, clenching and unclenching his fists. Sweat beaded on his brow.

More and more people arrived from the village, including the priest, who crossed himself when he spied Abaddon, but no one dared intervene. Some were shocked at the scene that was unfolding, while others didn't seem in the least bit surprised.

"This man murdered your rightful king," Beatrice told the onlookers in a clear voice, pointing at William. "He was going to have my sons murdered because he wanted the throne for himself."

She half-turned to the magician. "Abaddon saved my children by casting a spell to keep them safe on the island, despite all the things I said and did to him because I believed the lies my dead husband's brother told me about him. I know now the true extent of Abaddon's loyalty, and William's treason toward my husband!"

A murmur went through the crowd.

"William tried to have my sons killed at Oak Castle a few days ago, but Abaddon prevented it. The curse has been lifted tonight, because now you councilmen have proof, and you can see for yourselves what kind of monster William really is."

"Don't believe a word of it! She's gone mad after all these years on that island!" William said.

Artemis stood next to Beatrice, observing the tremor in Jarlath's sword hand. There was practically nothing left of the self-assured young knight who'd guided them through the ancient forest. His guilt was smothering him.

"Jarlath," Artemis called out. "You were there – what happened at Oak Castle?"

He hesitated, and she watched his stare wander from his father to his brothers. She sensed his fear of them, and for a second, the panic in his eyes reminded her of Chiron. She had to force the image from her thoughts. This was a man who'd have watched them all perish at the hands of his father's soldiers.

The priest's housekeeper plowed her way into the yard. Tears spilled over her face.

"Speak up!" she yelled at the prince. "My son was there, too! We were told he died defending you against Abaddon!"

"Oh, but he did!" William said, and gestured at Abaddon. "This magician is an evil man who turned your son and five other good men into trout, and they were left in the moat to die!"

At this, Jarlath shook his head. His sword slipped from his hand, and he let it fall to the ground.

"That's not how it was, Father. It's over. You can't win this."

"Shut up, you fool!" William hissed, but Jarlath stepped away from him and his brothers.

"My father sent me to Oak Castle with my aunt and cousins. The soldiers were told that my aunt's family still suffered from their affliction. They were to be killed out of mercy so their souls would finally be free and they couldn't infect others. I was supposed to give the order. The magician stopped me. I don't know how he did it, but the men turned into trout, and I fled. My aunt is telling the truth."

Several of the councilmen who had arrived on the first wagons talked among themselves in hushed voices, and the two younger princes threw down their swords. William glared at them. Then he picked up the keg and uncorked the valve. Wine spilled out and colored the snow red at his feet. Before anyone could stop him, he lifted the keg to his face and drank from the spurting spout. Then his gaze moved upward, and he waited for the poison to take effect.

Artemis followed his stare and watched it catch on a bat that was crossing the space between the roofed shelter and the stable. He observed the creature for a moment, and then dropped the keg. His coat fell in on itself as his body shrank, and a small black creature emerged from its neck, rose into the air, and flew away before anyone could get ahold of it.

"It's sparked by the first living thing you see or think of, isn't it...?" Artemis mumbled, realizing that the magician and the crayfish-people had been bluffing. The poisoned wine was still at the landing. Abaddon had merely procured a keg that resembled the ones on the pier and spiked it with the same powder she and Elnathan had taken.

An image of her brothers flashed in her mind. She saw them fishing for pikes on the lake around the time Abaddon cast his spell, three in the boat and four on the barge, drinking apple juice – from Abaddon's stock. Another memory showed her William's soldiers standing out in the bailey at Oak Castle by the sculpted well with the trout, and the earthenware mugs and pitchers of ale that had been scattered on the flagstones.

How long had Abaddon been stealing Uncle Alphard's face? By the expression on Benedict's, she suspected perhaps for the past thirteen years.

I'll always be around, he'd promised, and he had been.

"Can William transform and come back?" she asked him, motioning to the trees where the bat had vanished into the darkness.

The magician shook his head and winked at her. "I put plenty of the powder in that wine. He won't remember how by morning, and he has neither hope nor wonder."

"What about Elnathan?" she said. The raven had not moved from his shoulder since the magician had stepped out into the yard.

Abaddon gently stroked the black bird's neck, and he looked first at Benedict and then at Artemis.

"I'm afraid his human body was very badly hurt. He barely made it home and wouldn't survive changing back."

Benedict seemed to wilt, and Artemis' chest throbbed. She had trouble gathering her thoughts with all the people who were talking and shouting at the same time around them, and the house that was still burning close by.

A few of the fishers were making a futile attempt at saving the building. The bear-man and several of the councilmen had backed the princes against the wall of the stable and were questioning them.

Everything was in motion, but her world had stopped turning.

She recalled sitting in her tower room only a few weeks ago, wishing on the countless stars for things to change. Now they had, but not the way she'd wanted them to. The boys were human again. Cas might be king. Her mother was free to live her life, and so was she – but she didn't want that freedom without Elnathan. She didn't want to move through space unless it was with him.

"I read up on ravens, you know," she said to the magician after a moment, and tried to smile.

The magician gave her his undivided attention, and all the noise around them faded away.

"I thought you might," he said softly. "And what did you learn?"

She exchanged a glance with the raven. She could tell he'd been listening by the way he tilted his head.

Once they find their mates, they stay together for the rest of their lives, she told the magician and the raven without speaking.

Are you sure? Abaddon replied. *A human life is so much longer and more valuable than that of a bird.*

Nothing is valuable if you're alone and without hope and wonder.

Not even the stars? the magician wanted to know.

What good are the stars if you're not free to fly to them?

Abaddon took her in his arms. "I'll always be around," he said.

She nodded and smiled at Beatrice before she let the raven hop on her shoulder and walked away from them. Behind the barn, she squeezed her eyes shut. The fine cloak and the beautiful dress fell off her body, and together, she and Elnathan took flight by the light of the moon, and the vanishing comet. This time, she led the way, and Elnathan followed.

ANGUISH

Mary broke into a run. The fog had consumed the woods that lay between the manor and the river where she'd played. It poured over the rockery at the far end of the garden in thick wads and flooded the lawn as the little girl passed the flower beds that lined the white-pebbled circular driveway in front of the house.

A foul smell with an undertone of something she just couldn't identify bit the inside of her nose and throat. She frantically gasped for air, stifling a scream as a spray of gravel exploded in her wake, raining down left and right. Then the forecourt and the tiered fountain vanished in the mist.

The front door would be locked. It always was – day and night – for some reason. There would be no time to knock and wait for one of the servants to come and open it.

She skittered around the building between the herb garden and the patio, and almost fell down the stone steps that led to one of the tradesman's entrances. An angry howl rang out behind her as she burst into the kitchen and slammed the door, bolting it from the inside.

The milky glass panes trembled slightly in their frames as the cold mist touched the arching segments that formed a rising sun in the top half of the panel. Icy fingertips reached just far enough inside to send a shiver down Mary's spine. Her breath came in gulps

as she sank down into a sitting position with her back against the solid wood that closed snugly at the bottom with a heavy draft stopper.

"What on earth has gotten into you, child?" Mrs. Lewis demanded, oblivious to the creature outside as all the adults in the house seemed to be.

"Just look at you! You're a disgrace." The elderly cook wiped her fingers on her apron and leaned over the girl, bewildered. "What ever will your mother say?"

Mrs. Lewis inspected Mary's face and rubbed at the filthy smudges on her cheeks with a corner of a rag, but Mary knew what she really needed was a good wash. She'd be safe now. The creature couldn't come into the house, even if there was a window open, but she hadn't found out yet why. Perhaps the being was afraid of the grown-ups, or maybe the building as such was simply off-limits to monsters.

Sweat beaded on her brow. The stove was on full blast, and the air in the kitchen was sweltering.

"Speak up, girl, and stop making a nuisance of yourself!"

The old cook's voice coasted a whole pitch above normal. Mary knew she was keeping her from her work. The two scullery maids who were helping her were already whispering, but neither of them seemed inclined to get back to it without Mrs. Lewis to drive them on. Mary had heard them calling her a dragon behind her back more than once.

The three women were in the middle of preparing cakes and desserts for the wedding that would take place at the weekend. Some kind of fruity goodness with raisins and rum was baking in the huge oven. Pots with berries and cream simmered on the stove. Rectangular tins sat in neat rows on the table, ready to receive their layers of strawberry, vanilla, and pistachio cream for Mrs. Lewis' famous Neapolitan ice blocks. The distinct scent of chocolate hung in the air, and the icehouse would be full of wonderful things tomorrow. The prospect of all these treats should have excited Mary, but tonight, the heavy sweet smell made her feel ill.

"Why does His Lordship always insist on letting them bring their children?" one of the scullery maids said, shaking her head.

Mrs. Lewis spun around and cast her a frosty glare that was still there when she turned back to Mary.

Mary had no idea what the maid meant by them bringing their children. Not counting the young stableboys, she hadn't seen any other children besides Amanda since she got here. All she wanted right now was to get out of the stifling heat.

Mumbling apologies, she wound out of the stout woman's grasp and scampered off into the hall and up the servants' staircase. There was nothing she could say to Mrs. Lewis that the old woman would believe, and the servants would only think she was trying to get attention. They'd gossip. It might get back to her mother and make her sad. Mother had spent too much time being sad already.

Mary's bedroom lay on the second floor, and she hoped to avoid running into any of the guests who had already arrived for the big day. They were roaming the entire house, populating every free space except their own rooms, where they should have been.

Stepping out into the wide hallway, she only glanced in one direction and bumped hard into a man coming from the other. She winced at the scowl on his angular face, or what of it was visible above his elaborate beard, as he held her at arms' length.

"Do be more careful, young lady," he gruffly told her, while his wife stared her up and down from disdainful winter-blue eyes.

Again, she found herself muttering apologies and wiggling out of an adult's grasp.

"What a plain little thing she is," Mary heard the woman saying in a voice much too loud to just be meant for her husband's ears.

"Probably one of the domestics' brats," the man replied. "Bartholomew hasn't got them under control."

"He's getting soft in his old age," the woman said. "Maybe it's time someone with more mettle took that in hand, since the community is growing. It's getting beyond him, and he lets this house go to rack and ruin every time he comes back with a new toy."

They both laughed. It was a mean kind of cackle.

A tear leaked from Mary's eye as she ran the rest of the way to her room. Mrs. Lewis was right: all she seemed to be doing at the moment was getting herself in trouble.

Her first instinct was to hide in the huge closet that connected her room with Amanda's, but then she thought better of it. Her new stepsister would hear her coming in – if she hadn't already been aware of the commotion in the hall – so she just sat between the bed and the window wall, out of sight.

It wouldn't do to let anyone else see how out of sorts she was, especially not the little pest. Mary didn't believe Amanda left her room very often except to come into hers and annoy her, so she never got herself into difficulties.

The little goody two shoes probably thought she was very smart. The affected way she spoke irritated Mary to no end, but Amanda didn't know everything. She likely didn't know about the creature in the gardens. If she did, she'd have told her days ago, because Amanda couldn't keep a secret.

The girl talked non-stop about all kinds of other things. She garbled on and on about her dolls, the flower drawings she spent hours doing, the wedding, the shoes she would wear, and the way she'd have her hair done up in curls.

Most nights, she'd even come to Mary's room long after Mother had said goodnight and turned their lights off. They were strictly forbidden to leave their rooms after they'd had their dinner, but that didn't bother Amanda. She just continued prattling where she'd left off earlier.

Lord Bartholomew probably didn't like children very much, and it seemed like it had been a long time since the little girl had another child to talk to. She couldn't go to sleep unless she'd told Mary all her news of the day and every bit of chitchat she'd snatched up from the servants. It was all Mary could do to get her back to her own bed again before she drifted off. Unlike Amanda, Mary was exhausted in the evenings.

Now that she thought about it, there was something strange about Amanda that went beyond just annoying: in the two weeks since Mary and her mother had arrived at Asterbury Hall, she hadn't even once gone outside to play with her. She would look out the window, and remark on how it was too wet, too sunny, or too windy, and that she didn't like the weather ruining her pretty clothes.

She'd even insist she wasn't fond of ponies whenever Mary suggested coming out to the stables with her, despite her large collection of carved wooden horses with real hair manes. She pretended to be appalled at the very thought of riding one of the animals. What if she got her shoes dirty?

Not that Mary missed Amanda's company outdoors. She'd made up her mind that her new little sister was bothersome in so many ways, she had to be grateful for every escape she could manage. Besides, she had to mind herself, and she could hardly watch out for the two of them with Amanda's constant jabber in her ear. Even on her own without anyone to distract her, she'd ventured too far this afternoon.

Oh, but the riverside had been so tempting. How she loved to skip stones in the shallow water and make mud pies on the pebble shore, even though she was too old for that kind of thing at eleven. Little fish scuttled through the deeper end of the brook, tiny silver shadows in the glistening water, and she could spend hours watching them. She'd never been in a more magical place, and this made up for a lot of things.

The being wasn't always around. Generally, Mary knew in plenty of time if it was nearby because it only came when the sun was hidden away behind the clouds, close to dusk, and only if it had been raining that day. Mary had the notion that it needed moisture to manifest and move around, but sometimes she just wanted to tell herself to stop imagining things, and sometimes she'd just forget. Twice now it had gotten too close for comfort while she was playing.

It seemed to reside beyond the rhododendron hedges and walls that marked the perimeter of the cultivated garden surrounding the manor, perhaps in the moors, perhaps in the mountains – there was no way of telling. It would just appear out of nowhere. The only direction it never came from was the house.

There wasn't a doubt in Mary's mind that it was dangerous. She'd known from the first time she'd sensed its presence in the woods near the pasture where Lord Bartholomew's Thoroughbreds got their exercise.

She'd been collecting pinecones there a week ago, when she'd suddenly felt cold and looked around to find that a few of the domestic geese had strayed into the little coppice. Flustered, they'd honked and hissed at the quickly gathering fog closing in on them, whiter and thicker by the second.

Mary had hidden behind an oak with a trunk so thick, it could have concealed Mrs. Lewis' pudgy form. From there, she'd watched the strange mist completely swallow up the poor birds. With their wings clipped, they couldn't fly away, so they hadn't stood the least chance of escape.

Then the screaming began, and Mary had dropped all her pinecones and run for the house.

The next day, she'd gone back into the woods, hoping she'd merely had a bad dream – but not far from where she'd left her pinecones behind, she'd found the geese's carcasses. The flesh had been stripped clean off the bones, and puddles of feathers lay all around.

She'd raced off to tell the stablemaster, Mr. Merriman. Of all the servants at Asterbury Hall, she knew him best and she trusted him. He was kind, always had time for her, and he told funny jokes.

He'd listened closely, abandoned his chores, and come with her straight away, but he'd taken one look at the carnage and grinned at her.

"These here ladies were tricked by old Reynard, Little Miss," he'd told her in his thick Yorkshire accent. Then he'd bent to pick up a particularly beautiful white quill.

"We have fox lairs nearby, and it was a good season for this year's young. The lad in charge of the fences mustn't have been doing his rounds properly, and the dogs are getting old and lazy. I'll need to have a chat with me boys and see if we can't remedy this neglect."

When Mary still didn't understand, he offered the feather to her and explained, "Foxes are crafty. When they're hungry, they will bite their way through a wire mesh in one night, or dig holes underneath, and our ladies here aren't too bright, I'm afraid."

"I always thought geese were really clever birds," Mary mumbled.

Merriman stooped down to her so they were seeing eye-to-eye.

"Oh, but they are clever – for birds. No doubt about that. But they're also used to being safe and having their food provided for them, while foxes have to go out and hunt for theirs. That's why they have teeth and claws, and they have to be a little bit smarter than the animals they hunt so they don't starve. They're predators."

That word was new to Mary, and she repeated it softly to herself. He tapped his right temple and winked at her.

"These three darlings must have mistaken a weakness in the fence for an invitation to morning tea, and Reynard was right there waiting for them.

He's probably been waiting for his chance for a while. About time Lord Bartholomew called in another hunt so he won't steal your Christmas dinner as well."

Mary knew what she'd seen the previous evening simply couldn't have been a fox. One fox couldn't kill three grown geese so quickly, and although she knew little about foxes, she didn't believe an animal that size would strip all those bones clean in one night. Wouldn't it rather carry at least some of its quarry off? But she didn't argue. Adults were convinced they were always right. There was no point. Merriman was just like the others.

Mary hung her head in defeat and felt the weight of the feather in her hand. After a moment, Merriman hummed and rooted around in the huge pockets of his coat.

"Tell you what, Little Miss," he said. "I've got something that might help you. I took it off one of the stableboys earlier today…"

He couldn't seem to find what he was looking for right away, and patted every pocket he had on him from the outside with the flat of his palms. Eventually, he produced a slingshot.

"The lad was doing no good with it around the fowl, but I know you're a proper young lady who'll appreciate how to apply it appropriately in times of danger – like when you come across another one of them foxes in the woods."

He held the catapult out to her. Mary had never owned such an item, but she knew what it was and how it worked. It was rather small, but the wooden Y-shaped frame was solid, and the rubber band thick and flawless. She didn't take it right away. Elizabeth would never approve.

"You don't have to hit him to frighten him off," Merriman said, renewing his offer by poking the air right under her nose with the grip. "You'd never kill him unless he was already skinned. And your mother doesn't have to know. It's a secret between the two of us, and strictly meant to further the safety of our feathered friends."

She raised her gaze to his and found him grinning again, eyebrows arched in a way that told her it was all right. He was shouldering the responsibility for this.

She smiled back at him, accepted the slingshot, and tucked it into the wide front pocket of her dress along with the quill.

Over the following days, she learned that any animal or bird with a decent sense of self-preservation fled from the fog-being as soon as they became aware of its presence. Even the peacocks never strayed far from the manor. They headed for their Persian-style miniature house near the chicken coop well before dusk without having to be shepherded inside, and the cats that hunted mice in the stables never left the back yard at all.

Mary found more bones in odd places – though nothing quite as spectacular as in the woods. A crow's skull had lain half-crushed in the middle of the paddock one morning, part of a rat's or a squirrel's skeleton had turned up near the hen house, and a small, fractured shoulder blade had protruded from the earth in the herb garden between the chives and the parsley.

Merriman must have forgotten to speak to Lord Bartholomew about calling in a hunt because it didn't happen. Maybe Bartholomew was too busy planning the wedding. Mary was glad.

She'd never witnessed a foxhunt before, but whatever else was going on here, she was convinced the foxes of the area were innocent of killing those geese, and it wasn't fair to hunt innocents.

She knew this from the manhunts that were all over the newspapers in London. Her father had been the victim of such a hunt, and he had most certainly been innocent of whatever they'd accused him of before they'd dragged him out of the house and shot him in a nearby alleyway with half the police constabulary looking on.

But Amanda wouldn't know of these things. Mary had never seen hide nor hair of a newspaper at Asterbury Hall, and the girl didn't leave the house for fear of muddying her shoes. Or was all this playacting, in the end? Maybe Amanda knew full well what was going on here, but didn't want to admit it.

Mary was afraid too – but that didn't stop her from going wherever she pleased. She had her slingshot, and she practiced with it every day, well out of sight of the house in case Mother saw, or someone else did and tattled.

She didn't know if slingshots were any good against creatures that could turn themselves into fog, but she wasn't about to let herself be cooped up. Not unless it was stormy enough outside to sweep her down a rabbit hole to Wonderland.

Their garden in London had been the size of a postage stamp, surrounded by a three-foot wall with a mile-high wrought iron fence perched on top of it. She hadn't been allowed off the town house property on her own ever, and the rockeries, rose beds, and tended lawns of her new stepfather's manor by themselves seemed bigger than all of Hyde Park – never mind the rest of the grounds.

Mother had said they'd be safe in Yorkshire, and free. If she let this being, whatever it was, shut her inside the manor, she'd be no better off than at home.

"Are you here?" a small voice asked into the silence.

Mary groaned inwardly and stayed still, squeezing her eyes shut as though that might make Amanda go away. With the adrenaline drained from her body, she was spent.

"Mary?" The voice came nearer.

"Why are you hiding behind your bed?" Amanda looked down at Mary. "And why are you so dirty?"

Mary forced a smile. "I was playing down by the river and slipped."

"I thought you were going to the greenhouses in the walled garden today."

Amanda's mother had grown exotic plants and flowers in two large buildings made from metal and glass. A fancy heating system beneath the floors kept the greenery alive and blooming even in winter. The buildings nestled together in one corner of a beautiful walled garden near the boathouse, about a quarter of a mile from the manor.

An extra building behind the greenhouses held the furnace and boiler that provided the warm water for the heating system. The furnace tended to roar without warning, and the noises coming from the underground pipes made Mary uncomfortable whenever she was there on her own.

Once she'd discovered that neither of the two landscapers who were responsible for the walled garden was there today, she'd quickly turned back and headed for the river instead. The sandy bank where she liked to play was closer to the manor, and there were bound to be people about. Sometimes her courage didn't go quite as far as she would have liked it to, but she wasn't about to tell Amanda this.

"The gate was locked," she lied, thinking it probably should have been.

Amanda sat down beside her, making sure she wasn't creasing her dress.

"You could have asked Miss Polly to take you, you know," she said matter-of-factly, as though she did this all the time.

Mary half-shrugged, half-nodded. Miss Polly was one of the younger maids who aired and cleaned the bedrooms, as well as the carpets in the upstairs halls. She was usually finished with her chores after lunch and only started turning down the beds in the early evening, so she wasn't disinclined to distractions such as games and walks in the afternoons, but Mary didn't like the prissy young woman enough to make her a constant companion.

After a long silence, she came right out and asked, "Why are you afraid to go outside?"

Amanda's eyelashes fluttered. "Why should I be?"

Mary shrugged. "Well, are you?"

"It's nicer indoors than out at this time of the year." Amanda smoothed out her skirt like an old woman. "There's lots to do."

Mary huffed. She'd seen all of the house, and the most exciting thing inside was probably the music room. Unfortunately, she wasn't allowed to touch anything in there. Mother had promised her piano lessons once they'd settled in properly. The private teacher she was hiring would teach Mary all the lessons she'd had at the girls' school in London, and he'd also give her piano lessons, so she'd be allowed to practice on it then. But apart from that…?

"I think this old museum is terribly boring."

Of course, the garden was anything but boring when there wasn't an adult around, but there had to be a way of dealing with it other than hiding in the house all day. And Mother was content here, if not happy. Elizabeth hadn't smiled since Mary's father had died, but she seemed more at ease here than she had in London, and she wasn't worried about money anymore.

Amanda stomped her foot and rose. "I don't understand why everyone always says it's boring here!"

"I don't know who everyone else is," Mary replied, "but that's just what I think."

Pouting, Amanda considered for a moment, but then held her hand out to Mary. When Mary didn't take it right away, aware of how grubby she was, Amanda pulled back and settled for a verbal summons.

"Come on, I'll show you."

Mary got to her feet and left a grimy handprint on the pastel pink bedspread. The servants would take care of it tomorrow.

Instead of leading her out into the wide corridor, Amanda guided her back the way she had come, through their shared closet and into her own room.

There, Amanda leaned her slight weight against the corner of a heavy mahogany dresser at the far end. She managed to push it diagonally away from the wall, revealing a square white door, set about four feet up from the ground. The mirror fastened to the dresser's top had only just hidden it from sight.

At first, Mary thought she was looking at a dumbwaiter. She hadn't seen one anywhere else at Asterbury Hall, but she knew what they were for. A lot of big houses had them, but they were usually higher up in the wall, and built into shafts that originated somewhere near the kitchen or the laundry room. It occurred to Mary that Amanda's bedroom was the last one on the west wing corridor, while the kitchen was on the east side of the house.

Amanda turned the little golden key in the lock and opened the door. Behind it lay a cavernous hole. There had to be a passageway or even a whole room behind it, though Mary was sure there couldn't be.

"Where does this go?" she asked.

Amanda grinned mischievously. "Come and find out."

The little girl set an upholstered stool in front of the hole, climbed in, and balanced on something that stood on the other side of the wall – possibly another stool or chair. Then she turned and motioned to Mary.

"Come on!"

Mary didn't think this was a good idea, but curiosity got the better of her, and she followed Amanda.

The drop to the stool on the other side was deeper than Mary expected, and the hem of her skirt caught on a nail that protruded from the crudely plastered wall as she got down from it. Amanda giggled.

"That's not very nice," Mary grumbled, trying to assess the damage in the half-light.

Dirty was one thing, tattered quite another. This would definitely get back to Mother.

"Oh, don't get your knickers in a twist," Amanda said, striking a match. "The washing lady will fix it. Mrs. Stanford can fix anything, and if it can't be fixed, she'll sew you a new one."

Mary frowned. This was very unlike Amanda – was she trying to prove something to her now?

Amanda held the match to the bare wick of a strangely shaped oil lamp. It didn't have a chimney or a shade, and Mary thought it resembled the lamp Aladdin had rubbed to summon the genie. Her father had read the story to her one evening when she'd been around Amanda's age, and shown her the picture of the wonderous lamp in a book titled Thousand and One Nights.

"Come on," Amanda repeated, leading the way through the musty passageway to their left.

Shadows danced as the child bobbed away from her, and Mary had a hard time keeping up as she swiped at the cobwebs that caught in her hair and the threads of dust billowing up from the walls.

Her skin crawled at the thought of the spiders and insects she might step on or gather on her clothes. She wasn't afraid of them – she felt sorry for them. It was different indoors than out: those creepy crawlies were out of place indoors and couldn't get away, so they clung to you, hoping for a ride back out, mercy, or – at the very least – a meal.

It occurred to her that the being outside might be out of place, too. She hadn't done anything to anger it. At least not that she knew of, so maybe it was just like with the bugs and spiders. Perhaps the creature was somehow trapped on the grounds and hoping for mercy… or it was hoping for a meal.

"You're so slow," Amanda called to her from the top of a narrow staircase at the end of the passage.

Mary hurried up the steps and through a new corridor. It seemed to go on forever until it branched off to the right, where the final flight of creaking stairs took them up to the attic.

This was a part of the topmost floor Mary hadn't seen before, because it was neither accessible by way of the main staircase, nor one of the servants' staircases. Apparently, Amanda's secret passageway was the only way in.

The section of the attic she had seen so far was a fairly tidy space, mostly free from dust and dead moths. It was obviously being cleaned routinely, and strictly off-limits to her, of course, but she'd gone exploring there on her second day at Asterbury Hall anyway.

She recalled that its floor was laid out with threadbare oriental rugs too shabby for the family's rooms, but too good to be thrown out. Old scorch marks blackened the top of the wooden stanchions that hadn't been replaced after a bolt of lightning had set the roof on fire over a hundred years ago.

Mary remembered small windows set at regular intervals throughout the long sides of the roof. Sunbeams speared in through the thick glass panes in their zinc-stained metal frames. Fine particles of dust danced along the shafts of light, adding silvery motion to the patterns on the rugs.

She had peeked inside most of the age-darkened wardrobes with chipped corners and bits of ornamental carvings missing from their doors. All of them held clothes and other items no one seemed to pine for: fur coats, huge old-fashioned ball gowns, and satin vests grown dull and greasy with age, buttons dangling by a thread.

This side of the attic, however, was completely different. There were no carpets on the deck, and no scorch marks on the stanchions. A grainy layer of grime rested uneasily on worn floorboards that had once been painted a dark shade of red. Oddly, the scent of cinnamon and cloves lingered in the air, as though the Ghost of Christmas Past had been to visit.

Wooden post-and-beam structures partitioned off tiny garret rooms to the left and right of the narrow corridor. There were doorframes, but no doors, and Mary could see inside. Each of the rooms had at least one cot with a lumpy mattress on it, a trunk, and a nightstand with a lamp.

As in the other part of the attic, rectangular windows in the roof provided natural light, but it wasn't as bright here, on the whole. It was also colder. Perhaps the sun didn't shine down on this side of the house in autumn.

"Where are we?" she asked.

"Servants' quarters," Amanda said, as though this had to be obvious, and continued skipping along the aisle. "I come up here to play all the time."

Mary bit her lip. "But the servants' quarters are down in the cellar," she said.

Amanda looked back over her shoulder. "Some of them are. Not all."

Lord Bartholomew's butler and one of the other higher-ranking servants had rooms in the east wing on the third floor, but most of the staff slept in tiny low-ceilinged accommodations in the semi-basement, behind the laundry and linen rooms. Mary hadn't been aware of anyone up in the attic. Maybe she hadn't spent enough time exploring the house after all.

She followed Amanda to the open common room located at the end of the corridor. Almost like an ordinary salon, it was furnished with comfortable timeworn chairs and coffee tables. Sturdy cabinets with open shelves on top held chipped crockery, and a tiled stove in the corner next to the chimney shaft would have supplied warmth, had it been lit.

An ancient chaise lounge idled on one side of the bay. Even though the glass hadn't been cleaned in a while, the view from the window was spectacular. In better light, Mary thought she might be able to see right to the moors from here.

A single threadbare rug of indiscernible origin sprawled on the floor beneath the window. Most of its tassels were missing, and its pattern had long since faded, but it was strewn with parts of a miniature tea set and an assortment of carved animals, a tin carousel, and drawing utensils. Little dolls sat in an attentive line along the wall, each with a tiny cup from the tea set in front of it, and the little girl immediately got to work refilling each of them from the teapot.

"This is Miss Armstrong," Amanda explained earnestly. "Beside her is Miss Roberts. Miss Granger is the high-born Duchess of York over there in the blue dress."

Mary sat on the chaise lounge, testing the dodgy springs while her stepsister played, happily chattering away.

"Ah, so I did hear correctly," a male voice said from the entrance of the common room, startling Mary. "How nice to see you, Miss Amanda."

A butler Mary wasn't familiar with stood in the entrance of the common room, carrying a tray with porcelain dishes. Laugh lines creased the corners of his eyes, and his white hair gave him the appearance of an old man, but he didn't move like one.

"So happy to welcome you here, Miss Mary. May I bring milk and biscuits?"

Mary sat bolt upright. She hadn't heard footsteps, but she was sure she should have. She caught the aroma of the freshly baked treats, but her spine tingled, and she shivered.

"How do you do, Mr. Smith," Amanda said, beaming at him. "A little something to eat would be wonderful. Mary hasn't had her dinner yet – isn't that right, Mary?"

Mary stared at the butler, even though she knew it was impolite. A servant wasn't entitled to take offense, but her mother had taught her not to taunt the staff. Staring was certainly taunting.

A maid bustled in behind Smith. Mary had never seen the young woman before in her life, but Amanda obviously knew her. She carried a lacey tablecloth and elegantly smoothed it down over one of the coffee tables.

Smith placed a plate of assorted cakes and shortbread in the middle and turned it this way and that until he was satisfied. Then he set cups on either side of it and poured milk from a jug before he and the maid retreated from the table.

Mary just stared at the plate, but Amanda bounced up from where she'd been playing and grabbed an éclair.

"Are you not hungry?" she asked, peeling off the top of the treat to reveal oodles of fresh cream with twists of strawberry syrup. "Mrs. Thompkins makes excellent pastries."

Mary shook her head. "Who's Mrs. Thompkins?"

Amanda didn't answer right away. She returned the éclair to the plate, chose a bun, and admired the

sprinkles on its icing before she dug her fingers in and broke off a sizable chunk.

Under different circumstances, Mary might have questioned her stepsister's manners, but right now, she was more concerned with the new faces she was seeing and all the new names she was hearing.

"Mr. Smith, have you been at Asterbury Hall long?" she asked. Servants were obliged to answer questions.

Smith smiled warmly, and his back straightened. "I have indeed, young Miss. Many years now, I'm proud to say."

He spoke with the same Yorkshire accent Merriman did, and Mary wanted to like him, but something was definitely strange about him, and she wasn't sure he was supposed to be here at all.

"Who is Mrs. Thompkins?"

Smith tilted his head. A hint of amusement played around his eyes. "Why, she's the cook, Miss."

"But Mrs. Lewis is the cook," Mary said, trying to make sense of this.

Smith hummed indulgingly, as if he knew full well it was she who was mistaken, but he would have been out of place to say so.

"Of course, Miss."

Amanda sighed. She put the ruined bun on the tablecloth next to her cup, crossed the floor to Smith, and broke the uncomfortable silence.

"Please," she said, and when he hesitated, she implored him with her huge, doll-like eyes. "Please."

He looked down at her, obviously pained. "You'll be lonely again," he replied, and then cast Mary a worried glance.

Amanda held out her hand to him, like a daughter might to her father. "I'm used to it, and it's not fair. Not really."

Sadness pooled in Smith's eyes. Mary wondered what Amanda was asking him for, but the importance of the moment made her feel like an intruder. She'd never seen one of her cousins or other family members plead with a servant before. It didn't seem appropriate, but Amanda's relationship to Smith went deeper than it should have gone, like an underground river you couldn't see on the surface but felt when you stood still and listened closely.

He reached into the pocket of his vest and retrieved a small object.

"Best you explain to Miss Mary soon," he said to Amanda, pushing the object into her hand. Then he and the maid left.

When Amanda didn't immediately turn to face her, Mary stood beside her.

"Explain what? And what's that?"

She tried to get a glimpse at the object Mr. Smith had given her, but Amanda's fingers were closed firmly around it. Her expression told Mary she wasn't going to give up her secret just yet. Typical.

"I'm going back." Mary huffed. "This is stupid."

"We'd better get going anyway," the younger girl said, ignoring Mary's tone.

Glancing around, Mary realized it really was getting late. Shadows rose from every corner. Daylight was fading. The sun seemed to set much quicker here than it did at home, and dusk turned to pitch-black night in the wink of an eye.

London never grew entirely dark. Every evening, a lamplighter lit the elegant gas lamps on the street where she'd lived, and the soft golden glow had kept her room well illuminated all through the dark hours until dawn. She missed those gas lamps.

Again, Amanda led the way. To Mary's surprise, the garret rooms weren't empty now. They seemed to fill with voices and the busy bustle of life as the children passed them by. Coats and blankets hung in doorframes. Mary had to dodge under laundry that dried on lines crisscrossing the corridor. Freshly polished shoes stood in rows along the walls, and the scent of soap and beeswax mingled with the smell of tobacco and sweat.

A young lad who looked like a stableboy stepped out in front of them, almost bowling Mary over. Several marbles fell from his hands, and Amanda helped him pick them up.

"Very kind of you, Miss," he said, tugging at his cap.

He gave both girls a shy smile, playfully hinted a bow, and was on his way before a stocky woman who might have been his grandmother emerged from the room behind him.

"Remember to see to those fences, George," she called after him. "Stablemaster's still very unhappy with you!"

"Old Merriman's never happy with anyone!" the lad responded.

The woman looked ready to launch a terrible tirade at the boy, but then she noticed the girls. Her mouth clamped shut, and she blushed, lowering her head.

Amanda gestured to Mary, urging her to make haste without leaving her time for questions. Mary had a lot of questions, but they were all tumbling in her head.

Before she knew it, they were back in Amanda's room. Filthy – even more so than before – and overwhelmed, she sat on Amanda's bed.

The younger girl lit the lamp on the table by the window. "You should go back to your own room before your mother's cross with you again."

"What's going on here?" Mary asked outright, fixing her gaze to the other child's. "I know that the servants' quarters are downstairs in the cellar. I know Mrs. Lewis is our cook. And I also know things that weren't there before don't just appear out of thin air."

She let that stand for a moment, waiting for Amanda to object, but the younger girl didn't.

"Who are those people up in the attic?"

The door opened, and Mary spun around.

"Here you are," Elizabeth said, fumbling with one of her earrings.

She always wore the sparkly, dangly ones to dinner with the adults, all gold and diamonds. They went well with most of the sleek new evening gowns Bartholomew had bought for her in London, but Mary couldn't stand the perfume she'd dabbed on her wrists and neck tonight.

The heavy fragrance made her cough, as if something flaky had lodged in her throat. Elizabeth now owned at least half a dozen flagons of similarly unspeakable and probably very pricey scents, and Mary missed the lighter bouquets her mother had preferred before. She missed the scents her father had carefully giftwrapped for her on her birthday or anniversaries.

Many of the changes Bartholomew's presence in their lives had prompted were good, but Mary wished he wouldn't try to change everything about Elizabeth – about them. She wanted her family to have dinner together, like they'd used to, which was only a small wish that wasn't impossible to grant, surely.

Unrecoverable – and she knew this just as well – was the warm feeling she'd always gotten out of reading stories with her father in the evenings, whether they'd been about the brave young robber Aladdin, the castaway Robinson Crusoe, Frankenstein's Monster, or the spooky Vampyre. Elizabeth had scolded him for bringing home the latter volumes from the library, but Mary and he had relished every goosebump.

She couldn't see Bartholomew reading to or with her, or even Amanda. Not ever. Not that she wanted him to. He wasn't her father, and those were not his stories.

"I've been looking for you." Shuddering, Elizabeth rubbed her arms. "I want to wish you a good night.

Come into your own room, dear. It's so cold in here."

Mary hadn't noticed. She turned back to Amanda, but her stepsister was gone.

"I've been told you didn't come in to have your dinner," Elizabeth continued, oblivious to Mary's bewilderment.

Her voice balanced on the edge of irritation as her gaze roamed over Mary's ruined dress.

"I see Mrs. Lewis wasn't exaggerating when she told me that you'd made a proper mess of yourself."

Ignoring her, Mary hurried to the closet, opened it, and peered inside. Amanda wasn't there.

"Are you listening to me, Mary?"

Mary felt a cool hand on her shoulder. She turned to find Elizabeth now attentive and studying her as though she was searching for signs of a fever, but there was no fondness in the way she examined her. The concern in her eyes didn't reflect a mother's worry for a child so much as it betrayed her frustration at being held up here with her nuisance of a daughter. Her expression reminded Mary of the woman she'd run into earlier in the hall. But that couldn't be, could it? She was imagining things.

"Did you just see Amanda?" she asked after a moment.

Her mother's lips turned to thin lines, and her hand wandered down to grip Mary's, but not in an affectionate way. She squeezed it too hard and yanked it upward. Mary cried out, but Elizabeth ignored her. Every hour of her life was meticulously organized now, and anything that threatened to disturb her newly learned routines upset her.

"You have your own room," Elizabeth said. "You're not to play in here, do you understand?"

She pulled Mary out into the hallway and shut Amanda's door firmly behind them.

"I'll have one of the servants bring you something to eat, dear."

"I don't know if Amanda's eaten yet either," Mary said in a small voice.

Elizabeth halted in midstride, staring at her. She clamped her mouth shut for a moment, but finally said, "All right. I'll have them bring a plate for Amanda as well, then."

It was like she didn't want to, but she didn't want to argue either. Elizabeth didn't like Amanda and treated her as though she wasn't there. She didn't even like to talk about her, and Mary couldn't explain why.

Back in her own room, a maid – probably Polly – had filled her washbasin with warm water, put out a fresh bar of soap and a towel for her, and turned down the covers. A new silky nightgown lay on her pillow. She didn't like the feel of the fabric on her skin, but the old linen ones she'd brought from home had been thrown away.

She looked down at her feet, eyes brimming. The knot in her stomach just kept tightening.

"Listen, Mimi," Elizabeth said after a strange silence. "I'm doing this for you, too."

Mimi was the name Elizabeth reserved for bruised knees and bad dreams. It did nothing to bridge the void between them right now. Mary desperately wanted her mother to take her in her arms, but the bride-to-be had already put on makeup that mustn't smear. Downstairs, the musicians Bartholomew had hired for the wedding started playing, giving everyone a taste of their repertoire.

"Bartholomew is a very kind man," Elizabeth went on, now fidgeting with the clasp of her new bracelet. "He's a godsend to us both. He all but saved us, and we must be grateful. He'll be a considerate father to you. You'll want for nothing."

She seemed to wait for Mary to be a good girl and agree with everything she'd said, but Mary couldn't bring herself to do so. Another silence dragged on and on until Elizabeth, obviously torn, began to massage one of her temples, as had become a habit of hers.

"Do you know you're giving me a headache?"

Mary didn't have the strength of will to apologize and have it over with.

"I understand that you don't feel at home here yet, but you will. In time. We both will. Do try to adjust. It's not as if we had choices. Maybe you will later, but only because we're doing this now. Can you please promise me you'll put in an effort?"

Cheeks burning, Mary nodded without raising her head, and a few seconds later, she heard the door closing softly. Elizabeth was running late, and Bartholomew didn't have much patience with tardiness. A whiff of the awful perfume still lingered in the air, but it was better than if nothing of her mother had remained in this room at all.

She sniffed and wiped a tear from the side of her nose. In London, she and her parents would not only have had dinner together right about now – they would have played a board game together afterward, too. No dangly earrings, no evening gowns, just the three of them in ordinary, comfortable clothes, having an ordinary, comfortable evening.

Before Father had been bitten in the arm by a stray animal on his way home and gotten ill.

Before the men had come to take him away.

Before Bartholomew had come to rescue them and be their godsend.

Mary's fingers closed around the pearl-shaped silver pendant dangling from the delicate chain her father had given her the morning before everything had changed.

"For good luck, Mimi," he'd told her.

Then he'd given her a conspiratorial wink, lowered his voice, and added, "Pure silver will kill even the Vampyre Ruthven."

After his death, Elizabeth had been poorly. They hadn't left the house anymore at all, and she'd sent Aunt Merideth and Uncle Henry away every time they'd come to their door. But she hadn't sent Bartholomew's secretary away when he'd handed her His Lordship's calling card.

"Who's Mimi?" Amanda teased, peeping out of the closet.

"Never you mind," Mary replied with an unintended sharpness in her voice.

Amanda ignored it and sat on her bed. "Anyway," she continued, "best everyone's back where they belong before the adults get upset. They always find something to get upset about, don't they!"

"Well, you're not back where you belong." Mary glared at her, but her words seemed to have rolled right off the other girl. "My mother never used to be like that."

Again, tears stung in the corners of her eyes. She couldn't help herself.

Amanda bit her lip. "My mother didn't, either. Not before we came here."

Mary studied her. "What do you mean?"

Amanda shrugged, rolling her eyes. "You never listen, do you? I told you before. Lord Bartholomew isn't my real father."

Mary felt her jaw drop. "You did not tell me that!"

Or had she? Could this information actually have gotten lost in all the prattle Amanda had hurled at her over the past weeks?

A huge painting with an old-fashioned frame on the wall above the fireplace in the downstairs study depicted a perfect family of three: Amanda, perhaps eight or nine years old, sitting by her mother's feet in a pink and white summer dress, and Bartholomew standing up straight and handsome

beside the chair the young woman was sitting on, one hand on her shoulder.

"I still remember Liverpool," Amanda said. "I didn't like it there. It was loud, smelly, and there were always lights on everywhere."

Mary had never been to Liverpool, but she had read about the big harbor town in a book at school.

"Was it just you and your mother who came here?"

Amanda shook her head. "A few others, too."

"You mean your mother brought some of your servants along?"

Elizabeth had let their housekeeper and cook go after Mary's father had died. She'd only kept on the girl who came in to clean twice a week for a while, so when they'd left London, it had only been the two of them.

"No. Mother let them all go when we left our house after the men came for Father. They took him when he became ill, and he never came back. Mother said he died in hospital, but I'm not sure they took him there."

Mary's jaw felt soft and unhinged. Would it be impolite to ask Amanda to elaborate? Maybe they had something in common after all.

She cast her stepsister a questioning glance, but the girl's sad eyes stared into space, as though she was trying to remember something but couldn't reach far enough back into her mind.

"I didn't know most of the people who came along then, and I don't know who comes and goes here all the time now. The only people who are always here are the servants." She paused. "And Bartholomew, of course, when he isn't traveling. He's been all over the world."

Her expression derailed for an instant when she said his name, but then she went back to her normal cheery self.

"I'm so happy you're here now."

She smiled, and straightened her shoulders, grinning that mischievous grin of hers, and added, "One of the benefits of the fact that Lord Bartholomew likes to surround himself with an ever-changing circle of interesting people."

This sounded like a quote she'd snatched up from an adult. Ten-year-old girls didn't speak like that. But one thing was for sure: Bartholomew was not a lonely man, despite his cold demeanor, and the fact that Asterbury Hall was far away from any big town. Mary couldn't imagine what made him so popular, but he obviously was, or he wouldn't have so many friends and acquaintances who were all willing to make the trip at any given day of the week.

His guests usually arrived in the early evenings in time for the big dinners he gave most nights, but quite a few came later, which couldn't be easy on the muddy roads in the darkness of the moors and the rocky mountainscapes that surrounded this place.

Mary heard the carriages at all hours. Talk and laughter permeated the floors and walls of the old manor until well after midnight. The guest rooms were always occupied, but unlike in London – when her father was still alive – she wasn't expected to meet any of the family's visitors, smiles and curtseys, a peck on the cheek for the aunts and uncles. Neither was Amanda. In truth, they were both required to stay out of sight.

"Is that why there are so many servants in this house?"

Amanda shrugged. "There are the day people, and there are the night people." She made it sound so logical, but Mary had never heard of such a thing. It seemed very extravagant, even to her.

A knock at the door interrupted the conversation, and one of the scullery maids bustled in, somewhat out of sorts as she carried a tray with two bowls of steaming stew, white bread, and fruit. She set it down on the table by the window and scanned the room nervously, pushing an unruly strand of hair from her face.

"I'll be in to collect the dishes later, Miss," she said and left, probably in a hurry to get back to the desserts they would be serving tonight, and the sweets they were likely still preparing in the kitchen.

Mary wasn't really hungry, but she spooned some of the stew anyway just for the warmth of it, while Amanda busied herself with an apple slice, peeling off the skin with the nail of her thumb.

"What's that thing out in the garden?" Mary asked when she was finished, trying to sound casual.

The meal had eased some of her tension away.

After their little excursion to the attic, she had a feeling Amanda knew more than she was letting on. Obviously, she was dealing with it and not quite as easy to frighten as Mary had assumed.

The other child smiled. "Oh, you mean our angel. She's the guardian who watches that you don't wander off too far."

The image of the monster that was killing geese and other animals and birds in the garden wouldn't match up with the word angel or guardian in Mary's mind.

"Angel? It's a monster."

"She's not a monster, or she would have eaten you by now, wouldn't she," Amanda said, sounding almost offended.

"She?" The lump in Mary's throat returned.

She'd never considered monsters in terms of gender before, and it made her skin crawl to think that Amanda knew the creature well enough to be sure it was a she. Amanda just blinked at her, and Mary wanted to shake her.

She leaned forward. "It chases me!"

"Well, of course she would." Amanda folded her arms in front of her chest. "She can't talk to you during the day, and she has to do something to make you come back inside before dark. It's not safe out there, you know. Especially on a full moon night. Not with all those…" She struggled to find the right word, but finally came up with an unsettling one

Mary didn't like at all. "Not with all those strangers out there."

This couldn't be right. Some of Bartholomew's guests were downright sinister – she was thinking of the couple she'd nearly bowled over in the hallway earlier – but that didn't make them dangerous, did it? Her stepfather wouldn't allow dangerous people in the house, would he?

In London, Mother had always been afraid of strangers – of bad people. The terms strangers and bad people had almost seemed interchangeable after her father had been taken away by strangers who'd come to their house late one night and shot him in the next alleyway.

They were bad people who'd mistaken him for someone else, Mother had told her. They'd thought he was one of those sick people who were roaming the streets at night, hurting others. This wasn't true, of course, but self-proclaimed deputy constables, who were really lynch mobs, were taking matters into their own hands, as the newspapers put it.

Not having to deal with this kind of riffraff and the chaos they caused in London was one of the reasons Mother had chosen to accept Bartholomew's marriage proposal and move to his Yorkshire estate within a month of meeting him. Asterbury Hall was the safest place on earth, and there was less crime here than anywhere else in all of England, he'd assured them. So even if Bartholomew had invited over two hundred guests to the wedding, he and Mother would know them all, Mary supposed, and none of the people coming and going at the manor were strangers.

And yet… the being in the garden was certainly not an angel.

She fixed her stare to Amanda's. "That monster is dangerous. It's not a friendly creature like a horse or one of the hunting dogs."

"Stop calling her a monster," Amanda shouted, jumping up. "She means you no harm!"

"It killed three geese."

"She doesn't kill geese. She can't even eat." Amanda had tears in her eyes, and her fists clenched as she paced the room's length.

Mary shook her head in disbelief and followed her. "What is this… this thing?"

"It's not a thing. And I've already told you. She's here to keep you safe."

"Me? Safe? It's scaring me!"

Amanda's lips twitched. "You don't have to be afraid as long as you stick to the rules. She'll protect you. She always protects me."

Mary shuddered. Her hands felt like ice clumps. "From what?"

Amanda wiped at her eyes. The red rims around them accentuated her pale face, and she looked ill in the dim artificial light of the oil lamps.

"We're just children, and we're not supposed to be here. We can't become one of them until we're thirteen or fourteen, but the others don't remember themselves once they've changed…"

Mary's heart raced. What was the little pest talking about? Where else would either of them be but here?

"I don't understand! You're talking nonsense."

"You don't have to understand. I don't want you to!"

Amanda threw the balled-up napkin at her and rushed for the closet, where she vanished between overcoats and cardigans, leaving hangers clattering in her wake.

Mary almost followed her, but instead, she shut the door and leaned against it, trying to sort through her thoughts. In the end, she decided Amanda had to be making up stories to frighten her. And she was angry with herself because it was working.

The little pest was probably sitting in her room right now, gloating, making fun of her, and maybe already thinking up a new preposterous tale for Daft Mary tomorrow.

The marauding beast in the garden, however, was real. She wasn't imagining it. It wasn't a fox, but it certainly had to be some sort of predator, if not like the one Mr. Merriman assumed, and all she had to ward it off with was her slingshot.

Her gaze caught on a shiny object on the upholstered seat of the chair where Amanda had been sitting. A key lay on the damask. She bent to inspect it more closely. Its ornate bow was shaped like a skull, and it gave her the creeps, but she picked it up anyway. Its long shaft told her that this wasn't an indoor key. It rather looked like it might fit into a bigger lock, like that of the main entrance, or one of the stable doors.

She wondered what Amanda had been doing with it, but then remembered the object the girl had begged off Smith in the attic earlier.

A soft knock at the door announced the maid's return. Mary closed her fingers tightly around the key and hid her hands behind her back. Whatever the key's purpose, she sure wasn't going to leave it lying around for anyone to see.

"Your mother asked me to remind you to wash yourself before you go to bed, Miss Mary," the maid said as she closed the heavy drapes and picked up the tray.

"Can't you leave those open?" Mary asked.

"No, Miss." The maid shook her head. "His Lordship's orders and your mother's wishes." She studied Mary and added, "There are still guests arriving for the wedding, and we don't want your night's sleep disturbed now, do we? Not with the big day you'll be having tomorrow."

The big day. Oh joy.

She gave a little nod and counted to ten after the maid had gone, locking the door behind her, as usual. Then she tucked the key into the single pocket on the front of her dress, turned down the oil lamps, pulled the drapes back as far as they would go, and stood in front of the tall sash window, looking out.

The eerie fog had dispersed, and a pale full moon was rising behind the treetops of the little coppice beyond the rockery. Its glow bathed the garden in cold silver. Distorted shadows stirred between the shrubs and the flower beds, but not in a threatening manner – nothing out there moved in the wrong direction or too quickly, and nothing seemed out of place. All was well.

She was about to get ready for bed when complete darkness engulfed the room.

Water sloshed from the washbasin onto the carpet and soaked her stockings as she bumped the corner of the dresser in turning to face the window. She froze. An undulating surge of blackness was propelling upward right in front of the glass, blocking out the light. Her jaw dropped, and she stood still, watching a swarm of bats rising into the sky.

Once her eyes had adjusted, she saw that the individual animals were huge. Her bladder stung. The hairs on her arms and neck stood up. What if one of them saw her? But they were gone just as quickly and as quietly as they'd appeared.

When she was sure there were no more of the creatures near the house, she huddled down beneath the windowsill just inside the drapes. Morbidly mesmerized, she peered out at the swarm twisting through the sky like black silk in the wind until it had completely blended into the night.

Without warning, eyes appeared in the window, winter-blue and glowing. Their penetrating gaze searched the room and came to rest on her face. She heard a scream. It took her a moment to realize it was her own, and she tumbled backward into the middle of the carpet, landing on her behind in full view of the creature, exposed and defenseless.

Those eyes... she had seen them before, but she was so dizzy with fear, she couldn't think.

The beast's breath misted the glass as it climbed around on the window frame, grasping the stucco with its claw-tipped toes and the boney horns of its angular wings. It seemed to be positioning itself, scratching the wooden rims, trying to ferret out the best place to get in, and ultimately preparing to pounce through the panes. It fixated her, drooling like a dog staring at its bowl while it was being filled.

The closet door opened behind Mary, but she barely heard it. She only took notice of Amanda when the other girl crouched down next to her and shook her by the shoulders.

Behind the giant bat, the moon's light transformed from silver-gray to white. The creature snarled, then yelped as though it was in pain. It twisted and turned, working its jaw, pointed teeth snatching and biting at the air in an attempt to get ahold of whatever was attacking it, searing its wings and skin, while at the same time trying to keep from falling. Mary could guess what was going on: the fog had returned.

Warped and roaring, the bat lost hold of the building's façade and plunged backward into the billowing white-out, chased by a rain of crumbling plaster. Mary couldn't avert her gaze and gaped, mouth wide open and dry. Her heart pounded in her throat.

"They'll know," Amanda shrieked. "We have to leave!"

Mary heard her, but she couldn't make herself respond straight away. Amanda tugged at her arms. She didn't think she could stand up. All she really wanted to do was hide under the bed or in the closet, but she knew this wouldn't do her any good. The place was crawling with monsters, and they knew this house better than she did.

Another noise shook her to the core and brought her to her feet in a split second: the turning of the doorknob behind them. It was just as bad as the snarls of the creature that had been in front of her window.

What started off as a metallic scratching sound soon turned into a rattling and banging. Whoever was out there obviously didn't have a key, but they were determined to get in, and soon they were assaulting the door with everything they had.

Mary's head felt like it was about to explode, but Amanda took her by the hand and pulled her through the closet and into her own room.

"We have to hurry," she said, breathless. "One of them is dead, and they must have heard its screams, even if they were far away. They'll know you saw. No one can protect you here now."

She closed the closet doors, and swiftly locked her side. The curtains were drawn, and the room was dark, but Mary's eyes quickly adapted.

Amanda shoved the dresser aside just far enough to push the stool back underneath the little square door. Mary climbed into the passageway without question and Amanda followed her. There was nothing either of them could do about the stool and the dresser, but Amanda shut the little door behind them, at least.

Mary couldn't see a thing in here, but she was sure that the secret corridor would give them a realistic chance of getting away from whoever – or whatever – was breaking into her room. Who would think of looking for them in the upstairs servants' quarters?

She groped for the lamp Amanda had left behind on a hook in the wall earlier, but Amanda seized her arm.

"Leave it! There's no time."

There was no time to argue either. Glass shattered behind them. Mary felt Amanda's hand in her own, and she let her stepsister rush her off to the left instead of the right. They were not heading for the attic.

More splintering noises, and furniture crashed to the floor behind them. It was all Mary could do to keep up with Amanda as she stumbled blindly after her.

"Where are we going?" Mary wailed.

They had to get help. At least one of the adults or servants must have heard the destruction on the second floor, even with the music that was still playing down in the parlor.

"Careful, we're going down a flight of stairs now. We have to get out of the house."

Mary halted briefly, wavering. Wouldn't it be smarter to hide inside the house, with so many of those creatures outside the building?

"No time to explain," Amanda said, as if she could read her thoughts. "Just hurry, and try not to make too much noise. They'll hear."

"Are those things devils? Or demons?"

No answer, but Mary didn't have a chance to insist on one. The stairs were steeper than steep, and they went on forever. She kept thinking she was going to miss a tread. If she did, they'd probably both break their necks tumbling all the way down into the cellar. It was like walking on the air in a bad dream.

They had just reached the bottom when a thin shaft of light appeared above them. Someone had discovered the secret passage, and by the sound of it, they weren't alone. Shuffling and shifting, scraping and rustling, something tried to force its way down between the walls. Mary could imagine what it was.

Amanda pushed open a narrow door to her left. They slipped through, and she shut it firmly behind them, leaning against it. Desperately, she searched for a bolt, but there was no handle on this side, never mind a lock. The door looked like part of the wall's dark wooden paneling. It was merely held in place by a catch.

Mary scanned the empty corridor and recognized it as part of the downstairs servants' quarters in the semi-basement near the kitchen – the only servants' quarters she'd seen up until today. She was aware of how lucky they were to have made it this far without being caught.

Bordering on a miracle, no one was around down here. With a house full of guests, this was practically impossible, but she didn't have a moment to waste wondering where the domestic workers might have gone.

The two girls passed the kitchen and the servants hall, and ran for the exit that opened into the courtyard opposite the stables and the poultry coops.

Amanda turned to Mary. "Give me the skeleton key."

Mary was stunted.

"You did find the key I left in your room, didn't you?"

Panic seized her stomach as she rummaged in her pocket, trembling fingers inept and useless, fumbling away precious seconds. At last, there it was, between the rubber band of her slingshot, the goose feather, and a handkerchief that still smelled remotely of her father's Eau de Cologne.

She handed the key to Amanda, and Amanda unlocked the door.

Mary shivered in the chilly night air. The external alcove with the stairs leading up into the courtyard didn't allow for a view of what was going on at ground level. Despite the bright moonlight, they couldn't see past the railing. Anything could be waiting for them up there.

Her chest heaved. "I want my mother. We have to let her know!"

Amanda took her hand again. "She's not in the house–"

Mary cut her off. "How do you know?"

"I just do, and I can take you to her, but we must hurry!"

For an instant, Amanda directed her gaze up at the starlit sky, and Mary's followed. The coiling shape of the swarm was nowhere to be seen, but Mary felt a presence. Every fiber of her body told her to run faster as she and Amanda scuttled toward the stairs.

A noise behind them turned Mary's head. She glanced around at the house and up to the roof of the building. A man-sized bat just like the one that had been at her window was clinging to the rain gutter above them, watching them, gigantic wings unfurled and ready to swoop. Another was crawling over the shingles down toward it, postured like a cat stalking a mouse. More followed over the roof's ridge.

"Please, no!" Amanda's voice whimpered.

The girl's face was a mask of fear. Pulling Mary with her, she sprinted around the side of the stairs instead of going up and out into the courtyard. Running was no longer an option.

At the same time, Mary observed thin whisps of fog creeping around the corner of the building toward them. They were lost.

Amanda fidgeted with the skeleton key and unlocked the Hobbit-sized door underneath the stairs.

Hiding in there had to be insane. Even if the fog couldn't get in, the bat-creatures knew where they were. They didn't stand a chance. Mary had seen that door open, and she wasn't even sure if they would both fit into the tiny storage room behind it. It was cram-packed with cleaning utensils.

Still, Amanda kept pulling her along as she advanced into the cubby hole, again shutting them into complete darkness.

"What are those creatures?" Mary asked.

Amanda stubbornly held her silence. She rummaged around at the back of the room, shifting things from left to right.

All at once, Mary felt a draft, and the room's volume increased.

"Quickly," Amanda said, guiding her. "They can smell us."

How did chatty little Amanda become so bricky? Shouldn't she, Mary, be the one to get them to safety? She was the older of them, after all – and yet it was Amanda who was leading the way. But even at eleven, Mary had more sense than to object.

The other girl's hand felt tiny in her own – and so cold – but Mary trusted her enough to follow her into the entrance of what seemed to be a tunnel at the far end of the storage space. Once inside, she could stand up straight without bumping her head, but if she veered just a little to the left or the right, her shoulders brushed against cool, damp rock.

"This leads to the walled garden," Amanda said softly. "We have to get to the boathouse."

"Will my mother be there?"

Amanda hesitated, and doubt's icy fingers crept up Mary's spine.

"Are you sure she'll be there?" she repeated, louder this time.

"She will be there!"

Mary heard the click and hiss of a match being struck, and the small flame of an oil lamp flickered to life. The muffled sound of snarling, fighting, and things falling over penetrated the door. A deafening screech. A howl of pain. Then everything went quiet again. Too quiet.

Horrified, Mary forgot to ask what her mother was doing at the boathouse, and she let Amanda usher her deep into the passageway.

The tunnel became almost too narrow to pass through in several places because of rubble where parts of the ceiling had collapsed. Stones and grit bit into the soles of Mary's stockinged feet. Every now and then, her frozen toes caught on roots, and she stumbled. Twice, she fell to her knees, but Amanda always helped her up and kept her going.

Eventually, they heard the low growl of the awful furnace, and the tunnel ended in a vertical shaft. Rusty iron rungs led upward. Amanda put down the lamp and began climbing. Mary grabbed her arm.

"You promised you'd tell me what's going on."

"I will!" Amanda paused, pale and harried. "But not down here."

"I don't want to go up there if I don't know what's waiting for us outside. We're safe in here, aren't we? We could just wait…"

"Wait for what?"

Amanda gave her room to think about it, as though she was genuinely hoping Mary would come up with an alternative plan. There wasn't one. At least none that didn't include the adults in the house or her mother – but if Elizabeth was at the boathouse, for whatever reason, she wouldn't know they were coming, and Mary no longer believed anyone was going to help them.

All down the dark, dreadful passageway, she'd tried to find explanations for the gigantic bats she'd seen, for the kitchen and the servants hall being empty, and for all the other strange things she'd been trying so hard to understand. But there were none.

"Someone must have seen," she brabbled.

"They're all like the one you saw outside your window," Amanda said.

"But what about Bartholomew? And why is my mother at the boathouse? She could be looking for me!"

Of course Elizabeth would be searching for her. There was no way she wouldn't be – or had the beasts already gotten her and the others?

Her mother had been searching for a safe place for them since Father's death, somewhere they would be protected from bad people. Now they were surrounded by things she wouldn't have believed

existed just a few weeks ago. Things that wanted to hurt her – kill her.

Amanda looked at her feet. Tears streaked her face.

"She was with the others when they changed, but she isn't anymore."

Mary was too shocked to speak.

Amanda brushed her sleeve across her face and started climbing again. "Let's go find her. Are you coming?"

Mary didn't think she had a choice.

Located beneath a workbench within the building that housed the boiler for the greenhouses' heating system, the opening at the top of the shaft turned out to be a hatch door – thankfully without a bolt or lock on it. It was heavy and would only lift about halfway, but that was far enough for the girls to slip out.

The skeleton key came in handy with the next locked door they encountered, and its magic worked even on the gate to the walled garden. They were almost there now. Mary heard the gush of the river, but before they reached the shore, the night seemed to darken once again. Mary felt sick. The sky was teeming with man-sized bats, and the fog was drawing in from the river. They were cut off from the boathouse, but Amanda kept running – straight into the white.

She wanted to tear free of Amanda's hand, and she almost did, but the younger girl held on to her so fiercely, they were shrouded in mist before Mary could think of heading back to the garden.

The moist air was heavy with the sickly sweet smell of rotting meat and cinnamon. Mary gagged, and the two children huddled down instinctively, making themselves as small as possible. Oddly, the damp droplets then seemed to retreat from them, forming a dome around them. Inside, the air cleared, and Mary instantly felt better.

Outside their bubble, shots rang out, and someone shouted. Distantly, they could hear shrieks, like the ones they'd heard in the courtyard, and angry snarls. Then cries and other sounds of life-and-death struggles penetrated the mist's delicate tissue as though there was a terrible storm going on beyond the strata that surrounded the children.

Whoever had loosed the shots seemed to have missed, because more and more distant shadows moved outside or on the outer seams of the fog bank. Without relent, the enormous bats tried to fight their way down to the girls.

Mary realized Amanda had been telling the truth: the fog wasn't there to harm them. It was protecting them from the beasts.

Hands reached for the children, and Mary recognized Smith and George, the boy she'd bumped into in the attic. Both were so pale against the backdrop of the mist, they were almost transparent, and she recoiled.

"Come now, child," Smith said gently, helping her up against her will. "We have to get you away from this terrible place."

"Where's my mother?" she said, still trying to back away from him and unable to stop sobbing.

The butler and the stableboy looked like ghosts from the books in her father's library. Perhaps they were ghosts. She had seen so many unreal things tonight, she had no trouble believing it.

"Mary, you have to go now," Amanda told her in a firm, but soothing voice.

Mary turned to her and found herself gazing into a wispy two-dimensional face with the same pallor as Smith and George. Amanda was hardly there at all. Mary shook her head in disbelief.

"You told me she'd be here!" she shouted, stomach on fire.

Amanda flinched, small and lost all of a sudden, and Mary was caught between being sorry she'd shouted at her and wanting to do it again.

Her gaze darted over the immediate area around them, and then to the boy. George was holding on to a coat that was much too big to be his own. A burlap sack was strapped across his shoulders. He didn't seem to know what to do with the coat and handed it to Mary. It was one of Elizabeth's. She briefly thought of draping it around Amanda, but then consciously resolved to be selfish, and hugged it tightly to her chest.

At that moment, an elbow and a boot pushed through the wall of mist to Mary's left, followed by a shoulder, and then an entire man emerged and stepped into their space, clothes torn and bloodied, face battered. He was carrying one of the creatures in his arms, and a huge, oddly shaped rifle on his back.

Mary knew the tall, bearded figure all too well, but she wasn't sure if she was happy to see him. The stablemaster winked a smile at her, but she couldn't bring herself to smile back.

The creature's tattered wings hung like a cloak from its shoulders, and its head lay limp against his breast. Its fur was covered in blood.

"Done a little fox hunting, Merriman?" Smith said, relieving him of the rifle.

Merriman barked a laugh and carefully laid the creature down on the ground.

"I have indeed, Sir, and with success. It wasn't easy, mind you. Lead that would kill an elephant will hardly leave a mark on our friends."

Smith nodded, processing the information as he inspected Merriman's prize, searching it for bullet holes.

At first, Mary thought the fiend was dead, but then it stirred in a series of painful stretching movements, and it began to change into a human being. From where she was standing, she could see that its fur was fading away to reveal pale skin, and its wings retracted. Its wounds scabbed over and closed. Naked, human legs formed from black taloned limbs, and its grotesque snout morphed into the nose and lips of a woman.

She kept tearing at a small pouch someone – perhaps Merriman – had secured around her neck with a leather band. It seemed to cause her great pain, but between them, Smith and the stablemaster managed to keep her hands off it. By the time Mary had found the courage to edge closer for a better look, Elizabeth was all human again, breathing hard as her eyelids fluttered open.

Mary stood rooted to the spot. Her feet wouldn't move. She had no words. George beamed at Merriman.

"You really did it! You found her!"

Then he faced Mary. "She's safe now. You're both going to be all right."

"See? Just like I told you," Amanda said, cheery as if nothing out of the ordinary was going on.

"Welcome back, Ma'am," Smith said to Elizabeth, and held out his hand for the coat Mary was still holding.

She gave it to him, and he wrapped it around her mother as best he could while she tried to stand on wobbly legs, obviously disoriented to the point of not knowing where she was, or who was there with her.

"We must get her to the boat," he said to Merriman, and the stablemaster took Elizabeth's arm and braced her weight against him.

Left to her own devices, Mary couldn't have told what direction the boathouse was in, but Merriman confidently led the way, more carrying than supporting Elizabeth. Mary hastened after them with Amanda in her wake.

The mist shielded them until they reached the boathouse, and Amanda made good use of her key once again.

Inside the building, Merriman settled Elizabeth into the nearest of the five or six rowboats that were tethered to the U-shaped wooden landing. He bent over her, cupped her face in his hands so she had to look straight at him, and quietly said something to her. Mary couldn't hear his words, but she saw that a little leather pouch identical to her mother's dangled from a strap around his neck, and wondered if they had something to do with what was inside.

When Merriman had finished speaking, Elizabeth clutched at her pouch, but this time, without intention of ripping it off. She fondled it as though it was her most prized possession.

George placed the burlap sack in the boat, fitting it snugly into the front seat well. Then he helped Mary climb in. She'd witnessed the transformation, but she wasn't afraid. This was her mother, and Elizabeth pulled her into a firm embrace.

"I'm so sorry I got you into this, Mimi," she whispered. "So sorry…"

Mary sank into her arms and hot tears streamed down her cheeks. She didn't know what would come next, but the lad's words rung in her ears: she and Elizabeth were both going to be all right now.

The mist that had floated silently over the water just inside the river-facing open side of the structure grew thicker. It crept inside and advanced toward them, gathering and solidifying in the middle of the U-structure. From it, a figure materialized, shapeless at first, but then Mary recognized the woman from the portrait in the study, and Amanda's mother emerged from the haze.

She was less visible than Smith or the boy as she walked over the water toward them. Long silky hair floated around her head as if it were being swept up by the wind even though the air was still. Her white bridal gown reflected the silver sparkle of the moonlight and the stars in the same way the river did. Mary wanted to keep looking at her translucent shape – and didn't want to at the same time. Was this the true form of the creature she'd been so afraid of?

This woman was no angel, but she was no demon either. She was both life and death rolled into one as she passed them by and drifted to Amanda, where she halted and bent down to the child.

"I've missed you, little bunny," she said, and took the girl in her arms.

Amanda burrowed into the woman's dress, and it struck Mary that the girl she had secretly been calling a little pest was dealing with much bigger challenges than the death of a parent.

She'd been so wrong about Amanda. Without her, she wouldn't be here now. Perhaps her mother wouldn't, either. The memory of Amanda and Smith up in the attic flashed before her mind. Please, she'd said to him.

"We have to get them going, Ma'am," Merriman said to the specter.

Smith stood next to him, briefly bowing his head to the spirit. "Merriman's right, Ma'am. His Lordship will have guessed what you're planning on doing by now. He'll be trying to force his way in."

"He can't go through me any more than I can get into his house," the specter said, but the worry creases around Smith's brows deepened.

Amanda's mother turned to Mary and Elizabeth, studying them both, as though she had no idea what to do about them.

Elizabeth cleared her throat and said in a soft voice, "I don't know how to thank you."

The specter huffed a laugh. "Oh, I'm not doing this for you. I don't believe in salvaging souls who come here of their own free will anymore. There have been far too many. I'm doing this for her." She gestured at Mary. "Your daughter didn't have a choice, any more than mine did."

She hugged Amanda closer, and the child clung to the ghost of her mother, half-hiding behind her. Mary's heart went out to her.

Elizabeth lowered her gaze. "I thought it would be a way out. Bartholomew said there was no hope for us. My husband passed the illness on to me before we even knew he had it. I have no control over it, and I was all alone after the deputy constables came for him."

There was bitterness in her voice, and Mary finally comprehended what had happened. The constables had killed her father because he had become a shapechanger. They had not mistaken him for someone else.

"Bartholomew said he'd make sure Mary was protected until she was old enough to join us," Elizabeth went on. "He said there was no other way."

"You were and are naïve." This didn't sound like an accusation. It was merely a statement.

Despite her young age and confusion about her mother's confession, Mary understood that the specter spoke from personal experience. Something similar to what had happened to her family had also happened to Amanda's parents.

The specter motioned at the pouch that lay against Elizabeth's chest. "You can control it," she said, as though this should have been clear to Elizabeth from the start.

"I can take you away from here and give you a day's head start, but Bartholomew is invested in you. He will search for you," the being went on. "Get as far away from this place as you can." She paused and looked at Mary, and the hard lines of her face softened. "She will be worth the struggle."

"I don't know how we'll survive," Elizabeth whimpered. "What if this doesn't work?"

The ghost's eyes flashed, and she was suddenly in the boat with them, her face only inches from Elizabeth's, glaring at her, all fury and storm.

"Remember what has become of me, and learn."

Mary wasn't afraid, but she startled and jerked away at the penetrating stench of cinnamon and decay. She accidentally touched the white dress, and her hand went right through. It came away icy and wet, skin crawling.

"I wish I'd had someone to help me find the courage to save my girl. Instead, I ended my life in this river on my wedding day a hundred and four years ago. The servants hid my daughter from the shapechangers, but Bartholomew was so angry, he blocked all the exits to the attic and set his own house on fire. Most of the men and women who were up there burned, and those who got away through the secret passage were hunted down in the moors."

She cast Smith and the boy a glance that spoke volumes of guilt and regret.

"There is no easy way out."

Elizabeth nodded, tears leaking down her face, and the specter retreated from them. Her gaze fell on the little girl standing farther back on the pier.

"You must be Amanda," she said, and Mary realized this was the first time Elizabeth actually saw her. "Thank you for saving my daughter."

Amanda nodded, and smiled, then looked at Mary.

"I'll miss you," she said.

"Can't she come with us?" Mary said on impulse, not sure whom to address.

Elizabeth closed her eyes for the space of a heartbeat and shook her head. "Mimi, Amanda can't leave this place."

Amanda came closer and knelt on the wooden boards. Her skin was almost as transparent as her mother's out here. It dawned on Mary that she would have noticed this if Amanda had gone outside to play in the garden with her – but she'd seemed so real in the house, and Mary had been so busy with herself, perhaps, deep down inside, she hadn't wanted to notice.

"I'll be all right," Amanda said, batting her pretty dark eyelashes. "I never get bored in the house."

Mary sniffed back a tear. "They can't hurt you, can they?"

Amanda shook her head. "They can only hurt people who are still alive. I'm not. But I'm glad you are." She forced a smile. "I didn't want you to have to stay, like George did, even if I'll miss you."

"Oh, I don't mind. I never get bored either," George said, peeping over Amanda's shoulder.

His grin made Mary's heart lighter.

"Have to be going now, Ma'am," Smith said to the ghost with more urgency.

The specter whispered in Amanda's ear, and Amanda stepped back from the boat, mouthing a goodbye as Smith took charge of her and George like a kindly grandfather.

The fog thickened once more, and the denser it became, the less visible Amanda's mother was, until she faded out entirely. Merriman untied the boat and gave it a soft nudge with the tip of his toe to set it in motion. It drifted for a few feet, then abruptly came to a halt.

Without warning, the river rose, and an unnatural wave surged through the opening of the boathouse, violently tossing the little vessel. Mary held on to the gunwale as the boat bounced, threatening to capsize.

Three shapechangers shot from the water mere feet from them, sending explosive sprays up left and right that splashed high into the rafters of the structure.

Two of the man-bats plunged back into the water, skin steaming and bubbling as they sank below the water's surface to their deaths.

One didn't.

Wet to the bone and shaking, Mary tried to see where the third creature had gone. Its blazing red eyes quickly betrayed it. Claws sunk deep into the lumber, it clung to one of the beams above, dripping water, molten skin, and infinite, ancient rage.

Gracelessly, it twisted and turned to maneuver itself into a position that would allow it to hurl itself at them. Then, for a moment, it glared down at them. Its entire body was an open wound of scorched flesh, and its wings had been reduced to a mess of frayed matter clinging to bone and sinew, but despite its warped appearance, Mary identified Bartholomew's features.

Gone was the neatly trimmed beard, and a hole gaped where his prominent nose should have been, but his angular face and the way he tilted his head to study them gave him away.

His flight through the mist had ruined him, perhaps permanently, and he had to be lost in an ocean of pain. Yet the cool, controlled way he assessed them left no doubt in her mind that it was him, and that he would kill them.

"You are nothing without me," he roared at Elizabeth through cracked lips. They split open when he bared his teeth, and strings of saliva mingled with the blood that oozed from his mouth.

Frantically, Mary searched through the contents of her dress pocket. Her fingers closed around the slingshot. She didn't have a pebble, but she had her father's silver pendant.

For protection, she heard his voice saying in her head as she broke the delicate chain around her neck with one sharp yank. If pure silver could kill the Vampyre Ruthven, then it might also kill the so much less cultivated Lord of Asterbury Hall.

"You will not leave!" Bartholomew screamed, plunging at them. "No one leaves me!"

Mary ducked out from under her mother's arms before Elizabeth could grab her, and she stood up in the still swaying boat.

She took aim, arms and hands perfectly calm. She only had one shot.

She fired. Her silver pearl penetrated Bartholomew's left eye at the same moment as Merriman's bullet tore through his middle.

He dropped like a stone before he reached them and disappeared into the black water, bobbed up gasping for air, reaching for an imperceptible hold, and went under again, drowning as his already burned flesh fell off his bones and dissolved like lard in a frying pan. A foul gas rose from the water, hissing. Then he was gone.

On the landing, Merriman lowered his elephant gun and gave her a slow nod.

A ferocious outburst of screeching was audible from outside the boathouse. It sounded as though some of the man-bats were throwing themselves at the roof. Amanda hid behind Smith's leg. Merriman didn't appear too worried as he glanced up, but Mary couldn't stop trembling, and she knew the odds weren't on his side once those creatures had pounded, clawed, and torn their way through the wooden shingles.

She wanted to help the stablemaster, but she didn't know how. She was so spent, she hardly felt Elizabeth dragging her down onto her seat and into her arms.

"Go!" Smith yelled. "That'll draw some of them away from us!"

The boat began to move forward once more, out onto the open river, pushed along by a powerful invisible current and shielded within a safe bubble in the mist. Mary knew the boathouse was now no longer protected, and she tried to look back, but Elizabeth wouldn't let her.

More shots rang out behind them as they moved away, but the reports soon became distant and stopped altogether after the vessel passed the first bend in the river. Shadows flitted behind their thick white curtain every now and again, becoming fewer and less erratic the more distance they put between themselves and Asterbury Hall. Finally, they ceased.

The fog shrouded Mary and Elizabeth until they reached the boundary of Bartholomew's property just before night gave way to steel-gray dawn. For an instant, Mary thought she could see Amanda and her mother in the haze, both waving to her. Then, the mist dwindled out of existence, as did the two translucent figures.

With a thud, the little boat drifted to shore near the mountain pass that accommodated the only fastened country road in the valley. It ran almost parallel to the river all the way to Asterbury Hall in one direction and the area's only town worth mentioning in the other. They'd passed through it on their way here when they'd first arrived from London, but Mary didn't remember its name.

They'd be safe there for the moment, Elizabeth told her, throwing the burlap sack George had tucked into the seat well out onto the pebble bank ahead of her as she jumped into the shallow water.

Alarm bells shrilled in Mary's mind. They didn't know anyone there, so the townspeople would be strangers to them, or worse, perhaps friends of Bartholomew's. Any stranger could be a hunter, and any friend of Bartholomew's a shapechanger.

Did her mother – of all people – not realize this? Going into that town meant taking an unfathomable risk, especially after last night. A searing spearhead of dread and fear lodged deep inside Mary, and she didn't know if she could cope.

Elizabeth reached for her hand, but Mary couldn't bring herself to take it.

They couldn't very well stay here or go into the marshes, but Amanda was no longer around to show them another way out if things went badly, and Merriman wouldn't come to save them again. He could be dead, for all she knew, and the creatures he hadn't managed to take with him would be after Elizabeth and her in human form by day and in their bat form by night, no matter where they went, but they'd likely begin their hunt in that town.

And… whatever the stablemaster had put into the pouch on the strap around Elizabeth's neck – it was working now, but what if it didn't tomorrow?

"You've been very brave," Elizabeth said, reading her. "I know you hardly have reason to trust me when I don't know if I can trust myself. All I can do is promise you that I'll do everything I can to get us as far away from here as possible, as fast as possible. For that, we'll need transport, because we won't get

very far on foot. I don't ever want to put our fate in anyone else's hands again, Mimi, but we have to be quick about everything we do now. That's our only chance. Do you understand?"

Mary studied her for a second. Then she nodded and climbed out of the boat.

The sack contained traveling clothes, which Elizabeth pulled on immediately, shoes for them both, and a huge wad of money. Lips pinched, Elizabeth unraveled the wad and swiftly counted the crisp banknotes. Mary guessed it had to be a small fortune, because some of the worry creases on her mother's face melted away.

In town, they hired a driver to take them to Liverpool in his carriage, and there, Elizabeth booked them on a first-class passage to New York. Their ship was ready to leave that same day, and the agent who took down their names was surprised at their lack of papers and luggage, but he did not argue any further when Elizabeth pushed a substantial number of those banknotes at him in addition to their fare. He shoved them out of sight under his ledger, and congratulated Margarete and Victoria Smith to their first voyage across the Atlantic.

First-class meant a spacious outer cabin for them both, but it also necessitated formal dining attire and sitting in the big dining room with what felt like hundreds of people every night so they wouldn't appear suspicious to the other passengers or the crew. Everyone on board was mindful of the illness, and halfway there, they were informed of a new mandatory two-week quarantine in the port of New York.

The cabin passengers were asked to make arrangements for themselves with yet another agent ahead of arrival for the duration of those two weeks, and the best Bartholomew's money could buy for Mary and Elizabeth was a room on the mainland instead of on Hoffman Island, where conditions were said to be appalling. The illness had not spread to the New World yet, and the authorities were making a determined effort to keep it that way.

After their two weeks were up, Elizabeth rented a one-room apartment for them and found unlikely work in a store that sold Asian foods and spices on Mott Street in Chinatown. This kept the little leather pouch on the strap around her neck reliably filled, despite all the freight ships from the East Indies that were being held up even longer in the harbor than the passenger ships from Europe.

Over the following twelve months, the drastic measures being taken across the British Isles and continental Europe stopped the spread of the illness. Much to the people's – and the economy's – relief, it vanished as though it had never existed, and life there went back to a new kind of normal.

An extraordinary number of old manors and residential castles burned to the ground in the Old World at that time, and a hunter named Merriman published two unsuccessful books on natural remedies for the affliction that had held Europe hostage for so long. His mixtures with their exotic ingredients never gained scientific recognition.

Eventually, the New York Daily News moved on to new headlines, and people began to forget.

Mary did not. But as she grew older, her nightmares became less frequent, and the memory of the things she'd been through receded into the farthest corner of her subconscious mind. Sometimes, when she caught a whiff of the cinnamon in her mother's leather pouch, she thought about the stablemaster who'd risked his own life to save Elizabeth, and she wondered what had become of the little pest who'd turned out to be their salvation.

Other than that, the horrors of her time at Asterbury Hall resurfaced to the forefront of her thoughts vividly only once, when she was married and had children of her own, long after Elizabeth's death.

She was rummaging the shelves for new books in the East Village Library on 2nd Avenue when her youngest daughter showed her a new publication by an Irish author Mary hadn't heard of before. Its bright yellow cover with the red title over the top – some foreign name she wasn't sure how to pronounce – didn't strike her as promising, but the child was captivated.

"Can I take this?" Mandy asked.

Mary skimmed the first few pages and noticed that they were written in the form of a journal. A young solicitor was telling the story of how he was traveling to meet a peculiar client in Transylvania.

She froze for a moment, and her mouth went dry. Then she snapped the book shut and shoved it back in its place. Mandy's shoulders sagged.

"You know what?" Mary said, dancing her fingers across the spines of the books on the next shelf over. "Take this one instead."

She handed the girl a tatty old volume about a mad doctor and his monster. "It's not quite as far-fetched."

Mandy smiled.

Other titles by the same author:

Trading Darkness – A Dark Fairytale

An ancient curse. A stolen child. A deal with the devil.

Sacrificed to the Century Demon as a part of a bargain to save her father's people, Louisa of Blackvale has survived half a lifetime of darkness in the netherworld. Without the malevolent creature's knowledge, she learns to utilize her prison's ancient magic and make it her own.

When the demon sets a well-laid plan in motion and plunges Blackvale into war, Louisa knows it's time to fight and take back her life. It's time to strike a bargain of her own, even if it costs her soul.

But would she also trade in the life of the man she loves to win this battle?

If you enjoy fantasy with a bitter-sweet taste of darkness and a touch of fairytale magic, you'll love Trading Darkness.

Stealing the Light – Dies Irae Book One

The gravedigger's daughter has high ambitions. She also has a secret, no control over her magic, and she is about to make a fatal mistake.

Catherine, the village gravedigger's daughter, lives in a world where sorcery is forbidden under penalty of death. When she finds out she is descended from *tainted* nobility, she is determined to learn more and escape the misery of her father's home. Then she steals from the wrong man, and tragedy takes its course.

At the same time, a deeply scarred but highly gifted refugee boy arrives at The Fair – a haven for magic-wielders, well disguised as a traveling carnival. The lad's father, a resentful trickster, puts the community's existence in jeopardy, and when disaster strikes, he leaves his son to shoulder the blame.

Haunted by repression, murder, and betrayal, Catherine and Lorcan's powers unfold – but they are dangerous even to their own kind. Can the people of The Fair help them find their place and gain control over their *talents*, or will the two plunge headlong into the darkness that is consuming the realm?

If you love vivid world building and character-driven medieval fantasy, buy Stealing the Light to find out how the gravedigger's daughter and the trickster's son's fates connect in this Writer's Digest top-rated first book of the series.

Also available in the Dies Irae Series:

Into the Dark – *Dies Irae Book Two*
Gates of Eventide – *Dies Irae Book Three*
Fairyflies – *A Short Dies Irae Series Story*
Fire – *A Short Dies Irae Series Story*
Fairypeople – *A Short Dies Irae Series Story*

For more background and details,
you can visit the author's homepage at

https://www.lisahofmann.net

Made in United States
Orlando, FL
27 September 2022

22831265R00267